PENGUIN

The Master and Margarita

Mikhail Bulgakov was born in Kiev in May 1891. He studied and briefly practised medicine and, after indigent wanderings through revolutionary Russia and the Caucasus, he settled in Moscow in 1921. His sympathetic portrayal of White characters in his stories, in the plays *The Days of the Turbins (The White Guard)*, which enjoyed great success at the Moscow Art Theatre in 1926, and *Flight* (1927), and his satirical treatment of the officials of the New Economic Plan, led to growing criticism, which became violent after the play *The Purple Island*. His later works treat the subject of the artist and the tyrant under the guise of historical characters, with plays such as *Molière*, staged in 1936, *Don Quixote*, staged in 1940, and *Pushkin*, staged in 1943. He also wrote a brilliant biography, highly original in form, of his literary hero, Molière, but *The Master and Margarita*, a fantasy novel about the devil and his henchmen set in modern Moscow, is generally considered his masterpiece. Fame, at home and abroad, was not to come until a quarter of a century after his death at Moscow in 1940.

Richard Pevear was born in Waltham, Massachusetts, in 1943. He has published translations of Alain, Yves Bonnefoy and Alberto Savinio, as well as two books of poetry. He and his wife, Larissa Volokhonsky, who was born in Leningrad, have translated works by Pavel Florensky, Samuel Marshak, Daniil Kharms, Henri Volohonsky, Alexei Khvostenko, Fyodor Dostoyevsky and Nikolai Gogol. Their translation of *The Brothers Karamazov* received the PEN translation award in 1991, and they translated Tolstoy's *What is Art?* for Penguin Classics. They live in France.

MIKHAIL BULGAKOV

The Master and Margarita

TRANSLATED AND WITH NOTES BY
RICHARD PEVEAR AND LARISSA VOLOKHONSKY
WITH AN INTRODUCTION BY RICHARD PEVEAR

PENGUIN BOOKS

PENGUIN CLASSICS

Published by the Penguin Group

Penguin Books Ltd, 80 Strand, London WC2R ORL, England

Penguin Group (USA) Inc., 375 Hudson Street, New York, New York 10014, USA

Penguin Group (Canada), 90 Eglinton Avenue East, Suite 700, Toronto, Ontario, Canada M4P 2Y3
(a division of Pearson Penguin Canada Inc.)

Penguin Ireland, 25 St Stephen's Green, Dublin 2, Ireland
(a division of Penguin Books Ltd)

Penguin Group (Australia), 250 Camberwell Road, Camberwell, Victoria 3124, Australia
(a division of Pearson Australia Group Pty Ltd)

Penguin Books India Pvt Ltd, 11 Community Centre, Panchsheel Park, New Delhi – 110 017, India

Penguin Group (NZ), 67 Apollo Drive, Rosedale, North Shore 0632, New Zealand
(a division of Pearson New Zealand Ltd)

Penguin Books (South Africa) (Pty) Ltd, 24 Sturdee Avenue, Rosebank, Johannesburg 2196, South Africa

Penguin Books Ltd, Registered Offices: 80 Strand, London WC2R ORL, England

www.penguin.com

First published as *Master i Margarita* in serial form in *Moskva*, 1966–7
This translation published in Penguin Books 1997
Reprinted in Penguin Classics 2000
Reprinted with a new Chronology 2007

017

Text copyright © Mikhail Bulgakov, 1966, 1967
Translation, Further Reading and Notes copyright © Richard Pevear and
Larissa Volokhonsky, 1997
Introduction copyright © Richard Pevear, 1997
Chronology copyright © Andrew Bromfield, 2007
All rights reserved

The moral right of the author and translators has been asserted

Set in 10/12pt Monotype Garamond
Typeset by Rowland Phototypesetting Ltd,
Bury St Edmunds, Suffolk
Printed and bound in Great Britain by Clays Ltd, Elcograf S.p.A.

ISBN: 978-0-140-45546-5

www.greenpenguin.co.uk

Penguin Books is committed to a sustainable
future for our business, our readers and our planet.
This book is made from Forest Stewardship
Council™ certified paper.

Contents

Chronology

1871–8 Russo-Turkish war.

1881 Alexander II assassinated. Alexander III ascends the throne.

1891 Mikhail Afanasievich Bulgakov born on 15 May to the family of a professor at the Kiev Theological Academy.

1894 Nicholas II ascends the throne.

1898 The Moscow Art Theatre stages Chekhov's *Seagull*. First Congress of the Russian Social-Democratic Party (RSDP).

1901 The Moscow Art Theatre stages Chekhov's *Three Sisters*.

1903 At its Second Congress, the RSDP splits into Bolsheviks and Mensheviks.

1904–5 Russo-Japanese War.

1905 The 1905 Revolution.

1906 The first Duma (Russian Parliament).

April: Russia's first Constitution enacted.

1907 Bulgakov's family moves to 13 Andreevsky Spusk, which later inspires the setting for his novel *The White Guard* and his play *The Days of the Turbins*.

1909 Bulgakov graduates from the First Alexandrov Gymnasium (i.e. grammar school) and begins his medical studies at Kiev University.

1910 Leo Tolstoy dies.

1913 Bulgakov marries Tatyana Nikolaevna Lappa.

1914 The First World War begins. St Petersburg renamed Petrograd. Bulgakov and his wife work in front-line hospitals.

1916 Bulgakov graduates from the university and works in rural hospitals in Nikolsk and Vyazma in Smolensk Province.

1917 Bulgakov starts writing *A Country Doctor's Notebook*, based on his own experience.

The February Revolution (23 February–8 March). The State Duma is convened in Petrograd.

March: Nicholas II abdicates the throne in favour of Grand Prince Mikhail. Mikhail transfers power to the Provisional Government. Lenin returns from abroad.

June: The election of the Constituent Assembly is set for September.

August: The election is postponed to November.

25 October–7 November: The October Revolution.

December: The Constituent Assembly elections begin. The Cheka (Soviet secret police) is established.

1918 Bulgakov returns to Kiev and establishes his own private medical practice.

January: The Constituent Assembly is dissolved.

March: The Treaty of Brest-Litovsk is signed with Germany.

April: The British land at Murmansk, heralding numerous other attempts at foreign intervention in Russia.

June: Russian industry is nationalized.

November: The First World War ends. Russia repudiates the Treaty of Brest-Litovsk.

1919 Bulgakov moves to Vladikavkaz, where he gives up medicine and devotes himself to journalism and literature.

March: The Comintern is founded. Admiral Kolchak launches his campaign against the Bolsheviks.

October: Allied forces withdraw from Murmansk and Archangel.

1920 March: The Allied blockade is lifted.

November: The civil war ends in Russia.

1921 The Bulgakovs move to Moscow, where they live for several years in the apartment which is the model for the 'evil apartment' in *The Master and Margarita*.

March: The New Economic Policy (NEP) is introduced to replace the rigours of 'War Communism'.

1922 February: The Cheka is replaced by the OGPU.

April: Stalin becomes Secretary General of the Communist Party.

1923 Bulgakov works on the novel *The White Guard* and stories for the cycle *The Diaboliad*.

December: The Treaty of the Creation of the Union of Soviet Socialist Republics is signed.

1924 Bulgakov is divorced from Tatyana Lappa and marries Lyubov Belozerskaya. He writes the story *The Fatal Eggs*.

January: Lenin dies. The Constitution of the USSR is ratified.

The USSR gains wide international recognition.

1925 Several chapters from *The White Guard* are published. Bulgakov works on his story *A Dog's Heart* and the plays *The Days of the Turbins* and *Zoyka's Apartment*.

1926 *The Days of the Turbins* premieres at Stanislavsky and Nemirovich-Danchenko's Moscow Art Theatre and *Zoyka's Apartment* at the Vakhtangov Theatre. Following a search at the Bulgakovs' apartment, the manuscript of *A Dog's Heart* is confiscated.

1927 The Fifteenth Communist Party Congress is held. Stalin assumes control of the Party.

1928 Bulgakov's plays *Flight, The Days of the Turbins* and *Zoyka's Apartment* are all banned from performance.

The First Five-Year Plan is adopted.

1929 Bulgakov starts work on his *Theatrical Novel* (*A Dead Man's Memoir*) and the play *Molière*. The production of *The Days of the Turbins* at the Moscow Art Theatre is closed down. He meets Elena Shilovskaya, later to be his third wife, the prototype for Margarita in *The Master and Margarita*.

1930 Bulgakov receives a phone call from Stalin, always an admirer of his talent. Stalin apparently helped him obtain a position with the Moscow Art Theatre. Bulgakov works on a stage adaptation of Gogol's novel *Dead Souls* for the theatre.

The drive for the collectivization of agriculture and industrialization is launched.

1932 Bulgakov's play *The Days of the Turbins* is revived at the Moscow Art Theatre. Bulgakov is divorced from Lyubov Belozerskaya and marries Elena Shilovskaya. He works on the novel *The Master and Margarita*.

There is famine in Ukraine.

The 'Russian Association of Proletarian Writers' is disbanded.

1933 The USA recognizes the USSR.

1934 The Second Five-Year Plan.

The First Congress of Russian Writers.

The Soviet Union joins the League of Nations.

1935 Bulgakov completes his play *Alexander Pushkin*.

The Stalinist purges begin, following the assassination of Kirov.

1936 Bulgakov's play *Molière* opens at the Moscow Art Theatre and is banned after seven performances. He leaves the Moscow Art Theatre and works as a librettist at the Bolshoi Theatre.

Gorky dies.

The new 'Stalin' constitution is promulgated.

The show trials of Zinoviev and others begin.

1938 Bulgakov completes the manuscript of *The Master and Margarita* and his stage adaptation of *Don Quixote*.

The Third Five-Year Plan begins.

1939 Bulgakov works on the play *Batumi* and reads the entire text of *The Master and Margarita* to friends.

The Nazi–Soviet non-aggression pact is signed.

1940 Bulgakov dictates the final corrections to *The Master and Margarita*.

The Soviet Union attacks Poland and Finland.

Bulgakov dies of nephrosclerosis on 10 March.

1941 On 22 June Germany invades the USSR.

Introduction

Mikhail Bulgakov worked on this luminous book throughout one of the darkest decades of the century. His last revisions were dictated to his wife a few weeks before his death in 1940 at the age of forty-nine. For him, there was never any question of publishing the novel. The mere existence of the manuscript, had it come to the knowledge of Stalin's police, would almost certainly have led to the permanent disappearance of its author. Yet the book was of great importance to him, and he clearly believed that a time would come when it could be published. Another twenty-six years had to pass before events bore out that belief and *The Master and Margarita*, by what seems a surprising oversight in Soviet literary politics, finally appeared in print. The effect was electrifying.

The monthly magazine *Moskva*, otherwise a rather cautious and quiet publication, carried the first part of *The Master and Margarita* in its November 1966 issue. The 150,000 copies sold out within hours. In the weeks that followed, group readings were held, people meeting each other would quote and compare favourite passages, there was talk of little else. Certain sentences from the novel immediately became proverbial. The very language of the novel was a contradiction of everything wooden, official, imposed. It was a joy to speak.

When the second part appeared in the January 1967 issue of *Moskva*, it was greeted with the same enthusiasm. Yet this was not the excitement caused by the emergence of a new writer, as when Aleksandr Solzhenitsyn's *One Day in the Life of Ivan Denisovich* appeared in the magazine *Novy Mir* in 1962. Bulgakov was neither unknown nor forgotten. His plays had begun to be revived in theatres during the late fifties and were published in 1962. His superb *Life of Monsieur de Molière* came out in that same year. His early stories were reprinted. Then, in 1965, came the *Theatrical Novel*, based on his years of experience with Stanislavsky's renowned Moscow Art Theatre. And finally in 1966 a volume of *Selected Prose* was published, containing the complete text of Bulgakov's first novel, *The White Guard*, written in the twenties and dealing with the nearly contemporary events of the Russian civil war in his native Kiev and the Ukraine, a book which in its clear-sighted portrayal of human courage and weakness ranks among the truest depictions of war in all of literature.

Bulgakov was known well enough, then. But, outside a very small group, the existence of *The Master and Margarita* was completely unsuspected. That certainly accounts for some of the amazement caused by its publication. It was thought that virtually all of Bulgakov had found its way into print. And here was not some minor literary remains but a major novel, the author's crowning work. Then there were the qualities of the novel itself – its formal originality, its devastating satire of Soviet life, and of Soviet literary life in particular, its 'theatrical' rendering of the Great Terror of the thirties, the audacity of its portrayal of Jesus Christ and Pontius Pilate, not to mention Satan. But, above all, the novel breathed an air of freedom, artistic and spiritual, which had become rare indeed, not only in Soviet Russia. We sense it in the special tone of Bulgakov's writing, a combination of laughter (satire, caricature, buffoonery) and the most unguarded vulnerability. Two aphorisms detachable from the novel may suggest something of the complex nature of this freedom and how it may have struck the novel's first readers. One is the much-quoted 'Manuscripts don't burn', which seems to express an absolute trust in the triumph of poetry, imagination, the free word, over terror and oppression, and could thus become a watchword of the intelligentsia. The publication of *The Master and Margarita* was taken as a proof of the assertion. In fact, during a moment of fear early in his work on the novel, Bulgakov did burn what he had written. And yet, as we see, it refused to stay burned. This moment of fear, however, brings me to the second aphorism – 'Cowardice is the most terrible of vices' – which is repeated with slight variations several times in the novel. More penetrating than the defiant 'Manuscripts don't burn', this word touched the inner experience of generations of Russians. To portray that experience with such candour required another sort of freedom and a love for something more than 'culture'. Gratitude for such perfect expression of this other, deeper freedom must surely have been part of the enthusiastic response of readers to the novel's first appearance.

And then there was the sheer unlikeliness of its publication. By 1966 the 'thaw' that had followed Stalin's death was over and a new freeze was coming. The hopes awakened by the publication of *One Day in the Life of Ivan Denisovich*, the first public acknowledgement of the existence of the Gulag, had been disappointed. In 1964 came the notorious trial of the poet Joseph Brodsky, and a year later the trial of the writers Andrei Sinyavsky and Yuli Daniel, both sentenced to terms in that same Gulag. Solzhenitsyn saw a new Stalinization approaching, made worse by the terrible sense of repetition, stagnation and helplessness. Such was the monotonously grim atmosphere of the Brezhnev era. And in the midst of it there suddenly burst *The Master and Margarita*, not only an anomaly but an impossibility, a sort of cosmic error, evidence of some hidden but fatal crack in the system of Soviet power. People kept asking, how could they have let it happen?

Bulgakov began work on the first version of the novel early in 1929, or possibly at the end of 1928. It was abandoned, taken up again, burned, resurrected, recast and revised many times. It accompanied Bulgakov through the period of greatest suffering for his people – the period of forced collectivization and the first five-year plan, which decimated Russia's peasantry and destroyed her agriculture, the period of expansion of the system of 'corrective labour camps', of the penetration of the secret police into all areas of life, of the liquidation of the intelligentsia, of vast party purges and the Moscow 'show trials'. In literature the same struggle went on in miniature, and with the same results. Bulgakov was not arrested, but by 1930 he found himself so far excluded that he could no longer publish or produce his work. In an extraordinarily forthright letter to the central government, he asked for permission to emigrate, since the hostility of the literary powers made it impossible for him to live. If emigration was not permitted, 'and if I am condemned to keep silent in the Soviet Union for the rest of my days, then I ask the Soviet government to give me a job in my speciality and assign me to a theatre as a titular director.' Stalin himself answered this letter by telephone on 17 April, and shortly afterwards the Moscow Art Theatre hired Bulgakov as an assistant director and literary consultant. However, during the thirties only his stage adaptations of Gogol's *Dead Souls* and Cervantes' *Don Quixote* were granted a normal run. His own plays either were not staged at all or were quickly withdrawn, and his *Life of Monsieur de Molière*, written in 1932–3 for the collection Lives of Illustrious Men, was rejected by the publisher. These circumstances are everywhere present in *The Master and Margarita*, which was in part Bulgakov's challenge to the rule of terror in literature. The successive stages of his work on the novel, his changing evaluations of the nature of the book and its characters, reflect events in his life and his deepening grasp of what was at stake in the struggle. I will briefly sketch what the study of his archives has made known of this process.

The novel in its definitive version is composed of two distinct but interwoven parts, one set in contemporary Moscow, the other in ancient Jerusalem (called Yershalaim). Its central characters are Woland (Satan) and his retinue, the poet Ivan Homeless, Pontius Pilate, an unnamed writer known as 'the master', and Margarita. The Pilate story is condensed into four chapters and focused on four or five large-scale figures. The Moscow story includes a whole array of minor characters. The Pilate story, which passes through a succession of narrators, finally joins the Moscow story at the end, when the fates of Pilate and the master are simultaneously decided. The earliest version, narrated by a first-person 'chronicler' and entitled *The Engineer's Hoof*, was written in the first few months of 1929. It contained no trace of Margarita and only a faint hint of the master in a minor character representing the old intelligentsia. The Pilate story was confined to a single chapter. This version included the essentials of the Moscow satire, which afterwards underwent only minor revisions and rearrangements. It began in much the same way as the definitive version, with a dialogue between a people's poet and an editor (here of an anti-religious magazine, *The Godless*) on the correct portrayal of Christ as an exploiter of the proletariat. A stranger (Woland) appears and, surprised at their unbelief, astounds them with an eyewitness account of Christ's crucifixion. This account forms the second chapter, entitled 'The Gospel of Woland'.

Clearly, what first spurred Bulgakov to write the novel was his outrage at the portrayals of Christ in Soviet anti-religious propaganda (*The Godless* was an actual monthly magazine of atheism, published from 1922 to 1940). His response was based on a simple reversal – a vivid circumstantial narrative of what was thought to be a 'myth' invented by the ruling class, and a breaking down of the self-evident reality of Moscow life by the intrusion of the 'stranger'. This device, fundamental to the novel, would be more fully elaborated in its final form. Literary satire was also present from the start. The fifth chapter of the definitive version, entitled 'There were Doings at Griboedov's', already appeared intact in this earliest draft, where it was entitled 'Mania Furibunda'. In May of 1929, Bulgakov sent this chapter to a publisher, who rejected it. This was his only attempt to publish anything from the novel.

The second version, from later in the same year, was a reworking of the first four chapters, filling out certain episodes and adding the death of Judas to the second chapter, which also began to detach itself from Woland and become a more autonomous narrative. According to the author's wife, Elena Sergeevna, Bulgakov partially destroyed these two versions in the spring of 1930 – 'threw them in the fire', in the writer's own words. What survived were two large notebooks with many pages torn out. This was at the height of the attacks on Bulgakov in the press, the moment of his letter to the government.

After that came some scattered notes in two notebooks, kept intermittently over the next two years, which was a very difficult time for Bulgakov. In the upper-right-hand corner of the second, he wrote: 'Lord, help me to finish my novel, 1931.' In a fragment of a later chapter, entitled 'Woland's Flight', there is a reference to someone addressed familiarly as *ty*, who is told that he 'will meet with Schubert and clear mornings'. This is obviously the master, though he is not called so. There is also the first mention of the name of Margarita. In Bulgakov's mind, the main outlines of a new conception of the novel were evidently already clear.

This new version he began to write in earnest in October of 1932, during a visit to Leningrad with Elena Sergeevna, whom he had just married. (The 'model' for Margarita, who had now entered the composition, she was previously married to a high-ranking military official, who for some time opposed her wish to leave him for the writer, leading Bulgakov to think he would never see her again.) His wife was surprised that he could set to work without having any notes or earlier drafts with him, but Bulgakov explained, 'I know it by heart.' He continued working, not without long interruptions, until 1936. Various new titles occurred to him, all still referring to Satan as the central figure – *The Great Chancellor, Satan, Here I Am, The Black Theologian, He Has Come, The Hoofed Consultant*. As in the earliest version, the time of the action is 24–5 June, the feast of St John, traditionally a time of magic enchantments (later it was moved to the time of the spring full moon). The nameless friend of Margarita is called 'Faust' in some notes, though not in the text itself. He is also called 'the poet', and is made the author of a novel which corresponds to the 'Gospel of Woland' from the first drafts. This historical section is now broken up and moved to a later place in the novel, coming closer to what would be the arrangement in the final version.

Bulgakov laboured especially over the conclusion of the novel and what reward to give the master. The ending appears for the first time in a chapter entitled 'Last Flight', dating from July 1936. It differs little from the final version. In it, however, the master is told explicitly and directly:

> The house on Sadovaya and the horrible Bosoy will vanish from your memory, but with them will go Ha-Nozri and the forgiven hegemon. These things are not for your spirit. You will never raise yourself higher, you will not see Yeshua, you will never leave your refuge.

In an earlier note, Bulgakov had written even more tellingly: 'You will not hear the liturgy. But you will listen to the romantics . . .' These words, which do not appear in the definitive text, tell us how painfully Bulgakov weighed the question of cowardice and guilt in considering the fate of his hero, and how we should understand the ending of the final version. They also indicate a thematic link between Pilate, the master, and the author himself, connecting the historical and contemporary parts of the novel.

In a brief reworking from 1936–7, Bulgakov brought the beginning of the Pilate story back to the second chapter, where it would remain, and in another reworking from 1937–8 he finally found the definitive title for the novel. In this version, the original narrator, a characterized 'chronicler', is removed. The new narrator is that fluid voice – moving freely from detached observation to ironic double voicing, to the most personal interjection – which is perhaps the finest achievement of Bulgakov's art.

The first typescript of *The Master and Margarita*, dating to 1938, was dictated to the typist by Bulgakov from this last revision, with many changes along the way. In 1939 he made further alterations in the typescript, the most important of which concerns the fate of the hero and heroine. In the last manuscript version, the fate of the master and Margarita, announced to them by Woland, is to follow Pilate up the path of moonlight to find Yeshua and peace. In the typescript, the fate of the master, announced to Woland by Matthew Levi, speaking for

Yeshua, is not to follow Pilate but to go to his 'eternal refuge' with Margarita, in a rather German-Romantic setting, with Schubert's music and blossoming cherry trees. Asked by Woland, 'But why don't you take him with you into the light?' Levi replies in a sorrowful voice, 'He does not deserve the light, he deserves peace.' Bulgakov, still pondering the problem of the master's guilt (and his own, for what he considered various compromises, including his work on a play about Stalin's youth), went back to his notes and revisions from 1936, but lightened their severity with an enigmatic irony. This was to be the definitive resolution. Clearly, the master is not to be seen as a heroic martyr for art or a 'Christ-figure'. Bulgakov's gentle irony is a warning against the mistake, more common in our time than we might think, of equating artistic mastery with a sort of saintliness, or, in Kierkegaard's terms, of confusing the aesthetic with the ethical.

In the evolution of *The Master and Margarita*, the Moscow satire of Woland and his retinue versus the literary powers and the imposed normality of Soviet life in general is there from the first, and comes to involve the master when he appears, acquiring details from the writer's own life and with them a more personal tone alongside the bantering irreverence of the demonic retinue. The Pilate story, on the other hand, the story of an act of cowardice and an interrupted dialogue, gains in weight and independence as Bulgakov's work progresses. From a single inset episode, it becomes the centrepiece of the novel, setting off the contemporary events and serving as their measure. In style and form it is a counterpoint to the rest of the book. Finally, rather late in the process, the master and Margarita appear, with Margarita coming to dominate the second part of the novel. Her story is a romance in the old sense – the celebration of a beautiful woman, of a true love, and of personal courage.

These three stories, in form as well as content, embrace virtually all that was excluded from official Soviet ideology and its literature. But if the confines of 'socialist realism' are utterly exploded, so are the confines of more traditional novelistic realism. *The Master and Margarita* as a whole is a consistently free verbal construction which, true to its own premises, can re-create ancient Jerusalem in the smallest physical detail, but can also alter the specifics of the New Testament and play variations on its principal figures, can combine the realities of Moscow life with witchcraft, vampirism, the tearing off and replacing of heads, can describe for several pages the sensation of flight on a broomstick or the gathering of the infamous dead at Satan's annual spring ball, can combine the most acute sense of the fragility of human life with confidence in its indestructibility. Bulgakov underscores the continuity of this verbal world by having certain phrases – 'Oh, gods, my gods', 'Bring me poison', 'Even by moonlight I have no peace' – migrate from one character to another, or to the narrator. A more conspicuous case is the Pilate story itself, successive parts of which are told by Woland, dreamed by the poet Homeless, written by the master, and read by Margarita, while the whole preserves its stylistic unity. Narrow notions of the 'imitation of reality' break down here. But *The Master and Margarita* is true to the broader sense of the novel as a freely developing form embodied in the works of Dostoevsky and Gogol, of Swift and Sterne, of Cervantes, Rabelais and Apuleius. The mobile but personal narrative voice of the novel, the closest model for which Bulgakov may have found in Gogol's *Dead Souls*, is the perfect medium for this continuous verbal construction. There is no multiplicity of narrators in the novel. The voice is always the same. But it has unusual range, picking up, parodying, or ironically undercutting the tones of the novel's many characters, with undertones of lyric and epic poetry and old popular tales.

Bulgakov always loved clowning and agreed with E. T. A. Hoffmann that irony and buffoonery are expressions of 'the deepest contemplation of life in all its conditionality'. It is not by chance that his stage adaptations of the comic masterpieces of Gogol and Cervantes coincided with the writing of *The Master and Margarita*. Behind such specific 'influences' stands the age-old tradition of folk humour with its carnivalized world-view, its reversals and dethronings, its relativizing of worldly absolutes – a tradition that was the subject of a monumental study by Bulgakov's countryman and contemporary Mikhail Bakhtin. Bakhtin's *Rabelais and His World*, which in its way was as much an explosion of Soviet reality as Bulgakov's novel, appeared in 1965, a year before *The Master and Margarita*. The coincidence was not lost on Russian readers. Commenting on it, Bulgakov's wife noted that, while there had never been any direct link between the two men, they were both responding to the same historical situation from the same cultural basis.

Many observations from Bakhtin's study seem to be aimed directly at Bulgakov's intentions, none more so than his comment on Rabelais's travesty of the 'hidden meaning', the 'secret', the 'terrifying mysteries' of religion, politics and economics: 'Laughter must liberate the gay truth of the world from the veils of gloomy lies spun by the seriousness of fear, suffering, and violence.' The settling of scores is also part of the tradition of carnival laughter. Perhaps the most pure example is the *Testament* of the poet François Villon, who in the liveliest verse handed out appropriate 'legacies' to all his enemies, thus entering into tradition and even earning himself a place in the fourth book of Rabelais's *Gargantua and Pantagruel.* So, too, Bakhtin says of Rabelais:

In his novel ... he uses the popular-festive system of images with its charter of freedoms consecrated by many centuries; and he uses it to inflict a severe punishment upon his foe, the Gothic age ... In this setting of consecrated rights Rabelais attacks the fundamental dogmas and sacraments, the holy of holies of medieval ideology.

And he comments further on the broad nature of this tradition:

For thousands of years the people have used these festive comic images to express their criticism, their deep distrust of official truth, and their highest hopes and aspirations. Freedom was not so much an exterior right as it was the inner content of these images. It was the thousand-year-old language of fearlessness, a language with no reservations and omissions, about the world and about power.

Bulgakov drew on this same source in settling his scores with the custodians of official literature and official reality.

The novel's form excludes psychological analysis and historical commentary. Hence the quickness and pungency of Bulgakov's writing. At the same time, it allows Bulgakov to exploit all the theatricality of its great scenes – storms, flight, the attack of vampires, all the antics of the demons Koroviev and Behemoth, the séance in the Variety theatre, the ball at Satan's, but also the meeting of Pilate and Yeshua, the crucifixion as witnessed by Matthew Levi, the murder of Judas in the moonlit garden of Gethsemane.

Bulgakov's treatment of Gospel figures is the most controversial aspect of *The Master and Margarita* and has met with the greatest incomprehension. Yet his premises are made clear in the very first pages of the novel, in the dialogue between Woland and the atheist Berlioz. By the deepest irony of all, the 'prince of this world' stands as guarantor of the 'other' world. It exists, since he exists. But he says nothing directly about it. Apart from divine revelation, the only language able to speak of the 'other' world is the language of parable. Of this language Kafka wrote, in his parable 'On Parables':

Many complain that the words of the wise are always merely parables and of no use in daily life, which is the only life we have. When the sage says: 'Go over,' he does not mean that we should cross to some actual place, which we could do anyhow if it was worth the trouble; he means some fabulous yonder, something unknown to us, something, too, that he cannot designate more precisely, and therefore cannot help us here in the least. All these parables really set out to say simply that the incomprehensible is incomprehensible, and we know that already. But the cares we have to struggle with every day: that is a different matter.

Concerning this a man once said: Why such reluctance? If you only followed the parables, you yourselves would become parables and with that rid of all your daily cares.

Another said: I bet that is also a parable.

The first said: You win.

The second said: But unfortunately only in parable.

The first said: No, in reality. In parable you lose.

A similar dialogue lies at the heart of Bulgakov's novel. In it there are those who belong to parable and those who belong to reality. There are those who go over and those who do not. There are those who win in parable and become parables themselves, and there are those who win in reality. But this reality belongs to Woland. Its nature is made chillingly clear in the brief scene when he and Margarita contemplate his special globe. Woland says:

'For instance, do you see this chunk of land, washed on one side by the ocean? Look, it's filling with fire. A war has started there. If you look closer, you'll see the details.'

Margarita leaned towards the globe and saw the little square of land spread out, get painted in many colours, and turn as it were into a relief map. And then she saw the little ribbon of a river, and some village near it. A little house the size of a pea grew and became the size of a matchbox. Suddenly and noiselessly the roof of this house flew up along with a cloud of black smoke, and the walls collapsed, so that nothing was left of the little two-storey box except a small heap with black smoke pouring from it. Bringing her eye still closer, Margarita made out a small female figure lying on the ground, and next to her, in a pool of blood, a little child with outstretched arms.

'That's it,' Woland said, smiling, 'he had no time to sin. Abaddon's work is impeccable.'

When Margarita asks which side this Abaddon is on, Woland replies: 'He is of a rare impartiality and sympathizes equally with both sides of the fight. Owing to that, the results are always the same for both sides.'

There are others who dispute Woland's claim to the power of this world. They are absent or all but absent from *The Master and Margarita*. But the reality of the world seems to be at their disposal, to be shaped by them and to bear their imprint. Their names are Caesar and Stalin. Though absent in person, they are omnipresent. Their imposed will has become the measure of normality and self-evidence. In other words, the normality of this world is imposed terror. And, as the story of Pilate shows, this is by no means a twentieth-century phenomenon. Once terror is identified with the world, it becomes invisible. Bulgakov's portrayal of Moscow under Stalin's terror is remarkable precisely for its weightless, circus-like theatricality and lack of pathos. It is a substanceless reality, an empty suit writing at a desk. The citizens have adjusted to it and learned to play along as they always do. The mechanism of this forced adjustment is revealed in the chapter recounting 'Nikanor Ivanovich's Dream', in which prison, denunciation and betrayal become yet another theatre with a kindly and helpful master of ceremonies. Berlioz, the comparatist, is the spokesman for this 'normal' state of affairs, which is what makes his conversation with Woland so interesting. In it he is confronted with another reality which he cannot recognize. He becomes 'unexpectedly mortal'. In the story of Pilate, however, a moment of recognition does come. It occurs during Pilate's conversation with Yeshua, when he sees the wandering philosopher's head float off and in its place the toothless head of the aged Tiberius Caesar. This is the pivotal moment of the novel. Pilate breaks off his dialogue with Yeshua, he does not 'go over', and afterwards must sit like a stone for two thousand years waiting to continue their conversation.

Parable cuts through the normality of this world only at moments.

These moments are preceded by a sense of dread, or else by a presentiment of something good. The first variation is Berlioz's meeting with Woland. The second is Pilate's meeting with Yeshua. The third is the 'self-baptism' of the poet Ivan Homeless before he goes in pursuit of the mysterious stranger. The fourth is the meeting of the master and Margarita. These chance encounters have eternal consequences, depending on the response of the person, who must act without foreknowledge and then becomes the consequences of that action.

The touchstone character of the novel is Ivan Homeless, who is there at the start, is radically changed by his encounters with Woland and the master, becomes the latter's 'disciple' and continues his work, is present at almost every turn of the novel's action, and appears finally in the epilogue. He remains an uneasy inhabitant of 'normal' reality, as a historian who 'knows everything', but each year, with the coming of the spring full moon, he returns to the parable which for this world looks like folly.

Richard Pevear

A Note on the Text and Acknowledgements

At his death, Bulgakov left *The Master and Margarita* in a slightly unfinished state. It contains, for instance, certain inconsistencies – two versions of the 'departure' of the master and Margarita, two versions of Yeshua's entry into Yershalaim, two names for Yeshua's native town. His final revisions, undertaken in October of 1939, broke off near the start of Book Two. Later he dictated some additions to his wife, Elena Sergeevna, notably the opening paragraph of Chapter 32 ('Gods, my gods! How sad the evening earth!'). Shortly after his death in 1940, Elena Sergeevna made a new typescript of the novel. In 1963, she prepared another typescript for publication, which differs slightly from her 1940 text. This 1963 text was published by *Moskva* in November 1966 and January 1967. However, the editors of the magazine made cuts in it amounting to some sixty typed pages. These cut portions immediately appeared in *samizdat* (unofficial Soviet 'self-publishing'), were published by Scherz Verlag in Switzerland in 1967, and were then included in the Possev Verlag edition (Frankfurt-am-Main, 1969) and the YMCA-Press edition (Paris, 1969). In 1973 a new and now complete edition came out in Russia, the result of a comparison of the already published editions with materials in the Bulgakov archive. It included additions and changes taken from written corrections on other existing typescripts. The latest Russian edition (1990) has removed the most important of those additions, bringing the text close once again to Elena Sergeevna's 1963 typescript. Given the absence of a definitive authorial text, this process of revision is virtually endless. However, it involves changes that in most cases have little bearing for a translator.

The present translation has been made from the text of the original magazine publication, based on Elena Sergeevna's 1963 typescript, with all cuts restored as in the Possev and YMCA-Press editions. It is complete and unabridged.

The translators wish to express their gratitude to M. O. Chudakova for her advice on the text and to Irina Kronrod for her help in preparing the Further Reading.

R. P., L. V.

Further Reading

WORKS OF MIKHAIL BULGAKOV IN RUSSIAN

Bulgakov, M. A., *Sobraniye sochinenii v pyati tomakh*, Khudozhestvennaya Literatura, Moscow, 1989–90 (collected works in five volumes.)

WORKS ON MIKHAIL BULGAKOV AND *THE MASTER AND MARGARITA*

In Russian

Bulgakova, E. S., *Dnevnik*, Moscow, 1990 (diaries of Bulgakov's third wife)

Chudakova, M. O., *Zhizneopisanie Mikhaila Bulgakova*, Moscow, 1988

Gasparov, Boris, *Iz nabliudenii nad motivnoi strukturoi romana M. A. Bulgakova 'Master i Margarita'*, Riga, 1989

Kreps, Mikhail, *Bulgakov i Pasternak kak romanisty*, Ann Arbor, 1984

Vospominaniya o Mikhaile Bulgakove, Moscow, 1988 (memoirs by various hands)

Yanovskaya, L., *Tvorcheskiy put' Mikhaila Bulgakova*, Moscow, 1983

In English

Barratt, Andrew, *Between Two Worlds. A Critical Introduction to 'The Master and Margarita'*, Oxford, 1987

Curtis, Julie A., *Bulgakov's Last Decade: The Writer as Hero*, Cambridge, 1987

—— *Manuscripts Don't Burn: Mikhail Bulgakov, a Life in Letters and Diaries*, Woodstock, NY, 1992

Milne, Lesley, *The Master and Margarita: A Comedy of Victory*, Birmingham, 1977

—— *Mikhail Bulgakov: A Critical Biography*, Cambridge and New York, 1990

Proffer, Ellendea, *Bulgakov: Life and Work*, Ann Arbor, 1984

Wright, A. Colin, *Mikhail Bulgakov: Life and Interpretations*, Toronto, Buffalo and London, 1978

In French

Gourg, M., *Mikhail Boulgakov 1891–1940. Un maître et son destin*, Paris, 1992

'. . . who are you, then?'

'I am part of that power which eternally
wills evil and eternally works good.'

Goethe, *Faust*[1]

BOOK ONE

CHAPTER I

Never Talk with Strangers

At the hour of the hot spring sunset two citizens appeared at the Patriarch's Ponds.[1] One of them, approximately forty years old, dressed in a grey summer suit, was short, dark-haired, plump, bald, and carried his respectable fedora hat in his hand. His neatly shaven face was adorned with black horn-rimmed glasses of a supernatural size. The other, a broad-shouldered young man with tousled reddish hair, his checkered cap cocked back on his head, was wearing a cowboy shirt, wrinkled white trousers and black sneakers.

The first was none other than Mikhail Alexandrovich Berlioz,[2] editor of a fat literary journal and chairman of the board of one of the major Moscow literary associations, called Massolit[3] for short, and his young companion was the poet Ivan Nikolaevich Ponyrev, who wrote under the pseudonym of Homeless.[4]

Once in the shade of the barely greening lindens, the writers dashed first thing to a brightly painted stand with the sign: 'Beer and Soft Drinks.'

Ah, yes, note must be made of the first oddity of this dreadful May evening. There was not a single person to be seen, not only by the stand, but also along the whole walk parallel to Malaya Bronnaya Street. At that hour when it seemed no longer possible to breathe, when the sun, having scorched Moscow, was collapsing in a dry haze somewhere beyond Sadovoye Ring, no one came under the lindens, no one sat on a bench, the walk was empty.

'Give us seltzer,' Berlioz asked.

'There is no seltzer,' the woman in the stand said, and for some reason became offended.

'Is there beer?' Homeless inquired in a rasping voice.

'Beer'll be delivered towards evening,' the woman replied.

'Then what is there?' asked Berlioz.

'Apricot soda, only warm,' said the woman.

'Well, let's have it, let's have it! . . .'

The soda produced an abundance of yellow foam, and the air began to smell of a barber-shop. Having finished drinking, the writers immediately started to hiccup, paid, and sat down on a bench face to the pond and back to Bronnaya.

Here the second oddity occurred, touching Berlioz alone. He suddenly stopped hiccuping, his heart gave a thump and dropped away somewhere for an instant, then came back, but with a blunt needle lodged in it. Besides that, Berlioz was gripped by fear, groundless, yet so strong that he wanted to flee the Ponds at once without looking back.

Berlioz looked around in anguish, not understanding what had frightened him. He paled, wiped his forehead with a handkerchief, thought: 'What's the matter with me? This has never happened before. My heart's acting up ... I'm overworked ... Maybe it's time to send it all to the devil and go to Kislovodsk ...'[5]

And here the sweltering air thickened before him, and a transparent citizen of the strangest appearance wove himself out of it. A peaked jockey's cap on his little head, a short checkered jacket also made of air ... A citizen seven feet tall, but narrow in the shoulders, unbelievably thin, and, kindly note, with a jeering physiognomy.

The life of Berlioz had taken such a course that he was unaccustomed to extraordinary phenomena. Turning paler still, he goggled his eyes and thought in consternation: 'This can't be! ...'

But, alas, it was, and the long, see-through citizen was swaying before him to the left and to the right without touching the ground.

Here terror took such possession of Berlioz that he shut his eyes. When he opened them again, he saw that it was all over, the phantasm had dissolved, the checkered one had vanished, and with that the blunt needle had popped out of his heart.

'Pah, the devil!' exclaimed the editor. 'You know, Ivan, I nearly had heatstroke just now! There was even something like a hallucination ...' He attempted to smile, but alarm still jumped in his eyes and his hands trembled. However, he gradually calmed down, fanned himself with his handkerchief and, having said rather cheerfully: 'Well, and so ...', went on with the conversation interrupted by their soda-drinking.

This conversation, as was learned afterwards, was about Jesus Christ. The thing was that the editor had commissioned from the poet a long anti-religious poem for the next issue of his journal. Ivan Nikolaevich had written this poem, and in a very short time, but unfortunately the

8

editor was not at all satisfied with it. Homeless had portrayed the main character of his poem – that is, Jesus – in very dark colours, but nevertheless the whole poem, in the editor's opinion, had to be written over again. And so the editor was now giving the poet something of a lecture on Jesus, with the aim of underscoring the poet's essential error.

It is hard to say what precisely had let Ivan Nikolaevich down – the descriptive powers of his talent or a total unfamiliarity with the question he was writing about – but his Jesus came out, well, completely alive, the once-existing Jesus, though, true, a Jesus furnished with all negative features.

Now, Berlioz wanted to prove to the poet that the main thing was not how Jesus was, good or bad, but that this same Jesus, as a person, simply never existed in the world, and all the stories about him were mere fiction, the most ordinary mythology.

It must be noted that the editor was a well-read man and in his conversation very skilfully pointed to ancient historians – for instance, the famous Philo of Alexandria[6] and the brilliantly educated Flavius Josephus[7] – who never said a word about the existence of Jesus. Displaying a solid erudition, Mikhail Alexandrovich also informed the poet, among other things, that the passage in the fifteenth book of Tacitus's famous *Annals*,[8] the forty-fourth chapter, where mention is made of the execution of Jesus, was nothing but a later spurious interpolation.

The poet, for whom everything the editor was telling him was new, listened attentively to Mikhail Alexandrovich, fixing his pert green eyes on him, and merely hiccuped from time to time, cursing the apricot soda under his breath.

'There's not a single Eastern religion,' Berlioz was saying, 'in which, as a rule, an immaculate virgin did not give birth to a god. And in just the same way, without inventing anything new, the Christians created their Jesus, who in fact never lived. It's on this that the main emphasis should be placed . . .'

Berlioz's high tenor rang out in the deserted walk, and as Mikhail Alexandrovich went deeper into the maze, which only a highly educated man can go into without risking a broken neck, the poet learned more and more interesting and useful things about the Egyptian Osiris,[9] a benevolent god and the son of Heaven and Earth, and about the

Phoenician god Tammuz,[10] and about Marduk,[11] and even about a lesser known, terrible god, Vitzliputzli,[12] once greatly venerated by the Aztecs in Mexico. And just at the moment when Mikhail Alexandrovich was telling the poet how the Aztecs used to fashion figurines of Vitzliputzli out of dough – the first man appeared in the walk.

Afterwards, when, frankly speaking, it was already too late, various institutions presented reports describing this man. A comparison of them cannot but cause amazement. Thus, the first of them said that the man was short, had gold teeth, and limped on his right leg. The second, that the man was enormously tall, had platinum crowns, and limped on his left leg. The third laconically averred that the man had no distinguishing marks. It must be acknowledged that none of these reports is of any value.

First of all, the man described did not limp on any leg, and was neither short nor enormous, but simply tall. As for his teeth, he had platinum crowns on the left side and gold on the right. He was wearing an expensive grey suit and imported shoes of a matching colour. His grey beret was cocked rakishly over one ear; under his arm he carried a stick with a black knob shaped like a poodle's head.[13] He looked to be a little over forty. Mouth somehow twisted. Clean-shaven. Dark-haired. Right eye black, left – for some reason – green. Dark eyebrows, but one higher than the other. In short, a foreigner.[14]

Having passed by the bench on which the editor and the poet were placed, the foreigner gave them a sidelong look, stopped, and suddenly sat down on the next bench, two steps away from the friends.

'A German . . .' thought Berlioz. 'An Englishman . . .' thought Homeless. 'My, he must be hot in those gloves.'

And the foreigner gazed around at the tall buildings that rectangularly framed the pond, making it obvious that he was seeing the place for the first time and that it interested him. He rested his glance on the upper floors, where the glass dazzlingly reflected the broken-up sun which was for ever departing from Mikhail Alexandrovich, then shifted it lower down to where the windows were beginning to darken before evening, smiled condescendingly at something, narrowed his eyes, put his hands on the knob and his chin on his hands.

'For instance, Ivan,' Berlioz was saying, 'you portrayed the birth of Jesus, the son of God, very well and satirically, but the gist of it is that a whole series of sons of God were born before Jesus, like, say, the

Phoenician Adonis,[15] the Phrygian Attis,[16] the Persian Mithras.[17] And, to put it briefly, not one of them was born or ever existed, Jesus included, and what's necessary is that, instead of portraying his birth or, suppose, the coming of the Magi,[18] you portray the absurd rumours of their coming. Otherwise it follows from your story that he really was born! . . .'

Here Homeless made an attempt to stop his painful hiccuping by holding his breath, which caused him to hiccup more painfully and loudly, and at that same moment Berlioz interrupted his speech, because the foreigner suddenly got up and walked towards the writers. They looked at him in surprise.

'Excuse me, please,' the approaching man began speaking, with a foreign accent but without distorting the words, 'if, not being your acquaintance, I allow myself . . . but the subject of your learned conversation is so interesting that . . .'

Here he politely took off his beret, and the friends had nothing left but to stand up and make their bows.

'No, rather a Frenchman . . .' thought Berlioz.

'A Pole? . . .' thought Homeless.

It must be added that from his first words the foreigner made a repellent impression on the poet, but Berlioz rather liked him – that is, not liked but . . . how to put it . . . was interested, or whatever.

'May I sit down?' the foreigner asked politely, and the friends somehow involuntarily moved apart; the foreigner adroitly sat down between them and at once entered into the conversation:

'Unless I heard wrong, you were pleased to say that Jesus never existed?' the foreigner asked, turning his green left eye to Berlioz.

'No, you did not hear wrong,' Berlioz replied courteously, 'that is precisely what I was saying.'

'Ah, how interesting!' exclaimed the foreigner.

'What the devil does he want?' thought Homeless, frowning.

'And you were agreeing with your interlocutor?' inquired the stranger, turning to Homeless on his right.

'A hundred per cent!' confirmed the man, who was fond of whimsical and figurative expressions.

'Amazing!' exclaimed the uninvited interlocutor and, casting a thievish glance around and muffling his low voice for some reason, he said: 'Forgive my importunity, but, as I understand, along with everything else, you also do not believe in God?' He made frightened eyes and added: 'I swear I won't tell anyone!'

'No, we don't believe in God,' Berlioz replied, smiling slightly at the foreign tourist's fright, 'but we can speak of it quite freely.'

The foreigner sat back on the bench and asked, even with a slight shriek of curiosity:

'You are – atheists?!'

'Yes, we're atheists,' Berlioz smilingly replied, and Homeless thought, getting angry: 'Latched on to us, the foreign goose!'

'Oh, how lovely!' the astonishing foreigner cried out and began swivelling his head, looking from one writer to the other.

'In our country atheism does not surprise anyone,' Berlioz said with diplomatic politeness. 'The majority of our population consciously and long ago ceased believing in the fairy tales about God.'

Here the foreigner pulled the following stunt: he got up and shook the amazed editor's hand, accompanying it with these words:

'Allow me to thank you with all my heart!'

'What are you thanking him for?' Homeless inquired, blinking.

'For some very important information, which is of great interest to me as a traveller,' the outlandish fellow explained, raising his finger significantly.

The important information apparently had indeed produced a strong impression on the traveller, because he passed his frightened glance over the buildings, as if afraid of seeing an atheist in every window.

'No, he's not an Englishman . . .' thought Berlioz, and Homeless thought: 'Where'd he pick up his Russian, that's the interesting thing!' and frowned again.

'But, allow me to ask you,' the foreign visitor spoke after some anxious reflection, 'what, then, about the proofs of God's existence, of which, as is known, there are exactly five?'

'Alas!' Berlioz said with regret. 'Not one of these proofs is worth anything, and mankind shelved them long ago. You must agree that in the realm of reason there can be no proof of God's existence.'

'Bravo!' cried the foreigner. 'Bravo! You have perfectly repeated restless old Immanuel's[19] thought in this regard. But here's the hitch: he roundly demolished all five proofs, and then, as if mocking himself, constructed a sixth of his own.'

'Kant's proof,' the learned editor objected with a subtle smile, 'is equally unconvincing. Not for nothing did Schiller[20] say that the Kantian reasoning on this question can satisfy only slaves, and Strauss[21] simply laughed at this proof.'

Berlioz spoke, thinking all the while: 'But, anyhow, who is he? And why does he speak Russian so well?'

'They ought to take this Kant and give him a three-year stretch in Solovki[22] for such proofs!' Ivan Nikolaevich plumped quite unexpectedly.

'Ivan!' Berlioz whispered, embarrassed.

But the suggestion of sending Kant to Solovki not only did not shock the foreigner, but even sent him into raptures.

'Precisely, precisely,' he cried, and his green left eye, turned to Berlioz, flashed. 'Just the place for him! Didn't I tell him that time at breakfast: "As you will, Professor, but what you've thought up doesn't hang together. It's clever, maybe, but mighty unclear. You'll be laughed at."'

Berlioz goggled his eyes. 'At breakfast ... to Kant? ... What is this drivel?' he thought.

'But,' the outlander went on, unembarrassed by Berlioz's amazement and addressing the poet, 'sending him to Solovki is unfeasible, for the simple reason that he has been abiding for over a hundred years now in places considerably more remote than Solovki, and to extract him from there is in no way possible, I assure you.'

'Too bad!' the feisty poet responded.

'Yes, too bad!' the stranger agreed, his eye flashing, and went on: 'But here is a question that is troubling me: if there is no God, then, one may ask, who governs human life and, in general, the whole order of things on earth?'

'Man governs it himself,' Homeless angrily hastened to reply to this admittedly none-too-clear question.

'Pardon me,' the stranger responded gently, 'but in order to govern, one needs, after all, to have a precise plan for a certain, at least some-what decent, length of time. Allow me to ask you, then, how can man govern, if he is not only deprived of the opportunity of making a plan for at least some ridiculously short period – well, say, a thousand years – but cannot even vouch for his own tomorrow?

'And in fact,' here the stranger turned to Berlioz, 'imagine that you, for instance, start governing, giving orders to others and yourself, generally, so to speak, acquire a taste for it, and suddenly you get ...

hem ... hem ... lung cancer ...' – here the foreigner smiled sweetly, as if the thought of lung cancer gave him pleasure – 'yes, cancer' – narrowing his eyes like a cat, he repeated the sonorous word – 'and so your governing is over!

'You are no longer interested in anyone's fate but your own. Your family starts lying to you. Feeling that something is wrong, you rush to learned doctors, then to quacks, and sometimes to fortune-tellers as well. Like the first, so the second and third are completely sense-less, as you understand. And it all ends tragically: a man who still recently thought he was governing something, suddenly winds up lying motionless in a wooden box, and the people around him, seeing that the man lying there is no longer good for anything, burn him in an oven.

'And sometimes it's worse still: the man has just decided to go to Kislovodsk' – here the foreigner squinted at Berlioz – 'a trifling matter, it seems, but even this he cannot accomplish, because suddenly, no one knows why, he slips and falls under a tram-car! Are you going to say it was he who governed himself that way? Would it not be more correct to think that he was governed by someone else entirely?' And here the unknown man burst into a strange little laugh.

Berlioz listened with great attention to the unpleasant story about the cancer and the tram-car, and certain alarming thoughts began to torment him. 'He's not a foreigner ... he's not a foreigner ...' he thought, 'he's a most peculiar specimen ... but, excuse me, who is he then? ...'

'You'd like to smoke, I see?' the stranger addressed Homeless unexpectedly. 'Which kind do you prefer?'

'What, have you got several?' the poet, who had run out of cigarettes, asked glumly.

'Which do you prefer?' the stranger repeated.

'Okay – Our Brand,' Homeless replied spitefully.

The unknown man immediately took a cigarette case from his pocket and offered it to Homeless:

'Our Brand ...'

Editor and poet were both struck, not so much by Our Brand precisely turning up in the cigarette case, as by the cigarette case itself. It was of huge size, made of pure gold, and, as it was opened, a diamond triangle flashed white and blue fire on its lid.

Here the writers thought differently. Berlioz: 'No, a foreigner!', and Homeless: 'Well, devil take him, eh! . . .'

The poet and the owner of the cigarette case lit up, but the non-smoker Berlioz declined.

'I must counter him like this,' Berlioz decided, 'yes, man is mortal, no one disputes that. But the thing is . . .'

However, before he managed to utter these words, the foreigner spoke:

'Yes, man is mortal, but that would be only half the trouble. The worst of it is that he's sometimes unexpectedly mortal – there's the trick! And generally he's unable to say what he's going to do this same evening.'

'What an absurd way of putting the question . . .' Berlioz thought and objected:

'Well, there's some exaggeration here. About this same evening I do know more or less certainly. It goes without saying, if a brick should fall on my head on Bronnaya . . .'

'No brick,' the stranger interrupted imposingly, 'will ever fall on anyone's head just out of the blue. In this particular case, I assure you, you are not in danger of that at all. You will die a different death.'

'Maybe you know what kind precisely?' Berlioz inquired with perfectly natural irony, getting drawn into an utterly absurd conversation. 'And will tell me?'

'Willingly,' the unknown man responded. He looked Berlioz up and down as if he were going to make him a suit, muttered through his teeth something like: 'One, two . . . Mercury in the second house . . . moon gone . . . six – disaster . . . evening – seven . . .' then announced loudly and joyfully: 'Your head will be cut off!'

Homeless goggled his eyes wildly and spitefully at the insouciant stranger, and Berlioz asked, grinning crookedly:

'By whom precisely? Enemies? Interventionists?'[23]

'No,' replied his interlocutor, 'by a Russian woman, a Komsomol[24] girl.'

'Hm . . .' Berlioz mumbled, vexed at the stranger's little joke, 'well, excuse me, but that's not very likely.'

'And I beg you to excuse me,' the foreigner replied, 'but it's so. Ah, yes, I wanted to ask you, what are you going to do tonight, if it's not a secret?'

'It's not a secret. Right now I'll stop by my place on Sadovaya, and then at ten this evening there will be a meeting at Massolit, and I will chair it.'

'No, that simply cannot be,' the foreigner objected firmly.

'Why not?'

'Because,' the foreigner replied and, narrowing his eyes, looked into the sky, where, anticipating the cool of the evening, black birds were tracing noiselessly, 'Annushka has already bought the sunflower oil, and has not only bought it, but has already spilled it. So the meeting will not take place.'

Here, quite understandably, silence fell under the lindens.

'Forgive me,' Berlioz spoke after a pause, glancing at the drivel-spouting foreigner, 'but what has sunflower oil got to do with it . . . and which Annushka?'

'Sunflower oil has got this to do with it,' Homeless suddenly spoke, obviously deciding to declare war on the uninvited interlocutor. 'Have you ever happened, citizen, to be in a hospital for the mentally ill?'

'Ivan! . . .' Mikhail Alexandrovich exclaimed quietly.

But the foreigner was not a bit offended and burst into the merriest laughter.

'I have, I have, and more than once!' he cried out, laughing, but without taking his unlaughing eye off the poet. 'Where haven't I been! Only it's too bad I didn't get around to asking the professor what schizophrenia is. So you will have to find that out from him yourself, Ivan Nikolaevich!'

'How do you know my name?'

'Gracious, Ivan Nikolaevich, who doesn't know you?' Here the foreigner took out of his pocket the previous day's issue of the *Literary Gazette*, and Ivan Nikolaevich saw his own picture on the very first page and under it his very own verses. But the proof of fame and popularity, which yesterday had delighted the poet, this time did not delight him a bit.

'Excuse me,' he said, and his face darkened, 'could you wait one little moment? I want to say a couple of words to my friend.'

'Oh, with pleasure!' exclaimed the stranger. 'It's so nice here under the lindens, and, by the way, I'm not in any hurry.'

'Listen here, Misha,' the poet whispered, drawing Berlioz aside, 'he's no foreign tourist, he's a spy. A Russian émigré[25] who has crossed back over. Ask for his papers before he gets away . . .'

'You think so?' Berlioz whispered worriedly, and thought: 'Why, he's right . . .'

'Believe me,' the poet rasped into his ear, 'he's pretending to be a fool in order to find out something or other. Just hear how he speaks Russian.' As he spoke, the poet kept glancing sideways, to make sure the stranger did not escape. 'Let's go and detain him, or he'll get away . . .'

And the poet pulled Berlioz back to the bench by the arm.

The unknown man was not sitting, but was standing near it, holding in his hands some booklet in a dark-grey binding, a sturdy envelope made of good paper, and a visiting card.

'Excuse me for having forgotten, in the heat of our dispute, to introduce myself. Here is my card, my passport, and an invitation to come to Moscow for a consultation,' the stranger said weightily, giving both writers a penetrating glance.

They were embarrassed. 'The devil, he heard everything . . .' Berlioz thought, and with a polite gesture indicated that there was no need to show papers. While the foreigner was pushing them at the editor, the poet managed to make out the word 'Professor' printed in foreign type on the card, and the initial letter of the last name – a double 'V' – 'W'.

'My pleasure,' the editor meanwhile muttered in embarrassment, and the foreigner put the papers back in his pocket.

Relations were thus restored, and all three sat down on the bench again.

'You've been invited here as a consultant, Professor?' asked Berlioz.

'Yes, as a consultant.'

'You're German?' Homeless inquired.

'I? . . .' the professor repeated and suddenly fell to thinking. 'Yes, perhaps I am German . . .' he said.

'You speak real good Russian,' Homeless observed.

'Oh, I'm generally a polyglot and know a great number of languages,' the professor replied.

'And what is your field?' Berlioz inquired.

'I am a specialist in black magic.'

'There he goes! . . .' struck in Mikhail Alexandrovich's head.

'And ... and you've been invited here in that capacity?' he asked, stammering.

'Yes, in that capacity,' the professor confirmed, and explained: 'In a state library here some original manuscripts of the tenth-century necromancer Gerbert of Aurillac[26] have been found. So it is necessary for me to sort them out. I am the only specialist in the world.'

'Aha! You're a historian?' Berlioz asked with great relief and respect.

'I am a historian,' the scholar confirmed, and added with no rhyme or reason: 'This evening there will be an interesting story at the Ponds!'

Once again editor and poet were extremely surprised, but the professor beckoned them both to him, and when they leaned towards him, whispered:

'Bear in mind that Jesus did exist.'

'You see, Professor,' Berlioz responded with a forced smile, 'we respect your great learning, but on this question we hold to a different point of view.'

'There's no need for any points of view,' the strange professor replied, 'he simply existed, that's all.'

'But there's need for some proof...' Berlioz began.

'There's no need for any proofs,' replied the professor, and he began to speak softly, while his accent for some reason disappeared: 'It's all very simple: In a white cloak with blood-red lining, with the shuffling gait of a cavalryman, early in the morning of the fourteenth day of the spring month of Nisan...'[27]

CHAPTER 2

Pontius Pilate

In a white cloak with blood-red lining, with the shuffling gait of a cavalryman, early in the morning of the fourteenth day of the spring month of Nisan, there came out to the covered colonnade between the two wings of the palace of Herod the Great[1] the procurator of Judea,[2] Pontius Pilate.[3]

More than anything in the world the procurator hated the smell of rose oil, and now everything foreboded a bad day, because this smell had been pursuing the procurator since dawn.

It seemed to the procurator that a rosy smell exuded from the cypresses and palms in the garden, that the smell of leather trappings and sweat from the convoy was mingled with the cursed rosy flux.

From the outbuildings at the back of the palace, where the first cohort of the Twelfth Lightning legion,[4] which had come to Yershalaim[5] with the procurator, was quartered, a whiff of smoke reached the colonnade across the upper terrace of the palace, and this slightly acrid smoke, which testified that the centuries' mess cooks had begun to prepare dinner, was mingled with the same thick rosy scent.

'Oh, gods, gods, why do you punish me? . . . Yes, no doubt, this is it, this is it again, the invincible, terrible illness . . . hemicrania, when half of the head aches . . . there's no remedy for it, no escape . . . I'll try not to move my head . . .'

On the mosaic floor by the fountain a chair was already prepared, and the procurator, without looking at anyone, sat in it and reached his hand out to one side. His secretary deferentially placed a sheet of parchment in this hand. Unable to suppress a painful grimace, the procurator ran a cursory, sidelong glance over the writing, returned the parchment to the secretary, and said with difficulty:

'The accused is from Galilee?[6] Was the case sent to the tetrarch?'

'Yes, Procurator,' replied the secretary.

'And what then?'

'He refused to make a decision on the case and sent the Sanhedrin's[7] death sentence to you for confirmation,' the secretary explained.

The procurator twitched his cheek and said quietly:

'Bring in the accused.'

And at once two legionaries brought a man of about twenty-seven from the garden terrace to the balcony under the columns and stood him before the procurator's chair. The man was dressed in an old and torn light-blue chiton. His head was covered by a white cloth with a leather band around the forehead, and his hands were bound behind his back. Under the man's left eye there was a large bruise, in the corner of his mouth a cut caked with blood. The man gazed at the procurator with anxious curiosity.

The latter paused, then asked quietly in Aramaic:[8]

'So it was you who incited the people to destroy the temple of Yershalaim?'[9]

The procurator sat as if made of stone while he spoke, and only his lips moved slightly as he pronounced the words. The procurator was as if made of stone because he was afraid to move his head, aflame with infernal pain.

The man with bound hands leaned forward somewhat and began to speak:

'Good man! Believe me . . .'

But the procurator, motionless as before and not raising his voice in the least, straight away interrupted him:

'Is it me that you are calling a good man? You are mistaken. It is whispered about me in Yershalaim that I am a fierce monster, and that is perfectly correct.' And he added in the same monotone: 'Bring the centurion Ratslayer.'

It seemed to everyone that it became darker on the balcony when the centurion of the first century, Mark, nicknamed Ratslayer, presented himself before the procurator. Ratslayer was a head taller than the tallest soldier of the legion and so broad in the shoulders that he completely blocked out the still-low sun.

The procurator addressed the centurion in Latin:

'The criminal calls me "good man". Take him outside for a moment, explain to him how I ought to be spoken to. But no maiming.'

And everyone except the motionless procurator followed Mark Ratslayer with their eyes as he motioned to the arrested man, indicating that he should go with him. Everyone generally followed Ratslayer with their eyes wherever he appeared, because of his height, and those who were seeing him for the first time also because the centurion's face was disfigured: his nose had once been smashed by a blow from a Germanic club.

Mark's heavy boots thudded across the mosaic, the bound man noiselessly went out with him, complete silence fell in the colonnade, and one could hear pigeons cooing on the garden terrace near the balcony and water singing an intricate, pleasant song in the fountain.

The procurator would have liked to get up, put his temple under the spout, and stay standing that way. But he knew that even that would not help him.

Having brought the arrested man from under the columns out to the garden, Ratslayer took a whip from the hands of a legionary who was standing at the foot of a bronze statue and, swinging easily, struck the arrested man across the shoulders. The centurion's movement was casual and light, yet the bound man instantly collapsed on the ground as if his legs had been cut from under him; he gasped for air, the colour drained from his face, and his eyes went vacant.

With his left hand only, Mark heaved the fallen man into the air like an empty sack, set him on his feet, and spoke nasally, in poorly pronounced Aramaic:

'The Roman procurator is called Hegemon.[10] Use no other words. Stand at attention. Do you understand me, or do I hit you?'

The arrested man swayed, but got hold of himself, his colour returned, he caught his breath and answered hoarsely:

'I understand. Don't beat me.'

A moment later he was again standing before the procurator.

A lustreless, sick voice sounded:

'Name?'

'Mine?' the arrested man hastily responded, his whole being expressing a readiness to answer sensibly, without provoking further wrath.

The procurator said softly:

'I know my own. Don't pretend to be stupider than you are. Yours.'

'Yeshua,'[11] the prisoner replied promptly.

'Any surname?'

'Ha-Nozri.'

'Where do you come from?'

'The town of Gamala,'[12] replied the prisoner, indicating with his head

21

that there, somewhere far off to his right, in the north, was the town of Gamala.

'Who are you by blood?'

'I don't know exactly,' the arrested man replied animatedly, 'I don't remember my parents. I was told that my father was a Syrian . . .'

'Where is your permanent residence?'

'I have no permanent home,' the prisoner answered shyly, 'I travel from town to town.'

'That can be put more briefly, in a word – a vagrant,' the procurator said, and asked:

'Any family?'

'None. I'm alone in the world.'

'Can you read and write?'

'Yes.'

'Do you know any language besides Aramaic?'

'Yes. Greek.'

A swollen eyelid rose, an eye clouded with suffering fixed the arrested man. The other eye remained shut.

Pilate spoke in Greek.

'So it was you who was going to destroy the temple building and called on the people to do that?'

Here the prisoner again became animated, his eyes ceased to show fear, and he spoke in Greek:

'Never, goo . . .' Here terror flashed in the prisoner's eyes, because he had nearly made a slip. 'Never, Hegemon, never in my life was I going to destroy the temple building, nor did I incite anyone to this senseless act.'

Surprise showed on the face of the secretary, hunched over a low table and writing down the testimony. He raised his head, but immediately bent it to the parchment again.

'All sorts of people gather in this town for the feast. Among them there are magicians, astrologers, diviners and murderers,' the procurator spoke in monotone, 'and occasionally also liars. You, for instance, are a liar. It is written clearly: "Incited to destroy the temple". People have testified to it.'

'These good people,' the prisoner spoke and, hastily adding 'Hegemon', went on: '. . . haven't any learning and have confused everything I told them. Generally, I'm beginning to be afraid that this confusion may go on for a very long time. And all because he writes down the things I say incorrectly.'

Silence fell. By now both sick eyes rested heavily on the prisoner.

'I repeat to you, but for the last time, stop pretending that you're a madman, robber,' Pilate said softly and monotonously, 'there's not much written in your record, but what there is is enough to hang you.'

'No, no, Hegemon,' the arrested man said, straining all over in his wish to convince, 'there's one with a goatskin parchment who follows me, follows me and keeps writing all the time. But once I peeked into this parchment and was horrified. I said decidedly nothing of what's written there. I implored him: "Burn your parchment, I beg you!" But he tore it out of my hands and ran away.'

'Who is that?' Pilate asked squeamishly and touched his temple with his hand.

'Matthew Levi,'[13] the prisoner explained willingly. 'He used to be a tax collector, and I first met him on the road in Bethphage,[14] where a fig grove juts out at an angle, and I got to talking with him. He treated me hostilely at first and even insulted me – that is, thought he insulted me – by calling me a dog.' Here the prisoner smiled. 'I personally see nothing bad about this animal, that I should be offended by this word . . .'

The secretary stopped writing and stealthily cast a surprised glance, not at the arrested man, but at the procurator.

'. . . However, after listening to me, he began to soften,' Yeshua went on, 'finally threw the money down in the road and said he would go journeying with me . . .'

Pilate grinned with one cheek, baring yellow teeth, and said, turning his whole body towards the secretary:

'Oh, city of Yershalaim! What does one not hear in it! A tax collector, do you hear, threw money down in the road!'

Not knowing how to reply to that, the secretary found it necessary to repeat Pilate's smile.

'He said that henceforth money had become hateful to him,' Yeshua explained Matthew Levi's strange action and added: 'And since then he has been my companion.'

His teeth still bared, the procurator glanced at the arrested man, then at the sun, steadily rising over the equestrian statues of the hippodrome, which lay far below to the right, and suddenly, in some sickening anguish, thought that the simplest thing would be to drive this strange robber off the balcony by uttering just two words: 'Hang him.' To drive the convoy away as well, to leave the colonnade, go into the palace, order the room darkened, collapse on the bed, send for cold water, call in a plaintive voice for his dog Banga, and complain to him about the hemicrania. And the thought of poison suddenly flashed temptingly in the procurator's sick head.

He gazed with dull eyes at the arrested man and was silent for a time, painfully trying to remember why there stood before him in the pitiless morning sunlight of Yershalaim this prisoner with his face disfigured by beating, and what other utterly unnecessary questions he had to ask him.

'Matthew Levi?' the sick man asked in a hoarse voice and closed his eyes.

'Yes, Matthew Levi,' the high, tormenting voice came to him.

'And what was it in any case that you said about the temple to the crowd in the bazaar?'

The responding voice seemed to stab at Pilate's temple, was inexpressibly painful, and this voice was saying:

'I said, Hegemon, that the temple of the old faith would fall and a new temple of truth would be built. I said it that way so as to make it more understandable.'

'And why did you stir up the people in the bazaar, you vagrant, talking about the truth, of which you have no notion? What is truth?'[15]

And here the procurator thought: 'Oh, my gods! I'm asking him about something unnecessary at a trial . . . my reason no longer serves me . . .' And again he pictured a cup of dark liquid. 'Poison, bring me poison . . .'

And again he heard the voice:

'The truth is, first of all, that your head aches, and aches so badly that you're having faint-hearted thoughts of death. You're not only unable to speak to me, but it is even hard for you to look at me. And I am now your unwilling torturer, which upsets me. You can't even think about anything and only dream that your dog should come, apparently the one being you are attached to. But your suffering will soon be over, your headache will go away.'

The secretary goggled his eyes at the prisoner and stopped writing in mid-word.

Pilate raised his tormented eyes to the prisoner and saw that the sun already stood quite high over the hippodrome, that a ray had penetrated the colonnade and was stealing towards Yeshua's worn sandals, and that the man was trying to step out of the sun's way.

Here the procurator rose from his chair, clutched his head with his hands, and his yellowish, shaven face expressed dread. But he instantly suppressed it with his will and lowered himself into his chair again.

The prisoner meanwhile continued his speech, but the secretary was no longer writing it down, and only stretched his neck like a goose, trying not to let drop a single word.

'Well, there, it's all over,' the arrested man said, glancing benevolently at Pilate, 'and I'm extremely glad of it. I'd advise you, Hegemon, to leave the palace for a while and go for a stroll somewhere in the vicinity – say, in the gardens on the Mount of Olives.[16] A storm will come . . .' the prisoner turned, narrowing his eyes at the sun, '. . . later on, towards evening. A stroll would do you much good, and I would be glad to accompany you. Certain new thoughts have occurred to me, which I think you might find interesting, and I'd willingly share them with you, the more so as you give the impression of being a very intelligent man.'

The secretary turned deathly pale and dropped the scroll on the floor.

'The trouble is,' the bound man went on, not stopped by anyone, 'that you are too closed off and have definitively lost faith in people. You must agree, one can't place all one's affection in a dog. Your life is impoverished, Hegemon.' And here the speaker allowed himself to smile.

The secretary now thought of only one thing, whether to believe his ears or not. He had to believe. Then he tried to imagine precisely what whimsical form the wrath of the hot-tempered procurator would take at this unheard-of impudence from the prisoner. And this the secretary was unable to imagine, though he knew the procurator well.

Then came the cracked, hoarse voice of the procurator, who said in Latin:

'Unbind his hands.'

One of the convoy legionaries rapped with his spear, handed it to another, went over and took the ropes off the prisoner. The secretary picked up his scroll, having decided to record nothing for now, and to be surprised at nothing.

'Admit,' Pilate asked softly in Greek, 'that you are a great physician?'

'No, Procurator, I am not a physician,' the prisoner replied, delightedly rubbing a crimped and swollen purple wrist.

Scowling deeply, Pilate bored the prisoner with his eyes, and these eyes were no longer dull, but flashed with sparks familiar to all.

'I didn't ask you,' Pilate said, 'maybe you also know Latin?'

'Yes, I do,' the prisoner replied.

Colour came to Pilate's yellowish cheeks, and he asked in Latin:

'How did you know I wanted to call my dog?'

'It's very simple,' the prisoner replied in Latin. 'You were moving your hand in the air' – and the prisoner repeated Pilate's gesture – 'as if you wanted to stroke something, and your lips . . .'

'Yes,' said Pilate.

There was silence. Then Pilate asked a question in Greek:

'And so, you are a physician?'

'No, no,' the prisoner replied animatedly, 'believe me, I'm not a physician.'

'Very well, then, if you want to keep it a secret, do so. It has no direct bearing on the case. So you maintain that you did not incite anyone to destroy . . . or set fire to, or in any other way demolish the temple?'

'I repeat, I did not incite anyone to such acts, Hegemon. Do I look like a halfwit?'

'Oh, no, you don't look like a halfwit,' the procurator replied quietly and smiled some strange smile. 'Swear, then, that it wasn't so.'

'By what do you want me to swear?' the unbound man asked, very animated.

'Well, let's say, by your life,' the procurator replied. 'It's high time you swore by it, since it's hanging by a hair, I can tell you.'

'You don't think it was you who hung it, Hegemon?' the prisoner asked. 'If so, you are very mistaken.'

Pilate gave a start and replied through his teeth:

'I can cut that hair.'

'In that, too, you are mistaken,' the prisoner retorted, smiling brightly and shielding himself from the sun with his hand. 'You must agree that surely only he who hung it can cut the hair?'

'So, so,' Pilate said, smiling, 'now I have no doubts that the idle loafers of Yershalaim followed at your heels. I don't know who hung such a tongue on you, but he hung it well. Incidentally, tell me, is it true that you entered Yershalaim by the Susa gate[17] riding on an ass,[18] accompanied by a crowd of riff-raff who shouted greetings to you as some kind of prophet?' Here the procurator pointed to the parchment scroll.

The prisoner glanced at the procurator in perplexity.

'I don't even have an ass, Hegemon,' he said. 'I did enter Yershalaim by the Susa gate, but on foot, accompanied only by Matthew Levi, and no one shouted anything to me, because no one in Yershalaim knew me then.'

'Do you happen to know,' Pilate continued without taking his eyes off the prisoner, 'such men as a certain Dysmas, another named Gestas, and a third named Bar-Rabban?'[19]

'I do not know these good people,' the prisoner replied.

'Truly?'

'Truly.'

'And now tell me, why is it that you use the words "good people" all the time? Do you call everyone that, or what?'

'Everyone,' the prisoner replied. 'There are no evil people in the world.'

'The first I hear of it,' Pilate said, grinning. 'But perhaps I know too little of life! . . . You needn't record any more,' he addressed the secretary, who had not recorded anything anyway, and went on talking with the prisoner. 'You read that in some Greek book?'

'No, I figured it out for myself.'

'And you preach it?'

'Yes.'

'But take, for instance, the centurion Mark, the one known as Ratslayer – is he good?'

'Yes,' replied the prisoner. 'True, he's an unhappy man. Since the good people disfigured him, he has become cruel and hard. I'd be curious to know who maimed him.'

'I can willingly tell you that,' Pilate responded, 'for I was a witness to it. The good people fell on him like dogs on a bear. There were Germani fastened on his neck, his arms, his legs. The infantry maniple was encircled, and if one flank hadn't been cut by a cavalry turm, of which I was the commander – you, philosopher, would not have had the chance to speak with the Ratslayer. That was at the battle of Idistaviso,[20] in the Valley of the Virgins.'

'If I could speak with him,' the prisoner suddenly said musingly, 'I'm sure he'd change sharply.'

'I don't suppose,' Pilate responded, 'that you'd bring much joy to the legate of the legion if you decided to talk with any of his officers or soldiers. Anyhow, it's also not going to happen, fortunately for everyone, and I will be the first to see to it.'

At that moment a swallow swiftly flitted into the colonnade, described a circle under the golden ceiling, swooped down, almost brushed the face of a bronze statue in a niche with its pointed wing, and disappeared behind the capital of a column. It may be that it thought of nesting there.

During its flight, a formula took shape in the now light and lucid head of the procurator. It went like this: the hegemon has looked into the case of the vagrant philosopher Yeshua, alias Ha-Nozri, and found in it no grounds for indictment. In particular, he has found not the slightest connection between the acts of Yeshua and the disorders that have lately taken place in Yershalaim. The vagrant philosopher has proved to be mentally ill. Consequently, the procurator has not confirmed the death sentence on Ha-Nozri passed by the Lesser Sanhedrin. But seeing that Ha-Nozri's mad utopian talk might cause disturbances in Yershalaim, the procurator is removing Yeshua from Yershalaim and putting him under confinement in Stratonian Caesarea on the Mediterranean – that is, precisely where the procurator's residence was.

It remained to dictate it to the secretary.

The swallow's wings whiffled right over the hegemon's head, the bird darted to the fountain basin and then flew out into freedom. The procurator raised his eyes to the prisoner and saw the dust blaze up in a pillar around him.

'Is that all about him?' Pilate asked the secretary.

'Unfortunately not,' the secretary replied unexpectedly and handed Pilate another piece of parchment.

'What's this now?' Pilate asked and frowned.

Having read what had been handed to him, he changed countenance even more. Either the dark blood rose to his neck and face, or something else happened, only his skin lost its yellow tinge, turned brown, and his eyes seemed to sink.

Again it was probably owing to the blood rising to his temples and throbbing in them, only something happened to the procurator's vision. Thus, he imagined that the prisoner's head floated off somewhere, and another appeared in its place.[21] On this bald head sat a scant-pointed golden diadem. On the forehead was a round canker, eating into the skin and smeared with ointment. A sunken, toothless mouth with a pendulous, capricious lower lip. It seemed to Pilate that the pink columns of the balcony and the rooftops of Yershalaim far below, beyond the garden, vanished, and everything was drowned in the thickest green of Caprean gardens. And something strange also happened to his hearing: it was as if trumpets sounded far away, muted and menacing, and a nasal voice was very clearly heard, arrogantly drawling: 'The law of lese-majesty . . .'

Thoughts raced, short, incoherent and extraordinary: 'I'm lost! . . .' then: 'We're lost! . . .' And among them a totally absurd one, about some immortality, which immortality for some reason provoked unendurable anguish.

Pilate strained, drove the apparition away, his gaze returned to the balcony, and again the prisoner's eyes were before him.

'Listen, Ha-Nozri,' the procurator spoke, looking at Yeshua somehow strangely: the procurator's face was menacing, but his eyes were alarmed, 'did you ever say anything about the great Caesar? Answer! Did you? . . . Yes . . . or . . . no?' Pilate drew the word 'no' out somewhat longer than is done in court, and his glance sent Yeshua some thought that he wished as if to instil in the prisoner.

'To speak the truth is easy and pleasant,' the prisoner observed.

'I have no need to know,' Pilate responded in a stifled, angry voice, 'whether it is pleasant or unpleasant for you to speak the truth. You will have to speak it anyway. But, as you speak, weigh every word, unless you want a not only inevitable but also painful death.'

No one knew what had happened with the procurator of Judea, but he allowed himself to raise his hand as if to protect himself from a ray of sunlight, and from behind his hand, as from behind a shield, to send the prisoner some sort of prompting look.

'Answer, then,' he went on speaking, 'do you know a certain Judas from Kiriath,[22] and what precisely did you say to him about Caesar, if you said anything?'

'It was like this,' the prisoner began talking eagerly. 'The evening before last, near the temple, I made the acquaintance of a young man who called himself Judas, from the town of Kiriath. He invited me to his place in the Lower City and treated me to . . .'

'A good man?' Pilate asked, and a devilish fire flashed in his eyes.

'A very good man and an inquisitive one,' the prisoner confirmed. 'He showed the greatest interest in my thoughts and received me very cordially . . .'

'Lit the lamps . . .'[23] Pilate spoke through his teeth, in the same tone as the prisoner, and his eyes glinted.

'Yes,' Yeshua went on, slightly surprised that the procurator was so well informed, 'and asked me to give my view of state authority. He was extremely interested in this question.'

'And what did you say?' asked Pilate. 'Or are you going to reply that you've forgotten what you said?' But there was already hopelessness in Pilate's tone.

'Among other things,' the prisoner recounted, 'I said that all authority is violence over people, and that a time will come when there will be no authority of the Caesars, nor any other authority. Man will pass into the kingdom of truth and justice, where generally there will be no need for any authority.'

'Go on!'

'I didn't go on,' said the prisoner. 'Here men ran in, bound me, and took me away to prison.'

The secretary, trying not to let drop a single word, rapidly traced the words on his parchment.

'There never has been, is not, and never will be any authority in this world greater or better for people than the authority of the emperor Tiberius!' Pilate's cracked and sick voice swelled. For some reason the procurator looked at the secretary and the convoy with hatred.

'And it is not for you, insane criminal, to reason about it!' Here Pilate shouted: 'Convoy, off the balcony!' And turning to the secretary, he added: 'Leave me alone with the criminal, this is a state matter!'

The convoy raised their spears and with a measured tramp of hob-nailed caligae walked off the balcony into the garden, and the secretary followed the convoy.

For some time the silence on the balcony was broken only by the water singing in the fountain. Pilate saw how the watery dish blew up over the spout, how its edges broke off, how it fell down in streams.

The prisoner was the first to speak.

'I see that some misfortune has come about because I talked with that young man from Kiriath. I have a foreboding, Hegemon, that he will come to grief, and I am very sorry for him.'

'I think,' the procurator replied, grinning strangely, 'that there is now someone else in the world for whom you ought to feel sorrier than for Judas of Kiriath, and who is going to have it much worse than Judas! ... So, then, Mark Ratslayer, a cold and convinced torturer, the people who, as I see,' the procurator pointed to Yeshua's disfigured face, 'beat you for your preaching, the robbers Dysmas and Gestas, who with their confrères killed four soldiers, and, finally, the dirty traitor Judas – are all good people?'

'Yes,' said the prisoner.

'And the kingdom of truth will come?'

'It will, Hegemon,' Yeshua answered with conviction.

'It will never come!' Pilate suddenly cried out in such a terrible voice that Yeshua drew back. Thus, many years before, in the Valley of the Virgins, Pilate had cried to his horsemen the words: 'Cut them down! Cut them down! The giant Ratslayer is trapped!' He raised his voice, cracked with commanding, still more, and called out so that his words could be heard in the garden: 'Criminal! Criminal! Criminal!' And then, lowering his voice, he asked: 'Yeshua Ha-Nozri, do you believe in any gods?'

'God is one,' replied Yeshua, 'I believe in him.'

'Then pray to him! Pray hard! However . . .' here Pilate's voice gave out, 'that won't help. No wife?' Pilate asked with anguish for some reason, not understanding what was happening to him.

'No, I'm alone.'

'Hateful city . . .' the procurator suddenly muttered for some reason, shaking his shoulders as if he were cold, and rubbing his hands as though washing them, 'if they'd put a knife in you before your meeting with Judas of Kiriath, it really would have been better.'

'Why don't you let me go, Hegemon?' the prisoner asked unexpectedly, and his voice became anxious. 'I see they want to kill me.'

A spasm contorted Pilate's face, he turned to Yeshua the inflamed, red-veined whites of his eyes and said:

'Do you suppose, wretch, that the Roman procurator will let a man go who has said what you have said? Oh, gods, gods! Or do you think I'm ready to take your place? I don't share your thoughts! And listen to me: if from this moment on you say even one word, if you speak to anyone at all, beware of me! I repeat to you – beware!'

'Hegemon . . .'

'Silence!' cried Pilate, and his furious gaze followed the swallow that had again fluttered on to the balcony. 'To me!' Pilate shouted.

And when the secretary and the convoy returned to their places, Pilate announced that he confirmed the death sentence passed at the meeting of the Lesser Sanhedrin on the criminal Yeshua Ha-Nozri, and the secretary wrote down what Pilate said.

A moment later Mark Ratslayer stood before the procurator. The procurator ordered him to hand the criminal over to the head of the secret service, along with the procurator's directive that Yeshua Ha-Nozri was to be separated from the other condemned men, and also that the soldiers of the secret service were to be forbidden, on pain of severe punishment, to talk with Yeshua about anything at all or to answer any of his questions.

At a sign from Mark, the convoy closed around Yeshua and led him from the balcony.

Next there stood before the procurator a handsome, light-bearded man with eagle feathers on the crest of his helmet, golden lions' heads shining on his chest, and golden plaques on his sword belt, wearing triple-soled boots laced to the knees, and with a purple cloak thrown over his left shoulder. This was the legate in command of the legion.

The procurator asked him where the Sebastean cohort was stationed at the moment. The legate told him that the Sebasteans had cordoned off the square in front of the hippodrome, where the sentencing of the criminals was to be announced to the people.

Then the procurator ordered the legate to detach two centuries from the Roman cohort. One of them, under the command of Ratslayer, was to convoy the criminals, the carts with the implements for the execution and the executioners as they were transported to Bald Mountain,[24] and on arrival was to join the upper cordon. The other was to be sent at once to Bald Mountain and immediately start forming the cordon. For the same purpose, that is, to guard the mountain, the procurator asked the legate to send an auxiliary cavalry regiment – the Syrian ala.

After the legate left the balcony, the procurator ordered the secretary to summon to the palace the president of the Sanhedrin, two of its members, and the head of the temple guard in Yershalaim, adding that he asked things to be so arranged that before conferring with all these people, he could speak with the president previously and alone.

The procurator's order was executed quickly and precisely, and the sun, which in those days was scorching Yershalaim with an extraordinary fierceness, had not yet had time to approach its highest point when, on the upper terrace of the garden, by the two white marble lions that guarded the stairs, a meeting took place between the procurator and the man fulfilling the duties of president of the Sanhedrin, the high priest of the Jews, Joseph Kaifa.[25]

It was quiet in the garden. But when he came out from under the colonnade to the sun-drenched upper level of the garden with its palm trees on monstrous elephant legs, from which there spread before the procurator the whole of hateful Yershalaim, with its hanging bridges, fortresses, and, above all, that utterly indescribable heap of marble with golden dragon scales for a roof – the temple of Yershalaim – the procurator's sharp ear caught, far below, where the stone wall separated the lower terraces of the palace garden from the city square, a low rumble over which from time to time there soared feeble, thin moans or cries.

The procurator understood that there, on the square, a numberless crowd of Yershalaim citizens, agitated by the recent disorders, had already gathered, that this crowd was waiting impatiently for the announcement of the sentences, and that restless water sellers were crying in its midst.

The procurator began by inviting the high priest on to the balcony, to take shelter from the merciless heat, but Kaifa politely apologized[26] and explained that he could not do that on the eve of the feast. Pilate covered his slightly balding head with a hood and began the conversation. This conversation took place in Greek.

Pilate said that he had looked into the case of Yeshua Ha-Nozri and confirmed the death sentence.

Thus, three robbers – Dysmas, Gestas and Bar-Rabban – and this Yeshua Ha-Nozri besides, were condemned to be executed, and it was to be done that day. The first two, who had ventured to incite the people to rebel against Caesar, had been taken in armed struggle by the Roman authorities, were accounted to the procurator, and, consequently, would not be talked about here. But the second two, Bar-Rabban and Ha-Nozri, had been seized by the local authorities and condemned by the Sanhedrin. According to the law, according to custom, one of these two criminals had to be released in honour of the great feast of Passover, which would begin that day. And so the procurator wished to know which of the two criminals the Sanhedrin intended to set free: Bar-Rabban or Ha-Nozri?[27]

Kaifa inclined his head to signify that the question was clear to him, and replied:

'The Sanhedrin asks that Bar-Rabban be released.'

The procurator knew very well that the high priest would give precisely that answer, but his task consisted in showing that this answer provoked his astonishment.

This Pilate did with great artfulness. The eyebrows on the arrogant face rose, the procurator looked with amazement straight into the high priest's eyes.

'I confess, this answer stuns me,' the procurator began softly, 'I'm afraid there may be some misunderstanding here.'

Pilate explained himself. Roman authority does not encroach in the least upon the rights of the local spiritual authorities, the high priest knows that very well, but in the present case we are faced with an obvious error. And this error Roman authority is, of course, interested in correcting.

In fact, the crimes of Bar-Rabban and Ha-Nozri are quite incomparable in their gravity. If the latter, obviously an insane person, is guilty of uttering preposterous things in Yershalaim and some other places, the former's burden of guilt is more considerable. Not only did he allow himself to call directly for rebellion, but he also killed a guard during the attempt to arrest him. Bar-Rabban is incomparably more dangerous than Ha-Nozri.

On the strength of all the foregoing, the procurator asks the high priest to reconsider the decision and release the less harmful of the two condemned men, and that is without doubt Ha-Nozri. And so? . . .

Kaifa said in a quiet but firm voice that the Sanhedrin had thoroughly familiarized itself with the case and informed him a second time that it intended to free Bar-Rabban.

'What? Even after my intercession? The intercession of him through whose person Roman authority speaks? Repeat it a third time, High Priest.'

'And a third time I repeat that we are setting Bar-Rabban free,' Kaifa said softly.

It was all over, and there was nothing more to talk about. Ha-Nozri was departing for ever, and there was no one to cure the dreadful, wicked pains of the procurator, there was no remedy for them except death. But it was not this thought which now struck Pilate. The same incomprehensible anguish that had already visited him on the balcony pierced his whole being. He tried at once to explain it, and the explanation was a strange one: it seemed vaguely to the procurator that there was something he had not finished saying to the condemned man, and perhaps something he had not finished hearing.

Pilate drove this thought away, and it flew off as instantly as it had come flying. It flew off, and the anguish remained unexplained, for it could not well be explained by another brief thought that flashed like lightning and at once went out – 'Immortality ... immortality has come ...' Whose immortality had come? That the procurator did not understand, but the thought of this enigmatic immortality made him grow cold in the scorching sun.

'Very well,' said Pilate, 'let it be so.'

Here he turned, gazed around at the world visible to him, and was surprised at the change that had taken place. The bush laden with roses had vanished, vanished were the cypresses bordering the upper terrace, and the pomegranate tree, and the white statue amidst the greenery, and the greenery itself. In place of it all there floated some purple mass,[28] water weeds swayed in it and began moving off somewhere, and Pilate himself began moving with them. He was carried along now, smothered and burned, by the most terrible wrath – the wrath of impotence.

'Cramped,' said Pilate, 'I feel cramped!'

With a cold, moist hand he tore at the clasp on the collar of his cloak, and it fell to the sand.

'It's sultry today, there's a storm somewhere,' Kaifa responded, not taking his eyes off the procurator's reddened face, and foreseeing all the torments that still lay ahead, he thought: 'Oh, what a terrible month of Nisan we're having this year!'

'No,' said Pilate, 'it's not because of the sultriness, I feel cramped with you here, Kaifa.' And, narrowing his eyes, Pilate smiled and added: 'Watch out for yourself, High Priest.'

The high priest's dark eyes glinted, and with his face – no less artfully than the procurator had done earlier – he expressed amazement.

'What do I hear, Procurator?' Kaifa replied proudly and calmly. 'You threaten me after you yourself have confirmed the sentence passed? Can that be? We are accustomed to the Roman procurator choosing his words before he says something. What if we should be overheard, Hegemon?'

Pilate looked at the high priest with dead eyes and, baring his teeth, produced a smile.

'What's your trouble, High Priest? Who can hear us where we are now? Do you think I'm like that young vagrant holy fool who is to be executed today? Am I a boy, Kaifa? I know what I say and where I say it. There is a cordon around the garden, a cordon around the palace, so that a mouse couldn't get through any crack! Not only a mouse, but even that one, what's his name ... from the town of Kiriath, couldn't get through. Incidentally, High Priest, do you know him? Yes ... if that one got in here, he'd feel bitterly sorry for himself, in this you will, of course, believe me? Know, then, that from now on, High Priest, you will have no peace! Neither you nor your people' – and Pilate pointed far off to the right, where the temple blazed on high – 'it is I who tell you so, Pontius Pilate, equestrian of the Golden Spear!'[29]

'I know, I know!' the black-bearded Kaifa fearlessly replied, and his eyes flashed. He raised his arm to heaven and went on: 'The Jewish people know that you hate them with a cruel hatred, and will cause them much suffering, but you will not destroy them utterly! God will protect them! He will hear us, the almighty Caesar will hear, he will protect us from Pilate the destroyer!'

'Oh, no!' Pilate exclaimed, and he felt lighter and lighter with every word: there was no more need to pretend, no more need to choose his words. 'You have complained about me too much to Caesar, and now my hour has come, Kaifa! Now the message will fly from me, and not to the governor in Antioch, and not to Rome, but directly to Capreae, to the emperor himself, the message of how you in Yershalaim are sheltering known criminals from death. And then it will not be water from Solomon's Pool that I give Yershalaim to drink, as I wanted to do for your own good! No, not water! Remember how on account of you I had to remove the shields with the emperor's insignia from the walls, had to transfer troops, had, as you see, to come in person to look into what goes on with you here! Remember my words: it is not just one cohort that you will see here in Yershalaim, High Priest – no! The whole Fulminata legion will come under the city walls, the Arabian cavalry will arrive, and then you will hear bitter weeping and wailing! You will remember Bar-Rabban then, whom you saved, and you will regret having sent to his death a philosopher with his peaceful preaching!'

The high priest's face became covered with blotches, his eyes burned. Like the procurator, he smiled, baring his teeth, and replied:

'Do you yourself believe what you are saying now, Procurator? No, you do not! It is not peace, not peace, that the seducer of the people of Yershalaim brought us, and you, equestrian, understand that perfectly well. You wanted to release him so that he could disturb the people, outrage the faith, and bring the people under Roman swords! But I, the high priest of the Jews, as long as I live, will not allow the faith to be outraged and will protect the people! Do you hear, Pilate?' And Kaifa raised his arm menacingly: 'Listen, Procurator!'

Kaifa fell silent, and the procurator again heard a noise as if of the sea, rolling up to the very walls of the garden of Herod the Great. The noise rose from below to the feet and into the face of the procurator. And behind his back, there, beyond the wings of the palace, came alarming trumpet calls, the heavy crunch of hundreds of feet, the clanking of iron. The procurator understood that the Roman infantry was already setting out, on his orders, speeding to the parade of death so terrible for rebels and robbers.

'Do you hear, Procurator?' the high priest repeated quietly. 'Are you going to tell me that all this' – here the high priest raised both arms and the dark hood fell from his head – 'has been caused by the wretched robber Bar-Rabban?'

The procurator wiped his wet, cold forehead with the back of his hand, looked at the ground, then, squinting at the sky, saw that the red-hot ball was almost over his head and that Kaifa's shadow had shrunk to nothing by the lion's tail, and said quietly and indifferently:

'It's nearly noon. We got carried away by our conversation, and yet we must proceed.'

Having apologized in refined terms before the high priest, he invited him to sit down on a bench in the shade of a magnolia and wait until he summoned the other persons needed for the last brief conference and gave one more instruction connected with the execution.

Kaifa bowed politely, placing his hand on his heart, and stayed in the garden while Pilate returned to the balcony. There he told the secretary, who had been waiting for him, to invite to the garden the legate of the legion and the tribune of the cohort, as well as the two members of the Sanhedrin and the head of the temple guard, who had been awaiting his summons on the lower garden terrace, in a round gazebo with a fountain. To this Pilate added that he himself would come out to the garden at once, and withdrew into the palace.

While the secretary was gathering the conference, the procurator met, in a room shielded from the sun by dark curtains, with a certain man, whose face was half covered by a hood, though he could not have been bothered by the sun's rays in this room. The meeting was a very short one. The procurator quietly spoke a few words to the man, after which he withdrew and Pilate walked out through the colonnade to the garden.

There, in the presence of all those he had desired to see, the procurator solemnly and drily stated that he confirmed the death sentence on Yeshua Ha-Nozri, and officially inquired of the members of the Sanhedrin as to whom among the criminals they would like to grant life. Having received the reply that it was Bar-Rabban, the procurator said:

'Very well,' and told the secretary to put it into the record at once, clutched in his hand the clasp that the secretary had picked up from the sand, and said solemnly: 'It is time!'

Here all those present started down the wide marble stairway between walls of roses that exuded a stupefying aroma, descending lower and lower towards the palace wall, to the gates opening on to the big, smoothly paved square, at the end of which could be seen the columns and statues of the Yershalaim stadium.

As soon as the group entered the square from the garden and mounted the spacious stone platform that dominated the square, Pilate, looking around through narrowed eyelids, assessed the situation.

The space he had just traversed, that is, the space from the palace wall to the platform, was empty, but before him Pilate could no longer see the square – it had been swallowed up by the crowd, which would have poured over the platform and the cleared space as well, had it not been kept at bay by a triple row of Sebastean soldiers to the left of Pilate and soldiers of the auxiliary Iturean cohort to his right.

And so, Pilate mounted the platform, mechanically clutching the useless clasp in his fist and squinting his eyes. The procurator was squinting not because the sun burned his eyes – no! For some reason he did not want to see the group of condemned men who, as he knew perfectly well, were now being brought on to the platform behind him.

As soon as the white cloak with crimson lining appeared high up on the stone cliff over the verge of the human sea, the unseeing Pilate was struck in the ears by a wave of sound: 'Ha-a-a . . .' It started mutedly, arising somewhere far away by the hippodrome, then became thunderous and, having held out for a few seconds, began to subside. 'They've seen me,' the procurator thought. The wave had not reached its lowest point before it started swelling again unexpectedly and, sway-ing, rose higher than the first, and as foam boils up on the billows of the sea, so a whistling boiled up on this second wave and, separate, distinguishable from the thunder, the wails of women. 'They've been led on to the platform,' thought Pilate, 'and the wails mean that several women got crushed as the crowd surged forward.'

He waited for some time, knowing that no power could silence the crowd before it exhaled all that was pent up in it and fell silent of itself.

And when this moment came, the procurator threw up his right arm, and the last noise was blown away from the crowd.

Then Pilate drew into his breast as much of the hot air as he could and shouted, and his cracked voice carried over thousands of heads:

'In the name of the emperor Caesar! . . .'

Here his ears were struck several times by a clipped iron shout: the cohorts of soldiers raised high their spears and standards and shouted out terribly:

'Long live Caesar!'

Pilate lifted his face and thrust it straight into the sun. Green fire flared up behind his eyelids, his brain took flame from it, and hoarse Aramaic words went flying over the crowd:

'Four criminals, arrested in Yershalaim for murder, incitement to rebellion, and outrages against the laws and the faith, have been sen-tenced to a shameful execution – by hanging on posts! And this execution will presently be carried out on Bald Mountain! The names of the criminals are Dysmas, Gestas, Bar-Rabban and Ha-Nozri. Here they stand before you!'

Pilate pointed to his right, not seeing any criminals, but knowing they were there, in place, where they ought to be.

The crowd responded with a long rumble as if of surprise or relief. When it died down, Pilate continued:

'But only three of them will be executed, for, in accordance with law and custom, in honour of the feast of Passover, to one of the condemned, as chosen by the Lesser Sanhedrin and confirmed by Roman authority, the magnanimous emperor Caesar will return his contemptible life!'

Pilate cried out the words and at the same time listened as the rumble was replaced by a great silence. Not a sigh, not a rustle reached his ears now, and there was even a moment when it seemed to Pilate that everything around him had vanished altogether. The hated city died, and he alone is standing there, scorched by the sheer rays, his face set against the sky. Pilate held the silence a little longer, and then began to cry out:

'The name of the one who will now be set free before you is . . .'

He made one more pause, holding back the name, making sure he had said all, because he knew that the dead city would resurrect once the name of the lucky man was spoken, and no further words would be heard.

'All?' Pilate whispered soundlessly to himself. 'All. The name!'

And, rolling the letter 'r' over the silent city, he cried:

'Bar-Rabban!'

Here it seemed to him that the sun, clanging, burst over him and flooded his ears with fire. This fire raged with roars, shrieks, wails, guffaws and whistles.

Pilate turned and walked back across the platform to the stairs, looking at nothing except the multicoloured squares of the flooring under his feet, so as not to trip. He knew that behind his back the platform was being showered with bronze coins, dates, that people in the howling mob were climbing on shoulders, crushing each other, to see the miracle with their own eyes – how a man already in the grip of death escaped that grip! How the legionaries take the ropes off him, involuntarily causing him burning pain in his arms, dislocated during his interrogation; how he, wincing and groaning, nevertheless smiles a senseless, crazed smile.

He knew that at the same time the convoy was already leading the three men with bound arms to the side stairs, so as to take them to the road going west from the city, towards Bald Mountain. Only when he was off the platform, to the rear of it, did Pilate open his eyes, knowing that he was now safe – he could no longer see the condemned men.

Mingled with the wails of the quieting crowd, yet distinguishable from them, were the piercing cries of heralds repeating, some in Aramaic, others in Greek, all that the procurator had cried out from the platform. Besides that, there came to his ears the tapping, clattering and approaching thud of hoofs, and a trumpet calling out something brief and merry. These sounds were answered by the drilling whistles of boys on the roofs of houses along the street that led from the bazaar to the hippodrome square, and by cries of 'Look out!'

A soldier, standing alone in the cleared space of the square with a standard in his hand, waved it anxiously, and then the procurator, the legate of the legion, the secretary and the convoy stopped.

A cavalry ala, at an ever-lengthening trot, flew out into the square, so as to cross it at one side, bypassing the mass of people, and ride down a lane under a stone wall covered with creeping vines, taking the shortest route to Bald Mountain.

At a flying trot, small as a boy, dark as a mulatto, the commander of the ala, a Syrian, coming abreast of Pilate, shouted something in a high voice and snatched his sword from its sheath. The angry, sweating black horse shied and reared. Thrusting his sword back into its sheath, the commander struck the horse's neck with his crop, brought him down, and rode off into the lane, breaking into a gallop. After him, three by three, horsemen flew in a cloud of dust, the tips of their light bamboo lances bobbing, and faces dashed past the procurator – looking especially swarthy under their white turbans – with merrily bared, gleaming teeth.

Raising dust to the sky, the ala burst into the lane, and the last to ride past Pilate was a soldier with a trumpet slung on his back, blazing in the sun.

Shielding himself from the dust with his hand and wrinkling his face discontentedly, Pilate started on in the direction of the gates to the palace garden, and after him came the legate, the secretary, and the convoy.

It was around ten o'clock in the morning.

CHAPTER 3

The Seventh Proof

'Yes, it was around ten o'clock in the morning, my esteemed Ivan Nikolaevich,' said the professor.

The poet passed his hand over his face like a man just coming to his senses, and saw that it was evening at the Patriarch's Ponds. The water in the pond had turned black, and a light boat was now gliding on it, and one could hear the splash of oars and the giggles of some citizeness in the little boat. The public appeared on the benches along the walks, but again on the other three sides of the square, and not on the side where our interlocutors were.

The sky over Moscow seemed to lose colour, and the full moon could be seen quite distinctly high above, not yet golden but white. It was much easier to breathe, and the voices under the lindens now sounded softer, eveningish.

'How is it I didn't notice that he'd managed to spin a whole story? . . .' Homeless thought in amazement. 'It's already evening! . . . Or maybe he wasn't telling it, but I simply fell asleep and dreamed it all?'

But it must be supposed that the professor did tell the story after all, otherwise it would have to be assumed that Berlioz had had the same dream, because he said, studying the foreigner's face attentively:

'Your story is extremely interesting, Professor, though it does not coincide at all with the Gospel stories.'

'Good heavens,' the professor responded, smiling condescendingly, 'you of all people should know that precisely nothing of what is written in the Gospels ever actually took place, and if we start referring to the Gospels as a historical source . . .' he smiled once more, and Berlioz stopped short, because this was literally the same thing he had been saying to Homeless as they walked down Bronnaya towards the Patriarch's Ponds.

'That's so,' Berlioz replied, 'but I'm afraid no one can confirm that what you've just told us actually took place either.'

'Oh, yes! That there is one who can!' the professor, beginning to speak in broken language, said with great assurance, and with unexpected mysteriousness he motioned the two friends to move closer.

They leaned towards him from both sides, and he said, but again without any accent, which with him, devil knows why, now appeared, now disappeared:

'The thing is . . .' here the professor looked around fearfully and spoke in a whisper, 'that I was personally present at it all. I was on Pontius Pilate's balcony, and in the garden when he talked with Kaifa, and on the platform, only secretly, incognito, so to speak, and therefore I beg you – not a word to anyone, total secrecy, shh . . .'

Silence fell, and Berlioz paled.

'You . . . how long have you been in Moscow?' he asked in a quavering voice.

'I just arrived in Moscow this very minute,' the professor said perplexedly, and only here did it occur to the friends to take a good look in his eyes, at which they became convinced that his left eye, the green one, was totally insane, while the right one was empty, black and dead.

'There's the whole explanation for you!' Berlioz thought in bewilderment. 'A mad German has turned up, or just went crazy at the Ponds. What a story!'

Yes, indeed, that explained the whole thing: the most strange breakfast with the late philosopher Kant, the foolish talk about sunflower oil and Annushka, the predictions about his head being cut off and all the rest – the professor was mad.

Berlioz realized at once what had to be done. Leaning back on the bench, he winked to Homeless behind the professor's back – meaning, don't contradict him – but the perplexed poet did not understand these signals.

'Yes, yes, yes,' Berlioz said excitedly, 'incidentally it's all possible . . . even very possible, Pontius Pilate, and the balcony, and so forth . . . Did you come alone or with your wife?'

'Alone, alone, I'm always alone,' the professor replied bitterly.

'And where are your things, Professor?' Berlioz asked insinuatingly. 'At the Metropol?[1] Where are you staying?'

'I? . . . Nowhere,' the half-witted German answered, his green eye wandering in wild anguish over the Patriarch's Ponds.

'How's that? But . . . where are you going to live?'

'In your apartment,' the madman suddenly said brashly, and winked.

'I . . . I'm very glad . . .' Berlioz began muttering, 'but, really, you won't be comfortable at my place . . . and they have wonderful rooms at the Metropol, it's a first-class hotel . . .'

'And there's no devil either?' the sick man suddenly inquired merrily of Ivan Nikolaevich.

'No devil . . .'

'Don't contradict him,' Berlioz whispered with his lips only, dropping behind the professor's back and making faces.

'There isn't any devil!' Ivan Nikolaevich, at a loss from all this balderdash, cried out not what he ought. 'What a punishment! Stop playing the psycho!'

Here the insane man burst into such laughter that a sparrow flew out of the linden over the seated men's heads.

'Well, now that is positively interesting!' the professor said, shaking with laughter. 'What is it with you – no matter what one asks for, there isn't any!' He suddenly stopped laughing and, quite understandably for a mentally ill person, fell into the opposite extreme after laughing, became vexed and cried sternly: 'So you mean there just simply isn't any?'

'Calm down, calm down, calm down, Professor,' Berlioz muttered, for fear of agitating the sick man. 'You sit here for a little minute with Comrade Homeless, and I'll just run to the corner to make a phone call, and then we'll take you wherever you like. You don't know the city . . .'

Berlioz's plan must be acknowledged as correct: he had to run to the nearest public telephone and inform the foreigners' bureau, thus and so, there's some consultant from abroad sitting at the Patriarch's Ponds in an obviously abnormal state. So it was necessary to take measures, lest some unpleasant nonsense result.

'To make a call? Well, then make your call,' the sick man agreed sadly, and suddenly begged passionately: 'But I implore you, before you go, at least believe that the devil exists! I no longer ask you for anything more. Mind you, there exists a seventh proof of it, the surest of all! And it is going to be presented to you right now!'

'Very good, very good,' Berlioz said with false tenderness and, winking to the upset poet, who did not relish at all the idea of guarding the mad German, set out for the exit from the Ponds at the corner of Bronnaya and Yermolaevsky Lane.

And the professor seemed to recover his health and brighten up at once.

'Mikhail Alexandrovich!' he shouted after Berlioz.

The latter gave a start, looked back, but reassured himself with the thought that the professor had also learned his name and patronymic from some newspaper.

Then the professor called out, cupping his hands like a megaphone:

'Would you like me to have a telegram sent at once to your uncle in Kiev?'

And again Berlioz winced. How does the madman know about the existence of a Kievan uncle? That has certainly never been mentioned in any newspapers. Oh-oh, maybe Homeless is right after all? And suppose his papers are phoney? Ah, what a strange specimen . . . Call, call! Call at once! They'll quickly explain him!

And, no longer listening to anything, Berlioz ran on.

Here, just at the exit to Bronnaya, there rose from a bench to meet the editor exactly the same citizen who in the sunlight earlier had formed himself out of the thick swelter. Only now he was no longer made of air, but ordinary, fleshly, and Berlioz clearly distinguished in the beginning twilight that he had a little moustache like chicken feathers, tiny eyes, ironic and half drunk, and checkered trousers pulled up so high that his dirty white socks showed.

Mikhail Alexandrovich drew back, but reassured himself by reflecting that it was a stupid coincidence and that generally there was no time to think about it now.

'Looking for the turnstile, citizen?' the checkered type inquired in a cracked tenor. 'This way, please! Straight on and you'll get where you're going. How about a little pint pot for my information . . . to set up an ex-choirmaster! . . .' Mugging, the specimen swept his jockey's cap from his head.

Berlioz, not stopping to listen to the cadging and clowning choirmaster, ran up to the turnstile and took hold of it with his hand. He turned it and was just about to step across the rails when red and white light splashed in his face. A sign lit up in a glass box: 'Caution Tram-Car!'

And right then this tram-car came racing along, turning down the newly laid line from Yermolaevsky to Bronnaya. Having turned, and coming to the straight stretch, it suddenly lit up inside with electricity, whined, and put on speed.

The prudent Berlioz, though he was standing in a safe place, decided to retreat behind the stile, moved his hand on the crossbar, and stepped back. And right then his hand slipped and slid, one foot, unimpeded, as if on ice, went down the cobbled slope leading to the rails, the other was thrust into the air, and Berlioz was thrown on to the rails.

Trying to get hold of something, Berlioz fell backwards, the back of his head lightly striking the cobbles, and had time to see high up – but whether to right or left he no longer knew – the gold-tinged moon. He managed to turn on his side, at the same moment drawing his legs to his stomach in a frenzied movement, and, while turning, to make out the face, completely white with horror, and the crimson armband of the woman driver bearing down on him with irresistible force. Berlioz did not cry out, but around him the whole street screamed with desperate female voices.

The woman driver tore at the electric brake, the car dug its nose into the ground, then instantly jumped up, and glass flew from the windows with a crash and a jingle. Here someone in Berlioz's brain cried desperately: 'Can it be? . . .' Once more, and for the last time, the moon flashed, but now breaking to pieces, and then it became dark.

The tram-car went over Berlioz, and a round dark object was thrown up the cobbled slope below the fence of the Patriarch's walk. Having rolled back down this slope, it went bouncing along the cobblestones of the street.

It was the severed head of Berlioz.

CHAPTER 4

The Chase

The hysterical women's cries died down, the police whistles stopped drilling, two ambulances drove off – one with the headless body and severed head, to the morgue, the other with the beautiful driver, wounded by broken glass; street sweepers in white aprons removed the broken glass and poured sand on the pools of blood, but Ivan Nikolaevich just stayed on the bench as he had dropped on to it before reaching the turnstile. He tried several times to get up, but his legs would not obey him – something akin to paralysis had occurred with Homeless.

The poet had rushed to the turnstile as soon as he heard the first scream, and had seen the head go bouncing along the pavement. With that he so lost his senses that, having dropped on to the bench, he bit his hand until it bled. Of course, he forgot about the mad German and tried to figure out one thing only: how it could be that he had just been talking with Berlioz, and a moment later – the head . . .

Agitated people went running down the walk past the poet, exclaiming something, but Ivan Nikolaevich was insensible to their words. However, two women unexpectedly ran into each other near him, and one of them, sharp-nosed and bare-headed, shouted the following to the other, right next to the poet's ear:

'. . . Annushka, our Annushka! From Sadovaya! It's her work . . . She bought sunflower oil at the grocery, and went and broke the whole litre-bottle on the turnstile! Messed her skirt all up, and swore and swore! . . . And he, poor man, must have slipped and – right on to the rails . . .'

Of all that the woman shouted, one word lodged itself in Ivan Nikolaevich's upset brain: 'Annushka' . . .

'Annushka . . . Annushka?' the poet muttered, looking around anxiously. 'Wait a minute, wait a minute . . .'

The word 'Annushka' got strung together with the words 'sunflower oil', and then for some reason with 'Pontius Pilate'. The poet dismissed Pilate and began linking up the chain that started from the word

'Annushka'. And this chain got very quickly linked up and led at once to the mad professor.

'Excuse me! But he did say the meeting wouldn't take place because Annushka had spilled the oil. And, if you please, it won't take place! What's more, he said straight out that Berlioz's head would be cut off by a woman?! Yes, yes, yes! And the driver was a woman! What is all this, eh?!'

There was not a grain of doubt left that the mysterious consultant had known beforehand the exact picture of the terrible death of Berlioz. Here two thoughts pierced the poet's brain. The first: 'He's not mad in the least, that's all nonsense!' And the second: 'Then didn't he set it all up himself?'

'But in what manner, may we ask?! Ah, no, this we're going to find out!'

Making a great effort, Ivan Nikolaevich got up from the bench and rushed back to where he had been talking with the professor. And, fortunately, it turned out that the man had not left yet.

The street lights were already lit on Bronnaya, and over the Ponds the golden moon shone, and in the ever-deceptive light of the moon it seemed to Ivan Nikolaevich that he stood holding a sword, not a walking stick, under his arm.

The ex-choirmaster was sitting in the very place where Ivan Nikolaevich had sat just recently. Now the busybody had perched on his nose an obviously unnecessary pince-nez, in which one lens was missing altogether and the other was cracked. This made the checkered citizen even more repulsive than he had been when he showed Berlioz the way to the rails.

With a chill in his heart, Ivan approached the professor and, glancing into his face, became convinced that there were not and never had been any signs of madness in that face.

'Confess, who are you?' Ivan asked in a hollow voice.

The foreigner scowled, looked at the poet as if he were seeing him for the first time, and answered inimically:

'No understand ... no speak Russian ...'

'The gent don't understand,' the choirmaster mixed in from the bench, though no one had asked him to explain the foreigner's words.

'Don't pretend!' Ivan said threateningly, and felt cold in the pit of his stomach. 'You spoke excellent Russian just now. You're not a

German and you're not a professor! You're a murderer and a spy! . . . Your papers!' Ivan cried fiercely.

The mysterious professor squeamishly twisted his mouth, which was twisted to begin with, then shrugged his shoulders.

'Citizen!' the loathsome choirmaster butted in again. 'What're you doing bothering a foreign tourist? For that you'll incur severe punishment!'

And the suspicious professor made an arrogant face, turned, and walked away from Ivan. Ivan felt himself at a loss. Breathless, he addressed the choirmaster:

'Hey, citizen, help me to detain the criminal! It's your duty!'

The choirmaster became extraordinarily animated, jumped up and hollered:

'What criminal? Where is he? A foreign criminal?' The choirmaster's eyes sparkled gleefully. 'That one? If he's a criminal, the first thing to do is shout "Help!" Or else he'll get away. Come on, together now, one, two!' – and here the choirmaster opened his maw.

Totally at a loss, Ivan obeyed the trickster and shouted 'Help!' but the choirmaster bluffed him and did not shout anything.

Ivan's solitary, hoarse cry did not produce any good results. Two girls shied away from him, and he heard the word 'drunk'.

'Ah, so you're in with him!' Ivan cried out, waxing wroth. 'What are you doing, jeering at me? Out of my way!'

Ivan dashed to the right, and so did the choirmaster; Ivan dashed to the left, and the scoundrel did the same.

'Getting under my feet on purpose?' Ivan cried, turning ferocious. 'I'll hand you over to the police!'

Ivan attempted to grab the blackguard by the sleeve, but missed and caught precisely nothing: it was as if the choirmaster fell through the earth.

Ivan gasped, looked into the distance, and saw the hateful stranger. He was already at the exit to Patriarch's Lane; moreover, he was not alone. The more than dubious choirmaster had managed to join him. But that was still not all: the third in this company proved to be a tom-cat, who appeared out of nowhere, huge as a hog, black as soot or as a rook, and with a desperate cavalryman's whiskers. The trio set off down Patriarch's Lane, the cat walking on his hind legs.

Ivan sped after the villains and became convinced at once that it would be very difficult to catch up with them.

The trio shot down the lane in an instant and came out on Spiri-donovka. No matter how Ivan quickened his pace, the distance between him and his quarry never diminished. And before the poet knew it, he emerged, after the quiet of Spiridonovka, by the Nikitsky Gate, where his situation worsened. The place was swarming with people. Besides, the gang of villains decided to apply the favourite trick of bandits here: a scattered getaway.

The choirmaster, with great dexterity, bored his way on to a bus speeding towards the Arbat Square and slipped away. Having lost one of his quarry, Ivan focused his attention on the cat and saw this strange cat go up to the footboard of an 'A' tram waiting at a stop, brazenly elbow aside a woman, who screamed, grab hold of the handrail, and even make an attempt to shove a ten-kopeck piece into the conduc-tress's hand through the window, open on account of the stuffiness.

Ivan was so struck by the cat's behaviour that he froze motionless by the grocery store on the corner, and here he was struck for a second time, but much more strongly, by the conductress's behaviour. As soon as she saw the cat getting into the tram-car, she shouted with a malice that even made her shake:

'No cats allowed! Nobody with cats allowed! Scat! Get off, or I'll call the police!'

Neither the conductress nor the passengers were struck by the essence of the matter: not just that a cat was boarding a tram-car, which would have been good enough, but that he was going to pay!

The cat turned out to be not only a solvent but also a disciplined animal. At the very first shout from the conductress, he halted his advance, got off the footboard, and sat down at the stop, rubbing his whiskers with the ten-kopeck piece. But as soon as the conductress yanked the cord and the tram-car started moving off, the cat acted like anyone who has been expelled from a tram-car but still needs a ride. Letting all three cars go by, the cat jumped on to the rear coupling-pin of the last one, wrapped its paws around some hose sticking out of the side, and rode off, thus saving himself ten kopecks.

Occupied with the obnoxious cat, Ivan almost lost the main one of the three – the professor. But, fortunately, the man had not managed to slip away. Ivan saw the grey beret in the throng at the head of

Bolshaya Nikitskaya, now Herzen, Street. In the twinkling of an eye, Ivan arrived there himself. However, he had no luck. The poet would quicken his pace, break into a trot, shove passers-by, yet not get an inch closer to the professor.

Upset as he was, Ivan was still struck by the supernatural speed of the chase. Twenty seconds had not gone by when, after the Nikitsky Gate, Ivan Nikolaevich was already dazzled by the lights of the Arbat Square. Another few seconds, and here was some dark lane with slanting sidewalks, where Ivan Nikolaevich took a tumble and hurt his knee. Again a lit-up thoroughfare – Kropotkin Street – then a lane, then Ostozhenka, then another lane, dismal, vile and sparsely lit. And it was here that Ivan Nikolaevich definitively lost him whom he needed so much. The professor disappeared.

Ivan Nikolaevich was perplexed, but not for long, because he suddenly realized that the professor must unfailingly be found in house no. 13, and most assuredly in apartment 47.

Bursting into the entrance, Ivan Nikolaevich flew up to the second floor, immediately found the apartment, and rang impatiently. He did not have to wait long. Some little girl of about five opened the door for Ivan and, without asking him anything, immediately went away somewhere.

In the huge, extremely neglected front hall, weakly lit by a tiny carbon arc lamp under the high ceiling, black with grime, a bicycle without tyres hung on the wall, a huge iron-bound trunk stood, and on a shelf over the coat rack a winter hat lay, its long ear-flaps hanging down. Behind one of the doors, a resonant male voice was angrily shouting something in verse from a radio set.

Ivan Nikolaevich was not the least at a loss in the unfamiliar surroundings and rushed straight into the corridor, reasoning thus: 'Of course, he's hiding in the bathroom.' The corridor was dark. Having bumped into the wall a few times, Ivan saw a faint streak of light under a door, felt for the handle, and pulled it gently. The hook popped out, and Ivan found himself precisely in the bathroom and thought how lucky he was.

However, his luck was not all it might have been! Ivan met with a wave of humid heat and, by the light of the coals smouldering in the boiler, made out big basins hanging on the walls, and a bath tub, all black frightful blotches where the enamel had chipped off. And there, in this bath tub, stood a naked citizeness, all soapy and with a scrubber in her hand. She squinted near-sightedly at the bursting-in Ivan and, obviously mistaking him in the infernal light, said softly and gaily:

'Kiriushka! Stop this tomfoolery! Have you lost your mind? ... Fyodor Ivanych will be back any minute. Get out right now!' and she waved at Ivan with the scrubber.

The misunderstanding was evident, and Ivan Nikolaevich was, of course, to blame for it. But he did not want to admit it and, exclaiming reproachfully: 'Ah, wanton creature! ...', at once found himself for some reason in the kitchen. No one was there, and on the oven in the semi-darkness silently stood about a dozen extinguished primuses.[1] A single moonbeam, having seeped through the dusty, perennially unwashed window, shone sparsely into the corner where, in dust and cobwebs, a forgotten icon hung, with the ends of two wedding candles[2] peeking out from behind its casing. Under the big icon, pinned to it, hung a little one made of paper.

No one knows what thought took hold of Ivan here, but before running out the back door, he appropriated one of these candles, as well as the paper icon. With these objects, he left the unknown apartment, muttering something, embarrassed at the thought of what he had just experienced in the bathroom, involuntarily trying to guess who this impudent Kiriushka might be and whether the disgusting hat with ear-flaps belonged to him.

In the desolate, joyless lane the poet looked around, searching for the fugitive, but he was nowhere to be seen. Then Ivan said firmly to himself:

'Why, of course, he's at the Moscow River! Onward!'

Someone ought, perhaps, to have asked Ivan Nikolaevich why he supposed that the professor was precisely at the Moscow River and not in some other place. But the trouble was that there was no one to ask him. The loathsome lane was completely empty.

In the very shortest time, Ivan Nikolaevich could be seen on the granite steps of the Moscow River amphitheatre.[3]

Having taken off his clothes, Ivan entrusted them to a pleasant, bearded fellow who was smoking a hand-rolled cigarette, sitting beside a torn white Tolstoy blouse and a pair of unlaced, worn boots. After waving his arms to cool off, Ivan dived swallow-fashion into the water.

It took his breath away, so cold the water was, and the thought even flashed in him that he might not manage to come up to the surface. However, he did manage to come up, and, puffing and snorting, his eyes rounded in terror, Ivan Nikolaevich began swimming through the black, oil-smelling water among the broken zigzags of street lights on the bank.

When the wet Ivan came dancing back up the steps to the place where the bearded fellow was guarding his clothes, it became clear that not only the latter, but also the former – that is, the bearded fellow himself – had been stolen. In the exact spot where the pile of clothes had been, a pair of striped drawers, the torn Tolstoy blouse, the candle, the icon and a box of matches had been left. After threatening someone in the distance with his fist in powerless anger, Ivan put on what was left for him.

Here two considerations began to trouble him: first, that his Massolit identification card, which he never parted with, was gone, and, second, whether he could manage to get through Moscow unhindered looking the way he did now? In striped drawers, after all ... True, it was nobody's business, but still there might be some hitch or delay.

Ivan tore off the buttons where the drawers fastened at the ankle, figuring that this way they might pass for summer trousers, gathered up the icon, the candle and the matches, and started off, saying to himself:

'To Griboedov's! Beyond all doubt, he's there.'

The city was already living its evening life. Trucks flew through the dust, chains clanking, and on their platforms men lay sprawled belly up on sacks. All windows were open. In each of these windows a light burned under an orange lampshade, and from every window, every door, every gateway, roof, and attic, basement and courtyard blared the hoarse roar of the polonaise from the opera *Evgeny Onegin*.[4]

Ivan Nikolaevich's apprehensions proved fully justified: passers-by did pay attention to him and turned their heads. As a result, he took the decision to leave the main streets and make his way through back lanes, where people are not so importunate, where there were fewer chances of them picking on a barefoot man, pestering him with questions about his drawers, which stubbornly refused to look like trousers.

This Ivan did, and, penetrating the mysterious network of lanes around the Arbat, he began making his way along the walls, casting fearful sidelong glances, turning around every moment, hiding in gateways from time to time, avoiding intersections with traffic lights and the grand entrances of embassy mansions.

And all along his difficult way, he was for some reason inexpressibly tormented by the ubiquitous orchestra that accompanied the heavy basso singing about his love for Tatiana.

CHAPTER 5

There were Doings at Griboedov's

The old, two-storeyed, cream-coloured house stood on the ring boulevard, in the depths of a seedy garden, separated from the sidewalk by a fancy cast-iron fence. The small terrace in front of the house was paved with asphalt, and in wintertime was dominated by a snow pile with a shovel stuck in it, but in summertime turned into the most magnificent section of the summer restaurant under a canvas tent.

The house was called 'The House of Griboedov' on the grounds that it was alleged to have once belonged to an aunt of the writer Alexander Sergeevich Griboedov.[1] Now, whether it did or did not belong to her, we do not exactly know. On recollection, it even seems that Griboedov never had any such house-owning aunt . . . Nevertheless, that was what the house was called. Moreover, one Moscow liar had it that there, on the second floor, in a round hall with columns, the famous writer had supposedly read passages from *Woe From Wit* to this very aunt while she reclined on a sofa. However, devil knows, maybe he did, it's of no importance.

What is important is that at the present time this house was owned by that same Massolit which had been headed by the unfortunate Mikhail Alexandrovich Berlioz before his appearance at the Patriarch's Ponds.

In the casual manner of Massolit members, no one called the house 'The House of Griboedov', everyone simply said 'Griboedov's': 'I spent two hours yesterday knocking about Griboedov's.' 'Well, and so?' 'Got myself a month in Yalta.' 'Bravo!' Or: 'Go to Berlioz, he receives today from four to five at Griboedov's . . .' and so on.

Massolit had settled itself at Griboedov's in the best and cosiest way imaginable. Anyone entering Griboedov's first of all became involuntarily acquainted with the announcements of various sports clubs, and with group as well as individual photographs of the members of Massolit, hanging (the photographs) on the walls of the staircase leading to the second floor.

On the door to the very first room of this upper floor one could see a big sign: 'Fishing and Vacation Section', along with the picture of a carp caught on a line.

On the door of room no. 2 something not quite comprehensible was written: 'One-day Creative Trips. Apply to M. V. Spurioznaya.'

The next door bore a brief but now totally incomprehensible inscription: 'Perelygino'.[2] After which the chance visitor to Griboedov's would not know where to look from the motley inscriptions on the aunt's walnut doors: 'Sign up for Paper with Poklevkina', 'Cashier', 'Personal Accounts of Sketch-Writers' . . .

If one cut through the longest line, which already went downstairs and out to the doorman's lodge, one could see the sign 'Housing Question' on a door which people were crashing every second.

Beyond the housing question there opened out a luxurious poster on which a cliff was depicted and, riding on its crest, a horseman in a felt cloak with a rifle on his shoulder. A little lower – palm trees and a balcony; on the balcony – a seated young man with a forelock, gazing somewhere aloft with very lively eyes, holding a fountain pen in his hand. The inscription: 'Full-scale Creative Vacations from Two Weeks (Story/Novella) to One Year (Novel/Trilogy). Yalta, Suuk-Su, Borovoe, Tsikhidziri, Makhindzhauri, Leningrad (Winter Palace).'[3] There was also a line at this door, but not an excessive one – some hundred and fifty people.

Next, obedient to the whimsical curves, ascents and descents of the Griboedov house, came the 'Massolit Executive Board', 'Cashiers nos. 2, 3, 4, 5', 'Editorial Board', 'Chairman of Massolit', 'Billiard Room', various auxiliary institutions and, finally, that same hall with the colonnade where the aunt had delighted in the comedy of her genius nephew.

Any visitor finding himself in Griboedov's, unless of course he was a total dim-wit, would realize at once what a good life those lucky fellows, the Massolit members, were having, and black envy would immediately start gnawing at him. And he would immediately address bitter reproaches to heaven for not having endowed him at birth with literary talent, lacking which there was naturally no dreaming of owning a Massolit membership card, brown, smelling of costly leather, with a wide gold border – a card known to all Moscow.

Who will speak in defence of envy? This feeling belongs to the nasty category, but all the same one must put oneself in the visitor's position. For what he had seen on the upper floor was not all, and was far from all. The entire ground floor of the aunt's house was occupied by a restaurant, and what a restaurant! It was justly considered the best in Moscow. And not only because it took up two vast halls with arched ceilings, painted with violet, Assyrian-maned horses, not only because on each table there stood a lamp shaded with a shawl, not only because it was not accessible to just anybody coming in off the street, but because in the quality of its fare Griboedov's beat any restaurant in Moscow up and down, and this fare was available at the most reasonable, by no means onerous, price.

Hence there was nothing surprising, for instance, in the following conversation, which the author of these most truthful lines once heard near the cast-iron fence of Griboedov's:

'Where are you dining today, Amvrosy?'

'What a question! Why, here, of course, my dear Foka! Archibald Archibaldovich whispered to me today that there will be perch au naturel done to order. A virtuoso little treat!'

'You sure know how to live, Amvrosy!' skinny, run-down Foka, with a carbuncle on his neck, replied with a sigh to the ruddy-lipped giant, golden-haired, plump-cheeked Amvrosy-the-poet.

'I have no special knowledge,' Amvrosy protested, 'just the ordinary wish to live like a human being. You mean to say, Foka, that perch can be met with at the Coliseum as well. But at the Coliseum a portion of perch costs thirteen roubles fifteen kopecks, and here – five-fifty! Besides, at the Coliseum they serve three-day-old perch, and, besides, there's no guarantee you won't get slapped in the mug with a bunch of grapes at the Coliseum by the first young man who bursts in from Theatre Alley. No, I'm categorically opposed to the Coliseum,' the gastronome Amvrosy boomed for the whole boulevard to hear. 'Don't try to convince me, Foka!'

'I'm not trying to convince you, Amvrosy,' Foka squeaked. 'One can also dine at home.'

'I humbly thank you,' trumpeted Amvrosy, 'but I can imagine your wife, in the communal kitchen at home, trying to do perch au naturel to order in a saucepan! Hee, hee, hee! ... Aurevwar, Foka!' And, humming, Amvrosy directed his steps to the veranda under the tent.

Ahh, yes! ... Yes, there was a time! ... Old Muscovites will remember the renowned Griboedov's! What is poached perch done to order!

Cheap stuff, my dear Amvrosy! But sterlet, sterlet in a silvery chafing dish, sterlet slices interlaid with crayfish tails and fresh caviar? And eggs en cocotte with mushroom purée in little dishes? And how did you like the fillets of thrush? With truffles? Quail à la génoise? Nine-fifty! And the jazz, and the courteous service! And in July, when the whole family is in the country, and you are kept in the city by urgent literary business – on the veranda, in the shade of the creeping vines, in a golden spot on the cleanest of tablecloths, a bowl of soup printanier? Remember, Amvrosy? But why ask! I can see by your lips that you do. What is your whitefish, your perch! But the snipe, the great snipe, the jack snipe, the woodcock in their season, the quail, the curlew? Cool seltzer fizzing in your throat?! But enough, you are getting distracted, reader! Follow me! . . .

At half past ten on the evening when Berlioz died at the Patriarch's Ponds, only one room was lit upstairs at Griboedov's, and in it languished twelve writers who had gathered for a meeting and were waiting for Mikhail Alexandrovich.

Sitting on chairs, and on tables, and even on the two window-sills in the office of the Massolit executive board, they suffered seriously from the heat. Not a single breath of fresh air came through the open windows. Moscow was releasing the heat accumulated in the asphalt all day, and it was clear that night would bring no relief. The smell of onions came from the basement of the aunt's house, where the restaurant kitchen was at work, they were all thirsty, they were all nervous and angry.

The belletrist Beskudnikov – a quiet, decently dressed man with attentive and at the same time elusive eyes – took out his watch. The hand was crawling towards eleven. Beskudnikov tapped his finger on the face and showed it to the poet Dvubratsky, who was sitting next to him on the table and in boredom dangling his feet shod in yellow shoes with rubber treads.

'Anyhow,' grumbled Dvubratsky.

'The laddie must've got stuck on the Klyazma,' came the thick-voiced response of Nastasya Lukinishna Nepremenova, orphan of a Moscow merchant, who had become a writer and wrote stories about sea battles under the pen-name of Bos'n George.

'Excuse me!' boldly exclaimed Zagrivov, an author of popular sketches, 'but I personally would prefer a spot of tea on the balcony to stewing in here. The meeting was set for ten o'clock, wasn't it?'

'It's nice now on the Klyazma,' Bos'n George needled those present, knowing that Perelygino on the Klyazma, the country colony for writers, was everybody's sore spot. 'There's nightingales singing already. I always work better in the country, especially in spring.'

'It's the third year I've paid in so as to send my wife with goitre to this paradise, but there's nothing to be spied amidst the waves,' the novelist Ieronym Poprikhin said venomously and bitterly.

'Some are lucky and some aren't,' the critic Ababkov droned from the window-sill.

Bos'n George's little eyes lit up with glee, and she said, softening her contralto:

'We mustn't be envious, comrades. There's twenty-two dachas[4] in all, and only seven more being built, and there's three thousand of us in Massolit.'

'Three thousand one hundred and eleven,' someone put in from the corner.

'So you see,' the Bos'n went on, 'what can be done? Naturally, it's the most talented of us that got the dachas . . .'

'The generals!' Glukharev the scenarist cut right into the squabble.

Beskudnikov, with an artificial yawn, walked out of the room.

'Five rooms to himself in Perelygino,' Glukharev said behind him.

'Lavrovich has six to himself,' Deniskin cried out, 'and the dining room's panelled in oak!'

'Eh, that's not the point right now,' Ababkov droned, 'it's that it's half past eleven.'

A clamour arose, something like rebellion was brewing. They started telephoning hated Perelygino, got the wrong dacha, Lavrovich's, found out that Lavrovich had gone to the river, which made them totally upset. They called at random to the commission on fine literature, extension 930, and of course found no one there.

'He might have called!' shouted Deniskin, Glukharev and Quant.

Ah, they were shouting in vain: Mikhail Alexandrovich could not call anywhere. Far, far from Griboedov's, in an enormous room lit by thousand-watt bulbs, on three zinc tables, lay what had still recently been Mikhail Alexandrovich.

On the first lay the naked body, covered with dried blood, one arm broken, the chest caved in; on the second, the head with the front teeth knocked out, with dull, open eyes unafraid of the brightest light; and on the third, a pile of stiffened rags.

Near the beheaded body stood a professor of forensic medicine, a pathological anatomist and his dissector, representatives of the investigation, and Mikhail Alexandrovich's assistant in Massolit, the writer Zheldybin, summoned by telephone from his sick wife's side.

A car had come for Zheldybin and first of all taken him together with the investigators (this was around midnight) to the dead man's apartment, where the sealing of his papers had been carried out, after which they all went to the morgue.

And now those standing by the remains of the deceased were debating what was the better thing to do: to sew the severed head to the neck, or to lay out the body in the hall at Griboedov's after simply covering the dead man snugly to the chin with a black cloth?

No, Mikhail Alexandrovich could not call anywhere, and Deniskin, Glukharev and Quant, along with Beskudnikov, were being indignant and shouting quite in vain. Exactly at midnight, all twelve writers left the upper floor and descended to the restaurant. Here again they silently berated Mikhail Alexandrovich: all the tables on the veranda, naturally, were occupied, and they had to stay for supper in those beautiful but airless halls.

And exactly at midnight, in the first of these halls, something crashed, jangled, spilled, leaped. And all at once a high male voice desperately cried out 'Hallelujah!' to the music. The famous Griboedov jazz band struck up. Sweat-covered faces seemed to brighten, it was as if the horses painted on the ceiling came alive, the lamps seemed to shine with added light, and suddenly, as if tearing loose, both halls broke into dance, and following them the veranda broke into dance.

Glukharev danced with the poetess Tamara Polumesyats, Quant danced, Zhukopov the novelist danced with some movie actress in a yellow dress. Dragunsky danced, Cherdakchi danced, little Deniskin danced with the enormous Bos'n George, the beautiful Semeikina-Gall, an architect, danced in the tight embrace of a stranger in white canvas trousers. Locals and invited guests danced, Muscovites and out-of-towners, the writer Johann from Kronstadt, a certain Vitya Kuftik from Rostov, apparently a stage director, with a purple spot all over his cheek, the most eminent representatives of the poetry section of Massolit danced – that is, Baboonov, Blasphemsky, Sweetkin, Smatchstik and

Adelphina Buzdyak – young men of unknown profession, in crew cuts, with cotton-padded shoulders, danced, someone very elderly danced, a shred of green onion stuck in his beard, and with him danced a sickly, anaemia-consumed girl in a wrinkled orange silk dress.

Streaming with sweat, waiters carried sweating mugs of beer over their heads, shouting hoarsely and with hatred: 'Excuse me, citizen!' Somewhere through a megaphone a voice commanded: 'One Karsky shashlik! Two Zubrovkas! Home-style tripe!' The high voice no longer sang, but howled 'Hallelujah!' The clashing of golden cymbals in the band sometimes even drowned out the clashing of dishes which the dishwashers sent down a sloping chute to the kitchen. In short – hell.

And at midnight there came an apparition in hell. A handsome dark-eyed man with a dagger-like beard, in a tailcoat, stepped on to the veranda and cast a regal glance over his domain. They used to say, the mystics used to say, that there was a time when the handsome man wore not a tailcoat but a wide leather belt with pistol butts sticking from it, and his raven hair was tied with scarlet silk, and under his command a brig sailed the Caribbean under a black death flag with a skull and crossbones.

But no, no! The seductive mystics are lying, there are no Caribbean Seas in the world, no desperate freebooters sail them, no corvette chases after them, no cannon smoke drifts across the waves. There is nothing, and there was nothing! There is that sickly linden over there, there is the cast-iron fence, and the boulevard beyond it ... And the ice is melting in the bowl, and at the next table you see someone's bloodshot, bovine eyes, and you're afraid, afraid ... Oh, gods, my gods, poison, bring me poison! ...

And suddenly a word fluttered up from some table: 'Berlioz!!' The jazz broke up and fell silent, as if someone had hit it with a fist. 'What, what, what, what?!!' 'Berlioz!!!' And they began jumping up, exclaiming ...

Yes, a wave of grief billowed up at the terrible news about Mikhail Alexandrovich. Someone fussed about, crying that it was necessary at once, straight away, without leaving the spot, to compose some collective telegram and send it off immediately.

But what telegram, may we ask, and where? And why send it? And where, indeed? And what possible need for any telegram does someone have whose flattened pate is now clutched in the dissector's rubber hands, whose neck the professor is now piercing with curved needles? He's dead, and has no need of any telegrams. It's all over, let's not burden the telegraph wires any more.

Yes, he's dead, dead ... But, as for us, we're alive!

Yes, a wave of grief billowed up, held out for a while, but then began to subside, and somebody went back to his table and – sneakily at first, then openly – drank a little vodka and ate a bite. And, really, can one let chicken cutlets de volaille perish? How can we help Mikhail Alexandrovich? By going hungry? But, after all, we're alive!

Naturally, the grand piano was locked, the jazz band dispersed, several journalists left for their offices to write obituaries. It became known that Zheldybin had come from the morgue. He had installed himself in the deceased's office upstairs, and the rumour spread at once that it was he who would replace Berlioz. Zheldybin summoned from the restaurant all twelve members of the board, and at the urgently convened meeting in Berlioz's office they started a discussion of the pressing questions of decorating the hall with columns at Griboedov's, of transporting the body from the morgue to that hall, of opening it to the public, and all else connected with the sad event.

And the restaurant began to live its usual nocturnal life and would have gone on living it until closing time, that is, until four o'clock in the morning, had it not been for an occurrence which was completely out of the ordinary and which struck the restaurant's clientele much more than the news of Berlioz's death.

The first to take alarm were the coachmen[5] waiting at the gates of the Griboedov house. One of them, rising on his box, was heard to cry out:

'Hoo-ee! Just look at that!'

After which, from God knows where, a little light flashed by the cast-iron fence and began to approach the veranda. Those sitting at the tables began to get up and peer at it, and saw that along with the little light a white ghost was marching towards the restaurant. When it came right up to the trellis, everybody sat as if frozen at their tables, chunks of sterlet on their forks, eyes popping. The doorman, who at that moment had stepped out of the restaurant coat room to have a smoke in the yard, stamped out his cigarette and made for the ghost with the obvious intention of barring its way into the restaurant, but for some reason did not do so, and stopped, smiling stupidly.

And the ghost, passing through an opening in the trellis, stepped unhindered on to the veranda. Here everyone saw that it was no ghost at all, but Ivan Nikolaevich Homeless, the much-renowned poet.

He was barefoot, in a torn, whitish Tolstoy blouse, with a paper icon bearing the image of an unknown saint pinned to the breast of it with a safety pin, and was wearing striped white drawers. In his hand Ivan Nikolaevich carried a lighted wedding candle. Ivan Nikolaevich's right cheek was freshly scratched. It would even be difficult to plumb the depths of the silence that reigned on the veranda. Beer could be seen running down on to the floor from a mug tilted in one waiter's hand.

The poet raised the candle over his head and said loudly:

'Hail, friends!' After which he peeked under the nearest table and exclaimed ruefully: 'No, he's not there!'

Two voices were heard. A basso said pitilessly:

'That's it. Delirium tremens.'

And the second, a woman's, frightened, uttered the words:

'How could the police let him walk the streets like that?'

This Ivan Nikolaevich heard, and replied:

'They tried to detain me twice, in Skaterny and here on Bronnaya, but I hopped over the fence and, as you can see, cut my cheek!' Here Ivan Nikolaevich raised the candle and cried out: 'Brethren in literature!' (His hoarse voice grew stronger and more fervent.) 'Listen to me everyone! He has appeared. Catch him immediately, otherwise he'll do untold harm!'

'What? What? What did he say? Who has appeared?' voices came from all sides.

'The consultant,' Ivan replied, 'and this consultant just killed Misha Berlioz at the Patriarch's Ponds.'

Here people came flocking to the veranda from the inner rooms, a crowd gathered around Ivan's flame.

'Excuse me, excuse me, be more precise,' a soft and polite voice said over Ivan Nikolaevich's ear, 'tell me, what do you mean "killed"? Who killed?'

'A foreign consultant, a professor, and a spy,' Ivan said, looking around.

'And what is his name?' came softly to Ivan's ear.

'That's just it – his name!' Ivan cried in anguish. 'If only I knew his name! I didn't make out his name on his visiting card ... I only remember the first letter, "W", his name begins with "W"! What last name begins with "W"?' Ivan asked himself, clutching his forehead, and suddenly started muttering: 'Wi, we, wa ... Wu ... Wo ... Washner? Wagner? Weiner? Wegner? Winter?' The hair on Ivan's head began to crawl with the tension.

'Wolf?' some woman cried pitifully.

Ivan became angry.

'Fool!' he cried, seeking the woman with his eyes. 'What has Wolf got to do with it? Wolf's not to blame for anything! Wo, wa ... No, I'll never remember this way! Here's what, citizens: call the police at once, let them send out five motor cycles with machine-guns to catch the professor. And don't forget to tell them that there are two others with him: a long checkered one, cracked pince-nez, and a cat, black and fat ... And meanwhile I'll search Griboedov's, I sense that he's here!'

Ivan became anxious, pushed away the people around him, started waving the candle, pouring wax on himself, and looking under the tables. Here someone said: 'Call a doctor!' and someone's benign, fleshy face, clean shaven and well nourished, in horn-rimmed glasses, appeared before Ivan.

'Comrade Homeless,' the face began in a guest speaker's voice, 'calm down! You're upset at the death of our beloved Mikhail Alexandrovich ... no, say just Misha Berlioz. We all understand that perfectly well. You need rest. The comrades will take you home to bed right now, you'll forget ...'

'You,' Ivan interrupted, baring his teeth, 'but don't you understand that the professor has to be caught? And you come at me with your foolishness! Cretin!'

'Pardon me, Comrade Homeless! ...' the face replied, blushing, retreating, and already repentant at having got mixed up in this affair.

'No, anyone else, but you I will not pardon,' Ivan Nikolaevich said with quiet hatred.

A spasm distorted his face, he quickly shifted the candle from his right hand to his left, swung roundly and hit the compassionate face on the ear.

Here it occurred to them to fall upon Ivan – and so they did. The candle went out, and the glasses that had fallen from the face were instantly trampled. Ivan let out a terrible war cry, heard, to the temptation of all, even on the boulevard, and set about defending himself. Dishes fell clattering from the tables, women screamed.

All the while the waiters were tying up the poet with napkins, a conversation was going on in the coat room between the commander of the brig and the doorman.

'Didn't you see he was in his underpants?' the pirate inquired coldly.

'But, Archibald Archibaldovich,' the doorman replied, cowering, 'how could I not let him in, if he's a member of Massolit?'

'Didn't you see he was in his underpants?' the pirate repeated.

'Pardon me, Archibald Archibaldovich,' the doorman said, turning purple, 'but what could I do? I understand, there are ladies sitting on the veranda . . .'

'Ladies have nothing to do with it, it makes no difference to the ladies,' the pirate replied, literally burning the doorman up with his eyes, 'but it does to the police! A man in his underwear can walk the streets of Moscow only in this one case, that he's accompanied by the police, and only to one place – the police station! And you, if you're a doorman, ought to know that on seeing such a man, you must, without a moment's delay, start blowing your whistle. Do you hear? Do you hear what's going on on the veranda?'

Here the half-crazed doorman heard some sort of hooting coming from the veranda, the smashing of dishes and women's screams.

'Now, what's to be done with you for that?' the freebooter asked.

The skin on the doorman's face acquired a typhoid tinge, his eyes went dead. It seemed to him that the black hair, now combed and parted, was covered with flaming silk. The shirt-front and tailcoat disappeared and a pistol butt emerged, tucked into a leather belt. The doorman pictured himself hanging from the fore-topsail yard. His eyes saw his own tongue sticking out and his lifeless head lolling on his shoulder, and even heard the splash of waves against the hull. The doorman's knees gave way. But here the freebooter took pity on him and extinguished his sharp gaze.

'Watch out, Nikolai, this is the last time! We have no need of such doormen in the restaurant. Go find yourself a job as a beadle.' Having said this, the commander commanded precisely, clearly, rapidly: 'Get Pantelei from the snack bar. Police. Protocol. A car. To the psychiatric clinic.' And added: 'Blow your whistle!'

In a quarter of an hour an extremely astounded public, not only in the restaurant but on the boulevard itself and in the windows of houses looking on to the restaurant garden, saw Pantelei, the doorman, a policeman, a waiter and the poet Riukhin carry through the gates of Griboedov's a young man swaddled like a doll, dissolved in tears, who spat, aiming precisely at Riukhin, and shouted for all the boulevard to hear:

'You bastard! . . . You bastard! . . .'

A truck-driver with a spiteful face was starting his motor. Next to him a coachman, rousing his horse, slapping it on the croup with violet reins, shouted:

'Have a run for your money! I've taken 'em to the psychics before!'

Around them the crowd buzzed, discussing the unprecedented event. In short, there was a nasty, vile, tempting, swinish scandal, which ended only when the truck carried away from the gates of Griboedov's the unfortunate Ivan Nikolaevich, the policeman, Pantelei and Riukhin.

CHAPTER 6

Schizophrenia, as was Said

It was half past one in the morning when a man with a pointed beard and wearing a white coat came out to the examining room of the famous psychiatric clinic, built recently on the outskirts of Moscow by the bank of the river. Three orderlies had their eyes fastened on Ivan Nikolaevich, who was sitting on a couch. The extremely agitated poet Riukhin was also there. The napkins with which Ivan Nikolaevich had been tied up lay in a pile on the same couch. Ivan Nikolaevich's arms and legs were free.

Seeing the entering man, Riukhin turned pale, coughed, and said timidly:

'Hello, Doctor.'

The doctor bowed to Riukhin but, as he bowed, looked not at him but at Ivan Nikolaevich. The latter sat perfectly motionless, with an angry face and knitted brows, and did not even stir at the doctor's entrance.

'Here, Doctor,' Riukhin began speaking, for some reason, in a mysterious whisper, glancing timorously at Ivan Nikolaevich, 'is the renowned poet Ivan Homeless ... well, you see ... we're afraid it might be delirium tremens ...'

'Was he drinking hard?' the doctor said through his teeth.

'No, he drank, but not really so ...'

'Did he chase after cockroaches, rats, little devils, or slinking dogs?'

'No,' Riukhin replied with a shudder, 'I saw him yesterday and this morning ... he was perfectly well.'

'And why is he in his drawers? Did you get him out of bed?'

'No, Doctor, he came to the restaurant that way ...'

'Aha, aha,' the doctor said with great satisfaction, 'and why the scratches? Did he have a fight?'

'He fell off a fence, and then in the restaurant he hit somebody ... and then somebody else ...'

'So, so, so,' the doctor said and, turning to Ivan, added: 'Hello there!'

'Greetings, saboteur!'[1] Ivan replied spitefully and loudly.

Riukhin was so embarrassed that he did not dare raise his eyes to the courteous doctor. But the latter, not offended in the least, took off his glasses with a habitual, deft movement, raised the skirt of his coat, put them into the back pocket of his trousers, and then asked Ivan:

'How old are you?'

'You can all go to the devil!' Ivan shouted rudely and turned away.

'But why are you angry? Did I say anything unpleasant to you?'

'I'm twenty-three years old,' Ivan began excitedly, 'and I'll file a complaint against you all. And particularly against you, louse!' he adverted separately to Riukhin.

'And what do you want to complain about?'

'About the fact that I, a healthy man, was seized and dragged by force to a madhouse!' Ivan replied wrathfully.

Here Riukhin looked closely at Ivan and went cold: there was decidedly no insanity in the man's eyes. No longer dull as they had been at Griboedov's, they were now clear as ever.

'Good God!' Riukhin thought fearfully. 'So he's really normal! What nonsense! Why, in fact, did we drag him here? He's normal, normal, only his mug got scratched . . .'

'You are,' the doctor began calmly, sitting down on a white stool with a shiny foot, 'not in a madhouse, but in a clinic, where no one will keep you if it's not necessary.'

Ivan Nikolaevich glanced at him mistrustfully out of the corner of his eye, but still grumbled:

'Thank the Lord! One normal man has finally turned up among the idiots, of whom the first is that giftless goof Sashka!'

'Who is this giftless Sashka?' the doctor inquired.

'This one here – Riukhin,' Ivan replied, jabbing his dirty finger in Riukhin's direction.

The latter flushed with indignation. 'That's the thanks I get,' he thought bitterly, 'for showing concern for him! What trash, really!'

'Psychologically, a typical little kulak,'[2] Ivan Nikolaevich began, evidently from an irresistible urge to denounce Riukhin, 'and, what's more, a little kulak carefully disguising himself as a proletarian. Look at his lenten physiognomy, and compare it with those resounding verses he wrote for the First of May[3] – heh, heh, heh . . . "Soaring up!" and "Soaring down!!" But if you could look inside him and see what he thinks ... you'd gasp!' And Ivan Nikolaevich burst into sinister laughter.

Riukhin was breathing heavily, turned red, and thought of just one thing, that he had warmed a serpent on his breast, that he had shown concern for a man who turned out to be a vicious enemy. And, above all, there was nothing to be done: there's no arguing with the mentally ill!

'And why, actually, were you brought here?' the doctor asked, after listening attentively to Homeless's denunciations.

'Devil take them, the numskulls! They seized me, tied me up with some rags, and dragged me away in a truck!'

'May I ask why you came to the restaurant in just your underwear?'

'There's nothing surprising about that,' Ivan replied. 'I went for a swim in the Moscow River, so they filched my clothes and left me this trash! I couldn't very well walk around Moscow naked! I put it on because I was hurrying to Griboedov's restaurant.'

The doctor glanced questioningly at Riukhin, who muttered glumly:

'The name of the restaurant.'

'Aha,' said the doctor, 'and why were you in such a hurry? Some business meeting?'

'I'm trying to catch the consultant,' Ivan Nikolaevich said and looked around anxiously.

'What consultant?'

'Do you know Berlioz?' Ivan asked significantly.

'The ... composer?'

Ivan got upset.

'What composer? Ah, yes ... Ah, no. The composer has the same name as Misha Berlioz.'

Riukhin had no wish to say anything, but was forced to explain:

'The secretary of Massolit, Berlioz, was run over by a tram-car tonight at the Patriarch's Ponds.'

'Don't blab about what you don't know!' Ivan got angry with Riukhin. 'I was there, not you! He got him under the tram-car on purpose!'

'Pushed him?'

' "Pushed him", nothing!' Ivan exclaimed, angered by the general obtuseness. 'His kind don't need to push! He can perform such stunts – hold on to your hat! He knew beforehand that Berlioz would get under the tram-car!'

'And did anyone besides you see this consultant?'

'That's the trouble, it was just Berlioz and I.'

'So. And what measures did you take to catch this murderer?' Here the doctor turned and sent a glance towards a woman in a white coat, who was sitting at a table to one side. She took out a sheet of paper and began filling in the blank spaces in its columns.

'Here's what measures: I took a little candle from the kitchen . . .'

'That one?' asked the doctor, pointing to the broken candle lying on the table in front of the woman, next to the icon.

'That very one, and . . .'

'And why the icon?'

'Ah, yes, the icon . . .' Ivan blushed. 'It was the icon that frightened them most of all.' He again jabbed his finger in the direction of Riukhin. 'But the thing is that he, the consultant, he . . . let's speak directly . . . is mixed up with the unclean powers . . . and you won't catch him so easily.'

The orderlies for some reason snapped to attention and fastened their eyes on Ivan.

'Yes, sirs,' Ivan went on, 'mixed up with them! An absolute fact. He spoke personally with Pontius Pilate. And there's no need to stare at me like that. I'm telling the truth! He saw everything – the balcony and the palm trees. In short, he was at Pontius Pilate's, I can vouch for it.'

'Come, come . . .'

'Well, so I pinned the icon on my chest and ran . . .'

Here the clock suddenly struck twice.

'Oh-oh!' Ivan exclaimed and got up from the couch. 'It's two o'clock, and I'm wasting time with you! Excuse me, where's the telephone?'

'Let him use the telephone,' the doctor told the orderlies.

Ivan grabbed the receiver, and the woman meanwhile quietly asked Riukhin:

'Is he married?'

'Single,' Riukhin answered fearfully.

'Member of a trade union?'

'Yes.'

'Police?' Ivan shouted into the receiver. 'Police? Comrade officer-on-duty, give orders at once for five motor cycles with machine-guns to be sent out to catch the foreign consultant. What? Come and pick me up, I'll go with you ... It's the poet Homeless speaking from the madhouse ... What's your address?' Homeless asked the doctor in a whisper, covering the receiver with his hand, and then again shouting into it: 'Are you listening? Hello! ... Outrageous!' Ivan suddenly screamed and hurled the receiver against the wall. Then he turned to the doctor, offered him his hand, said 'Goodbye' drily, and made as if to leave.

'For pity's sake, where do you intend to go?' the doctor said, peering into Ivan's eyes. 'In the dead of night, in your underwear ... You're not feeling well, stay with us.'

'Let me pass,' Ivan said to the orderlies, who closed ranks at the door. 'Will you let me pass or not?' the poet shouted in a terrible voice.

Riukhin trembled, but the woman pushed a button on the table and a shiny little box with a sealed ampoule popped out on to its glass surface.

'Ah, so?!' Ivan said, turning around with a wild and hunted look. 'Well, then ... Goodbye!' And he rushed head first into the window-blind.

The crash was rather forceful, but the glass behind the blind gave no crack, and in an instant Ivan Nikolaevich was struggling in the hands of the orderlies. He gasped, tried to bite, shouted:

'So that's the sort of windows you've got here! Let me go! Let me go! ...'

A syringe flashed in the doctor's hand, with a single movement the woman slit the threadbare sleeve of the shirt and seized the arm with unwomanly strength. There was a smell of ether, Ivan went limp in the hands of the four people, the deft doctor took advantage of this moment and stuck the needle into Ivan's arm. They held Ivan for another few seconds and then lowered him on to the couch.

'Bandits!' Ivan shouted and jumped up from the couch, but was installed on it again. The moment they let go of him, he again jumped up, but sat back down by himself. He paused, gazing around wildly, then unexpectedly yawned, then smiled maliciously.

'Locked me up after all,' he said, yawned again, unexpectedly lay down, put his head on the pillow, his fist under his head like a child, and muttered now in a sleepy voice, without malice: 'Very well, then ... you'll pay for it yourselves ... I've warned you, you can do as you

like ... I'm now interested most of all in Pontius Pilate ... Pilate ...',
and he closed his eyes.

'A bath, a private room, number 117, and a nurse to watch him,'
the doctor ordered as he put his glasses on. Here Riukhin again gave
a start: the white door opened noiselessly, behind it a corridor could
be seen, lit by blue night-lights. Out of the corridor rolled a stretcher
on rubber wheels, to which the quieted Ivan was transferred, and then
he rolled off down the corridor and the door closed behind him.

'Doctor,' the shaken Riukhin asked in a whisper, 'it means he's really
ill?'

'Oh, yes,' replied the doctor.

'But what's wrong with him, then?' Riukhin asked timidly.

The tired doctor glanced at Riukhin and answered listlessly:

'Locomotor and speech excitation ... delirious interpretations ...
A complex case, it seems. Schizophrenia, I suppose. Plus this
alcoholism ...'

Riukhin understood nothing from the doctor's words, except that
things were evidently not so great with Ivan Nikolaevich. He sighed
and asked:

'But what's all this talk of his about some consultant?'

'He must have seen somebody who struck his disturbed imagination.
Or maybe a hallucination ...'

A few minutes later the truck was carrying Riukhin off to Moscow.
Day was breaking, and the light of the street lights still burning along
the highway was now unnecessary and unpleasant. The driver was
vexed at having wasted the night, drove the truck as fast as he could,
and skidded on the turns.

Now the woods dropped off, stayed somewhere behind, and the
river went somewhere to the side, and an omnium gatherum came
spilling to meet the truck: fences with sentry boxes and stacks of wood,
tall posts and some sort of poles, with spools strung on the poles,
heaps of rubble, the earth scored by canals – in short, you sensed that
she was there, Moscow, right there, around the turn, and about to
heave herself upon you and engulf you.

Riukhin was jolted and tossed about; the sort of stump he had placed
himself on kept trying to slide out from under him. The restaurant
napkins, thrown in by the policeman and Pantelei, who had left earlier
by bus, moved all around the flatbed. Riukhin tried to collect them,

but then, for some reason hissing spitefully: 'Devil take them! What am I doing fussing like a fool? . . .', he spurned them aside with his foot and stopped looking at them.

The rider's state of mind was terrible. It was becoming clear that his visit to the house of sorrow had left the deepest mark on him. Riukhin tried to understand what was tormenting him. The corridor with blue lights, which had stuck itself to his memory? The thought that there is no greater misfortune in the world than the loss of reason? Yes, yes, of course, that, too. But that – that's only a general thought. There's something else. What is it? An insult, that's what. Yes, yes, insulting words hurled right in his face by Homeless. And the trouble is not that they were insulting, but that there was truth in them.

The poet no longer looked around, but, staring into the dirty, shaking floor, began muttering something, whining, gnawing at himself.

Yes, poetry . . . He was thirty-two years old! And, indeed, what then? So then he would go on writing his several poems a year. Into old age? Yes, into old age. What would these poems bring him? Glory? 'What nonsense! Don't deceive yourself, at least. Glory will never come to someone who writes bad poems. What makes them bad? The truth, he was telling the truth!' Riukhin addressed himself mercilessly. 'I don't believe in anything I write! . . .'

Poisoned by this burst of neurasthenia, the poet swayed, the floor under him stopped shaking. Riukhin raised his head and saw that he had long been in Moscow, and, what's more, that it was dawn over Moscow, that the cloud was underlit with gold, that his truck had stopped, caught in a column of other vehicles at the turn on to the boulevard, and that very close to him on a pedestal stood a metal man,[4] his head inclined slightly, gazing at the boulevard with indifference.

Some strange thoughts flooded the head of the ailing poet. 'There's an example of real luck . . .' Here Riukhin rose to his full height on the flatbed of the truck and raised his arm, for some reason attacking the cast-iron man who was not bothering anyone. 'Whatever step he made in his life, whatever happened to him, it all turned to his benefit, it all led to his glory! But what did he do? I can't conceive . . . Is there anything special in the words: "The snowstorm covers . . ."? I don't understand! . . . Luck, sheer luck!' Riukhin concluded with venom, and felt the truck moving under him. 'He shot him, that white guard shot him, smashed his hip, and assured his immortality . . .'

The column began to move. In no more than two minutes, the completely ill and even aged poet was entering the veranda of Griboedov's. It was now empty. In a corner some company was finishing its drinks, and in the middle the familiar master of ceremonies was bustling about, wearing a skullcap, with a glass of Abrau wine in his hand.

Riukhin, laden with napkins, was met affably by Archibald Archibaldovich and at once relieved of the cursed rags. Had Riukhin not become so worn out in the clinic and on the truck, he would certainly have derived pleasure from telling how everything had gone in the hospital and embellishing the story with invented details. But just then he was far from such things, and, little observant though Riukhin was, now, after the torture on the truck, he peered keenly at the pirate for the first time and realized that, though the man asked about Homeless and even exclaimed 'Ai-yai-yai!', he was essentially quite indifferent to Homeless's fate and did not feel a bit sorry for him. 'And bravo! Right you are!' Riukhin thought with cynical, self-annihilating malice and, breaking off the story about the schizophrenia, begged:

'Archibald Archibaldovich, a drop of vodka . . .'

The pirate made a compassionate face and whispered:

'I understand . . . this very minute . . .' and beckoned to a waiter.

A quarter of an hour later, Riukhin sat in complete solitude, hunched over his bream, drinking glass after glass, understanding and recognizing that it was no longer possible to set anything right in his life, that it was only possible to forget.

The poet had wasted his night while others were feasting and now understood that it was impossible to get it back. One needed only to raise one's head from the lamp to the sky to understand that the night was irretrievably lost. Waiters were hurriedly tearing the tablecloths from the tables. The cats slinking around the veranda had a morning look. Day irresistibly heaved itself upon the poet.

CHAPTER 7

A Naughty Apartment

If Styopa Likhodeev had been told the next morning: 'Styopa! You'll be shot if you don't get up this minute!' – Styopa would have replied in a languid, barely audible voice: 'Shoot me, do what you like with me, I won't get up.'

Not only not get up, it seemed to him that he could not open his eyes, because if he were to do so, there would be a flash of lightning, and his head would at once be blown to pieces. A heavy bell was booming in that head, brown spots rimmed with fiery green floated between his eyeballs and his closed eyelids, and to crown it all he was nauseous, this nausea, as it seemed to him, being connected with the sounds of some importunate gramophone.

Styopa tried to recall something, but only one thing would get recalled – that yesterday, apparently, and in some unknown place, he had stood with a napkin in his hand and tried to kiss some lady, promising her that the next day, and exactly at noon, he would come to visit her. The lady had declined, saying: 'No, no, I won't be home!', but Styopa had stubbornly insisted: 'And I'll just up and come anyway!'

Who the lady was, and what time it was now, what day, of what month, Styopa decidedly did not know, and, worst of all, he could not figure out where he was. He attempted to learn this last at least, and to that end unstuck the stuck-together lids of his left eye. Something gleamed dully in the semi-darkness. Styopa finally recognized the pier-glass and realized that he was lying on his back in his own bed – that is, the jeweller's wife's former bed – in the bedroom. Here he felt such a throbbing in his head that he closed his eyes and moaned.

Let us explain: Styopa Likhodeev, director of the Variety Theatre, had come to his senses that morning at home, in the very apartment which he shared with the late Berlioz, in a big, six-storeyed, U-shaped building on Sadovaya Street.

It must be said that this apartment – no. 50 – had long had, if not a bad, at least a strange reputation. Two years ago it had still belonged to the widow of the jeweller de Fougeray. Anna Frantsevna de Fougeray, a respectable and very practical fifty-year-old woman, let out three of the five rooms to lodgers: one whose last name was apparently Belomut, and another with a lost last name.

And then two years ago inexplicable events began to occur in this apartment: people began to disappear[1] from this apartment without a trace.

Once, on a day off, a policeman came to the apartment, called the second lodger (the one whose last name got lost) out to the front hall, and said he was invited to come to the police station for a minute to put his signature to something. The lodger told Anfisa, Anna Frantsevna's long-time and devoted housekeeper, to say, in case he received any telephone calls, that he would be back in ten minutes, and left together with the proper, white-gloved policeman. He not only did not come back in ten minutes, but never came back at all. The most surprising thing was that the policeman evidently vanished along with him.

The pious, or, to speak more frankly, superstitious Anfisa declared outright to the very upset Anna Frantsevna that it was sorcery and that she knew perfectly well who had stolen both the lodger and the policeman, only she did not wish to talk about it towards night-time.

Well, but with sorcery, as everyone knows, once it starts, there's no stopping it. The second lodger is remembered to have disappeared on a Monday, and that Wednesday Belomut seemed to drop from sight, though, true, under different circumstances. In the morning a car came, as usual, to take him to work, and it did take him to work, but it did not bring anyone back or come again itself.

Madame Belomut's grief and horror defied description. But, alas, neither the one nor the other continued for long. That same night, on returning with Anfisa from her dacha, which Anna Frantsevna had hurried off to for some reason, she did not find the wife of citizen Belomut in the apartment. And not only that: the doors of the two rooms occupied by the Belomut couple turned out to be sealed.

Two days passed somehow. On the third day, Anna Frantsevna, who had suffered all the while from insomnia, again left hurriedly for her dacha ... Needless to say, she never came back!

Left alone, Anfisa, having wept her fill, went to sleep past one o'clock in the morning. What happened to her after that is not known, but lodgers in other apartments told of hearing some sort of knocking all night in no. 50 and of seeing electric light burning in the windows till morning. In the morning it turned out that there was also no Anfisa!

For a long time all sorts of legends were repeated in the house about these disappearances and about the accursed apartment, such as, for instance, that this dry and pious little Anfisa had supposedly carried on her dried-up breast, in a suede bag, twenty-five big diamonds belonging to Anna Frantsevna. That in the woodshed of that very dacha to which Anna Frantsevna had gone so hurriedly, there supposedly turned up, of themselves, some inestimable treasures in the form of those same diamonds, plus some gold coins of tsarist minting ... And so on, in the same vein. Well, what we don't know, we can't vouch for.

However it may have been, the apartment stood empty and sealed for only a week. Then the late Berlioz moved in with his wife, and this same Styopa, also with his wife. It was perfectly natural that, as soon as they got into the malignant apartment, devil knows what started happening with them as well! Namely, within the space of a month both wives vanished. But these two not without a trace. Of Berlioz's wife it was told that she had supposedly been seen in Kharkov with some ballet-master, while Styopa's wife allegedly turned up on Bozhedomka Street, where wagging tongues said the director of the Variety, using his innumerable acquaintances, had contrived to get her a room, but on the one condition that she never show her face on Sadovaya ...

And so, Styopa moaned. He wanted to call the housekeeper Grunya and ask her for aspirin, but was still able to realize that it was foolish, and that Grunya, of course, had no aspirin. He tried to call Berlioz for help, groaned twice: 'Misha ... Misha ...', but, as you will understand, received no reply. The apartment was perfectly silent.

Moving his toes, Styopa realized that he was lying there in his socks, passed his trembling hand down his hip to determine whether he had his trousers on or not, but failed. Finally, seeing that he was abandoned and alone, and there was no one to help him, he decided to get up, however inhuman the effort it cost him.

Styopa unstuck his glued eyelids and saw himself reflected in the pier-glass as a man with hair sticking out in all directions, with a bloated physiognomy covered with black stubble, with puffy eyes, a dirty shirt, collar and necktie, in drawers and socks.

So he saw himself in the pier-glass, and next to the mirror he saw an unknown man, dressed in black and wearing a black beret.

Styopa sat up in bed and goggled his bloodshot eyes as well as he could at the unknown man. The silence was broken by this unknown man, who said in a low, heavy voice, and with a foreign accent, the following words:

'Good morning, my most sympathetic Stepan Bogdanovich!'

There was a pause, after which, making a most terrible strain on himself, Styopa uttered:

'What can I do for you?' – and was amazed, not recognizing his own voice. He spoke the word 'what' in a treble, 'can I' in a bass, and his 'do for you' did not come off at all.

The stranger smiled amicably, took out a big gold watch with a diamond triangle on the lid, rang eleven times, and said:

'Eleven. And for exactly an hour I've been waiting for you to wake up, since you made an appointment for me to come to your place at ten. Here I am!'[2]

Styopa felt for his trousers on the chair beside his bed, whispered: 'Excuse me . . .', put them on, and asked hoarsely: 'Tell me your name, please?'

He had difficulty speaking. At each word, someone stuck a needle into his brain, causing infernal pain.

'What! You've forgotten my name, too?' Here the unknown man smiled.

'Forgive me . . .' Styopa croaked, feeling that his hangover had presented him with a new symptom: it seemed to him that the floor beside his bed went away, and that at any moment he would go flying down to the devil's dam in the nether world.

'My dear Stepan Bogdanovich,' the visitor said, with a perspicacious smile, 'no aspirin will help you. Follow the wise old rule – cure like with like. The only thing that will bring you back to life is two glasses of vodka with something pickled and hot to go with it.'

Styopa was a shrewd man and, sick as he was, realized that since he had been found in this state, he would have to confess everything.

'Frankly speaking,' he began, his tongue barely moving, 'yesterday I got a bit . . .'

'Not a word more!' the visitor answered and drew aside with his chair.

Styopa, rolling his eyes, saw that a tray had been set on a small table, on which tray there were sliced white bread, pressed caviar in a little bowl, pickled mushrooms on a dish, something in a saucepan, and, finally, vodka in a roomy decanter belonging to the jeweller's wife. What struck Styopa especially was that the decanter was frosty with cold. This, however, was understandable: it was sitting in a bowl packed with ice. In short, the service was neat, efficient.

The stranger did not allow Styopa's amazement to develop to a morbid degree, but deftly poured him half a glass of vodka.

'And you?' Styopa squeaked.

'With pleasure!'

His hand twitching, Styopa brought the glass to his lips, while the stranger swallowed the contents of his glass at one gulp. Chewing a lump of caviar, Styopa squeezed out of himself the words:

'And you . . . a bite of something?'

'Much obliged, but I never snack,' the stranger replied and poured seconds. The saucepan was opened and found to contain frankfurters in tomato sauce.

And then the accursed green haze before his eyes dissolved, the words began to come out clearly, and, above all, Styopa remembered a thing or two. Namely, that it had taken place yesterday in Skhodnya, at the dacha of the sketch-writer Khustov, to which this same Khustov had taken Styopa in a taxi. There was even a memory of having hired this taxi by the Metropol, and there was also some actor, or not an actor . . . with a gramophone in a little suitcase. Yes, yes, yes, it was at the dacha! The dogs, he remembered, had howled from this gramophone. Only the lady Styopa had wanted to kiss remained unexplained . . . devil knows who she was . . . maybe she was in radio, maybe not . . .

The previous day was thus coming gradually into focus, but right now Styopa was much more interested in today's day and, particularly, in the appearance in his bedroom of a stranger, and with hors d'œuvres and vodka to boot. It would be nice to explain that!

'Well, I hope by now you've remembered my name?'

But Styopa only smiled bashfully and spread his arms.

'Really! I get the feeling that you followed the vodka with port wine! Good heavens, it simply isn't done!'

'I beg you to keep it between us,' Styopa said fawningly.

'Oh, of course, of course! But as for Khustov, needless to say, I can't vouch for him.'

'So you know Khustov?'

'Yesterday, in your office, I saw this individuum briefly, but it only takes a fleeting glance at his face to understand that he is a bastard, a squabbler, a trimmer and a toady.'

'Perfectly true!' thought Styopa, struck by such a true, precise and succinct definition of Khustov.

Yes, the previous day was piecing itself together, but, even so, anxiety would not take leave of the director of the Variety. The thing was that a huge black hole yawned in this previous day. Say what you will, Styopa simply had not seen this stranger in the beret in his office yesterday.

'Professor of black magic Woland,'[3] the visitor said weightily, seeing Styopa's difficulty, and he recounted everything in order.

Yesterday afternoon he arrived in Moscow from abroad, went immediately to Styopa, and offered his show to the Variety. Styopa telephoned the Moscow Regional Entertainment Commission and had the question approved (Styopa turned pale and blinked), then signed a contract with Professor Woland for seven performances (Styopa opened his mouth), and arranged that Woland should come the next morning at ten o'clock to work out the details ... And so Woland came. Having come, he was met by the housekeeper Grunya, who explained that she had just come herself, that she was not a live-in maid, that Berlioz was not home, and that if the visitor wished to see Stepan Bogdanovich, he should go to his bedroom himself. Stepan Bogdanovich was such a sound sleeper that she would not undertake to wake him up. Seeing what condition Stepan Bogdanovich was in, the artiste sent Grunya to the nearest grocery store for vodka and hors d'œuvres, to the druggist's for ice, and ...

'Allow me to reimburse you,' the mortified Styopa squealed and began hunting for his wallet.

'Oh, what nonsense!' the guest performer exclaimed and would hear no more of it.

And so, the vodka and hors d'œuvres got explained, but all the same Styopa was a pity to see: he remembered decidedly nothing about the contract and, on his life, had not seen this Woland yesterday. Yes, Khustov had been there, but not Woland.

'May I have a look at the contract?' Styopa asked quietly.

'Please do, please do ...'

Styopa looked at the paper and froze. Everything was in place: first of all, Styopa's own dashing signature . . . aslant the margin a note in the hand of the findirector[4] Rimsky authorizing the payment of ten thousand roubles to the artiste Woland, as an advance on the thirty-five thousand roubles due him for seven performances. What's more, Woland's signature was right there attesting to his receipt of the ten thousand!

'What is all this?!' the wretched Styopa thought, his head spinning. Was he starting to have ominous gaps of memory? Well, it went without saying, once the contract had been produced, any further expressions of surprise would simply be indecent. Styopa asked his visitor's leave to absent himself for a moment and, just as he was, in his stocking feet, ran to the front hall for the telephone. On his way he called out in the direction of the kitchen:

'Grunya!'

But no one responded. He glanced at the door to Berlioz's study, which was next to the front hall, and here he was, as they say, flabbergasted. On the door-handle he made out an enormous wax seal[5] on a string.

'Hel-lo!' someone barked in Styopa's head. 'Just what we needed!' And here Styopa's thoughts began running on twin tracks, but, as always happens in times of catastrophe, in the same direction and, generally, devil knows where. It is even difficult to convey the porridge in Styopa's head. Here was this devilry with the black beret, the chilled vodka, and the incredible contract . . . And along with all that, if you please, a seal on the door as well! That is, tell anyone you like that Berlioz has been up to no good – no one will believe it, by Jove, no one will believe it! Yet look, there's the seal! Yes, sir . . .

And here some most disagreeable little thoughts began stirring in Styopa's brain, about the article which, as luck would have it, he had recently inflicted on Mikhail Alexandrovich for publication in his journal. The article, just between us, was idiotic! And worthless. And the money was so little . . .

Immediately after the recollection of the article, there came flying a recollection of some dubious conversation that had taken place, he recalled, on the twenty-fourth of April, in the evening, right there in the dining room, while Styopa was having dinner with Mikhail Alexandrovich. That is, of course, this conversation could not have been called dubious in the full sense of the word (Styopa would not have ventured upon such a conversation), but it was on some unnecessary subject. He had been quite free, dear citizens, not to begin it. Before the seal, this conversation would undoubtedly have been considered a perfect trifle, but now, after the seal . . .

'Ah, Berlioz, Berlioz!' boiled up in Styopa's head. 'This is simply too much for one head!'

But it would not do to grieve too long, and Styopa dialled the number of the office of the Variety's findirector, Rimsky. Styopa's position was ticklish: first, the foreigner might get offended that Styopa was checking on him after the contract had been shown, and then to talk with the findirector was also exceedingly difficult. Indeed, he could not just ask him like that: 'Tell me, did I sign a contract for thirty-five thousand roubles yesterday with a professor of black magic?' It was no good asking like that!

'Yes!' Rimsky's sharp, unpleasant voice came from the receiver.

'Hello, Grigory Danilovich,' Styopa began speaking quietly, 'it's Likhodeev. There's a certain matter . . . hm . . . hm . . . I have this . . . er . . . artiste Woland sitting here . . . So you see . . . I wanted to ask, how about this evening? . . .'

'Ah, the black magician?' Rimsky's voice responded in the receiver. 'The posters will be ready shortly.'

'Uh-huh . . .' Styopa said in a weak voice, 'well, 'bye . . .'

'And you'll be coming in soon?' Rimsky asked.

'In half an hour,' Styopa replied and, hanging up the receiver, pressed his hot head in his hands. Ah, what a nasty thing to have happen! What was wrong with his memory, citizens? Eh?

However, to go on lingering in the front hall was awkward, and Styopa formed a plan straight away: by all means to conceal his incredible forgetfulness, and now, first off, contrive to get out of the foreigner what, in fact, he intended to show that evening in the Variety, of which Styopa was in charge.

Here Styopa turned away from the telephone and saw distinctly in the mirror that stood in the front hall, and which the lazy Grunya had not wiped for ages, a certain strange specimen, long as a pole, and in a pince-nez (ah, if only Ivan Nikolaevich had been there! He would have recognized this specimen at once!). The figure was reflected and then disappeared. Styopa looked further down the hall in alarm and was rocked a second time, for in the mirror a stalwart black cat passed and also disappeared.

Styopa's heart skipped a beat, he staggered.

'What is all this?' he thought. 'Am I losing my mind? Where are these reflections coming from?!' He peeked into the front hall and cried timorously:

'Grunya! What's this cat doing hanging around here?! Where did he come from? And the other one?!'

'Don't worry, Stepan Bogdanovich,' a voice responded, not Grunya's but the visitor's, from the bedroom. 'The cat is mine. Don't be nervous. And Grunya is not here, I sent her off to Voronezh. She complained you diddled her out of a vacation.'

These words were so unexpected and preposterous that Styopa decided he had not heard right. Utterly bewildered, he trotted back to the bedroom and froze on the threshold. His hair stood on end and small beads of sweat broke out on his brow.

The visitor was no longer alone in the bedroom, but had company: in the second armchair sat the same type he had imagined in the front hall. Now he was clearly visible: the feathery moustache, one lens of the pince-nez gleaming, the other not there. But worse things were to be found in the bedroom: on the jeweller's wife's ottoman, in a casual pose, sprawled a third party – namely, a black cat of uncanny size, with a glass of vodka in one paw and a fork, on which he had managed to spear a pickled mushroom, in the other.

The light, faint in the bedroom anyway, now began to grow quite dark in Styopa's eyes. 'This is apparently how one loses one's mind . . .' he thought and caught hold of the doorpost.

'I see you're somewhat surprised, my dearest Stepan Bogdanovich?' Woland inquired of the teeth-chattering Styopa. 'And yet there's nothing to be surprised at. This is my retinue.'

Here the cat tossed off the vodka, and Styopa's hand began to slide down the doorpost.

'And this retinue requires room,' Woland continued, 'so there's just one too many of us in the apartment. And it seems to us that this one too many is precisely you.'

'Theirself, theirself!' the long checkered one sang in a goat's voice, referring to Styopa in the plural. 'Generally, theirself has been up to some terrible swinishness lately. Drinking, using their position to have liaisons with women, don't do devil a thing, and can't do anything, because they don't know anything of what they're supposed to do. Pulling the wool over their superiors' eyes.'

'Availing hisself of a government car!' the cat snitched, chewing a mushroom.

And here occurred the fourth and last appearance in the apartment, as Styopa, having slid all the way to the floor, clawed at the doorpost with an enfeebled hand.

Straight from the pier-glass stepped a short but extraordinarily broad-shouldered man, with a bowler hat on his head and a fang sticking out of his mouth, which made still uglier a physiognomy unprecedentedly loathsome without that. And with flaming red hair besides.

'Generally,' this new one entered into the conversation, 'I don't understand how he got to be a director,' the redhead's nasal twang was growing stronger and stronger, 'he's as much a director as I'm a bishop.'

'You don't look like a bishop, Azazello,'[6] the cat observed, heaping his plate with frankfurters.

'That's what I mean,' twanged the redhead and, turning to Woland, he added deferentially: 'Allow me, Messire, to chuck him the devil out of Moscow?'

'Scat!' the cat barked suddenly, bristling his fur.

And then the bedroom started spinning around Styopa, he hit his head against the doorpost, and, losing consciousness, thought: 'I'm dying . . .'

But he did not die. Opening his eyes slightly, he saw himself sitting on something made of stone. Around him something was making noise. When he opened his eyes properly, he realized that the noise was being made by the sea and, what's more, that the waves were rocking just at his feet, that he was, in short, sitting at the very end of a jetty, that over him was a brilliant blue sky and behind him a white city on the mountains.

Not knowing how to behave in such a case, Styopa got up on his trembling legs and walked along the jetty towards the shore.

Some man was standing on the jetty, smoking and spitting into the sea. He looked at Styopa with wild eyes and stopped spitting.

Then Styopa pulled the following stunt: he knelt down before the unknown smoker and said:

'I implore you, tell me what city is this?'

'Really!' said the heartless smoker.

'I'm not drunk,' Styopa replied hoarsely, 'something's happened to me . . . I'm ill . . . Where am I? What city is this?'

'Well, it's Yalta . . .'

Styopa quietly gasped and sank down on his side, his head striking the warm stone of the jetty. Consciousness left him.

CHAPTER 8

The Combat between the Professor and the Poet

At the same time that consciousness left Styopa in Yalta, that is, around half past eleven in the morning, it returned to Ivan Nikolaevich Homeless, who woke up after a long and deep sleep. He spent some time pondering how it was that he had wound up in an unfamiliar room with white walls, with an astonishing night table made of some light metal, and with white blinds behind which one could sense the sun.

Ivan shook his head, ascertained that it did not ache, and remembered that he was in a clinic. This thought drew after it the remembrance of Berlioz's death, but today it did not provoke a strong shock in Ivan. Having had a good sleep, Ivan Nikolaevich became calmer and began to think more clearly. After lying motionless for some time in this most clean, soft and comfortable spring bed, Ivan noticed a bell button beside him. From a habit of touching things needlessly, Ivan pressed it. He expected the pressing of the button to be followed by some ringing or appearance, but something entirely different happened. A frosted glass cylinder with the word 'Drink' on it lit up at the foot of Ivan's bed. After pausing for a while, the cylinder began to rotate until the word 'Nurse' popped out. It goes without saying that the clever cylinder amazed Ivan. The word 'Nurse' was replaced by the words 'Call the Doctor.'

'Hm . . .' said Ivan, not knowing how to proceed further with this cylinder. But here he happened to be lucky. Ivan pressed the button a second time at the word 'Attendant'. The cylinder rang quietly in response, stopped, the light went out, and a plump, sympathetic woman in a clean white coat came into the room and said to Ivan:

'Good morning!'

Ivan did not reply, considering such a greeting inappropriate under the circumstances. Indeed, they lock up a healthy man in a clinic, and pretend that that is how it ought to be!

The woman meanwhile, without losing her good-natured expression, brought the blinds up with one push of a button, and sun flooded the room through a light and wide-meshed grille which reached right to the floor. Beyond the grille a balcony came into view, beyond that the bank of a meandering river, and on its other bank a cheerful pine wood.

'Time for our bath,' the woman invited, and under her hands the inner wall parted, revealing behind it a bathroom and splendidly equipped toilet.

Ivan, though he had resolved not to talk to the woman, could not help himself and, on seeing the water gush into the tub in a wide stream from the gleaming faucet, said ironically:

'Looky there! Just like the Metropol! . . .'

'Oh, no,' the woman answered proudly, 'much better. There is no such equipment even anywhere abroad. Scientists and doctors come especially to study our clinic. We have foreign tourists every day.'

At the words 'foreign tourists', Ivan at once remembered yesterday's consultant. Ivan darkened, looked sullen, and said:

'Foreign tourists . . . How you all adore foreign tourists! But among them, incidentally, you come across all sorts. I, for instance, met one yesterday – quite something!'

And he almost started telling about Pontius Pilate, but restrained himself, realizing that the woman had no use for these stories, that in any case she could not help him.

The washed Ivan Nikolaevich was straight away issued decidedly everything a man needs after a bath: an ironed shirt, drawers, socks. And not only that: opening the door of a cupboard, the woman pointed inside and asked:

'What would you like to put on – a dressing gown or some nice pyjamas?'

Attached to his new dwelling by force, Ivan almost clasped his hands at the woman's casualness and silently pointed his finger at the crimson flannel pyjamas.

After this, Ivan Nikolaevich was led down the empty and noiseless corridor and brought to an examining room of huge dimensions. Ivan, having decided to take an ironic attitude towards everything to be found in this wondrously equipped building, at once mentally christened this room the 'industrial kitchen'.

And with good reason. Here stood cabinets and glass cases with gleaming nickel-plated instruments. There were chairs of extraordinarily complex construction, some pot-bellied lamps with shiny shades, a myriad of phials, Bunsen burners, electric cords and appliances quite unknown to anyone.

In the examining room Ivan was taken over by three persons – two women and a man – all in white. First, they led Ivan to a corner, to a little table, with the obvious purpose of getting something or other out of him.

Ivan began to ponder the situation. Three ways stood before him. The first was extremely tempting: to hurl himself at all these lamps and sophisticated little things, make the devil's own wreck of them, and thereby express his protest at being detained for nothing. But today's Ivan already differed significantly from the Ivan of yesterday, and this first way appeared dubious to him: for all he knew, the thought might get rooted in them that he was a violent madman. Therefore Ivan rejected the first way. There was a second: immediately to begin his account of the consultant and Pontius Pilate. However, yesterday's experience showed that this story either was not believed or was taken somehow perversely. Therefore Ivan renounced this second way as well, deciding to choose the third way – withdrawal into proud silence.

He did not succeed in realizing it fully, and had willy-nilly to answer, though charily and glumly, a whole series of questions. Thus they got out of Ivan decidedly everything about his past life, down to when and how he had fallen ill with scarlet fever fifteen years ago. A whole page having been covered with writing about Ivan, it was turned over, and the woman in white went on to questions about Ivan's relatives. Some sort of humdrum started: who died when and why, and whether he drank or had venereal disease, and more of the same. In conclusion he was asked to tell about yesterday's events at the Patriarch's Ponds, but they did not pester him too much, and were not surprised at the information about Pontius Pilate.

Here the woman yielded Ivan up to the man, who went to work on him differently and no longer asked any questions. He took the temperature of Ivan's body, counted his pulse, looked in Ivan's eyes, directing some sort of lamp into them. Then the second woman came to the man's assistance, and they pricked Ivan in the back with something, but not painfully, drew some signs on the skin of his chest with the handle of a little hammer, tapped his knees with the hammer, which made Ivan's legs jump, pricked his finger and took his blood, pricked him inside his bent elbow, put some rubber bracelets on his arms . . .

Ivan just smiled bitterly to himself and reflected on how stupidly and strangely it had all happened. Just think! He had wanted to warn them all of the danger threatening from the unknown consultant, had intended to catch him, and all he had achieved was to wind up in some mysterious room, telling all sorts of hogwash about Uncle Fyodor, who had done some hard drinking in Vologda. Insufferably stupid!

Finally Ivan was released. He was escorted back to his room, where he was given a cup of coffee, two soft-boiled eggs and white bread with butter. Having eaten and drunk all that was offered him, Ivan decided to wait for whoever was chief of this institution, and from this chief to obtain both attention for himself and justice.

And he did come, and very soon after Ivan's breakfast. Unexpectedly, the door of Ivan's room opened, and in came a lot of people in white coats. At their head walked a man of about forty-five, as carefully shaven as an actor, with pleasant but quite piercing eyes and courteous manners. The whole retinue showed him tokens of attention and respect, and his entrance therefore came out very solemn. 'Like Pontius Pilate!' thought Ivan.

Yes, this was unquestionably the chief. He sat down on a stool, while everyone else remained standing.

'Doctor Stravinsky,' the seated man introduced himself to Ivan and gave him a friendly look.

'Here, Alexander Nikolaevich,' someone with a trim beard said in a low voice, and handed the chief Ivan's chart, all covered with writing.

'They've sewn up a whole case!' Ivan thought. And the chief ran through the chart with a practised eye, muttered 'Mm-hm, mm-hm . . .', and exchanged a few phrases with those around him in a little-known language. 'And he speaks Latin like Pilate,' Ivan thought sadly. Here one word made him jump; it was the word 'schizophrenia' – alas, already uttered yesterday by the cursed foreigner at the Patriarch's Ponds, and now repeated today by Professor Stravinsky. 'And he knew that, too!' Ivan thought anxiously.

The chief apparently made it a rule to agree with and rejoice over everything said to him by those around him, and to express this with the words 'Very nice, very nice . . .'

'Very nice!' said Stravinsky, handing the chart back to someone, and he addressed Ivan:

'You are a poet?'

'A poet,' Ivan replied glumly, and for the first time suddenly felt some inexplicable loathing for poetry, and his own verses, coming to mind at once, seemed to him for some reason distasteful.

Wrinkling his face, he asked Stravinsky in turn:

'You are a professor?'

To this, Stravinsky, with obliging courtesy, inclined his head.

'And you're the chief here?' Ivan continued.

Stravinsky nodded to this as well.

'I must speak with you,' Ivan Nikolaevich said meaningly.

'That is what I'm here for,' returned Stravinsky.

'The thing is,' Ivan began, feeling his hour had come, 'that I've been got up as a madman, and nobody wants to listen to me! . . .'

'Oh, no, we shall hear you out with great attention,' Stravinsky said seriously and soothingly, 'and by no means allow you to be got up as a madman.'

'Listen, then: yesterday evening I met a mysterious person at the Patriarch's Ponds, maybe a foreigner, maybe not, who knew beforehand about Berlioz's death and has seen Pontius Pilate in person.'

The retinue listened to the poet silently and without stirring.

'Pilate? The Pilate who lived in the time of Jesus Christ?' Stravinsky asked, narrowing his eyes at Ivan.

'The same.'

'Aha,' said Stravinsky, 'and this Berlioz died under a tram-car?'

'Precisely, he's the one who in my presence was killed by a tram-car yesterday at the Ponds, and this same mysterious citizen . . .'

'The acquaintance of Pontius Pilate?' asked Stravinsky, apparently distinguished by great mental alacrity.

'Precisely him,' Ivan confirmed, studying Stravinsky. 'Well, so he said beforehand that Annushka had spilled the sunflower oil . . . And he slipped right on that place! How do you like that?' Ivan inquired significantly, hoping to produce a great effect with his words.

But the effect did not ensue, and Stravinsky quite simply asked the following question:

'And who is this Annushka?'

This question upset Ivan a little; his face twitched.

'Annushka is of absolutely no importance here,' he said nervously. 'Devil knows who she is. Just some fool from Sadovaya. What's important is that he knew beforehand, you see, beforehand, about the sunflower oil! Do you understand me?'

'Perfectly,' Stravinsky replied seriously and, touching the poet's knee, added: 'Don't get excited, just continue.'

'To continue,' said Ivan, trying to fall in with Stravinsky's tone, and knowing already from bitter experience that only calm would help him, 'so, then, this horrible type (and he's lying that he's a consultant) has some extraordinary power! ... For instance, you chase after him and it's impossible to catch up with him ... And there's also a little pair with him – good ones, too, but in their own way: some long one in broken glasses and, besides him, a cat of incredible size who rides the tram all by himself. And besides,' interrupted by no one, Ivan went on talking with ever increasing ardour and conviction, 'he was personally on Pontius Pilate's balcony, there's no doubt of it. So what is all this, eh? He must be arrested immediately, otherwise he'll do untold harm.'

'So you're trying to get him arrested? Have I understood you correctly?' asked Stravinsky.

'He's intelligent,' thought Ivan. 'You've got to admit, even among intellectuals you come across some of rare intelligence, there's no denying it,' and he replied:

'Quite correctly! And how could I not be trying, just consider for yourself! And meanwhile I've been forcibly detained here, they poke lamps into my eyes, give me baths, question me for some reason about my Uncle Fedya! ... And he departed this world long ago! I demand to be released immediately!'

'Well, there, very nice, very nice!' Stravinsky responded. 'Now everything's clear. Really, what's the sense of keeping a healthy man in a clinic? Very well, sir, I'll check you out of here right now, if you tell me you're normal. Not prove, but merely tell. So, then, are you normal?'

Here complete silence fell, and the fat woman who had taken care of Ivan in the morning looked at the professor with awe. Ivan thought once again: 'Positively intelligent!'

The professor's offer pleased him very much, yet before replying he thought very, very hard, wrinkling his forehead, and at last said firmly:

'I am normal.'

'Well, how very nice,' Stravinsky exclaimed with relief, 'and if so, let's reason logically. Let's take your day yesterday.' Here he turned and Ivan's chart was immediately handed to him. 'In search of an unknown man who recommended himself as an acquaintance of Pontius Pilate, you performed the following actions yesterday.' Here Stravinsky began holding up his long fingers, glancing now at the chart, now at Ivan. 'You hung a little icon on your chest. Did you?'

'I did,' Ivan agreed sullenly.

'You fell off a fence and hurt your face. Right? Showed up in a restaurant carrying a burning candle in your hand, in nothing but your underwear, and in the restaurant you beat somebody. You were brought here tied up. Having come here, you called the police and asked them to send out machine-guns. Then you attempted to throw yourself out the window. Right? The question is: can one, by acting in such fashion, catch or arrest anyone? And if you're a normal man, you yourself will answer: by no means. You wish to leave here? Very well, sir. But allow me to ask, where are you going to go?'

'To the police, of course,' Ivan replied, no longer so firmly, and somewhat at a loss under the professor's gaze.

'Straight from here?'

'Mm-hm . . .'

'Without stopping at your place?' Stravinsky asked quickly.

'I have no time to stop anywhere! While I'm stopping at places, he'll slip away!'

'So. And what will you tell the police to start with?'

'About Pontius Pilate,' Ivan Nikolaevich replied, and his eyes clouded with a gloomy mist.

'Well, how very nice!' the won-over Stravinsky exclaimed and, turning to the one with the little beard, ordered: 'Fyodor Vassilyevich, please check Citizen Homeless out for town. But don't put anyone in his room or change the linen. In two hours, Citizen Homeless will be back here. So, then,' he turned to the poet, 'I won't wish you success, because I don't believe one iota in that success. See you soon!' He stood up, and his retinue stirred.

'On what grounds will I be back here?' Ivan asked anxiously.

Stravinsky was as if waiting for this question, immediately sat down, and began to speak:

'On the grounds that as soon as you show up at the police station in your drawers and tell them you've seen a man who knew Pontius Pilate personally, you'll instantly be brought here, and you'll find yourself again in this very same room.'

'What have drawers got to do with it?' Ivan asked, gazing around in bewilderment.

'It's mainly Pontius Pilate. But the drawers, too. Because we'll take the clinic underwear from you and give you back your clothes. And you were delivered here in your drawers. And yet you were by no means going to stop at your place, though I dropped you a hint. Then comes Pilate . . . and that's it.'

Here something strange happened with Ivan Nikolaevich. His will seemed to crack, and he felt himself weak, in need of advice.

'What am I to do, then?' he asked, timidly this time.

'Well, how very nice!' Stravinsky replied. 'A most reasonable question. Now I am going to tell you what actually happened to you. Yesterday someone frightened you badly and upset you with a story about Pontius Pilate and other things. And so you, a very nervous and high-strung man, started going around the city, telling about Pontius Pilate. It's quite natural that you're taken for a madman. Your salvation now lies in just one thing – complete peace. And you absolutely must remain here.'

'But he has to be caught!' Ivan exclaimed, imploringly now.

'Very good, sir, but why should you go running around yourself? Explain all your suspicions and accusations against this man on paper. Nothing could be simpler than to send your declaration to the proper quarters, and if, as you think, we are dealing with a criminal, it will be clarified very quickly. But only on one condition: don't strain your head, and try to think less about Pontius Pilate. People say all kinds of things! One mustn't believe everything.'

'Understood!' Ivan declared resolutely. 'I ask to be given pen and paper.'

'Give him paper and a short pencil,' Stravinsky ordered the fat woman, and to Ivan he said: 'But I don't advise you to write today.'

'No, no, today, today without fail!' Ivan cried out in alarm.

'Well, all right. Only don't strain your head. If it doesn't come out today, it will tomorrow.'

'He'll escape.'

'Oh, no,' Stravinsky objected confidently, 'he won't escape anywhere, I guarantee that. And remember that here with us you'll be helped in all possible ways, and without us nothing will come of it. Do you hear me?' Stravinsky suddenly asked meaningly and took Ivan Nikolaevich by both hands. Holding them in his own, he repeated for a long time, his eyes fixed on Ivan's: 'You'll be helped here ... do you hear me? ... You'll be helped here ... you'll get relief ... it's quiet here, all peaceful ... you'll be helped here ...'

Ivan Nikolaevich unexpectedly yawned, and the expression on his face softened.

'Yes, yes,' he said quietly.

'Well, how very nice!' Stravinsky concluded the conversation in his usual way and stood up: 'Goodbye!' He shook Ivan's hand and, on his way out, turned to the one with the little beard and said: 'Yes, and try oxygen ... and baths.'

A few moments later there was no Stravinsky or his retinue before Ivan. Beyond the window grille, in the noonday sun, the joyful and springtime pine wood stood beautiful on the other bank and, closer by, the river sparkled.

CHAPTER 9

Koroviev's Stunts

Nikanor Ivanovich Bosoy, chairman of the tenants' association[1] of no. 302-bis on Sadovaya Street in Moscow, where the late Berlioz used to reside, had been having the most terrible troubles, starting from that Wednesday night.

At midnight, as we already know, a commission of which Zheldybin formed a part came to the house, summoned Nikanor Ivanovich, told him about the death of Berlioz, and together with him went to apartment no. 50.

There the sealing of the deceased's manuscripts and belongings was carried out. Neither Grunya, the daytime housekeeper, nor the light-minded Stepan Bogdanovich was there at the time. The commission announced to Nikanor Ivanovich that it would take the deceased's manuscripts for sorting out, that his living space, that is, three rooms (the former study, living room and dining room of the jeweller's wife), reverted to the disposal of the tenants' association, and that the belongings were to be kept in the aforementioned living space until the heirs were announced.

The news of Berlioz's death spread through the whole house with a sort of supernatural speed, and as of seven o'clock Thursday morning, Bosoy began to receive telephone calls and then personal visits with declarations containing claims to the deceased's living space. In the period of two hours, Nikanor Ivanovich received thirty-two such declarations.

They contained pleas, threats, libels, denunciations, promises to do renovations at their own expense, references to unbearable over-crowding and the impossibility of living in the same apartment with bandits. Among others there were a description, staggering in its artistic power, of the theft from apartment no. 31 of some meat dumplings, tucked directly into the pocket of a suit jacket, two vows to end life by suicide and one confession of secret pregnancy.

Nikanor Ivanovich was called out to the front hall of his apartment, plucked by the sleeve, whispered to, winked at, promised that he would not be left the loser.

This torture went on until noon, when Nikanor Ivanovich simply fled his apartment for the management office by the gate, but when he saw them lying in wait for him there, too, he fled that place as well. Having somehow shaken off those who followed on his heels across the asphalt-paved courtyard, Nikanor Ivanovich disappeared into the sixth entrance and went up to the fifth floor, where this vile apartment no. 50 was located.

After catching his breath on the landing, the corpulent Nikanor Ivanovich rang, but no one opened for him. He rang again, and then again, and started grumbling and swearing quietly. Even then no one opened. His patience exhausted, Nikanor Ivanovich took from his pocket a bunch of duplicate keys belonging to the house management, opened the door with a sovereign hand, and went in.

'Hey, housekeeper!' Nikanor Ivanovich cried in the semi-dark front hall. 'Grunya, or whatever your name is! . . . Are you here?'

No one responded.

Then Nikanor Ivanovich took a folding ruler from his briefcase, removed the seal from the door to the study, and stepped in. Stepped in, yes, but halted in amazement in the doorway and even gave a start.

At the deceased's desk sat an unknown, skinny, long citizen in a little checkered jacket, a jockey's cap, and a pince-nez . . . well, in short, that same one.

'And who might you be, citizen?' Nikanor Ivanovich asked fearfully.

'Hah! Nikanor Ivanovich!' the unexpected citizen yelled in a rattling tenor and, jumping up, greeted the chairman with a forced and sudden handshake. This greeting by no means gladdened Nikanor Ivanovich.

'Excuse me,' he said suspiciously, 'but who might you be? Are you an official person?'

'Eh, Nikanor Ivanovich!' the unknown man exclaimed soulfully. 'What are official and unofficial persons? It all depends on your point of view on the subject. It's all fluctuating and relative, Nikanor Ivanovich. Today I'm an unofficial person, and tomorrow, lo and behold, I'm an official one! And it also happens the other way round – oh, how it does!'

This argument in no way satisfied the chairman of the house management. Being a generally suspicious person by nature, he concluded that the man holding forth in front of him was precisely an unofficial person, and perhaps even an idle one.

'Yes, but who might you be? What's your name?' the chairman inquired with increasing severity and even began to advance upon the unknown man.

'My name,' the citizen responded, not a bit put out by the severity, 'well, let's say it's Koroviev. But wouldn't you like a little snack, Nikanor Ivanovich? No formalities, eh?'

'Excuse me,' Nikanor Ivanovich began, indignantly now, 'what have snacks got to do with it!' (We must confess, unpleasant as it is, that Nikanor Ivanovich was of a somewhat rude nature.) 'Sitting in the deceased's half is not permitted! What are you doing here?'

'Have a seat, Nikanor Ivanovich,' the citizen went on yelling, not a bit at a loss, and began fussing about offering the chairman a seat.

Utterly infuriated, Nikanor Ivanovich rejected the seat and screamed: 'But who are you?'

'I, if you please, serve as interpreter for a foreign individual who has taken up residence in this apartment,' the man calling himself Koroviev introduced himself and clicked the heels of his scuffed, unpolished shoes.

Nikanor Ivanovich opened his mouth. The presence of some foreigner in this apartment, with an interpreter to boot, came as a complete surprise to him, and he demanded explanations.

The interpreter explained willingly. A foreign artiste, Mr Woland, had been kindly invited by the director of the Variety, Stepan Bogdanovich Likhodeev, to spend the time of his performances, a week or so, in his apartment, about which he had written to Nikanor Ivanovich yesterday, requesting that he register the foreigner as a temporary resident, while Likhodeev himself took a trip to Yalta.

'He never wrote me anything,' the chairman said in amazement.

'Just look through your briefcase, Nikanor Ivanovich,' Koroviev suggested sweetly.

Nikanor Ivanovich, shrugging his shoulders, opened the briefcase and found Likhodeev's letter in it.

'How could I have forgotten about it?' Nikanor Ivanovich muttered, looking dully at the opened envelope.

'All sorts of things happen, Nikanor Ivanovich, all sorts!' Koroviev rattled. 'Absent-mindedness, absent-mindedness, fatigue and high blood pressure, my dear friend Nikanor Ivanovich! I'm terribly absent-minded myself! Someday, over a glass, I'll tell you a few facts from my biography – you'll die laughing!'

'And when is Likhodeev going to Yalta?'

'He's already gone, gone!' the interpreter cried. 'He's already wheeling along, you know! He's already devil knows where!' And here the interpreter waved his arms like the wings of a windmill.

Nikanor Ivanovich declared that he must see the foreigner in person, but got a refusal on that from the interpreter: quite impossible. He's busy. Training the cat.

'The cat I can show you, if you like,' Koroviev offered.

This Nikanor Ivanovich refused in his turn, and the interpreter straight away made the chairman an unexpected but quite interesting proposal: seeing that Mr Woland had no desire whatsoever to live in a hotel, and was accustomed to having a lot of space, why shouldn't the tenants' association rent to him, Woland, for one little week, the time of his performances in Moscow, the whole of the apartment, that is, the deceased's rooms as well?

'It's all the same to him – the deceased – you must agree, Nikanor Ivanovich,' Koroviev whispered hoarsely. 'He doesn't need the apartment now, does he?'

Nikanor Ivanovich, somewhat perplexed, objected that foreigners ought to live at the Metropol, and not in private apartments at all . . .

'I'm telling you, he's capricious as devil knows what!' Koroviev whispered. 'He just doesn't want to! He doesn't like hotels! I've had them up to here, these foreign tourists!' Koroviev complained confidentially, jabbing his finger at his sinewy neck. 'Believe me, they wring the soul right out of you! They come and either spy on you like the lowest son of a bitch, or else torment you with their caprices – this isn't right and that isn't right! . . . And for your association, Nikanor Ivanovich, it's a sheer gain and an obvious profit. He won't stint on money.' Koroviev looked around and then whispered into the chairman's ear: 'A millionaire!'

The interpreter's offer made clear practical sense, it was a very solid offer, yet there was something remarkably unsolid in his manner of speaking, and in his clothes, and in that loathsome, good-for-nothing pince-nez. As a result, something vague weighed on the chairman's soul, but he nevertheless decided to accept the offer. The thing was that the tenants' association, alas, had quite a sizeable deficit. Fuel had to be bought for the heating system by fall, but who was going to shell out for it – no one knew. But with the foreign tourist's money, it might be possible to wriggle out of it. However, the practical and prudent Nikanor Ivanovich said he would first have to settle the question with the foreign tourist bureau.

'I understand!' Koroviev cried out. 'You've got to settle it! Absolutely! Here's the telephone, Nikanor Ivanovich, settle it at once! And don't be shy about the money,' he added in a whisper, drawing the chairman to the telephone in the front hall, 'if he won't pay, who will! You should see the villa he's got in Nice! Next summer, when you go abroad, come especially to see it – you'll gasp!'

The business with the foreign tourist bureau was arranged over the phone with an extraordinary speed, quite amazing to the chairman. It turned out that they already knew about Mr Woland's intention of staying in Likhodeev's private apartment and had no objections to it.

'That's wonderful!' Koroviev yelled. Somewhat stunned by his chatter, the chairman announced that the tenants' association agreed to rent apartment no. 50 for a week to the artiste Woland, for ... Nikanor Ivanovich faltered a little, then said:

'For five hundred roubles a day.'

Here Koroviev utterly amazed the chairman. Winking thievishly in the direction of the bedroom, from which the soft leaps of a heavy cat could be heard, he rasped out:

'So it comes to three thousand five hundred for the week?'

To which Nikanor Ivanovich thought he was going to add: 'Some appetite you've got, Nikanor Ivanovich!' but Koroviev said something quite different:

'What kind of money is that? Ask five, he'll pay it.'

Grinning perplexedly, Nikanor Ivanovich, without noticing how, found himself at the deceased's writing desk, where Koroviev with great speed and dexterity drew up a contract in two copies. Then he flew to the bedroom with them and came back, both copies now bearing the foreigner's sweeping signature. The chairman also signed the contract. Here Koroviev asked for a receipt for five ...

'Write it out, write it out, Nikanor Ivanovich! ... thousand roubles ...' And with words somehow unsuited to serious business –

'Ein, zwei, drei!' – he laid out for the chairman five stacks of new banknotes.

The counting-up took place, interspersed with Koroviev's quips and quiddities, such as 'Cash loves counting', 'Your own eye won't lie', and others of the same sort.

After counting the money, the chairman received from Koroviev the foreigner's passport for temporary registration, put it, together with the contract and the money, into his briefcase, and, somehow unable to help himself, sheepishly asked for a free pass . . .

'Don't mention it!' bellowed Koroviev. 'How many tickets do you want, Nikanor Ivanovich – twelve, fifteen?'

The flabbergasted chairman explained that all he needed was a couple of passes, for himself and Pelageya Antonovna, his wife.

Koroviev snatched out a notebook at once and dashed off a pass for Nikanor Ivanovich, for two persons in the front row. And with his left hand the interpreter deftly slipped this pass to Nikanor Ivanovich, while with his right he put into the chairman's other hand a thick, crackling wad. Casting an eye on it, Nikanor Ivanovich blushed deeply and began to push it away.

'It isn't done . . .' he murmured.

'I won't hear of it,' Koroviev whispered right in his ear. 'With us it's not done, but with foreigners it is. You'll offend him, Nikanor Ivanovich, and that's embarrassing. You've worked hard . . .'

'It's severely punishable,' the chairman whispered very, very softly and glanced over his shoulder.

'But where are the witnesses?' Koroviev whispered into his other ear. 'I ask you, where are they? You don't think . . . ?'

Here, as the chairman insisted afterwards, a miracle occurred: the wad crept into his briefcase by itself. And then the chairman, somehow limp and even broken, found himself on the stairs. A whirlwind of thoughts raged in his head. There was the villa in Nice, and the trained cat, and the thought that there were in fact no witnesses, and that Pelageya Antonovna would be delighted with the pass. They were incoherent thoughts, but generally pleasant. But, all the same, somewhere, some little needle kept pricking the chairman in the very bottom of his soul. This was the needle of anxiety. Besides, right then on the stairs the chairman was seized, as with a stroke, by the thought: 'But how did the interpreter get into the study if the door was sealed?! And how was it that he, Nikanor Ivanovich, had not asked about it?' For some time the chairman stood staring like a sheep at the steps of the stairway, but then he decided to spit on it and not torment himself with intricate questions . . .

As soon as the chairman left the apartment, a low voice came from the bedroom:

'I didn't like this Nikanor Ivanovich. He is a chiseller and a crook. Can it be arranged so that he doesn't come any more?'

'Messire, you have only to say the word . . .' Koroviev responded from somewhere, not in a rattling but in a very clear and resounding voice.

And at once the accursed interpreter turned up in the front hall, dialled a number there, and for some reason began speaking very tearfully into the receiver:

'Hello! I consider it my duty to inform you that the chairman of our tenants' association at no. 302-bis on Sadovaya, Nikanor Ivanovich Bosoy, is speculating in foreign currency.[2] At the present moment, in his apartment no. 35, he has four hundred dollars wrapped up in newspaper in the ventilation of the privy. This is Timofei Kvastsov speaking, a tenant of the said house, apartment no. 11. But I adjure you to keep my name a secret. I fear the vengeance of the above-stated chairman.'

And he hung up, the scoundrel!

What happened next in apartment no. 50 is not known, but it is known what happened at Nikanor Ivanovich's. Having locked himself in the privy with the hook, he took from his briefcase the wad foisted on him by the interpreter and satisfied himself that it contained four hundred roubles. Nikanor Ivanovich wrapped this wad in a scrap of newspaper and put it into the ventilation duct.

Five minutes later the chairman was sitting at the table in his small dining room. His wife brought pickled herring from the kitchen, neatly sliced and thickly sprinkled with green onion. Nikanor Ivanovich poured himself a dram of vodka, drank it, poured another, drank it, picked up three pieces of herring on his fork . . . and at that moment the doorbell rang. Pelageya Antonovna was just bringing in a steaming pot which, one could tell at once from a single glance, contained, amidst a fiery borscht, that than which there is nothing more delicious in the world – a marrow bone.

Swallowing his spittle, Nikanor Ivanovich growled like a dog:

'Damn them all! Won't allow a man to eat ... Don't let anyone in, I'm not here, not here ... If it's about the apartment, tell them to stop blathering, there'll be a meeting next week.'

His wife ran to the front hall, while Nikanor Ivanovich, using a ladle, drew from the fire-breathing lake – it, the bone, cracked lengthwise. And at that moment two citizens entered the dining room, with Pelageya Antonovna following them, for some reason looking very pale. Seeing the citizens, Nikanor Ivanovich also turned white and stood up.

'Where's the jakes?' the first one, in a white side-buttoned shirt, asked with a preoccupied air.

Something thudded against the dining table (this was Nikanor Ivanovich dropping the ladle on to the oilcloth).

'This way, this way,' Pelageya Antonovna replied in a patter.

And the visitors immediately hastened to the corridor.

'What's the matter?' Nikanor Ivanovich asked quietly, going after the visitors. 'There can't be anything like that in our apartment ... And – your papers ... begging your pardon ...'

The first, without stopping, showed Nikanor Ivanovich a paper, and the second was at the same moment standing on a stool in the privy, his arm in the ventilation duct. Everything went dark in Nikanor Ivanovich's eyes. The newspaper was removed, but in the wad there were not roubles but some unknown money, bluish-greenish, and with the portrait of some old man. However, Nikanor Ivanovich saw it all dimly, there were some sort of spots floating in front of his eyes.

'Dollars in the ventilation ...' the first said pensively and asked Nikanor Ivanovich gently and courteously: 'Your little wad?'

'No!' Nikanor Ivanovich replied in a dreadful voice. 'Enemies stuck me with it!'

'That happens,' the first agreed and added, again gently: 'Well, you're going to have to turn in the rest.'

'I haven't got any! I swear to God, I never laid a finger on it!' the chairman cried out desperately.

He dashed to the chest, pulled a drawer out with a clatter, and from it the briefcase, crying out incoherently:

'Here's the contract ... that vermin of an interpreter stuck me with it ... Koroviev ... in a pince-nez! ...'

He opened the briefcase, glanced into it, put a hand inside, went blue in the face, and dropped the briefcase into the borscht. There was nothing in the briefcase: no letter from Styopa, no contract, no foreigner's passport, no money, no theatre pass. In short, nothing except a folding ruler.

'Comrades!' the chairman cried frenziedly. 'Catch them! There are unclean powers in our house!'

It is not known what Pelageya Antonovna imagined here, only she clasped her hands and cried:

'Repent, Ivanych! You'll get off lighter.'

His eyes bloodshot, Nikanor Ivanovich raised his fists over his wife's head, croaking:

'Ohh, you damned fool!'

Here he went slack and sank down on a chair, evidently resolved to submit to the inevitable.

During this time, Timofei Kondratievich Kvastsov stood on the landing, placing now his ear, now his eye to the keyhole of the door to the chairman's apartment, melting with curiosity.

Five minutes later the tenants of the house who were in the courtyard saw the chairman, accompanied by two other persons, proceed directly to the gates of the house. It was said that Nikanor Ivanovich looked awful, staggered like a drunk man as he passed, and was muttering something.

And an hour after that an unknown citizen appeared in apartment no. 11, just as Timofei Kondratievich, spluttering with delight, was telling some other tenants how the chairman got pinched, motioned to Timofei Kondratievich with his finger to come from the kitchen to the front hall, said something to him, and together they vanished.

CHAPTER 10

News From Yalta

At the same time that disaster struck Nikanor Ivanovich, not far away from no. 302-bis, on the same Sadovaya Street, in the office of the financial director of the Variety Theatre, Rimsky, there sat two men: Rimsky himself, and the administrator of the Variety, Varenukha.[1]

The big office on the second floor of the theatre had two windows on Sadovaya and one, just behind the back of the findirector, who was sitting at his desk, facing the summer garden of the Variety, where there were refreshment stands, a shooting gallery and an open-air stage. The furnishings of the office, apart from the desk, consisted of a bunch of old posters hanging on the wall, a small table with a carafe of water on it, four armchairs and, in the corner, a stand on which stood a dust-covered scale model of some past review. Well, it goes without saying that, in addition, there was in the office a small, shabby, peeling fireproof safe, to Rimsky's left, next to the desk.

Rimsky, now sitting at his desk, had been in bad spirits since morning, while Varenukha, on the contrary, was very animated and somehow especially restlessly active. Yet there was no outlet for his energy.

Varenukha was presently hiding in the findirector's office to escape the seekers of free passes, who poisoned his life, especially on days when the programme changed. And today was precisely such a day. As soon as the telephone started to ring, Varenukha would pick up the receiver and lie into it:

'Who? Varenukha? He's not here. He stepped out.'

'Please call Likhodeev again,' Rimsky asked vexedly.

'He's not home. I even sent Karpov, there's no one in the apartment.'

'Devil knows what's going on!' Rimsky hissed, clacking on the adding machine.

The door opened and an usher dragged in a thick stack of freshly printed extra posters; in big red letters on a green background was printed:

Today and Every Day at the Variety Theatre
an Additional Programme
PROFESSOR WOLAND
Séances of Black Magic and its Full Exposure

Varenukha stepped back from the poster, which he had thrown on to the scale model, admired it, and told the usher to send all the posters out immediately to be pasted up.

'Good ... Loud!' Varenukha observed on the usher's departure.

'And I dislike this undertaking extremely,' Rimsky grumbled, glancing spitefully at the poster through his horn-rimmed glasses, 'and generally I'm surprised he's been allowed to present it.'

'No, Grigory Danilovich, don't say so! This is a very subtle step. The salt is all in the exposure.'

'I don't know, I don't know, there's no salt, in my opinion ... and he's always coming up with things like this! ... He might at least show us his magician! Have you seen him? Where he dug him up, devil knows!'

It turned out that Varenukha had not seen the magician any more than Rimsky had. Yesterday Styopa had come running ('like crazy', in Rimsky's expression) to the findirector with the already written draft of a contract, ordered it copied straight away and the money handed over to Woland. And this magician had cleared out, and no one had seen him except Styopa himself.

Rimsky took out his watch, saw that it read five minutes past two, and flew into a complete rage. Really! Likhodeev had called at around eleven, said he'd come in half an hour, and not only had not come, but had disappeared from his apartment.

'He's holding up my business!' Rimsky was roaring now, jabbing his finger at a pile of unsigned papers.

'Might he have fallen under a tram-car like Berlioz?' Varenukha said as he held his ear to the receiver, from which came low, prolonged and utterly hopeless signals.

'Wouldn't be a bad thing ...' Rimsky said barely audibly through his teeth.

At that same moment a woman in a uniform jacket, visored cap, black skirt and sneakers came into the office. From a small pouch at her belt the woman took a small white square and a notebook and asked:

'Who here is Variety? A super-lightning telegram.[2] Sign here.'

Varenukha scribbled some flourish in the woman's notebook, and as soon as the door slammed behind her, he opened the square. After reading the telegram, he blinked and handed the square to Rimsky.

The telegram contained the following: 'Yalta to Moscow Variety. Today eleven thirty brown-haired man came criminal investigation nightshirt trousers shoeless mental case gave name Likhodeev Director Variety Wire Yalta criminal investigation where Director Likhodeev.'

'Hello and how do you do!' Rimsky exclaimed, and added: 'Another surprise!'

'A false Dmitri!'[3] said Varenukha, and he spoke into the receiver. 'Telegraph office? Variety account. Take a super-lightning telegram. Are you listening? "Yalta criminal investigation. Director Likhodeev Moscow Findirector Rimsky."'

Irrespective of the news about the Yalta impostor, Varenukha again began searching all over for Styopa by telephone, and naturally did not find him anywhere.

Just as Varenukha, receiver in hand, was pondering where else he might call, the same woman who had brought the first telegram came in and handed Varenukha a new envelope. Opening it hurriedly, Varenukha read the message and whistled.

'What now?' Rimsky asked, twitching nervously.

Varenukha silently handed him the telegram, and the findirector saw there the words: 'Beg believe thrown Yalta Woland hypnosis wire criminal investigation confirm identity Likhodeev.'

Rimsky and Varenukha, their heads touching, reread the telegram, and after rereading it, silently stared at each other.

'Citizens!' the woman got angry. 'Sign, and then be silent as much as you like! I deliver lightnings!'

Varenukha, without taking his eyes off the telegram, made a crooked scrawl in the notebook, and the woman vanished.

'Didn't you talk with him on the phone at a little past eleven?' the administrator began in total bewilderment.

'No, it's ridiculous!' Rimsky cried shrilly. 'Talk or not, he can't be in Yalta now! It's ridiculous!'

'He's drunk . . .' said Varenukha.

'Who's drunk?' asked Rimsky, and again the two stared at each other.

That some impostor or madman had sent telegrams from Yalta,

there was no doubt. But the strange thing was this: how did the Yalta mystifier know Woland, who had come to Moscow just the day before? How did he know about the connection between Likhodeev and Woland?

'Hypnosis . . .' Varenukha kept repeating the word from the telegram. 'How does he know about Woland?' He blinked his eyes and suddenly cried resolutely: 'Ah, no! Nonsense! . . . Nonsense, nonsense!'

'Where's he staying, this Woland, devil take him?' asked Rimsky.

Varenukha immediately got connected with the foreign tourist bureau and, to Rimsky's utter astonishment, announced that Woland was staying in Likhodeev's apartment. Dialling the number of the Likhodeev apartment after that, Varenukha listened for a long time to the low buzzing in the receiver. Amidst the buzzing, from somewhere far away, came a heavy, gloomy voice singing: '. . . rocks, my refuge . . .'[4] and Varenukha decided that the telephone lines had crossed with a voice from a radio show.

'The apartment doesn't answer,' Varenukha said, putting down the receiver, 'or maybe I should call . . .'

He did not finish. The same woman appeared in the door, and both men, Rimsky and Varenukha, rose to meet her, while she took from her pouch not a white sheet this time, but some sort of dark one.

'This is beginning to get interesting,' Varenukha said through his teeth, his eyes following the hurriedly departing woman. Rimsky was the first to take hold of the sheet.

On a dark background of photographic paper, some black handwritten lines were barely discernible:

'Proof my handwriting my signature wire urgently confirmation place secret watch Woland Likhodeev.'

In his twenty years of work in the theatre, Varenukha had seen all kinds of sights, but here he felt his mind becoming obscured as with a veil, and he could find nothing to say but the at once mundane and utterly absurd phrase:

'This cannot be!'

Rimsky acted otherwise. He stood up, opened the door, barked out to the messenger girl sitting on a stool:

'Let no one in except postmen!' – and locked the door with a key.

Then he took a pile of papers out of the desk and began carefully to compare the bold, back-slanting letters of the photogram with the letters in Styopa's resolutions and signatures, furnished with a corkscrew flourish. Varenukha, leaning his weight on the table, breathed hotly on Rimsky's cheek.

'It's his handwriting,' the findirector finally said firmly, and Varenukha repeated like an echo:

'His.'

Peering into Rimsky's face, the administrator marvelled at the change that had come over this face. Thin to begin with, the findirector seemed to have grown still thinner and even older, his eyes in their horn rims had lost their customary prickliness, and there appeared in them not only alarm, but even sorrow.

Varenukha did everything that a man in a moment of great astonishment ought to do. He raced up and down the office, he raised his arms twice like one crucified, he drank a whole glass of yellowish water from the carafe and exclaimed:

'I don't understand! I don't understand! I don't un-der-stand!'

Rimsky meanwhile was looking out the window, thinking hard about something. The findirector's position was very difficult. It was necessary at once, right on the spot, to invent ordinary explanations for extraordinary phenomena.

Narrowing his eyes, the findirector pictured to himself Styopa, in a nightshirt and shoeless, getting into some unprecedented super-high-speed airplane at around half past eleven that morning, and then the same Styopa, also at half past eleven, standing in his stocking feet at the airport in Yalta ... devil knew what to make of it!

Maybe it was not Styopa who talked with him this morning over the phone from his own apartment? No, it was Styopa speaking! Who if not he should know Styopa's voice? And even if it was not Styopa speaking today, it was no earlier than yesterday, towards evening, that Styopa had come from his office to this very office with this idiotic contract and annoyed the findirector with his light-mindedness. How could he have gone or flown away without leaving word at the theatre? But if he had flown away yesterday evening – he would not have arrived by noon today. Or would he?

'How many miles is it to Yalta?' asked Rimsky.

Varenukha stopped his running and yelled:

'I thought of that! I already thought of it! By train it's over nine hundred miles to Sebastopol, plus another fifty to Yalta! Well, but by air, of course, it's less.'

Hm . . . Yes . . . There could be no question of any trains. But what then? Some fighter plane? Who would let Styopa on any fighter plane without his shoes? What for? Maybe he took his shoes off when he got to Yalta? It's the same thing: what for? And even with his shoes on they wouldn't have let him on a fighter! And what has the fighter got to do with it? It's written that he came to the investigators at half past eleven in the morning, and he talked on the telephone in Moscow . . . excuse me . . . (the face of Rimsky's watch emerged before his eyes).

Rimsky tried to remember where the hands had been . . . Terrible! It had been twenty minutes past eleven!

So what does it boil down to? If one supposes that after the conversation Styopa instantly rushed to the airport, and reached it in, say, five minutes (which, incidentally, was also unthinkable), it means that the plane, taking off at once, covered nearly a thousand miles in five minutes. Consequently, it was flying at twelve thousand miles an hour!!! That cannot be, and that means he's not in Yalta!

What remains, then? Hypnosis? There's no hypnosis in the world that can fling a man a thousand miles away! So he's imagining that he's in Yalta? He may be imagining it, but are the Yalta investigators also imagining it? No, no, sorry, that can't be! . . . Yet they did telegraph from there?

The findirector's face was literally dreadful. The door handle was all the while being turned and pulled from outside, and the messenger girl could be heard through the door crying desperately:

'Impossible! I won't let you! Cut me to pieces! It's a meeting!'

Rimsky regained control of himself as well as he could, took the receiver of the phone, and said into it:

'A super-urgent call to Yalta, please.'

'Clever!' Varenukha observed mentally.

But the conversation with Yalta did not take place. Rimsky hung up the receiver and said:

'As luck would have it, the line's broken.'

It could be seen that the broken line especially upset him for some reason, and even made him lapse into thought. Having thought a little, he again took the receiver in one hand, and with the other began writing down what he said into it:

'Take a super-lightning. Variety. Yes. Yalta criminal investigation. Yes. "Today around eleven thirty Likhodeev talked me phone Moscow stop After that did not come work unable locate by phone stop Confirm handwriting stop Taking measures watch said artiste Findirector Rimsky."'

'Very clever!' thought Varenukha, but before he had time to think well, the words rushed through his head: 'Stupid! He can't be in Yalta!'

Rimsky meanwhile did the following: he neatly stacked all the received telegrams, plus the copy of his own, put the stack into an envelope, sealed it, wrote a few words on it, and handed it to Varenukha, saying:

'Go right now, Ivan Savelyevich, take it there personally.[5] Let them sort it out.'

'Now that is really clever!' thought Varenukha, and he put the envelope into his briefcase. Then, just in case, he dialled Styopa's apartment number on the telephone, listened, and began winking and grimacing joyfully and mysteriously. Rimsky stretched his neck.

'May I speak with the artiste Woland?' Varenukha asked sweetly.

'Mister's busy,' the receiver answered in a rattling voice, 'who's calling?'

'The administrator of the Variety, Varenukha.'

'Ivan Savelyevich?' the receiver cried out joyfully. 'Terribly glad to hear your voice! How're you doing?'

'Merci,' Varenukha replied in amazement, 'and with whom am I speaking?'

'His assistant, his assistant and interpreter, Koroviev!' crackled the receiver. 'I'm entirely at your service, my dearest Ivan Savelyevich! Order me around as you like. And so?'

'Excuse me, but . . . what, is Stepan Bogdanovich Likhodeev not at home now?'

'Alas, no! No!' the receiver shouted. 'He left!'

'For where?'

'Out of town, for a drive in the car.'

'Wh . . . what? A dr . . . drive? And when will he be back?'

'He said, I'll get a breath of fresh air and come back.'

'So . . .' said the puzzled Varenukha, 'merci . . . kindly tell Monsieur Woland that his performance is tonight in the third part of the programme.'

'Right. Of course. Absolutely. Urgently. Without fail. I'll tell him,' the receiver rapped out abruptly.

'Goodbye,' Varenukha said in astonishment.

'Please accept,' said the receiver, 'my best, warmest greetings and wishes! For success! Luck! Complete happiness! Everything!'

'But of course! Didn't I say so!' the administrator cried agitatedly. 'It's not any Yalta, he just went to the country!'

'Well, if that's so,' the findirector began, turning pale with anger, 'it's real swinishness, there's even no name for it!'

Here the administrator jumped up and shouted so that Rimsky gave a start:

'I remember! I remember! They've opened a new Georgian tavern in Pushkino called "Yalta"! It's all clear! He went there, got drunk, and now he's sending telegrams from there!'

'Well, now that's too much!' Rimsky answered, his cheek twitching, and deep, genuine anger burned in his eyes. 'Well, then, he's going to pay dearly for this little excursion! . . .' He suddenly faltered and added irresolutely: 'But what about the criminal investigation . . .'

'It's nonsense! His own little jokes,' the expansive administrator interrupted, and asked: 'Shall I take the envelope?'

'Absolutely,' replied Rimsky.

And again the door opened and in came that same . . . 'Her!' thought Rimsky, for some reason with anguish. And both men rose to meet the postwoman.

This time the telegram contained the words:

'Thank you confirmation send five hundred urgently criminal investigation my name tomorrow fly Moscow Likhodeev.'

'He's lost his mind . . .' Varenukha said weakly.

Rimsky jingled his key, took money from the fireproof safe, counted out five hundred roubles, rang the bell, handed the messenger the money, and sent him to the telegraph office.

'Good heavens, Grigory Danilovich,' Varenukha said, not believing his eyes, 'in my opinion you oughtn't to send the money.'

'It'll come back,' Rimsky replied quietly, 'but he'll have a hard time explaining this little picnic.' And he added, indicating the briefcase to Varenukha: 'Go, Ivan Savelyevich, don't delay.'

And Varenukha ran out of the office with the briefcase.

He went down to the ground floor, saw the longest line at the box office, found out from the box-office girl that she expected to sell out within the hour, because the public was simply pouring in since the additional poster had been put up, told the girl to earmark and hold thirty of the best seats in the gallery and the stalls, popped out of the box office, shook off importunate pass-seekers as he ran, and dived into his little office to get his cap. At that moment the telephone rattled.

'Yes!' Varenukha shouted.

'Ivan Savelyevich?' the receiver inquired in a most repulsive nasal voice.

'He's not in the theatre!' Varenukha was shouting, but the receiver interrupted him at once:

'Don't play the fool, Ivan Savelyevich, just listen. Do not take those telegrams anywhere or show them to anyone.'

'Who is this?' Varenukha bellowed. 'Stop these jokes, citizen! You'll be found out at once! What's your number?'

'Varenukha,' the same nasty voice returned, 'do you understand Russian? Don't take the telegrams anywhere.'

'Ah, so you won't stop?' the administrator cried furiously. 'Look out, then! You're going to pay for it!' He shouted some other threat, but fell silent, because he sensed that no one was listening to him any longer in the receiver.

Here it somehow began to grow dark very quickly in his little office. Varenukha ran out, slammed the door behind him, and rushed through the side entrance into the summer garden.

The administrator was agitated and full of energy. After the insolent phone call he had no doubts that it was a band of hooligans playing nasty tricks, and that these tricks were connected with the disappearance of Likhodeev. The administrator was choking with the desire to expose the malefactors, and, strange as it was, the anticipation of something enjoyable was born in him. It happens that way when a man strives to become the centre of attention, to bring sensational news somewhere.

In the garden the wind blew in the administrator's face and flung sand in his eyes, as if blocking his way, as if cautioning him. A window on the second floor slammed so that the glass nearly broke, the tops of the maples and lindens rustled alarmingly. It became darker and colder. The administrator rubbed his eyes and saw that a yellow-bellied storm cloud was creeping low over Moscow. There came a dense, distant rumbling.

However great Varenukha's hurry, an irrepressible desire pulled at him to run over to the summer toilet for a second on his way, to check whether the repairman had put a wire screen over the light-bulb.

Running past the shooting gallery, Varenukha came to a thick growth of lilacs where the light-blue toilet building stood. The repairman turned out to be an efficient fellow, the bulb under the roof of the gentlemen's side was covered with a wire screen, but the administrator was upset that even in the pre-storm darkness one could make out that the walls were already written all over in charcoal and pencil.

'Well, what sort of . . .' the administrator began and suddenly heard a voice purring behind him:

'Is that you, Ivan Savelyevich?'

Varenukha started, turned around, and saw before him a short, fat man with what seemed to him a cat-like physiognomy.

'So, it's me, Varenukha answered hostilely.'

'Very, very glad,' the cat-like fat man responded in a squeaky voice and, suddenly swinging his arm, gave Varenukha such a blow on the ear that the cap flew off the administrator's head and vanished without a trace down the hole in the seat.

At the fat man's blow, the whole toilet lit up momentarily with a tremulous light, and a roll of thunder echoed in the sky. Then came another flash and a second man emerged before the administrator – short, but with athletic shoulders, hair red as fire, albugo in one eye, a fang in his mouth . . . This second one, evidently a lefty, socked the administrator on the other ear. In response there was another roll of thunder in the sky, and rain poured down on the wooden roof of the toilet.

'What is it, comr . . .' the half-crazed administrator whispered, realized at once that the word 'comrades' hardly fitted bandits attacking a man in a public toilet, rasped out: 'citiz . . .' – figured that they did not merit this appellation either, and received a third terrible blow from he did not know which of them, so that blood gushed from his nose on to his Tolstoy blouse.

'What you got in the briefcase, parasite?' the one resembling a cat cried shrilly. 'Telegrams? Weren't you warned over the phone not to take them anywhere? Weren't you warned, I'm asking you?'

'I was wor . . . wer . . . warned . . .' the administrator answered, suffocating.

'And you skipped off anyway? Gimme the briefcase, vermin!' the second one cried in the same nasal voice that had come over the telephone, and he yanked the briefcase from Varenukha's trembling hands.

And the two picked the administrator up under the arms, dragged him out of the garden, and raced down Sadovaya with him. The storm raged at full force, water streamed with a noise and howling down the drains, waves bubbled and billowed everywhere, water gushed from the roofs past the drainpipes, foamy streams ran from gateways. Everything living got washed off Sadovaya, and there was no one to save Ivan Savelyevich. Leaping through muddy rivers, under flashes of lightning, the bandits dragged the half-alive administrator in a split second to no. 302-bis, flew with him through the gateway, where two barefoot women, holding their shoes and stockings in their hands, pressed themselves to the wall. Then they dashed into the sixth entrance, and Varenukha, nearly insane, was taken up to the fifth floor and thrown down in the semi-dark front hall, so well known to him, of Styopa Likhodeev's apartment.

Here the two robbers vanished, and in their place there appeared in the front hall a completely naked girl – red-haired, her eyes burning with a phosphorescent gleam.

Varenukha understood that this was the most terrible of all things that had ever happened to him and, moaning, recoiled against the wall. But the girl came right up to the administrator and placed the palms of her hands on his shoulders. Varenukha's hair stood on end, because even through the cold, water-soaked cloth of his Tolstoy blouse he could feel that those palms were still colder, that their cold was the cold of ice.

'Let me give you a kiss,' the girl said tenderly, and there were shining eyes right in front of his eyes. Then Varenukha fainted and never felt the kiss.

CHAPTER 11

Ivan Splits in Two

The woods on the opposite bank of the river, still lit up by the May sun an hour earlier, turned dull, smeary, and dissolved.

Water fell down in a solid sheet outside the window. In the sky, threads flashed every moment, the sky kept bursting open, and the patient's room was flooded with a tremulous, frightening light.

Ivan quietly wept, sitting on his bed and looking out at the muddy river boiling with bubbles. At every clap of thunder, he cried out pitifully and buried his face in his hands. Pages covered with Ivan's writing lay about on the floor. They had been blown down by the wind that flew into the room before the storm began.

The poet's attempts to write a statement concerning the terrible consultant had gone nowhere. As soon as he got the pencil stub and paper from the fat attendant, whose name was Praskovya Fyodorovna, he rubbed his hands in a business-like way and hastily settled himself at the little table. The beginning came out quite glibly.

'To the police. From Massolit member Ivan Nikolaevich Homeless. A statement. Yesterday evening I came to the Patriarch's Ponds with the deceased M. A. Berlioz ...'

And right there the poet got confused, mainly owing to the word 'deceased'. Some nonsensicality emerged at once: what's this – came with the deceased? The deceased don't go anywhere! Really, for all he knew, they might take him for a madman!

Having reflected thus, Ivan Nikolaevich began to correct what he had written. What came out this time was: '... with M. A. Berlioz, subsequently deceased ...' This did not satisfy the author either. He had to have recourse to a third redaction, which proved still worse than the first two: 'Berlioz, who fell under the tram-car ...' – and that namesake composer, unknown to anyone, was also dangling here, so he had to put in: 'not the composer ...'

After suffering over these two Berliozes, Ivan crossed it all out and decided to begin right off with something very strong, in order to attract the reader's attention at once, so he wrote that a cat had got on a tram-car, and then went back to the episode with the severed head. The head and the consultant's prediction led him to the thought of Pontius Pilate, and for greater conviction Ivan decided to tell the whole story of the procurator in full, from the moment he walked out in his white cloak with blood-red lining to the colonnade of Herod's palace.

Ivan worked assiduously, crossing out what he had written, putting in new words, and even attempted to draw Pontius Pilate and then a cat standing on its hind legs. But the drawings did not help, and the further it went, the more confusing and incomprehensible the poet's statement became.

By the time the frightening cloud with smoking edges appeared from far off and covered the woods, and the wind began to blow, Ivan felt that he was strengthless, that he would never be able to manage with the statement, and he would not pick up the scattered pages, and he wept quietly and bitterly. The good-natured nurse Praskovya Fyodorovna visited the poet during the storm, became alarmed on seeing him weeping, closed the blinds so that the lightning would not frighten the patient, picked up the pages from the floor, and ran with them for the doctor.

He came, gave Ivan an injection in the arm, and assured him that he would not weep any more, that everything would pass now, everything would change, everything would be forgotten.

The doctor proved right. Soon the woods across the river became as before. It was outlined to the last tree under the sky, which cleared to its former perfect blue, and the river grew calm. Anguish had begun to leave Ivan right after the injection, and now the poet lay calmly and looked at the rainbow that stretched across the sky.

So it went till evening, and he did not even notice how the rainbow melted away, how the sky saddened and faded, how the woods turned black.

Having drunk some hot milk, Ivan lay down again and marvelled himself at how changed his thinking was. The accursed, demonic cat somehow softened in his memory, the severed head did not frighten him any more, and, abandoning all thought of it, Ivan began to reflect that, essentially, it was not so bad in the clinic, that Stravinsky was a clever man and a famous one, and it was quite pleasant to deal with him. Besides, the evening air was sweet and fresh after the storm.

The house of sorrow was falling asleep. In quiet corridors the frosted white lights went out, and in their place, according to regulations, faint blue night-lights were lit, and the careful steps of attendants were heard more and more rarely on the rubber matting of the corridor outside the door.

Now Ivan lay in sweet languor, glancing at the lamp under its shade, shedding a softened light from the ceiling, then at the moon rising behind the black woods, and conversed with himself.

'Why, actually, did I get so excited about Berlioz falling under a tram-car?' the poet reasoned. 'In the final analysis, let him sink! What am I, in fact, his chum or in-law? If we air the question properly, it turns out that, in essence, I really did not even know the deceased. What, indeed, did I know about him? Nothing except that he was bald and terribly eloquent. And furthermore, citizens,' Ivan continued his speech, addressing someone or other, 'let's sort this out: why, tell me, did I get furious at this mysterious consultant, magician and professor with the black and empty eye? Why all this absurd chase after him in underpants and with a candle in my hand, and then those wild shenanigans in the restaurant?'

'Uh-uh-uh!' the former Ivan suddenly said sternly somewhere, either inside or over his ear, to the new Ivan. 'He did know beforehand that Berlioz's head would be cut off, didn't he? How could I not get excited?'

'What are we talking about, comrades?' the new Ivan objected to the old, former Ivan. 'That things are not quite proper here, even a child can understand. He's a one-hundred-per-cent outstanding and mysterious person! But that's the most interesting thing! The man was personally acquainted with Pontius Pilate, what could be more interesting than that? And, instead of raising a stupid rumpus at the Ponds, wouldn't it have been more intelligent to question him politely about what happened further on with Pilate and his prisoner Ha-Nozri? And I started devil knows what! A major occurrence, really – a magazine editor gets run over! And so, what, is the magazine going to shut down for that? Well, what can be done about it? Man is mortal and, as has rightly been said, unexpectedly mortal. Well, may he rest in peace! Well, so there'll be another editor, and maybe even more eloquent than the previous one!'

After dozing for a while, the new Ivan asked the old Ivan sarcastically: 'And what does it make me, in that case?'

'A fool!' a bass voice said distinctly somewhere, a voice not belonging to either of the Ivans and extremely like the bass of the consultant.

Ivan, for some reason not offended by the word 'fool', but even pleasantly surprised at it, smiled and drowsily grew quiet. Sleep was stealing over Ivan, and he was already picturing a palm tree on its elephant's leg, and a cat passing by – not scary, but merry – and, in short, sleep was just about to come over Ivan, when the grille suddenly moved noiselessly aside, and a mysterious figure appeared on the balcony, hiding from the moonlight, and shook its finger at Ivan.

Not frightened in the least, Ivan sat up in bed and saw that there was a man on the balcony. And this man, pressing a finger to his lips, whispered:

'Shhh! . . .'

CHAPTER 12

Black Magic and Its Exposure

A small man in a yellow bowler-hat full of holes and with a pear-shaped, raspberry-coloured nose, in checkered trousers and patent-leather shoes, rolled out on to the stage of the Variety on an ordinary two-wheeled bicycle. To the sounds of a foxtrot he made a circle, and then gave a triumphant shout, which caused his bicycle to rear up. After riding around on the back wheel, the little man turned upside down, contrived while in motion to unscrew the front wheel and send it backstage, and then proceeded on his way with one wheel, turning the pedals with his hands.

On a tall metal pole with a seat at the top and a single wheel, a plump blonde rolled out in tights and a little skirt strewn with silver stars, and began riding in a circle. As he met her, the little man uttered cries of greeting, doffing his bowler-hat with his foot.

Finally, a little eight-year-old with an elderly face came rolling out and began scooting about among the adults on a tiny two-wheeler furnished with an enormous automobile horn.

After making several loops, the whole company, to the alarming drum-beats of the orchestra, rolled to the very edge of the stage, and the spectators in the front rows gasped and drew back, because it seemed to the public that the whole trio with its vehicles was about to crash down into the orchestra pit.

But the bicycles stopped just at the moment when the front wheels threatened to slide into the abyss on the heads of the musicians. With a loud shout of 'Hup!' the cyclists jumped off their vehicles and bowed, the blonde woman blowing kisses to the public, and the little one tooting a funny signal on his horn.

Applause shook the building, the light-blue curtain came from both sides and covered the cyclists, the green 'Exit' lights by the doors went out, and in the web of trapezes under the cupola white spheres lit up like the sun. It was the intermission before the last part.

The only man who was not the least bit interested in the wonders of the Giulli family's cycling technique was Grigory Danilovich Rimsky.

In complete solitude he sat in his office, biting his thin lips, a spasm passing over his face from time to time. To the extraordinary disappearance of Likhodeev had now been added the wholly unforeseen disappearance of Varenukha.

Rimsky knew where he had gone, but he had gone and ... not come back! Rimsky shrugged his shoulders and whispered to himself:

'But what for?'

And it was strange: for such a practical man as the findirector, the simplest thing would, of course, have been to call the place where Varenukha had gone and find out what had befallen him, yet until ten o'clock at night he had been unable to force himself to do it.

At ten, doing outright violence to himself, Rimsky picked up the receiver and here discovered that his telephone was dead. The messenger reported that the other telephones in the building were also out of order. This certainly unpleasant, though hardly supernatural, occurrence for some reason thoroughly shocked the findirector, but at the same time he was glad: the need to call fell away.

Just as the red light over the findirector's head lit up and blinked, announcing the beginning of the intermission, a messenger came in and informed him of the foreign artiste's arrival. The findirector cringed for some reason, and, blacker than a storm cloud, went backstage to receive the visitor, since there was no one else to receive him.

Under various pretexts, curious people kept peeking into the big dressing room from the corridor, where the signal bell was already ringing. Among them were conjurers in bright robes and turbans, a skater in a white knitted jacket, a storyteller pale with powder and the make-up man.

The newly arrived celebrity struck everyone by his marvellously cut tailcoat, of a length never seen before, and by his having come in a black half-mask. But most remarkable of all were the black magician's two companions: a long checkered one with a cracked pince-nez, and a fat black cat who came into the dressing room on his hind legs and quite nonchalantly sat on the sofa squinting at the bare make-up lights.

Rimsky attempted to produce a smile on his face, which made it look sour and spiteful, and bowed to the silent black magician, who was seated on the sofa beside the cat. There was no handshake. Instead, the easygoing checkered one made his own introductions to the findirector, calling himself 'the gent's assistant'. This circumstance surprised the findirector, and unpleasantly so: there was decidedly no mention of any assistant in the contract.

Quite stiffly and drily, Grigory Danilovich inquired of this fallen-from-the-sky checkered one where the artiste's paraphernalia was.

'Our heavenly diamond, most precious mister director,' the magician's assistant replied in a rattling voice, 'the paraphernalia is always with us. Here it is! Ein, zwei, drei!' And, waving his knotty fingers before Rimsky's eyes, he suddenly took from behind the cat's ear Rimsky's own gold watch and chain, hitherto worn by the findirector in his waistcoat pocket, under his buttoned coat, with the chain through a buttonhole.

Rimsky inadvertently clutched his stomach, those present gasped, and the make-up man, peeking in the doorway, grunted approvingly.

'Your little watchie? Kindly take it,' the checkered one said, smiling casually and offering the bewildered Rimsky his own property on a dirty palm.

'No getting on a tram with that one,' the storyteller whispered quietly and merrily to the make-up man.

But the cat pulled a neater trick than the number with the stolen watch. Getting up from the sofa unexpectedly, he walked on his hind legs to the dressing table, pulled the stopper out of the carafe with his front paw, poured water into a glass, drank it, installed the stopper in its place, and wiped his whiskers with a make-up cloth.

Here no one even gasped, their mouths simply fell open, and the make-up man whispered admiringly:

'That's class!'

Just then the bells rang alarmingly for the third time, and everyone, agitated and anticipating an interesting number, thronged out of the dressing room.

A moment later the spheres went out in the theatre, the footlights blazed up, lending a reddish glow to the base of the curtain, and in the lighted gap of the curtain there appeared before the public a plump man, merry as a baby, with a clean-shaven face, in a rumpled tailcoat and none-too-fresh shirt. This was the master of ceremonies, well known to all Moscow – Georges Bengalsky.

'And now, citizens,' Bengalsky began, smiling his baby smile, 'there is about to come before you . . .' Here Bengalsky interrupted himself and spoke in a different tone: 'I see the audience has grown for the third part. We've got half the city here! I met a friend the other day and said to him: "Why don't you come to our show? Yesterday we had half the city." And he says to me: "I live in the other half!"' Bengalsky paused, waiting for a burst of laughter, but as no one laughed, he went on: '. . . And so, now comes the famous foreign artiste, Monsieur Woland, with a séance of black magic. Well, both you and I know,' here Bengalsky smiled a wise smile, 'that there's no such thing in the world, and that it's all just superstition, and Maestro Woland is simply a perfect master of the technique of conjuring, as we shall see from the most interesting part, that is, the exposure of this technique, and since we're all of us to a man both for technique and for its exposure, let's bring on Mr Woland! . . .'

After uttering all this claptrap, Bengalsky pressed his palms together and waved them in greeting through the slit of the curtain, which caused it to part with a soft rustle.

The entrance of the magician with his long assistant and the cat, who came on stage on his hind legs, pleased the audience greatly.

'An armchair for me,' Woland ordered in a low voice, and that same second an armchair appeared on stage, no one knew how or from where, in which the magician sat down. 'Tell me, my gentle Fagott,' Woland inquired of the checkered clown, who evidently had another appellation than Koroviev, 'what do you think, the Moscow populace has changed significantly, hasn't it?'

The magician looked out at the hushed audience, struck by the appearance of the armchair out of nowhere.

'That it has, Messire,' Fagott-Koroviev replied in a low voice.

'You're right. The city folk have changed greatly . . . externally, that is . . . as has the city itself, incidentally . . . Not to mention their clothing, these . . . what do you call them . . . trams, automobiles . . . have appeared . . .'

'Buses . . .' Fagott prompted deferentially.

The audience listened attentively to this conversation, thinking it constituted a prelude to the magic tricks. The wings were packed with performers and stage-hands, and among their faces could be seen the tense, pale face of Rimsky.

The physiognomy of Bengalsky, who had retreated to the side of the stage, began to show some perplexity. He raised one eyebrow slightly and, taking advantage of a pause, spoke:

'The foreign artiste is expressing his admiration for Moscow and its technological development, as well as for the Muscovites.' Here Bengalsky smiled twice, first to the stalls, then to the gallery.

Woland, Fagott and the cat turned their heads in the direction of the master of ceremonies.

'Did I express admiration?' the magician asked the checkered Fagott.

'By no means, Messire, you never expressed any admiration,' came the reply.

'Then what is the man saying?'

'He quite simply lied!' the checkered assistant declared sonorously, for the whole theatre to hear, and turning to Bengalsky, he added: 'Congrats, citizen, you done lied!'

Tittering spattered from the gallery, but Bengalsky gave a start and goggled his eyes.

'Of course, I'm not so much interested in buses, telephones and other . . .'

'Apparatuses,' the checkered one prompted.

'Quite right, thank you,' the magician spoke slowly in a heavy bass, 'as in a question of much greater importance: have the city folk changed inwardly?'

'Yes, that is the most important question, sir.'

There was shrugging and an exchanging of glances in the wings, Bengalsky stood all red, and Rimsky was pale. But here, as if sensing the nascent alarm, the magician said:

'However, we're talking away, my dear Fagott, and the audience is beginning to get bored. My gentle Fagott, show us some simple little thing to start with.'

The audience stirred. Fagott and the cat walked along the footlights to opposite sides of the stage. Fagott snapped his fingers, and with a rollicking 'Three, four!' snatched a deck of cards from the air, shuffled it, and sent it in a long ribbon to the cat. The cat intercepted it and sent it back. The satiny snake whiffled, Fagott opened his mouth like a nestling and swallowed it all card by card. After which the cat bowed, scraping his right hind paw, winning himself unbelievable applause.

'Class! Real class!' rapturous shouts came from the wings.

And Fagott jabbed his finger at the stalls and announced:

'You'll find that same deck, esteemed citizens, on citizen Parchevsky in the seventh row, just between a three-rouble bill and a summons to court in connection with the payment of alimony to citizen Zelkova.'

There was a stirring in the stalls, people began to get up, and finally some citizen whose name was indeed Parchevsky, all crimson with amazement, extracted the deck from his wallet and began sticking it up in the air, not knowing what to do with it.

'You may keep it as a souvenir!' cried Fagott. 'Not for nothing did you say at dinner yesterday that if it weren't for poker your life in Moscow would be utterly unbearable.'

'An old trick!' came from the gallery. 'The one in the stalls is from the same company.'

'You think so?' shouted Fagott, squinting at the gallery. 'In that case you're also one of us, because the deck is now in your pocket!'

There was movement in the balcony, and a joyful voice said:

'Right! He's got it! Here, here! . . . Wait! It's ten-rouble bills!'

Those sitting in the stalls turned their heads. In the gallery a bewildered citizen found in his pocket a bank-wrapped packet with 'One thousand roubles' written on it. His neighbours hovered over him, and he, in amazement, picked at the wrapper with his fingernail, trying to find out if the bills were real or some sort of magic ones.

'By God, they're real! Ten-rouble bills!' joyful cries came from the gallery.

'I want to play with the same kind of deck,' a fat man in the middle of the stalls requested merrily.

'Avec playzeer!' Fagott responded. 'But why just you? Everyone will warmly participate!' And he commanded: 'Look up, please! . . . One!' There was a pistol in his hand. He shouted: 'Two!' The pistol was pointed up. He shouted: 'Three!' There was a flash, a bang, and all at once, from under the cupola, bobbing between the trapezes, white strips of paper began falling into the theatre.

They twirled, got blown aside, were drawn towards the gallery, bounced into the orchestra and on to the stage. In a few seconds, the rain of money, ever thickening, reached the seats, and the spectators began snatching at it.

Hundreds of arms were raised, the spectators held the bills up to the lighted stage and saw the most true and honest-to-God watermarks. The smell also left no doubts: it was the incomparably delightful smell of freshly printed money. The whole theatre was seized first with merriment and then with amazement. The word 'money, money!'

hummed everywhere, there were gasps of 'ah, ah!' and merry laughter. One or two were already crawling in the aisles, feeling under the chairs. Many stood on the seats, trying to catch the flighty, capricious notes.

Bewilderment was gradually coming to the faces of the policemen, and performers unceremoniously began sticking their heads out from the wings.

In the dress circle a voice was heard: 'What're you grabbing at? It's mine, it flew to me!' and another voice: 'Don't shove me, or you'll get shoved back!' And suddenly there came the sound of a whack. At once a policeman's helmet appeared in the dress circle, and someone from the dress circle was led away.

The general agitation was increasing, and no one knows where it all would have ended if Fagott had not stopped the rain of money by suddenly blowing into the air.

Two young men, exchanging significant and merry glances, took off from their seats and made straight for the buffet. There was a hum in the theatre, all the spectators' eyes glittered excitedly. Yes, yes, no one knows where it all would have ended if Bengalsky had not summoned his strength and acted. Trying to gain better control of himself, he rubbed his hands, as was his custom, and in his most resounding voice spoke thus:

'Here, citizens, you and I have just beheld a case of so-called mass hypnosis. A purely scientific experiment, proving in the best way possible that there are no miracles in magic. Let us ask Maestro Woland to expose this experiment for us. Presently, citizens, you will see these supposed banknotes disappear as suddenly as they appeared.'

Here he applauded, but quite alone, while a confident smile played on his face, yet in his eyes there was no such confidence, but rather an expression of entreaty.

The audience did not like Bengalsky's speech. Total silence fell, which was broken by the checkered Fagott.

'And this is a case of so-called lying,' he announced in a loud, goatish tenor. 'The notes, citizens, are genuine.'

'Bravo!' a bass barked from somewhere on high.

'This one, incidentally,' here Fagott pointed to Bengalsky, 'annoys me. Keeps poking his nose where nobody's asked him, spoils the séance with false observations! What're we going to do with him?'

'Tear his head off!' someone up in the gallery said severely.

'What's that you said? Eh?' Fagott responded at once to this outrageous suggestion. 'Tear his head off? There's an idea! Behemoth!'
he shouted to the cat. 'Go to it! Ein, zwei, drei!'

And an unheard-of thing occurred. The fur bristled on the cat's
back, and he gave a rending miaow. Then he compressed himself into
a ball and shot like a panther straight at Bengalsky's chest, and from
there on to his head. Growling, the cat sank his plump paws into the
skimpy chevelure of the master of ceremonies and in two twists tore
the head from the thick neck with a savage howl.

The two and a half thousand people in the theatre cried out as one.
Blood spurted in fountains from the torn neck arteries and poured
over the shirt-front and tailcoat. The headless body paddled its feet
somehow absurdly and sat down on the floor. Hysterical women's cries
came from the audience. The cat handed the head to Fagott, who lifted
it up by the hair and showed it to the audience, and the head cried
desperately for all the theatre to hear:

'A doctor!'

'Will you pour out such drivel in the future?' Fagott asked the
weeping head menacingly.

'Never again!' croaked the head.

'For God's sake, don't torture him!' a woman's voice from a box
seat suddenly rose above the clamour, and the magician turned in the
direction of that voice.

'So, what then, citizens, shall we forgive him?' Fagott asked, addressing the audience.

'Forgive him, forgive him!' separate voices, mostly women's, spoke
first, then merged into one chorus with the men's.

'What are your orders, Messire?' Fagott asked the masked man.

'Well, now,' the latter replied pensively, 'they're people like any other
people ... They love money, but that has always been so ... Mankind
loves money, whatever it's made of – leather, paper, bronze, gold. Well,
they're light-minded ... well, what of it ... mercy sometimes knocks
at their hearts ... ordinary people ... In general, reminiscent of the
former ones ... only the housing problem has corrupted them...'
And he ordered loudly: 'Put the head on.'

The cat, aiming accurately, planted the head on the neck, and it sat
exactly in its place, as if it had never gone anywhere. Above all, there
was not even any scar left on the neck. The cat brushed Bengalsky's

tailcoat and shirt-front with his paws, and all traces of blood disappeared from them. Fagott got the sitting Bengalsky to his feet, stuck a packet of money into his coat pocket, and sent him from the stage with the words:

'Buzz off, it's more fun without you!'

Staggering and looking around senselessly, the master of ceremonies had plodded no farther than the fire post when he felt sick. He cried out pitifully:

'My head, my head! . . .'

Among those who rushed to him was Rimsky. The master of ceremonies wept, snatched at something in the air with his hands, and muttered:

'Give me my head, give me back my head . . . Take my apartment, take my paintings, only give me back my head! . . .'

A messenger ran for a doctor. They tried to lie Bengalsky down on a sofa in the dressing room, but he began to struggle, became violent. They had to call an ambulance. When the unfortunate master of ceremonies was taken away, Rimsky ran back to the stage and saw that new wonders were taking place on it. Ah, yes, incidentally, either then or a little earlier, the magician disappeared from the stage together with his faded armchair, and it must be said that the public took absolutely no notice of it, carried away as it was by the extraordinary things Fagott was unfolding on stage.

And Fagott, having packed off the punished master of ceremonies, addressed the public thus:

'All righty, now that we've kicked that nuisance out, let's open a ladies' shop!'

And all at once the floor of the stage was covered with Persian carpets, huge mirrors appeared, lit by greenish tubes at the sides, and between the mirrors – display windows, and in them the merrily astonished spectators saw Parisian ladies' dresses of various colours and cuts. In some of the windows, that is, while in others there appeared hundreds of ladies' hats, with feathers and without feathers, and – with buckles or without – hundreds of shoes, black, white, yellow, leather, satin, suede, with straps, with stones. Among the shoes there appeared cases of perfume, mountains of handbags of antelope hide, suede, silk, and among these, whole heaps of little elongated cases of gold metal such as usually contain lipstick.

A red-headed girl appeared from devil knows where in a black evening dress – a girl nice in all respects, had she not been marred by a queer scar on her neck – smiling a proprietary smile by the display windows.

Fagott, grinning sweetly, announced that the firm was offering perfectly gratis an exchange of the ladies' old dresses and shoes for Parisian models and Parisian shoes. The same held, he added, for the handbags and other things.

The cat began scraping with his hind paw, while his front paw performed the gestures appropriate to a doorman opening a door.

The girl sang out sweetly, though with some hoarseness, rolling her r's, something not quite comprehensible but, judging by the women's faces in the stalls, very tempting:

'Guérlain, Chanel, Mitsouko, Narcisse Noir, Chanel No. 5, evening gowns, cocktail dresses . . .'

Fagott wriggled, the cat bowed, the girl opened the glass windows. 'Welcome!' yelled Fagott. 'With no embarrassment or ceremony!'

The audience was excited, but as yet no one ventured on stage. Finally some brunette stood up in the tenth row of the stalls and, smiling as if to say it was all the same to her and she did not give a hoot, went and climbed on stage by the side stairs.

'Bravo!' Fagott shouted. 'Greetings to the first customer! Behemoth, a chair! Let's start with the shoes, madame.'

The brunette sat in the chair, and Fagott at once poured a whole heap of shoes on the rug in front of her. The brunette removed her right shoe, tried a lilac one, stamped on the rug, examined the heel.

'They won't pinch?' she asked pensively.

To this Fagott exclaimed with a hurt air:

'Come, come!' and the cat miaowed resentfully.

'I'll take this pair, m'sieur,' the brunette said with dignity, putting on the second shoe as well.

The brunette's old shoes were tossed behind a curtain, and she proceeded there herself, accompanied by the red-headed girl and Fagott, who was carrying several fashionable dresses on hangers. The cat bustled about, helped, and for greater importance hung a measuring tape around his neck.

A minute later the brunette came from behind the curtain in such a dress that the stalls all let out a gasp. The brave woman, who had become astonishingly prettier, stopped at the mirror, moved her bare shoulders, touched the hair on her nape and, twisting, tried to peek at her back.

'The firm asks you to accept this as a souvenir,' said Fagott, and he offered the brunette an open case with a flacon in it.

'Merci,' the brunette said haughtily and went down the steps to the stalls. As she walked, the spectators jumped up and touched the case.

And here there came a clean breakthrough, and from all sides women marched on to the stage. Amid the general agitation of talk, chuckles and gasps, a man's voice was heard: 'I won't allow it!' and a woman's: 'Despot and philistine! Don't break my arm!' Women disappeared behind the curtain, leaving their dresses there and coming out in new ones. A whole row of ladies sat on stools with gilded legs, stamping the carpet energetically with newly shod feet. Fagott was on his knees, working away with a metal shoehorn; the cat, fainting under piles of purses and shoes, plodded back and forth between the display windows and the stools; the girl with the disfigured neck appeared and disappeared, and reached the point where she started rattling away entirely in French, and, surprisingly, the women all understood her from half a word, even those who did not know a single word of French.

General amazement was aroused by a man edging his way on-stage. He announced that his wife had the flu, and he therefore asked that something be sent to her through him. As proof that he was indeed married, the citizen was prepared to show his passport. The solicitous husband's announcement was met with guffaws. Fagott shouted that he believed him like his own self, even without the passport, and handed the citizen two pairs of silk stockings, and the cat for his part added a little tube of lipstick.

Late-coming women tore on to the stage, and off the stage the lucky ones came pouring down in ball gowns, pyjamas with dragons, sober formal outfits, little hats tipped over one eyebrow.

Then Fagott announced that owing to the lateness of the hour, the shop would close in exactly one minute until the next evening, and an unbelievable scramble arose on-stage. Women hastily grabbed shoes without trying them on. One burst behind the curtain like a storm, got out of her dress there, took possession of the first thing that came to hand – a silk dressing-gown covered with huge bouquets – and managed to pick up two cases of perfume besides.

Exactly a minute later a pistol shot rang out, the mirrors disappeared, the display windows and stools dropped away, the carpet melted into air, as did the curtain. Last to disappear was the high mountain of old dresses and shoes, and the stage was again severe, empty and bare.

And it was here that a new character mixed into the affair. A pleasant, sonorous, and very insistent baritone came from box no. 2:

'All the same it is desirable, citizen artiste, that you expose the technique of your tricks to the spectators without delay, especially the trick with the paper money. It is also desirable that the master of ceremonies return to the stage. The spectators are concerned about his fate.'

The baritone belonged to none other than that evening's guest of honour, Arkady Apollonovich Sempleyarov, chairman of the Acoustics Commission of the Moscow theatres.

Arkady Apollonovich was in his box with two ladies: the older one dressed expensively and fashionably, the other one, young and pretty, dressed in a simpler way. The first, as was soon discovered during the drawing up of the report, was Arkady Apollonovich's wife, and the second was his distant relation, a promising débutante, who had come from Saratov and was living in the apartment of Arkady Apollonovich and his wife.

'Pardone!' Fagott replied. 'I'm sorry, there's nothing here to expose, it's all clear.'

'No, excuse me! The exposure is absolutely necessary. Without it your brilliant numbers will leave a painful impression. The mass of spectators demands an explanation.'

'The mass of spectators,' the impudent clown interrupted Sempleyarov, 'doesn't seem to be saying anything. But, in consideration of your most esteemed desire, Arkady Apollonovich, so be it – I will perform an exposure. But, to that end, will you allow me one more tiny number?'

'Why not?' Arkady Apollonovich replied patronizingly. 'But there must be an exposure.'

'Very well, very well, sir. And so, allow me to ask, where were you last evening, Arkady Apollonovich?'

At this inappropriate and perhaps even boorish question, Arkady Apollonovich's countenance changed, and changed quite drastically.

'Last evening Arkady Apollonovich was at a meeting of the Acoustics

Commission,' Arkady Apollonovich's wife declared very haughtily, 'but I don't understand what that has got to do with magic.'

'Ouee, madame!' Fagott agreed. 'Naturally you don't understand. As for the meeting, you are totally deluded. After driving off to the said meeting, which incidentally was not even scheduled for last night, Arkady Apollonovich dismissed his chauffeur at the Acoustics Commission building on Clean Ponds' (the whole theatre became hushed), 'and went by bus to Yelokhovskaya Street to visit an actress from the regional itinerant theatre, Militsa Andreevna Pokobatko, with whom he spent some four hours.'

'Aie!' someone cried out painfully in the total silence.

Arkady Apollonovich's young relation suddenly broke into a low and terrible laugh.

'It's all clear!' she exclaimed. 'And I've long suspected it. Now I see why that giftless thing got the role of Louisa!'[1]

And, swinging suddenly, she struck Arkady Apollonovich on the head with her short and fat violet umbrella.

Meanwhile, the scoundrelly Fagott, alias Koroviev, was shouting:

'Here, honourable citizens, is one case of the exposure Arkady Apollonovich so importunately insisted on!'

'How dare you touch Arkady Apollonovich, you vile creature!' Arkady Apollonovich's wife asked threateningly, rising in the box to all her gigantic height.

A second brief wave of satanic laughter seized the young relation.

'Who else should dare touch him,' she answered, guffawing, 'if not me!' And for the second time there came the dry, crackling sound of the umbrella bouncing off the head of Arkady Apollonovich.

'Police! Seize her!!' Sempleyarov's wife shouted in such a terrible voice that many hearts went cold.

And here the cat also leaped out to the footlights and suddenly barked in a human voice for all the theatre to hear:

'The séance is over! Maestro! Hack out a march!'

The half-crazed conductor, unaware of what he was doing, waved his baton, and the orchestra did not play, or even strike up, or even bang away at, but precisely, in the cat's loathsome expression, hacked out some incredible march of an unheard-of brashness.

For a moment there was an illusion of having heard once upon a time, under southern stars, in a café-chantant, some barely intelligible, half-blind, but rollicking words to this march:

>His Excellency reached the stage
>Of liking barnyard fowl.
>He took under his patronage
>Three young girls and an owl!!!

Or maybe these were not the words at all, but there were others to the same music, extremely indecent ones. That is not the important thing, the important thing is that, after all this, something like babel broke loose in the Variety. The police went running to Sempleyarov's box, people were climbing over the barriers, there were bursts of infernal guffawing and furious shouts, drowned in the golden clash of the orchestra's cymbals.

And one could see that the stage was suddenly empty, and that the hoodwinker Fagott, as well as the brazen tom-cat Behemoth, had melted into air, vanished as the magician had vanished earlier in his armchair with the faded upholstery.

CHAPTER 13

The Hero Enters

And so, the unknown man shook his finger at Ivan and whispered: 'Shhh!...'

Ivan lowered his legs from the bed and peered. Cautiously looking into the room from the balcony was a clean-shaven, dark-haired man of approximately thirty-eight, with a sharp nose, anxious eyes, and a wisp of hair hanging down on his forehead.

Having listened and made sure that Ivan was alone, the mysterious visitor took heart and stepped into the room. Here Ivan saw that the man was dressed as a patient. He was wearing long underwear, slippers on his bare feet, and a brown dressing-gown thrown over his shoulders.

The visitor winked at Ivan, hid a bunch of keys in his pocket, inquired in a whisper: 'May I sit down?' – and receiving an affirmative nod, placed himself in an armchair.

'How did you get here?' Ivan asked in a whisper, obeying the dry finger shaken at him. 'Aren't the balcony grilles locked?'

'The grilles are locked,' the guest agreed, 'but Praskovya Fyodorovna, while the dearest person, is also, alas, quite absent-minded. A month ago I stole a bunch of keys from her, and so gained the opportunity of getting out on to the common balcony, which runs around the entire floor, and so of occasionally calling on a neighbour.'

'If you can get out on to the balcony, you can escape. Or is it high up?' Ivan was interested.

'No,' the guest replied firmly, 'I cannot escape from here, not because it's high up, but because I have nowhere to escape to.' And he added, after a pause: 'So, here we sit.'

'Here we sit,' Ivan replied, peering into the man's brown and very restless eyes.

'Yes...' here the guest suddenly became alarmed, 'but you're not violent, I hope? Because, you know, I cannot stand noise, turmoil, force, or other things like that. Especially hateful to me are people's cries, whether cries of rage, suffering, or anything else. Set me at ease, tell me, you're not violent?'

'Yesterday in a restaurant I socked one type in the mug,' the transformed poet courageously confessed.

'Your grounds?' the guest asked sternly.

'No grounds, I must confess,' Ivan answered, embarrassed.

'Outrageous,' the guest denounced Ivan and added: 'And besides, what a way to express yourself: "socked in the mug" . . . It is not known precisely whether a man has a mug or a face. And, after all, it may well be a face. So, you know, using fists . . . No, you should give that up, and for good.'

Having thus reprimanded Ivan, the guest inquired:

'Your profession?'

'Poet,' Ivan confessed, reluctantly for some reason.

The visitor became upset.

'Ah, just my luck!' he exclaimed, but at once reconsidered, apologized, and asked: 'And what is your name?'

'Homeless.'

'Oh-oh . . .' the guest said, wincing.

'What, you mean you dislike my poetry?' Ivan asked with curiosity.

'I dislike it terribly.'

'And what have you read.'

'I've never read any of your poetry!' the visitor exclaimed nervously.

'Then how can you say that?'

'Well, what of it?' the guest replied. 'As if I haven't read others. Or else . . . maybe there's some miracle? Very well, I'm ready to take it on faith. Is your poetry good? You tell me yourself.'

'Monstrous!' Ivan suddenly spoke boldly and frankly.

'Don't write any more!' the visitor asked beseechingly.

'I promise and I swear!' Ivan said solemnly.

The oath was sealed with a handshake, and here soft footsteps and voices were heard in the corridor.

'Shh!' the guest whispered and, jumping out to the balcony, closed the grille behind him.

Praskovya Fyodorovna peeked in, asked Ivan how he was feeling and whether he wished to sleep in the dark or with a light. Ivan asked her to leave the light on, and Praskovya Fyodorovna withdrew, wishing the patient a good night. And when everything was quiet, the guest came back again.

He informed Ivan in a whisper that there was a new arrival in room

119 – some fat man with a purple physiognomy, who kept muttering something about currency in the ventilation and swearing that unclean powers were living in their place on Sadovaya.

'He curses Pushkin up and down and keeps shouting: "Kurolesov, encore, encore!"' the guest said, twitching nervously. Having calmed himself, he sat down, said: 'Anyway, God help him,' and continued his conversation with Ivan: 'So, how did you wind up here?'

'On account of Pontius Pilate,' Ivan replied, casting a glum look at the floor.

'What?!' the guest cried, forgetting all caution, and clapped his hand over his own mouth. 'A staggering coincidence! Tell me about it, I beg you, I beg you!'

Feeling trust in the unknown man for some reason, Ivan began, falteringly and timorously at first, then more boldly, to tell about the previous day's story at the Patriarch's Ponds. Yes, it was a grateful listener that Ivan Nikolaevich acquired in the person of the mysterious stealer of keys! The guest did not take Ivan for a madman, he showed great interest in what he was being told, and, as the story developed, finally became ecstatic. Time and again he interrupted Ivan with exclamations:

'Well, well, go on, go on, I beg you! Only, in the name of all that's holy, don't leave anything out!'

Ivan left nothing out in any case, it was easier for him to tell it that way, and he gradually reached the moment when Pontius Pilate, in a white mantle with blood-red lining, came out to the balcony.

Then the visitor put his hands together prayerfully and whispered:

'Oh, how I guessed! How I guessed it all!'

The listener accompanied the description of Berlioz's terrible death with an enigmatic remark, while his eyes flashed with spite:

'I only regret that it wasn't the critic Latunsky or the writer Mstislav Lavrovich instead of this Berlioz!', and he cried out frenziedly but soundlessly: 'Go on!'

The cat handing money to the woman conductor amused the guest exceedingly, and he choked with quiet laughter watching as Ivan, excited by the success of his narration, quietly hopped on bent legs, portraying the cat holding the coin up next to his whiskers.

'And so,' Ivan concluded, growing sad and melancholy after telling about the events at Griboedov's, 'I wound up here.'

The guest sympathetically placed a hand on the poor poet's shoulder and spoke thus:

'Unlucky poet! But you yourself, dear heart, are to blame for it all. You oughtn't to have behaved so casually and even impertinently with him. So you've paid for it. And you must still say thank you that you got off comparatively cheaply.'

'But who is he, finally?' Ivan asked, shaking his fists in agitation.

The guest peered at Ivan and answered with a question:

'You're not going to get upset? We're all unreliable here ... There won't be any calling for the doctor, injections, or other fuss?'

'No, no!' Ivan exclaimed. 'Tell me, who is he?'

'Very well,' the visitor replied, and he said weightily and distinctly: 'Yesterday at the Patriarch's Ponds you met Satan.'

Ivan did not get upset, as he had promised, but even so he was greatly astounded.

'That can't be! He doesn't exist!'

'Good heavens! Anyone else might say that, but not you. You were apparently one of his first victims. You're sitting, as you yourself understand, in a psychiatric clinic, yet you keep saying he doesn't exist. Really, it's strange!'

Thrown off, Ivan fell silent.

'As soon as you started describing him,' the guest went on, 'I began to realize who it was that you had the pleasure of talking with yesterday. And, really, I'm surprised at Berlioz! Now you, of course, are a virginal person,' here the guest apologized again, 'but that one, from what I've heard about him, had after all read at least something! The very first things this professor said dispelled all my doubts. One can't fail to recognize him, my friend! Though you ... again I must apologize, but I'm not mistaken, you are an ignorant man?'

'Indisputably,' the unrecognizable Ivan agreed.

'Well, so ... even the face, as you described it, the different eyes, the eyebrows! ... Forgive me, however, perhaps you've never even heard the opera *Faust*?'

Ivan became terribly embarrassed for some reason and, his face aflame, began mumbling something about some trip to a sanatorium ... to Yalta ...

'Well, so, so ... hardly surprising! But Berlioz, I repeat, astounds me ... He's not only a well-read man but also a very shrewd one.

Though I must say in his defence that Woland is, of course, capable of pulling the wool over the eyes of an even shrewder man.'

'What?!' Ivan cried out in his turn.

'Hush!'

Ivan slapped himself roundly on the forehead with his palm and rasped:

'I see, I see. He had the letter "W" on his visiting card. Ai-yai-yai, what a thing!' He lapsed into a bewildered silence for some time, peering at the moon floating outside the grille, and then spoke: 'So that means he might actually have been at Pontius Pilate's? He was already born then? And they call me a madman!' Ivan added indignantly, pointing to the door.

A bitter wrinkle appeared on the guest's lips.

'Let's look the truth in the eye.' And the guest turned his face towards the nocturnal luminary racing through a cloud. 'You and I are both madmen, there's no denying that! You see, he shocked you – and you came unhinged, since you evidently had the ground prepared for it. But what you describe undoubtedly took place in reality. But it's so extraordinary that even Stravinsky, a psychiatrist of genius, did not, of course, believe you. Did he examine you?' (Ivan nodded.) 'Your interlocutor was at Pilate's, and had breakfast with Kant, and now he's visiting Moscow.'

'But he'll be up to devil knows what here! Oughtn't we to catch him somehow?' the former, not yet definitively quashed Ivan still raised his head, though without much confidence, in the new Ivan.

'You've already tried, and that will do for you,' the guest replied ironically. 'I don't advise others to try either. And as for being up to something, rest assured, he will be! Ah, ah! But how annoying that it was you who met him and not I. Though it's all burned up, and the coals have gone to ashes, still, I swear, for that meeting I'd give Praskovya Fyodorovna's bunch of keys, for I have nothing else to give. I'm destitute.'

'But what do you need him for?'

The guest paused ruefully for a long time and twitched, but finally spoke:

'You see, it's such a strange story, I'm sitting here for the same reason you are – namely, on account of Pontius Pilate.' Here the guest looked around fearfully and said: 'The thing is that a year ago I wrote a novel about Pilate.'

'You're a writer?' the poet asked with interest.

The guest's face darkened and he threatened Ivan with his fist, then said:

'I am a master.' He grew stern and took from the pocket of his dressing-gown a completely greasy black cap with the letter 'M' embroidered on it in yellow silk. He put this cap on and showed himself to Ivan both in profile and full face, to prove that he was a master. 'She sewed it for me with her own hands,' he added mysteriously.

'And what is your name?'

'I no longer have a name,' the strange guest answered with gloomy disdain. 'I renounced it, as I generally did everything in life. Let's forget it.'

'Then at least tell me about the novel,' Ivan asked delicately.

'If you please, sir. My life, it must be said, has taken a not very ordinary course,' the guest began.

... A historian by education, he had worked until two years ago at one of the Moscow museums, and, besides that, had also done translations.

'From what languages?' Ivan interrupted curiously.

'I know five languages besides my own,' replied the guest, 'English, French, German, Latin and Greek. Well, I can also read Italian a little.'

'Oh, my!' Ivan whispered enviously.

... The historian had lived solitarily, had no family anywhere and almost no acquaintances in Moscow. And, just think, one day he won a hundred thousand roubles.

'Imagine my astonishment,' the guest in the black cap whispered, 'when I put my hand in the basket of dirty laundry and, lo and behold, it had the same number as in the newspaper. A state bond,'[1] he explained, 'they gave it to me at the museum.'

... Having won a hundred thousand roubles, Ivan's mysterious guest acted thus: bought books, gave up his room on Myasnitskaya ...

'Ohh, that accursed hole! ...' he growled.

... and rented from a builder, in a lane near the Arbat, two rooms in the basement of a little house in the garden. He left his work at the museum and began writing a novel about Pontius Pilate.

'Ah, that was a golden age!' the narrator whispered, his eyes shining. 'A completely private little apartment, plus a front hall with a sink in it,' he underscored for some reason with special pride, 'little windows just level with the paved walk leading from the gate. Opposite, only four steps away, near the fence, lilacs, a linden and a maple. Ah, ah, ah! In winter it was very seldom that I saw someone's black feet through my window and heard the snow crunching under them. And in my stove a fire was eternally blazing! But suddenly spring came and through the dim glass I saw lilac bushes, naked at first, then dressing themselves up in green. And it was then, last spring, that something happened far more delightful than getting a hundred thousand roubles. And that, you must agree, is a huge sum of money!'

'That's true,' acknowledged the attentively listening Ivan.

'I opened my little windows and sat in the second, quite minuscule room.' The guest began measuring with his arms: 'Here's the sofa, and another sofa opposite, and a little table between them, with a beautiful night lamp on it, and books nearer the window, and here a small writing table, and in the first room – a huge room, one hundred and fifty square feet! – books, books and the stove. Ah, what furnishings I had! The extraordinary smell of the lilacs! And my head was getting light with fatigue, and Pilate was flying to the end . . .'

'White mantle, red lining! I understand!' Ivan exclaimed.

'Precisely so! Pilate was flying to the end, to the end, and I already knew that the last words of the novel would be: ". . . the fifth procurator of Judea, the equestrian Pontius Pilate". Well, naturally, I used to go out for a walk. A hundred thousand is a huge sum, and I had an excellent suit. Or I'd go and have dinner in some cheap restaurant. There was a wonderful restaurant on the Arbat, I don't know whether it exists now.' Here the guest's eyes opened wide, and he went on whispering, gazing at the moon: 'She was carrying repulsive, alarming yellow flowers in her hand. Devil knows what they're called, but for some reason they're the first to appear in Moscow. And these flowers stood out clearly against her black spring coat. She was carrying yellow flowers! Not a nice colour. She turned down a lane from Tverskaya and then looked back. Well, you know Tverskaya! Thousands of people were walking along Tverskaya, but I can assure you that she saw me alone, and looked not really alarmed, but even as if in pain. And I was struck not so much by her beauty as by an extraordinary loneliness in her eyes, such as no one had ever seen before! Obeying this yellow sign, I also turned down the lane and followed her. We walked along the crooked, boring lane silently, I on one side, she on the other. And, imagine, there was not a soul in the lane. I was suffering, because it seemed to me that it was necessary to speak to her, and I worried that I wouldn't utter a single word, and she would leave, and I'd never see her again. And, imagine, suddenly she began to speak:

'"Do you like my flowers?"'

'I remember clearly the sound of her voice, rather low, slightly husky, and, stupid as it is, it seemed that the echo resounded in the lane and bounced off the dirty yellow wall. I quickly crossed to her side and, coming up to her, answered:

'"No!"'

'She looked at me in surprise, and I suddenly, and quite unexpectedly, understood that all my life I had loved precisely this woman! Quite a thing, eh? Of course, you'll say I'm mad?'

'I won't say anything,' Ivan exclaimed, and added: 'I beg you, go on!'

And the guest continued.

'Yes, she looked at me in surprise, and then, having looked, asked thus:

'"You generally don't like flowers?"'

'It seemed to me there was hostility in her voice. I was walking beside her, trying to keep in step, and, to my surprise, did not feel the least constraint.

'"No, I like flowers, but not this kind," I said.

'"Which, then?"'

'"I like roses."'

'Then I regretted having said it, because she smiled guiltily and threw the flowers into the gutter. Slightly at a loss, I nevertheless picked them up and gave them to her, but she, with a smile, pushed the flowers away, and I carried them in my hand.

'So we walked silently for some time, until she took the flowers from my hand and threw them to the pavement, then put her own hand in a black glove with a bell-shaped cuff under my arm, and we walked on side by side.'

'Go on,' said Ivan, 'and please don't leave anything out!'

'Go on?' repeated the visitor. 'Why, you can guess for yourself how it went on.' He suddenly wiped an unexpected tear with his right sleeve and continued: 'Love leaped out in front of us like a murderer in an alley leaping out of nowhere, and struck us both at once. As lightning strikes, as a Finnish knife strikes! She, by the way, insisted afterwards that it wasn't so, that we had, of course, loved each other for a long, long time, without knowing each other, never having seen each other, and that she was living with a different man ... as I was, too, then ... with that, what's her ...'

'With whom?' asked Homeless.

'With that ... well ... with ...' replied the guest, snapping his fingers. 'You were married?'

'Why, yes, that's why I'm snapping ... With that ... Varenka ... Manechka ... no, Varenka ... striped dress, the museum ... Anyhow, I don't remember.

'Well, so she said she went out that day with yellow flowers in her hand so that I would find her at last, and that if it hadn't happened, she would have poisoned herself, because her life was empty.

'Yes, love struck us instantly. I knew it that same day, an hour later, when, without having noticed the city, we found ourselves by the Kremlin wall on the embankment.

'We talked as if we had parted only the day before, as if we had known each other for many years. We arranged to meet the next day at the same place on the Moscow River, and we did. The May sun shone down on us. And soon, very soon, this woman became my secret wife.

'She used to come to me every afternoon, but I would begin waiting for her in the morning. This waiting expressed itself in the moving around of objects on the table. Ten minutes before, I would sit down by the little window and begin to listen for the banging of the decrepit gate. And how curious: before my meeting with her, few people came to our yard – more simply, no one came – but now it seemed to me that the whole city came flocking there.

'Bang goes the gate, bang goes my heart, and, imagine, it's inevitably somebody's dirty boots level with my face behind the window. A knife-grinder. Now, who needs a knife-grinder in our house? To sharpen what? What knives?

'She would come through the gate once, but my heart would pound no less than ten times before that, I'm not lying. And then, when her hour came and the hands showed noon, it even wouldn't stop pounding until, almost without tapping, almost noiselessly, her shoes would come even with my window, their black suede bows held tightly by steel buckles.

'Sometimes she would get mischievous, pausing at the second window and tapping the glass with her toe. That same instant I would be at the window, but the shoe would be gone, the black silk blocking the light would be gone – I'd go and open the door for her.

'No one knew of our liaison, I assure you of that, though it never happens. Her husband didn't know, her acquaintances didn't know. In the old house where I had that basement, people knew, of course, they saw that some woman visited me, but they didn't know her name.'

'But who is she?' asked Ivan, intrigued in the highest degree by this love story.

The guest made a gesture signifying that he would never tell that to anyone, and went on with his story.

Ivan learned that the master and the unknown woman loved each other so deeply that they became completely inseparable. Ivan could clearly picture to himself the two rooms in the basement of the house, where it was always twilight because of the lilacs and the fence. The worn red furniture, the bureau, the clock on it which struck every half hour, and books, books, from the painted floor to the sooty ceiling, and the stove.

Ivan learned that his guest and his secret wife, from the very first days of their liaison, had come to the conclusion that fate itself had thrown them together at the corner of Tverskaya and that lane, and that they had been created for each other for all time.

Ivan learned from the guest's story how the lovers would spend the day. She would come, and put on an apron first thing, and in the narrow front hall where stood that same sink of which the poor patient was for some reason so proud, would light the kerosene stove on the wooden table, prepare lunch, and set it out on the oval table in the first room. When the May storms came and water rushed noisily through the gateway past the near-sighted windows, threatening to flood their last refuge, the lovers would light the stove and bake potatoes in it. Steam rose from the potatoes, the black potato skins dirtied their fingers. Laughter came from the basement, the trees in the garden after rain shed broken twigs, white clusters.

When the storms ended and sultry summer came, there appeared in the vase the long-awaited roses they both loved. The man who called himself a master worked feverishly on his novel, and this novel also absorbed the unknown woman.

'Really, there were times when I'd begin to be jealous of it on account of her,' the night visitor come from the moonlit balcony whispered to Ivan.

Her slender fingers with sharply filed nails buried in her hair, she endlessly reread what he had written, and after rereading it would sit sewing that very same cap. Sometimes she crouched down by the lower shelves or stood by the upper ones and wiped the hundreds of dusty spines with a cloth. She foretold fame, she urged him on, and it was then that she began to call him a master. She waited impatiently for the already promised last words about the fifth procurator of Judea, repeated aloud in a sing-song voice certain phrases she liked, and said that her life was in this novel.

It was finished in the month of August, was given to some unknown typist, and she typed it in five copies. And finally the hour came when he had to leave his secret refuge and go out into life.

'And I went out into life holding it in my hands, and then my life ended,' the master whispered and drooped his head, and for a long time nodded the woeful black cap with the yellow letter 'M' on it. He continued his story, but it became somewhat incoherent, one could only understand that some catastrophe had then befallen Ivan's guest.

'For the first time I found myself in the world of literature, but now, when it's all over and my ruin is clear, I recall it with horror!' the master whispered solemnly and raised his hand. 'Yes, he astounded me greatly, ah, how he astounded me!'

'Who?' Ivan whispered barely audibly, fearing to interrupt the agitated narrator.

'Why, the editor, I tell you, the editor! Yes, he read it all right. He looked at me as if I had a swollen cheek, looked sidelong into the corner, and even tittered in embarrassment. He crumpled the manuscript needlessly and grunted. The questions he asked seemed crazy to me. Saying nothing about the essence of the novel, he asked me who I was, where I came from, and how long I had been writing, and why no one had heard of me before, and even asked what in my opinion was a totally idiotic question: who had given me the idea of writing a novel on such a strange theme? Finally I got sick of him and asked directly whether he would publish the novel or not. Here he started squirming, mumbled something, and declared that he could not decide the question on his own, that other members of the editorial board had to acquaint themselves with my work – namely, the critics Latunsky and Ariman, and the writer Mstislav Lavrovich.[2] He asked me to come in two weeks. I came in two weeks and was received by some girl whose eyes were crossed towards her nose from constant lying.'

'That's Lapshennikova, the editorial secretary,' Ivan said with a smirk. He knew very well the world described so wrathfully by his guest.

'Maybe,' the other snapped, 'and so from her I got my novel back, already quite greasy and dishevelled. Trying to avoid looking me in the eye, Lapshennikova told me that the publisher was provided with material for two years ahead, and therefore the question of printing my novel, as she put it, "did not arise".

'What do I remember after that?' the master muttered, rubbing his temple. 'Yes, red petals strewn across the title page, and also the eyes of my friend. Yes, those eyes I remember.'

The story of Ivan's guest was becoming more confused, more filled with all sorts of reticences. He said something about slanting rain and despair in the basement refuge, about having gone elsewhere. He exclaimed in a whisper that he did not blame her in the least for pushing him to fight – oh, no, he did not blame her!

Further on, as Ivan heard, something sudden and strange happened. One day our hero opened a newspaper and saw in it an article by the critic Ariman,[3] in which Ariman warned all and sundry that he, that is, our hero, had attempted to foist into print an apology for Jesus Christ.

'Ah, I remember, I remember!' Ivan cried out. 'But I've forgotten your name!'

'Let's leave my name out of it, I repeat, it no longer exists,' replied the guest. 'That's not the point. Two days later in another newspaper, over the signature of Mstislav Lavrovich, appeared another article, in which its author recommended striking, and striking hard, at Pilatism and at the icon-dauber who had ventured to foist it (again that accursed word!) into print.

'Dumbfounded by this unheard-of word "Pilatism", I opened a third newspaper. There were two articles in it, one by Latunsky, the other signed with the initials "N.E." I assure you, the works of Ariman and Lavrovich could be counted as jokes compared with what Latunsky wrote. Suffice it to say that Latunsky's article was entitled "A Militant Old Believer".[4] I got so carried away reading the article about myself that I didn't notice (I had forgotten to lock the door) how she came in and stood before me with a wet umbrella in her hand and wet newspapers as well. Her eyes flashed fire, her trembling hands were cold. First she rushed to kiss me, then, in a hoarse voice, and pounding the table with her fist, she said she would poison Latunsky.'

Ivan grunted somewhat embarrassedly, but said nothing.

'Joyless autumn days set in,' the guest went on. 'The monstrous failure with this novel seemed to have taken out a part of my soul. Essentially speaking, I had nothing more to do, and I lived from one meeting with her to the next. And it was at that time that something happened to me. Devil knows what, Stravinsky probably figured it out long ago. Namely, anguish came over me and certain forebodings appeared.

'The articles, please note, did not cease. I laughed at the first of them. But the more of them that appeared, the more my attitude towards them changed. The second stage was one of astonishment. Some rare falsity and insecurity could be sensed literally in every line of these articles, despite their threatening and confident tone. I had the feeling, and I couldn't get rid of it, that the authors of these articles were not saying what they wanted to say, and that their rage sprang precisely from that. And then, imagine, a third stage came – of fear. No, not fear of these articles, you understand, but fear of other things totally unrelated to them or to the novel. Thus, for instance, I began to be afraid of the dark. In short, the stage of mental illness came. It seemed to me, especially as I was falling asleep, that some very cold and pliant octopus was stealing with its tentacles immediately and directly towards my heart. And I had to sleep with the light on.

'My beloved changed very much (of course, I never told her about the octopus, but she could see that something was going wrong with me), she became thinner and paler, stopped laughing, and kept asking me to forgive her for having advised me to publish an excerpt. She said I should drop everything and go to the south, to the Black Sea, and spend all that was left of the hundred thousand on the trip.

'She was very insistent, and to avoid an argument (something told me I was not to go to the Black Sea), I promised her that I'd do it one of those days. But she said she would buy me the ticket herself. Then I took out all my money – that is, about ten thousand roubles – and gave it to her.

' "Why so much?" she was surprised.

'I said something or other about being afraid of thieves and asked her to keep the money until my departure. She took it, put it in her purse, began kissing me and saying that it would be easier for her to die than to leave me alone in such a state, but that she was expected, that she must bow to necessity, that she would come the next day. She begged me not to be afraid of anything.

'This was at dusk, in mid-October. And she left. I lay down on the sofa and fell asleep without turning on the light. I was awakened by the feeling that the octopus was there. Groping in the dark, I barely managed to turn on the light. My pocket watch showed two o'clock in the morning. I was falling ill when I went to bed, and I woke up sick. It suddenly seemed to me that the autumn darkness would push through the glass and pour into the room, and I would drown in it as in ink. I got up a man no longer in control of himself. I cried out, the thought came to me of running to someone, even if it was my landlord upstairs. I struggled with myself like a madman. I had strength enough to get to the stove and start a fire in it. When the wood began to crackle and the stove door rattled, I seemed to feel slightly better. I dashed to the front room, turned on the light there, found a bottle of white wine, uncorked it and began drinking from the bottle. This blunted the fear somewhat – at least enough to keep me from running to the landlord – and I went back to the stove. I opened the little door, so that the heat began to burn my face and hands, and whispered:

'"Guess that trouble has befallen me ... Come, come, come! ..."

'But no one came. The fire roared in the stove, rain lashed at the windows. Then the final thing happened. I took the heavy manuscript of the novel and the draft notebooks from the desk drawer and started burning them. This was terribly hard to do, because written-on paper burns reluctantly. Breaking my fingernails, I tore up the notebooks, stuck them vertically between the logs, and ruffled the pages with the poker. At times the ashes got the best of me, choking the flames, but I struggled with them, and the novel, though stubbornly resisting, was nevertheless perishing. Familiar words flashed before me, the yellow climbed steadily up the pages, but the words still showed through it. They would vanish only when the paper turned black, and I finished them off with the poker.

'Just then someone began scratching quietly at the window. My heart leaped, and having stuffed the last notebook into the fire, I rushed to open the door. Brick steps led up from the basement to the door on the yard. Stumbling, I ran up to it and asked quietly:

' "Who's there?"

'And that voice, her voice, answered:

' "It's me . . ."

'I don't remember how I managed with the chain and hook. As soon as she stepped inside, she clung to me, trembling, all wet, her cheeks wet and her hair uncurled. I could only utter the word:

' "You . . . you? . . .", and my voice broke, and we ran downstairs.

'She freed herself of her overcoat in the front hall, and we quickly went into the first room. With a soft cry, she pulled out of the stove with her bare hands and threw on to the floor the last of what was there, a sheaf that had caught fire from below. Smoke filled the room at once. I stamped out the fire with my feet, and she collapsed on the sofa and wept irrepressibly and convulsively.

'When she calmed down, I said:

' "I came to hate this novel, and I'm afraid. I'm ill. Frightened."

'She stood up and said:

' "God, how sick you are. Why is it, why? But I'll save you, I'll save you. What is all this?"

'I saw her eyes swollen with smoke and weeping, felt her cold hands stroke my forehead.

' "I'll cure you, I'll cure you," she was murmuring, clutching my shoulders. "You'll restore it. Why, why didn't I keep a copy?"

'She bared her teeth with rage, she said something else inarticulately. Then, compressing her lips, she began to collect and smooth out the burnt-edged pages. It was some chapter from the middle of the novel, I don't remember which. She neatly stacked the pages, wrapped them in paper, tied them with a ribbon. All her actions showed that she was full of determination, and that she had regained control of herself. She asked for wine and, having drunk it, spoke more calmly:

' "This is how one pays for lying," she said, "and I don't want to lie any more. I'd stay with you right now, but I'd rather not do it that way. I don't want it to remain for ever in his memory that I ran away from him in the middle of the night. He's never done me any wrong . . . He was summoned unexpectedly, there was a fire at the factory.

But he'll be back soon. I'll talk with him tomorrow morning, I'll tell him that I love another man and come back to you for ever. Or maybe you don't want that? Answer me."

'"Poor dear, my poor dear," I said to her. "I won't allow you to do it. Things won't go well for me, and I don't want you to perish with me."

'"Is that the only reason?" she asked, and brought her eyes close to mine.

'"The only one."

'She became terribly animated, she clung to me, put her arms around my neck and said:

'"I'm perishing with you. In the morning I'll be here."

'And so, the last thing I remember from my life is a strip of light from my front hall, and in that strip of light an uncurled strand of hair, her beret and her eyes filled with determination. I also remember the black silhouette in the outside doorway and the white package.

'"I'd see you home, but it's beyond my strength to come back alone. I'm afraid."

'"Don't be afraid. Bear with it for a few hours. Tomorrow morning I'll be here."

'Those were her last words in my life ... Shh! ...' the patient suddenly interrupted himself and raised a finger. 'It's a restless moonlit night tonight.'

He disappeared on to the balcony. Ivan heard little wheels roll down the corridor, someone sobbed or cried out weakly.

When everything grew still, the guest came back and announced that room 120 had received an occupant. Someone had been brought, and he kept asking to be given back his head. The two interlocutors fell anxiously silent, but, having calmed down, they returned to the interrupted story. The guest was just opening his mouth, but the night was indeed a restless one. There were still voices in the corridor, and the guest began to speak into Ivan's ear, so softly that what he told him was known only to the poet, apart from the first phrase:

'A quarter of an hour after she left me, there came a knock at my window ...'

What the patient whispered into Ivan's ear evidently agitated him very much. Spasms repeatedly passed over his face. Fear and rage swam and flitted in his eyes. The narrator pointed his hand somewhere in the direction of the moon, which had long since left the balcony. Only when all sounds from outside ceased to reach them did the guest move away from Ivan and begin to speak more loudly:

'Yes, and so in mid-January, at night, in the same coat but with the buttons torn off,[5] I was huddled with cold in my little yard. Behind me were snowdrifts that hid the lilac bushes, and before me and below – my little windows, dimly lit, covered with shades. I bent down to the first of them and listened – a gramophone was playing in my rooms. That was all I heard, but I could not see anything. I stood there a while, then went out the gate to the lane. A blizzard was frolicking in it. A dog, dashing under my feet, frightened me, and I ran away from it to the other side. The cold, and the fear that had become my constant companion, were driving me to frenzy. I had nowhere to go, and the simplest thing, of course, would have been to throw myself under a tram-car on the street where my lane came out. From far off I could see those light-filled, ice-covered boxes and hear their loathsome screeching in the frost. But, my dear neighbour, the whole thing was that fear possessed every cell of my body. And, just as I was afraid of the dog, so I was afraid of the tram-car. Yes, there is no illness in this place worse than mine, I assure you!'

'But you could have let her know,' said Ivan, sympathizing with the poor patient. 'Besides, she has your money. She did keep it, of course?'

'You needn't doubt that, of course she kept it. But you evidently don't understand me. Or, rather, I've lost the ability I once had for describing things. However, I'm not very sorry about that, since I no longer have any use for it. Before her,' the guest reverently looked out at the darkness of the night, 'there would lie a letter from a madhouse. How can one send letters from such an address . . . a mental patient? . . . You're joking, my friend! Make her unhappy? No, I'm not capable of that.'

Ivan was unable to object to this, but the silent Ivan sympathized with the guest, he commiserated with him. And the other, from the pain of his memories, nodded his head in the black cap and spoke thus:

'Poor woman . . . However, I have hopes that she has forgotten me . . .'

'But you may recover . . .' Ivan said timidly.

'I am incurable,' the guest replied calmly. 'When Stravinsky says he will bring me back to life, I don't believe him. He is humane and simply wants to comfort me. I don't deny, however, that I'm much better now. Yes, so where did I leave off? Frost, those flying trams ... I knew that this clinic had been opened, and set out for it on foot across the entire city. Madness! Outside the city I probably would have frozen to death, but chance saved me. A truck had broken down, I came up to the driver, it was some three miles beyond the city limits, and to my surprise he took pity on me. The truck was coming here. And he took me along. I got away with having my left toes frostbitten. But they cured that. And now this is the fourth month that I've been here. And, you know, I find it not at all bad here. One mustn't make grandiose plans, dear neighbour, really! I, for instance, wanted to go all around the globe. Well, so it turns out that I'm not going to do it. I see only an insignificant piece of that globe. I suppose it's not the very best there is on it, but, I repeat, it's not so bad. Summer is coming, the ivy will twine up on to the balcony. So Praskovya Fyodorovna promises. The keys have broadened my possibilities. There'll be the moon at night. Ah, it's gone! Freshness. It's falling past midnight. Time to go.'

'Tell me, what happened afterwards with Yeshua and Pilate?' Ivan asked. 'I beg you, I want to know.'

'Ah, no, no,' the guest replied with a painful twitch. 'I cannot recall my novel without trembling. And your acquaintance from the Patriarch's Ponds would do it better than I. Thank you for the conversation. Goodbye.'

And before Ivan could collect his senses, the grille closed with a quiet clang, and the guest vanished.

CHAPTER 14

Glory to the Cock!

His nerves gave out, as they say, and Rimsky fled to his office before they finished drawing up the report. He sat at his desk and stared with inflamed eyes at the magic banknotes lying before him. The findirector's wits were addled. A steady hum came from outside. The audience poured in streams from the Variety building into the street. Rimsky's extremely sharpened hearing suddenly caught the distant trill of a police-man. That in itself never bodes anything pleasant. But when it was repeated and, to assist it, another joined in, more authoritative and prolonged, and to them was added a clearly audible guffawing and even some hooting, the findirector understood at once that something else scandalous and vile had happened in the street. And that, however much he wanted to wave it away, it was closely connected with the repulsive séance presented by the black magician and his assistants.

The keen-eared findirector was not mistaken in the least. As soon as he cast a glance out the window on to Sadovaya, his face twisted, and he did not whisper but hissed:

'So I thought!'

In the bright glare of the strongest street lights he saw, just below him on the sidewalk, a lady in nothing but a shift and violet bloomers. True, there was a little hat on the lady's head and an umbrella in her hands. The lady, who was in a state of utter consternation, now crouching down, now making as if to run off somewhere, was surrounded by an agitated crowd, which produced the very guffawing that had sent a shiver down the fin-director's spine. Next to the lady some citizen was flitting about, trying to tear off his summer coat, and in his agitation simply unable to manage the sleeve in which his arm was stuck.

Shouts and roaring guffaws came from yet another place – namely, the left entrance – and turning his head in that direction, Grigory Danilovich saw a second lady, in pink underwear. She leaped from the street to the sidewalk, striving to hide in the hallway, but the audience pouring out blocked the way, and the poor victim of her own flightiness and passion for dressing up, deceived by vile Fagott's firm, dreamed of only one thing – falling through the earth. A policeman made for the unfortunate woman, drilling the air with his whistle, and after the policeman hastened some merry young men in caps. It was they who produced the guffawing and hooting.

A skinny, moustachioed cabby flew up to the first undressed woman and dashingly reined in his bony, broken-down nag. The moustached face was grinning gleefully.

Rimsky beat himself on the head with his fist, spat, and leaped back from the window. For some time he sat at his desk listening to the street. The whistling at various points reached its highest pitch, then began to subside. The scandal, to Rimsky's surprise, was somehow liquidated with unexpected swiftness.

It came time to act. He had to drink the bitter cup of responsibility. The telephones had been repaired during the third part. He had to make calls, to tell what had happened, to ask for help, lie his way out of it, heap everything on Likhodeev, cover up for himself, and so on. Pah, the devil!

Twice the upset director put his hand on the receiver, and twice he drew it back. And suddenly, in the dead silence of the office, the telephone burst out ringing by itself right in the findirector's face, and he gave a start and went cold. 'My nerves are really upset, though!' he thought, and picked up the receiver. He recoiled from it instantly and turned whiter than paper. A soft but at the same time insinuating and lewd female voice whispered into the receiver:

'Don't call anywhere, Rimsky, it'll be bad . . .'

The receiver straight away went empty. With goose-flesh prickling on his back, the findirector hung up the telephone and for some reason turned to look at the window behind him. Through the scant and still barely greening branches of a maple, he saw the moon racing in a transparent cloud. His eyes fixed on the branches for some reason, Rimsky went on gazing at them, and the longer he gazed, the more strongly he was gripped by fear.

With great effort, the findirector finally turned away from the moonlit window and stood up. There could no longer be any question of phone calls, and now the findirector was thinking of only one thing – getting out of the theatre as quickly as possible.

He listened: the theatre building was silent. Rimsky realized that he had long been the only one on the whole second floor, and a childish, irrepressible fear came over him at this thought. He could not think without shuddering of having to walk alone now along the empty corridors and down the stairs. Feverishly he seized the hypnotist's banknotes from the table, put them in his briefcase, and coughed so as to cheer himself up at least a little. The cough came out slightly hoarse, weak.

And here it seemed to him that a whiff of some putrid dankness was coming in under the office door. Shivers ran down the findirector's spine. And then the clock also rang out unexpectedly and began to strike midnight. And even its striking provoked shivers in the findirector. But his heart definitively sank when he heard the English key turning quietly in the lock. Clutching his briefcase with damp, cold hands, the findirector felt that if this scraping in the keyhole were to go on any longer, he would break down and give a piercing scream.

Finally the door yielded to someone's efforts, opened, and Varenukha noiselessly entered the office. Rimsky simply sank down into the armchair where he stood, because his legs gave way. Drawing a deep breath, he smiled an ingratiating smile, as it were, and said quietly:

'God, you frightened me . . .'

Yes, this sudden appearance might have frightened anyone you like, and yet at the same time it was a great joy: at least one little end peeped out in this tangled affair.

'Well, tell me quickly! Well? Well?' Rimsky wheezed, grasping at this little end. 'What does it all mean?!'

'Excuse me, please,' the entering man replied in a hollow voice, closing the door, 'I thought you had already left.'

And Varenukha, without taking his cap off, walked to the armchair and sat on the other side of the desk.

It must be said that Varenukha's response was marked by a slight oddity which at once needled the findirector, who could compete in sensitivity with the seismograph of any of the world's best stations. How could it be? Why did Varenukha come to the findirector's office if he thought he was not there? He had his own office, first of all. And second, whichever entrance to the building Varenukha had used, he would inevitably have met one of the night-watchmen, to all of whom it had been announced that Grigory Danilovich was staying late in his office. But the findirector did not spend long pondering this oddity – he had other problems.

'Why didn't you call? What are all these shenanigans about Yalta?'

'Well, it's as I was saying,' the administrator replied, sucking as if he were troubled by a bad tooth. 'He was found in the tavern in Pushkino.'

'In Pushkino?! You mean just outside Moscow?! What about the telegrams from Yalta?!'

'The devil they're from Yalta! He got a telegrapher drunk in Pushkino, and the two of them started acting up, sending telegrams marked "Yalta", among other things.'

'Aha . . . aha . . . Well, all right, all right . . .' Rimsky did not say but sang out. His eyes lit up with a yellow light. In his head there formed the festive picture of Styopa's shameful dismissal from his job. Deliverance! The findirector's long-awaited deliverance from this disaster in the person of Likhodeev! And maybe Stepan Bogdanovich would achieve something worse than dismissal . . . 'The details!' said Rimsky, banging the paperweight on the desk.

And Varenukha began giving the details. As soon as he arrived where the findirector had sent him, he was received at once and given a most attentive hearing. No one, of course, even entertained the thought that Styopa could be in Yalta. Everyone agreed at once with Varenukha's suggestion that Likhodeev was, of course, at the Yalta in Pushkino.

'Then where is he now?' the agitated findirector interrupted the administrator.

'Well, where else could he be?' the administrator replied, grinning crookedly. 'In a sobering-up cell, naturally!'

'Well, well. How nice!'

Varenukha went on with his story, and the more he told, the more vividly there unfolded before the findirector the long chain of Likhodeev's boorish and outrageous acts, and every link in this chain was worse than the one before. The drunken dancing in the arms of the telegrapher on the lawn in front of the Pushkino telegraph office to the sounds of some itinerant barrel-organ was worth something! The chase after some female citizens shrieking with terror! The attempt at a fight with the barman in the Yalta itself! Scattering green onions all over the floor of the same Yalta. Smashing eight bottles of dry white Ai-Danil. Breaking the meter when the taxi-driver refused to take Styopa in his cab. Threatening to arrest the citizens who attempted to stop Styopa's obnoxiousness . . . In short, black horror!

Styopa was well known in Moscow theatre circles, and everyone knew that the man was no gift. But all the same, what the administrator was telling about him was too much even for Styopa. Yes, too much. Even much too much . . .

Rimsky's needle-sharp glance pierced the administrator's face from across the desk, and the longer the man spoke, the grimmer those eyes became. The more lifelike and colourful the vile details with which the administrator furnished his story, the less the findirector believed the storyteller. And when Varenukha told how Styopa had let himself go so far as to try to resist those who came to bring him back to Moscow, the findirector already knew firmly that everything the administrator who had returned at midnight was telling him, everything, was a lie! A lie from first word to last!

Varenukha never went to Pushkino, and there was no Styopa in Pushkino. There was no drunken telegrapher, there was no broken glass in the tavern, Styopa did not get tied up with ropes . . . none of it happened.

As soon as the findirector became firmly convinced that the administrator was lying to him, fear crept over his body, starting from the legs, and twice again the findirector fancied that a putrid malarial dankness was wafting across the floor. Never for a moment taking his eyes off the administrator – who squirmed somehow strangely in his armchair, trying not to get out of the blue shade of the desk lamp, and screening himself with a newspaper in some remarkable fashion from the bothersome light – the findirector was thinking of only one thing: what did it all mean? Why was he being lied to so brazenly, in the silent and deserted building, by the administrator who was so late in coming back to him? And the awareness of danger, an unknown but menacing danger, began to gnaw at Rimsky's soul. Pretending to ignore Varenukha's dodges and tricks with the newspaper, the findirector studied his face, now almost without listening to the yarn Varenukha was spinning. There was something that seemed still more inexplicable than the calumny invented, God knows why, about adventures in Pushkino, and that something was the change in the administrator's appearance and manners.

No matter how the man pulled the duck-like visor of his cap over his eyes, so as to throw a shadow on his face, no matter how he fidgeted with the newspaper, the findirector managed to make out an enormous bruise on the right side of his face just by the nose. Besides that, the normally full-blooded administrator was now pale with a chalk-like, unhealthy pallor, and on this stifling night his neck was for some reason wrapped in an old striped scarf. Add to that the repulsive manner the administrator had acquired during the time of his absence of sucking and smacking, the sharp change in his voice, which had become hollow and coarse, and the furtiveness and cowardliness in his eyes, and one could boldly say that Ivan Savelyevich Varenukha had become unrecognizable.

Something else burningly troubled the findirector, but he was unable to grasp precisely what it was, however much he strained his feverish mind, however hard he peered at Varenukha. One thing he could affirm, that there was something unprecedented, unnatural in this combination of the administrator and the familiar armchair.

'Well, we finally overpowered him, loaded him into the car,' Varenukha boomed, peeking from behind the paper and covering the bruise with his hand.

Rimsky suddenly reached out and, as if mechanically, tapping his fingers on the table at the same time, pushed the electric-bell button with his palm and went numb. The sharp signal ought to have been heard without fail in the empty building. But no signal came, and the button sank lifelessly into the wood of the desk. The button was dead, the bell broken.

The findirector's stratagem did not escape the notice of Varenukha, who asked, twitching, with a clearly malicious fire flickering in his eyes:

'What are you ringing for?'

'Mechanically,' the findirector replied hollowly, jerking his hand back, and asked in turn, in an unsteady voice: 'What's that on your face?'

'The car skidded, I bumped against the door-handle,' Varenukha said, looking away.

'He's lying!' the findirector exclaimed mentally. And here his eyes suddenly grew round and utterly insane, and he stared at the back of the armchair.

Behind the chair on the floor two shadows lay criss-cross, one more dense and black, the other faint and grey. The shadow of the back of the chair and of its tapering legs could be seen distinctly on the floor, but there was no shadow of Varenukha's head above the back of the chair, or of the administrator's legs under its legs.

'He casts no shadow!' Rimsky cried out desperately in his mind. He broke into shivers.

Varenukha, following Rimsky's insane gaze, looked furtively behind him at the back of the chair, and realized that he had been found out.

He got up from the chair (the findirector did likewise) and made one step back from the desk, clutching his briefcase in his hands.

'He's guessed, damn him! Always was clever,' Varenukha said, grinning spitefully right in the findirector's face, and he sprang unexpectedly from the chair to the door and quickly pushed down the catch on the lock. The findirector looked desperately behind him, as he retreated to the window giving on to the garden, and in this window, flooded with moonlight, saw the face of a naked girl pressed against the glass and her naked arm reaching through the vent-pane and trying to open the lower latch. The upper one was already open.

It seemed to Rimsky that the light of the desk lamp was going out and the desk was tilting. An icy wave engulfed Rimsky, but – fortunately for him – he got control of himself and did not fall. He had enough strength left to whisper, but not cry out:

'Help . . .'

Varenukha, guarding the door, hopped up and down by it, staying in air for a long time and swaying there. Waving his hooked fingers in Rimsky's direction, he hissed and smacked, winking to the girl in the window.

She began to hurry, stuck her red-haired head through the vent, reached her arm down as far as she could, her nails clawing at the lower latch and shaking the frame. Her arm began to lengthen, rubber-like, and became covered with a putrid green. Finally the dead woman's green fingers got hold of the latch knob, turned it, and the frame began to open. Rimsky cried out weakly, leaned against the wall, and held his briefcase in front of him like a shield. He realized that his end had come.

The frame swung wide open, but instead of the night's freshness and the fragrance of the lindens, the smell of a cellar burst into the room. The dead woman stepped on to the window-sill. Rimsky clearly saw spots of decay on her breast.

And just then the joyful, unexpected crowing of a cock came from the garden, from that low building beyond the shooting gallery where birds participating in the programme were kept. A loud, trained cock trumpeted, announcing that dawn was rolling towards Moscow from the east.

Savage fury distorted the girl's face, she emitted a hoarse oath, and at the door Varenukha shrieked and dropped from the air to the floor.

The cock-crow was repeated, the girl clacked her teeth, and her red hair stood on end. With the third crowing of the cock, she turned and flew out. And after her, jumping up and stretching himself horizontally in the air, looking like a flying cupid, Varenukha slowly floated over the desk and out the window.

White as snow, with not a single black hair on his head, the old man who still recently had been Rimsky rushed to the door, undid the catch, opened the door, and ran hurtling down the dark corridor. At the turn to the stairs, moaning with fear, he felt for the switch, and the stairway lighted up. On the stairs the shaking, trembling old man fell because he imagined that Varenukha had softly tumbled on top of him.

Having run downstairs, Rimsky saw a watchman asleep on a chair by the box office in the lobby. Rimsky stole past him on tiptoe and slipped out the main entrance. Outside he felt slightly better. He recovered his senses enough to realize, clutching his head, that his hat had stayed behind in the office.

Needless to say, he did not go back for it, but, breathless, ran across the wide street to the opposite corner by the movie theatre, near which a dull reddish light hovered. In a moment he was there. No one had time to intercept the cab.

'Make the Leningrad express, I'll tip you well,' the old man said, breathing heavily and clutching his heart.

'I'm going to the garage,' the driver answered hatefully and turned away.

Then Rimsky unlatched his briefcase, took out fifty roubles, and handed them to the driver through the open front window.

A few moments later, the rattling car was flying like the wind down Sadovoye Ring. The passenger was tossed about on his seat, and in the fragment of mirror hanging in front of the driver, Rimsky saw now the driver's happy eyes, now his own insane ones.

Jumping out of the car in front of the train station, Rimsky cried to the first man he saw in a white apron with a badge:

'First class, single, I'll pay thirty,' he was pulling the banknotes from his briefcase, crumpling them, 'no first class, get me second . . . if not – a hard bench!'

The man with the badge kept glancing up at the lighted clock face as he tore the banknotes from Rimsky's hand.

Five minutes later the express train disappeared from under the glass vault of the train station and vanished clean away in the darkness. And with it vanished Rimsky.

CHAPTER 15

Nikanor Ivanovich's Dream

It is not difficult to guess that the fat man with the purple physiognomy who was put in room 119 of the clinic was Nikanor Ivanovich Bosoy.

He got to Professor Stravinsky not at once, however, but after first visiting another place.[1] Of this other place little remained in Nikanor Ivanovich's memory. He recalled only a desk, a bookcase and a sofa.

There a conversation was held with Nikanor Ivanovich, who had some sort of haze before his eyes from the rush of blood and mental agitation, but the conversation came out somehow strange, muddled, or, better to say, did not come out at all.

The very first question put to Nikanor Ivanovich was the following:

'Are you Nikanor Ivanovich Bosoy, chairman of the house committee at no. 302-bis on Sadovaya Street?'

To this Nikanor Ivanovich, bursting into terrible laughter, replied literally thus:

'I'm Nikanor, of course I'm Nikanor! But what the deuce kind of chairman am I?'

'Meaning what?' the question was asked with a narrowing of eyes.

'Meaning,' he replied, 'that if I was chairman, I should have determined at once that he was an unclean power! Otherwise – what is it? A cracked pince-nez, all in rags ... what kind of foreigner's interpreter could he be?'

'Who are you talking about?' Nikanor Ivanovich was asked.

'Koroviev!' Nikanor Ivanovich cried out. 'Got himself lodged in our apartment number fifty. Write it down – Koroviev! He must be caught at once. Write it down – the sixth entrance. He's there.'

'Where did you get the currency?' Nikanor Ivanovich was asked soulfully.

'As God is true, as God is almighty,' Nikanor Ivanovich began, 'he sees everything, and it serves me right. I never laid a finger on it, never even suspected what it was, this currency! God is punishing me for my iniquity,' Nikanor Ivanovich went on with feeling, now buttoning, now unbuttoning his shirt, now crossing himself. 'I took! I took, but

I took ours, Soviet money! I'd register people for money, I don't argue, it happened. Our secretary Bedsornev is a good one, too, another good one! Frankly speaking, there's nothing but thieves in the house management ... But I never took currency!'

To the request that he stop playing the fool and tell how the dollars got into the ventilation, Nikanor Ivanovich went on his knees and swayed, opening his mouth as if he meant to swallow a section of the parquet.

'If you want,' he mumbled, 'I'll eat dirt that I didn't do it! And Koroviev – he's the devil!'

All patience has its limits, and the voice at the desk was now raised, hinting to Nikanor Ivanovich that it was time he began speaking in human language.

Here the room with that same sofa resounded with Nikanor Ivanovich's wild roaring, as he jumped up from his knees:

'There he is! There, behind the bookcase! He's grinning! And his pince-nez ... Hold him! Spray the room with holy water!'

The blood left Nikanor Ivanovich's face. Trembling, he made crosses in the air, rushing to the door and back, intoned some prayer, and finally began spouting sheer gibberish.

It became perfectly clear that Nikanor Ivanovich was unfit for any conversation. He was taken out and put in a separate room, where he calmed down somewhat and only prayed and sobbed.

They did, of course, go to Sadovaya and visit apartment no. 50. But they did not find any Koroviev there, and no one in the house either knew or had seen any Koroviev. The apartment occupied by the late Berlioz, as well as by the Yalta-visiting Likhodeev, was empty, and in the study wax seals hung peacefully on the bookcases, unbroken by anyone. With that they left Sadovaya, and there also departed with them the perplexed and dispirited secretary of the house management, Bedsornev.

In the evening Nikanor Ivanovich was delivered to Stravinsky's clinic. There he became so agitated that an injection, made according to Stravinsky's recipe, had to be given him, and only after midnight did Nikanor Ivanovich fall asleep in room 119, every now and then emitting a heavy, painful moan.

But the longer he slept, the easier his sleep became. He stopped tossing and groaning, his breathing became easy and regular, and he was left alone. Then Nikanor Ivanovich was visited by a dream, at the basis of which undoubtedly lay the experience of that day. It began with Nikanor Ivanovich seeing as it were some people with golden trumpets in their hands leading him, and very solemnly, to a big lacquered door. At this door his companions played as it were a flourish for Nikanor Ivanovich, and then from the sky a resounding bass said merrily:

'Welcome, Nikanor Ivanovich, turn over your currency!'

Exceedingly astonished, Nikanor Ivanovich saw a black loudspeaker above him.

Then he found himself for some reason in a theatre house, where crystal chandeliers blazed under a gilded ceiling and Quinquet lamps[2] on the walls. Everything was as it ought to be in a small-sized but very costly theatre. There was a stage closed off by a velvet curtain, its dark cerise background spangled, as if with stars, with oversized gold pieces, there was a prompter's box, and there was even an audience.

What surprised Nikanor Ivanovich was that this audience was all of the same sex – male – and all for some reason bearded. Besides that, it was striking that there were no seats in the theatre, and the audience was all sitting on the floor, splendidly polished and slippery.

Abashed in this new and big company, Nikanor Ivanovich, after a brief hesitation, followed the general example and sat down on the parquet Turkish-fashion, huddled between some stalwart, bearded redhead and another citizen, pale and quite overgrown. None of the sitters paid any attention to the newly arrived spectator.

Here the soft ringing of a bell was heard, the lights in the house went out, and the curtain opened to reveal a lighted stage with an armchair, a little table on which stood a golden bell, and a solid black velvet backdrop.

An artiste came out from the wings in an evening jacket, smoothly shaven, his hair neatly parted, young and with very pleasant features. The audience in the house livened up, and everyone turned towards the stage. The artiste advanced to the prompter's box and rubbed his hands.

'All sitting?'[3] he asked in a soft baritone and smiled to the house.

'Sitting, sitting,' a chorus of tenors and basses answered from the house.

'Hm . . .' the artiste began pensively, 'and how you're not sick of it

I just don't understand! Everybody else is out walking around now, enjoying the spring sun and the warmth, and you're stuck in here on the floor of a stuffy theatre! Is the programme so interesting? Tastes differ, however,' the artiste concluded philosophically.

Then he changed both the timbre of his voice and its intonation, and announced gaily and resoundingly:

'And now for the next number on our programme – Nikanor Ivanovich Bosoy, chairman of a house committee and director of a dietetic kitchen. Nikanor Ivanovich, on-stage!'

General applause greeted the artiste. The surprised Nikanor Ivanovich goggled his eyes, while the master of ceremonies, blocking the glare of the footlights with his hand, located him among the sitters and tenderly beckoned him on-stage with his finger. And Nikanor Ivanovich, without knowing how, found himself on-stage. Beams of coloured light struck his eyes from in front and below, which at once caused the house and the audience to sink into darkness.

'Well, Nikanor Ivanovich, set us a good example, sir,' the young artiste said soulfully, 'turn over your currency.'

Silence ensued. Nikanor Ivanovich took a deep breath and quietly began to speak:

'I swear to God that I . . .'

But before he had time to get the words out, the whole house burst into shouts of indignation. Nikanor Ivanovich got confused and fell silent.

'As far as I understand you,' said the programme announcer, 'you wanted to swear to God that you haven't got any currency?', and he gazed sympathetically at Nikanor Ivanovich.

'Exactly right, I haven't,' replied Nikanor Ivanovich.

'Right,' responded the artiste, 'and . . . excuse the indiscretion, where did the four hundred dollars that were found in the privy of the apartment of which you and your wife are the sole inhabitants come from?'

'Magic!' someone in the dark house said with obvious irony.

'Exactly right – magic,' Nikanor Ivanovich timidly replied, vaguely addressing either the artiste or the dark house, and he explained: 'Unclean powers, the checkered interpreter stuck me with them.'

And again the house raised an indignant roar. When silence came, the artiste said:

'See what La Fontaine fables I have to listen to! Stuck him with four hundred dollars! Now, all of you here are currency dealers, so I address you as experts: is that conceivable?'

'We're not currency dealers,' various offended voices came from the theatre, 'but, no, it's not conceivable!'

'I'm entirely of the same mind,' the artiste said firmly, 'and let me ask you: what is it that one can be stuck with?'

'A baby!' someone cried from the house.

'Absolutely correct,' the programme announcer confirmed, 'a baby, an anonymous letter, a tract, an infernal machine, anything else, but no one will stick you with four hundred dollars, for such idiots don't exist in nature.' And turning to Nikanor Ivanovich, the artiste added reproachfully and sorrowfully: 'You've upset me, Nikanor Ivanovich, and I was counting on you. So, our number didn't come off.'

Whistles came from the house, addressed to Nikanor Ivanovich.

'He's a currency dealer,' they shouted from the house, 'and we innocent ones have to suffer for the likes of him!'

'Don't scold him,' the master of ceremonies said softly, 'he'll repent.' And turning to Nikanor Ivanovich, his blue eyes filled with tears, he added: 'Well, Nikanor Ivanovich, you may go to your place.'

After that the artiste rang the bell and announced loudly:

'Intermission, you blackguards!'

The shaken Nikanor Ivanovich, who unexpectedly for himself had become a participant in some sort of theatre programme, again found himself in his place on the floor. Here he dreamed that the house was plunged in total darkness, and fiery red words leaped out on the walls: 'Turn over your currency!' Then the curtain opened again and the master of ceremonies invited:

'I call Sergei Gerardovich Dunchil to the stage.'

Dunchil turned out to be a fine-looking but rather unkempt man of about fifty.

'Sergei Gerardovich,' the master of ceremonies addressed him, 'you've been sitting here for a month and a half now, stubbornly refusing to turn over the currency you still have, while the country is in need of it, and you have no use for it whatsoever. And still you persist. You're an intelligent man, you understand it all perfectly well, and yet you don't want to comply with me.'

'To my regret, there is nothing I can do, since I have no more currency,' Dunchil calmly replied.

'Don't you at least have some diamonds?' asked the artiste.

'No diamonds either.'

The artiste hung his head and pondered, then clapped his hands. A middle-aged lady came out from the wings, fashionably dressed – that is, in a collarless coat and a tiny hat. The lady looked worried, but Dunchil glanced at her without moving an eyebrow.

'Who is this lady?' the programme announcer asked Dunchil.

'That is my wife,' Dunchil replied with dignity and looked at the lady's long neck with a certain repugnance.

'We have troubled you, Madame Dunchil,' the master of ceremonies adverted to the lady, 'with regard to the following: we wanted to ask you, does your husband have any more currency?'

'He turned it all over the other time,' Madame Dunchil replied nervously.

'Right,' said the artiste, 'well, then, if it's so, it's so. If he turned it all over, then we ought to part with Sergei Gerardovich immediately, there's nothing else to do! If you wish, Sergei Gerardovich, you may leave the theatre.' And the artiste made a regal gesture.

Dunchil turned calmly and with dignity, and headed for the wings.

'Just a moment!' the master of ceremonies stopped him. 'Allow me on parting to show you one more number from our programme.' And again he clapped his hands.

The black backdrop parted, and on to the stage came a young beauty in a ball gown, holding in her hands a golden tray on which lay a fat wad tied with candy-box ribbon and a diamond necklace from which blue, yellow and red fire leaped in all directions.

Dunchil took a step back and his face went pale. The house froze.

'Eighteen thousand dollars and a necklace worth forty thousand in gold,' the artiste solemnly announced, 'kept by Sergei Gerardovich in the city of Kharkov, in the apartment of his mistress, Ida Herkulanovna Vors, whom we have the pleasure of seeing here before us and who so kindly helped in discovering these treasures – priceless, yet useless in the hands of a private person. Many thanks, Ida Herkulanovna!'

The beauty smiled, flashing her teeth, and her lush eyelashes fluttered.

'And under your so very dignified mask,' the artiste adverted to Dunchil, 'is concealed a greedy spider and an astonishing bamboozler and liar. You wore everyone out during this month and a half with your dull obstinacy. Go home now, and let the hell your wife sets up for you be your punishment.'

Dunchil swayed and, it seems, wanted to fall down, but was held up by someone's sympathetic hands. Here the front curtain dropped and concealed all those on-stage.

Furious applause shook the house, so much so that Nikanor Ivanovich fancied the lights were leaping in the chandeliers. When the front curtain went up, there was no one on-stage except the lone artiste. Greeted with a second burst of applause, he bowed and began to speak:

'In the person of this Dunchil, our programme has shown you a typical ass. I did have the pleasure of saying yesterday that the concealing of currency is senseless. No one can make use of it under any circumstances, I assure you. Let's take this same Dunchil. He gets a splendid salary and doesn't want for anything. He has a splendid apartment, a wife and a beautiful mistress. But no, instead of living quietly and peacefully without any troubles, having turned over the currency and stones, this mercenary blockhead gets himself exposed in front of everybody, and to top it off contracts major family trouble. So, who's going to turn over? Any volunteers? In that case, for the next number on our programme, a famous dramatic talent, the actor Kurolesov, Savva Potapovich, especially invited here, will perform excerpts from *The Covetous Knight*[4] by the poet Pushkin.'

The promised Kurolesov was not slow in coming on stage and turned out to be a strapping and beefy man, clean-shaven, in a tailcoat and white tie. Without any preliminaries, he concocted a gloomy face, knitted his brows, and began speaking in an unnatural voice, glancing sidelong at the golden bell:

'As a young scapegrace awaits a tryst with some sly strumpet...'[5]

And Kurolesov told many bad things about himself. Nikanor Ivanovich heard Kurolesov confess that some wretched widow had gone on her knees to him, howling, in the rain, but had failed to move the actor's callous heart.

Before his dream, Nikanor Ivanovich had been completely ignorant of the poet Pushkin's works, but the man himself he knew perfectly well and several times a day used to say phrases like: 'And who's going to pay the rent – Pushkin?'[6] or 'Then who did unscrew the bulb on the stairway – Pushkin?' or 'So who's going to buy the fuel – Pushkin?'

Now, having become acquainted with one of his works, Nikanor Ivanovich felt sad, imagined the woman on her knees, with her orphaned children, in the rain, and involuntarily thought: 'What a type, though, this Kurolesov!'

And the latter, ever raising his voice, went on with his confession and got Nikanor Ivanovich definitively muddled, because he suddenly started addressing someone who was not on-stage, and responded for this absent one himself, calling himself now dear sir, now baron, now father, now son, now formally, and now familiarly.

Nikanor Ivanovich understood only one thing, that the actor died an evil death, crying out: 'Keys! My keys!', after which he collapsed on the floor, gasping and carefully tearing off his tie.

Having died, Kurolesov got up, brushed the dust from his trousers, bowed with a false smile, and withdrew to the accompaniment of thin applause. And the master of ceremonies began speaking thus:

'We have just heard *The Covetous Knight* wonderfully performed by Savva Potapovich. This knight hoped that frolicking nymphs would come running to him, and that many other pleasant things in the same vein would occur. But, as you see, none of it happened, no nymphs came running to him, and the muses paid him no tribute, and he raised no mansions, but, on the contrary, ended quite badly, died of a stroke, devil take him, on his chest of currency and jewels. I warn you that the same sort of thing, if not worse, is going to happen to you if you don't turn over your currency!'

Whether Pushkin's poetry produced such an effect, or it was the prosaic speech of the master of ceremonies, in any case a shy voice suddenly came from the house:

'I'll turn over my currency.'

'Kindly come to the stage,' the master of ceremonies courteously invited, peering into the dark house.

On-stage appeared a short, fair-haired citizen, who, judging by his face, had not shaved in about three weeks.

'Beg pardon, what is your name?' the master of ceremonies inquired.

'Kanavkin, Nikolai,' the man responded shyly.

'Ah! Very pleased, Citizen Kanavkin. And so? . . .'

'I'll turn it over,' Kanavkin said quietly.

'How much?'

'A thousand dollars and twenty ten-rouble gold pieces.'

'Bravo! That's all, then?'

The programme announcer stared straight into Kanavkin's eyes, and it even seemed to Nikanor Ivanovich that those eyes sent out rays that penetrated Kanavkin like X-rays. The house stopped breathing.

'I believe you!' the artiste exclaimed finally and extinguished his gaze. 'I do! These eyes are not lying! How many times have I told you that your basic error consists in underestimating the significance of the human eye. Understand that the tongue can conceal the truth, but the eyes – never! A sudden question is put to you, you don't even flinch, in one second you get hold of yourself and know what you must say to conceal the truth, and you speak quite convincingly, and not a wrinkle on your face moves, but – alas – the truth which the question stirs up from the bottom of your soul leaps momentarily into your eyes, and it's all over! They see it, and you're caught!'

Having delivered, and with great ardour, this highly convincing speech, the artiste tenderly inquired of Kanavkin:

'And where is it hidden?'

'With my aunt, Porokhovnikova, on Prechistenka.'

'Ah! That's ... wait ... that's Klavdia Ilyinishna, isn't it?'

'Yes.'

'Ah, yes, yes, yes, yes! A separate little house? A little front garden opposite? Of course, I know, I know! And where did you put it there?'

'In the cellar, in a candy tin ...'

The artiste clasped his hands.

'Have you ever seen the like?' he cried out, chagrined. 'Why, it'll get damp and mouldy there! Is it conceivable to entrust currency to such people? Eh? Sheer childishness! By God! ...'

Kanavkin himself realized he had fouled up and was in for it, and he hung his tufty head.

'Money,' the artiste went on, 'must be kept in the state bank, in special dry and well-guarded rooms, and by no means in some aunt's cellar, where it may, in particular, suffer damage from rats! Really, Kanavkin, for shame! You're a grown-up!'

Kanavkin no longer knew what to do with himself, and merely picked at the lapel of his jacket with his finger.

'Well, all right,' the artiste relented, 'let bygones be ...' And he suddenly added unexpectedly: 'Ah, by the way ... so that in one ... to save a trip ... this same aunt also has some, eh?'

Kanavkin, never expecting such a turn of affairs, wavered, and the theatre fell silent.

'Ehh, Kanavkin...' the master of ceremonies said in tender reproach, 'and here I was praising him! Look, he just went and messed it up for no reason at all! It's absurd, Kanavkin! Wasn't I just talking about eyes? Can't we see that the aunt has got some? Well, then why do you torment us for nothing?'

'She has!' Kanavkin cried dashingly.

'Bravo!' cried the master of ceremonies.

'Bravo!' the house roared frightfully.

When things quieted down, the master of ceremonies congratulated Kanavkin, shook his hand, offered him a ride home to the city in a car, and told someone in the wings to go in that same car to fetch the aunt and ask her kindly to come for the programme at the women's theatre.

'Ah, yes, I wanted to ask you, has the aunt ever mentioned where she hides hers?' the master of ceremonies inquired, courteously offering Kanavkin a cigarette and a lighted match. As he lit up, the man grinned somehow wistfully.

'I believe you, I believe you,' the artiste responded with a sigh. 'Not just her nephew, the old pinchfist wouldn't tell the devil himself! Well, so, we'll try to awaken some human feelings in her. Maybe not all the strings have rotted in her usurious little soul. Bye-bye, Kanavkin!'

And the happy Kanavkin drove off. The artiste inquired whether there were any others who wished to turn over their currency, but was answered with silence.

'Odd birds, by God!' the artiste said, shrugging, and the curtain hid him.

The lights went out, there was darkness for a while, and in it a nervous tenor was heard singing from far away:

'There great heaps of gold do shine, and all those heaps of gold are mine...'[7]

Then twice the sound of subdued applause came from somewhere.

'Some little lady in the women's theatre is turning hers over,' Nikanor Ivanovich's red-bearded neighbour spoke up unexpectedly, and added with a sigh: 'Ah, if it wasn't for my geese! ... I've got fighting geese in Lianozovo, my dear fellow ... they'll die without me, I'm afraid. A fighting bird's delicate, it needs care ... Ah, if it wasn't for my geese!

... They won't surprise me with Pushkin ...' And again he began to sigh.

Here the house lit up brightly, and Nikanor Ivanovich dreamed that cooks in white chef's hats and with ladles in their hands came pouring from all the doors. Scullions dragged in a cauldron of soup and a stand with cut-up rye bread. The spectators livened up. The jolly cooks shuttled among the theatre buffs, ladled out bowls of soup, and distributed bread.

'Dig in, lads,' the cooks shouted, 'and turn over your currency! What's the point of sitting here? Who wants to slop up this swill! Go home, have a good drink, a little bite, that's the way!'

'Now, you, for instance, what're you doing sitting here, old man?' Nikanor Ivanovich was directly addressed by a fat cook with a raspberry-coloured neck, as he offered him a bowl in which a lone cabbage leaf floated in some liquid.

'I don't have any! I don't! I don't!' Nikanor Ivanovich cried out in a terrible voice. 'You understand, I don't!'

'You don't?' the cook bellowed in a menacing bass. 'You don't?' he asked in a tender woman's voice. 'You don't, you don't,' he murmured soothingly, turning into the nurse Praskovya Fyodorovna.

She was gently shaking Nikanor Ivanovich by the shoulder as he moaned in his sleep. Then the cooks melted away, and the theatre with its curtain broke up. Through his tears, Nikanor Ivanovich made out his room in the hospital and two people in white coats, who were by no means casual cooks getting at people with their advice, but the doctor and that same Praskovya Fyodorovna, who was holding not a bowl but a little dish covered with gauze, with a syringe lying on it.

'What is all this?' Nikanor Ivanovich said bitterly, as they were giving him the injection. 'I don't have any and that's that! Let Pushkin turn over his currency for them. I don't have any!'

'No, you don't, you don't,' the kind-hearted Praskovya Fyodorovna soothed him, 'and if you don't, there's no more to be said.'

After the injection, Nikanor Ivanovich felt better and fell asleep without any dreams.

But, thanks to his cries, alarm was communicated to room 120, where the patient woke up and began looking for his head, and to room 118, where the unknown master became restless and wrung his hands in anguish, looking at the moon, remembering the last bitter autumn night of his life, a strip of light under the basement door, and uncurled hair.

From room 118, the alarm flew by way of the balcony to Ivan, and he woke up and began to weep.

But the doctor quickly calmed all these anxious, sorrowing heads, and they began to fall asleep. Ivan was the last to become oblivious, as dawn was already breaking over the river. After the medicine, which suffused his whole body, calm came like a wave and covered him. His body grew lighter, his head basked in the warm wind of reverie. He fell asleep, and the last waking thing he heard was the pre-dawn chirping of birds in the woods. But they soon fell silent, and he began dreaming that the sun was already going down over Bald Mountain, and the mountain was cordoned off by a double cordon . . .

CHAPTER 16

The Execution

The sun was already going down over Bald Mountain, and the mountain was cordoned off by a double cordon.

The cavalry ala that had cut across the procurator's path around noon came trotting up to the Hebron gate of the city. Its way had already been prepared. The infantry of the Cappadocian cohort had pushed the conglomeration of people, mules and camels to the sides, and the ala, trotting and raising white columns of dust in the sky, came to an intersection where two roads met: the south road leading to Bethlehem, and the north-west road to Jaffa. The ala raced down the north-west road. The same Cappadocians were strung out along the sides of the road, and in good time had driven to the sides of it all the caravans hastening to the feast in Yershalaim. Crowds of pilgrims stood behind the Cappadocians, having abandoned their temporary striped tents, pitched right on the grass. Going on for about a half-mile, the ala caught up with the second cohort of the Lightning legion and, having covered another half-mile, was the first to reach the foot of Bald Mountain. Here they dismounted. The commander broke the ala up into squads, and they cordoned off the whole foot of the small hill, leaving open only the way up from the Jaffa road.

After some time, the ala was joined at the hill by the second cohort, which climbed one level higher and also encircled the hill in a wreath.

Finally the century under the command of Mark Ratslayer arrived. It went stretched out in files along the sides of the road, and between these files, convoyed by the secret guard, the three condemned men rode in a cart, white boards hanging around their necks with 'robber and rebel' written on each of them in two languages – Aramaic and Greek.

The cart with the condemned men was followed by others laden with freshly hewn posts with crosspieces, ropes, shovels, buckets and axes. Six executioners rode in these carts. They were followed on horseback by the centurion Mark, the chief of the temple guard of

Yershalaim, and that same hooded man with whom Pilate had had a momentary meeting in a darkened room of the palace.

A file of soldiers brought up the rear of the procession, and behind it walked about two thousand of the curious, undaunted by the infernal heat and wishing to be present at the interesting spectacle. The curious from the city were now joined by the curious from among the pilgrims, who were admitted without hindrance to the tail of the procession. Under the shrill cries of the heralds who accompanied the column and cried aloud what Pilate had cried out at around noon, the procession drew itself up Bald Mountain.

The ala admitted everyone to the second level, but the second century let only those connected with the execution go further up, and then, manoeuvring quickly, spread the crowd around the entire hill, so that people found themselves between the cordons of infantry above and cavalry below. Now they could watch the execution through the sparse line of the infantry.

And so, more than three hours had gone by since the procession climbed the mountain, and the sun was already going down over Bald Mountain, but the heat was still unbearable, and the soldiers in both cordons suffered from it, grew weary with boredom, and cursed the three robbers in their hearts, sincerely wishing them the speediest death.

The little commander of the ala, his brow moist and the back of his white shirt dark with sweat, having placed himself at the foot of the hill by the open passage, went over to the leather bucket of the first squad every now and then, scooped handfuls of water from it, drank and wetted his turban. Somewhat relieved by that, he would step away and again begin pacing back and forth on the dusty road leading to the top. His long sword slapped against his laced leather boot. The commander wished to give his cavalrymen an example of endurance, but, pitying his soldiers, he allowed them to stick their spears pyramid-like in the ground and throw their white cloaks over them. Under these tents, the Syrians hid from the merciless sun. The buckets were quickly emptied, and cavalrymen from different squads took turns going to fetch water in the gully below the hill, where in the thin shade of spindly mulberries a muddy brook was living out its last days in the devilish heat. There, too, catching the unsteady shade, stood the bored horse-handlers, holding the quieted horses.

The weariness of the soldiers and the abuse they aimed at the robbers were understandable. The procurator's apprehensions concerning the disorders that might occur at the time of the execution in the city of Yershalaim, so hated by him, fortunately were not borne out. And when the fourth hour of the execution came, there was, contrary to all expectations, not a single person left between the two files, the infantry above and the cavalry below. The sun had scorched the crowd and driven it back to Yershalaim. Beyond the file of two Roman centuries there were only two dogs that belonged to no one knew whom and had for some reason ended up on the hill. But the heat got to them, too, and they lay down with their tongues hanging out, panting and paying no attention to the green-backed lizards, the only beings not afraid of the sun, darting among the scorching stones and some sort of big-thorned plants that crept on the ground.

No one attempted to rescue the condemned men either in Yershalaim itself, flooded with troops, or here on the cordoned-off hill, and the crowd went back to the city, for indeed there was absolutely nothing interesting in this execution, while there in the city preparations were under way for the great feast of Passover, which was to begin that evening.

The Roman infantry on the second level suffered still more than the cavalry. The only thing the centurion Ratslayer allowed his soldiers was to take off their helmets and cover their heads with white headbands dipped in water, but he kept them standing, and with their spears in their hands. He himself, in the same kind of headband, but dry, not wet, walked about not far from the group of executioners, without even taking the silver plaques with lions' muzzles off his shirt, or removing his greaves, sword and knife. The sun beat straight down on the centurion without doing him any harm, and the lions' muzzles were impossible to look at – the eyes were devoured by the dazzling gleam of the silver which was as if boiling in the sun.

Ratslayer's mutilated face expressed neither weariness nor displeasure, and it seemed that the giant centurion was capable of pacing like that all day, all night and the next day – in short, for as long as necessary. Of pacing in the same way, holding his hands to the heavy belt with its bronze plaques, glancing in the same stern way now at the posts with the executed men, now at the file of soldiers, kicking aside with the toe of a shaggy boot in the same indifferent way human bones whitened by time or small flints that happened under his feet.

That man in the hood placed himself not far from the posts on a three-legged stool and sat there in complacent motionlessness, though poking the sand with a twig from time to time out of boredom.

What has been said about there not being a single person beyond the file of legionaries is not quite true. There was one person, but he simply could not be seen by everyone. He had placed himself, not on the side where the way up the mountain was open and from where it would have been most convenient to watch the execution, but on the north side, where the slope was not gentle and accessible, but uneven, with gaps and clefts, where in a crevice, clutching at the heaven-cursed waterless soil, a sickly fig tree was trying to live.

Precisely under it, though it gave no shade, this sole spectator who was not a participant in the execution had established himself, and had sat on a stone from the very beginning, that is, for over three hours now. Yes, he had chosen not the best but the worst position for watching the execution. But still, even from there the posts could be seen, and there could also be seen, beyond the file of soldiers, the two dazzling spots on the centurion's chest, and that was apparently quite enough for a man who obviously wished to remain little noticed and not be bothered by anyone.

But some four hours ago, at the start of the execution, this man had behaved quite differently, and might have been noticed very well, which was probably why he had now changed his behaviour and secluded himself.

It was only when the procession came to the very top, beyond the file, that he had first appeared, and as an obvious latecomer at that. He was breathing hard, and did not walk but ran up the hill, pushing his way, and, seeing the file close together before him as before everyone else, made a naive attempt, pretending he did not understand the angry shouts, to break through the soldiers to the very place of execution, where the condemned men were already being taken from the cart. For that he received a heavy blow in the chest with the butt end of a spear, and he leaped back from the soldiers, crying out not in pain but in despair. At the legionary who had dealt the blow he cast a dull glance, utterly indifferent to everything, like a man insensible to physical pain.

Coughing and breathless, clutching his chest, he ran around the hill, trying to find some gap in the file on the north side where he could slip through. But it was too late, the ring was closed. And the man, his face distorted with grief, was forced to renounce his attempts to break through to the carts, from which the posts had already been unloaded. These attempts would have led nowhere, except that he would have been seized, and to be arrested on that day by no means entered his plans.

And so he went to the side, towards the crevice, where it was quieter and nobody bothered him.

Now, sitting on the stone, this black-bearded man, his eyes festering from the sun and lack of sleep, was in anguish. First he sighed, opening his tallith, worn out in his wanderings, gone from light-blue to dirty grey, and bared his chest, which had been hurt by the spear and down which ran dirty sweat; then, in unendurable pain, he raised his eyes to the sky, following the three vultures that had long been floating in great circles on high, anticipating an imminent feast; then he peered with hopeless eyes into the yellow earth, and saw on it the half-destroyed skull of a dog and lizards scurrying around it.

The man's sufferings were so great that at times he began talking to himself.

'Oh, fool that I am . . .' he muttered, swaying on the stone in the pain of his heart and clawing his swarthy chest with his nails. 'Fool, senseless woman, coward! I'm not a man, I'm carrion!'

He would fall silent, hang his head, then, after drinking some warm water from a wooden flask, he would revive again and clutch now at the knife hidden on his chest under the tallith, now at the piece of parchment lying before him on the stone next to a stylus and a pot of ink.

On this parchment some notes had already been scribbled:

'The minutes run on, and I, Matthew Levi, am here on Bald Mountain, and still no death!'

Further:

'The sun is sinking, but no death.'

Now Matthew Levi wrote hopelessly with the sharp stylus:

'God! Why are you angry with him? Send him death.'

Having written this, he sobbed tearlessly and again wounded his chest with his nails.

The reason for Levi's despair lay in the terrible misfortune that had befallen Yeshua and him and, besides that, in the grave error that he,

Levi, in his own opinion, had committed. Two days earlier, Yeshua and Levi had been in Bethphage near Yershalaim, where they had visited a certain gardener who liked Yeshua's preaching very much. The two visitors had spent the whole morning working in the garden, helping their host, and planned to go to Yershalaim towards evening when it cooled off. But Yeshua began to hurry for some reason, said he had urgent business in the city, and left alone around noontime. Here lay Matthew Levi's first error. Why, why had he let him go alone!

Nor was Matthew Levi to go to Yershalaim that evening. He was struck by some unexpected and terrible ailment. He began to shake, his whole body was filled with fire, his teeth chattered, and he kept asking to drink all the time.

He could not go anywhere. He collapsed on a horse blanket in the gardener's shed and lay there till dawn on Friday, when the illness released Levi as unexpectedly as it had fallen upon him. Though he was still weak and his legs trembled, he took leave of his host and, oppressed by some foreboding of disaster, went to Yershalaim. There he learned that his foreboding had not deceived him – the disaster occurred. Levi was in the crowd and heard the procurator announce the sentence.

When the condemned men were led off to the mountain, Matthew Levi ran alongside the file in the crowd of the curious, trying to let Yeshua know in some inconspicuous way that at least he, Levi, was there with him, that he had not abandoned him on his last journey, and that he was praying that death would overtake Yeshua as soon as possible. But Yeshua, who was looking into the distance towards where he was being taken, of course did not see Levi.

And then, when the procession had gone about a half-mile along the road, a simple and ingenious thought dawned on Matthew, who was being jostled by the crowd just next to the file, and in his excitement he at once showered himself with curses for not having thought of it earlier. The file of soldiers was not solid, there were spaces between them. Given great dexterity and a precise calculation, one could bend down, slip between two legionaries, make it to the cart and jump into it. Then Yeshua would be saved from suffering.

One instant would be enough to stab Yeshua in the back with a knife, crying to him: 'Yeshua! I save you and go with you! I, Matthew, your faithful and only disciple!'

And if God granted him one more free instant, he would also have time to stab himself and avoid death on a post. This last, however, was of little interest to Levi, the former tax collector. He was indifferent to how he died. He wanted one thing, that Yeshua, who had never in his life done the least evil to anyone, should escape torture.

The plan was a very good one, but the fact of the matter was that Levi had no knife with him. Nor did he have a single piece of money.

Furious with himself, Levi got out of the crowd and ran back to the city. A single feverish thought was leaping in his burning head: how to procure a knife there in the city, in any way possible, and have time to overtake the procession.

He ran up to the city gate, manoeuvring amid the throng of caravans being sucked into the city, and saw to his left the open door of a little shop where bread was sold. Breathing hard after running down the scorched road, Levi got control of himself, entered the shop very sedately, greeted the woman behind the counter, asked her to take the top loaf from the shelf, which for some reason he liked better than the others, and when she turned around, silently and quickly took from the counter that than which there could be nothing better – a long, razor-sharp bread knife – and at once dashed out of the shop.

A few moments later he was again on the Jaffa road. But the procession was no longer in sight. He ran. At times he had to drop down right in the dust and lie motionless to recover his breath. And so he would lie there, to the astonishment of people riding on mules or walking on foot to Yershalaim. He would lie listening to his heart pounding not only in his chest but in his head and ears. Having recovered his breath a little, he would jump up and continue running, but ever slower and slower. When he finally caught sight of the long procession raising dust in the distance, it was already at the foot of the hill.

'Oh, God! . . .' Levi moaned, realizing that he was going to be too late. And he was too late.

When the fourth hour of the execution had gone by, Levi's torments reached their highest degree and he fell into a rage. Getting up from the stone, he flung to the ground the stolen knife – stolen in vain, as he now thought – crushed the flask with his foot, depriving himself of water, threw off his kefia, seized his thin hair, and began cursing himself.

He cursed himself, calling out meaningless words, growled and spat, abused his father and mother for bringing a fool into the world.

Seeing that curses and abuse had no effect and nothing in the sun-scorched place was changed by them, he clenched his dry fists, raised them, squinting, to the sky, to the sun that was sliding ever lower, lengthening the shadows and going to fall into the Mediterranean, and demanded an immediate miracle from God. He demanded that God at once send Yeshua death.

Opening his eyes, he became convinced that everything on the hill was unchanged, except that the blazing spots on the centurion's chest had gone out. The sun was sending its rays into the backs of the executed men, who were facing Yershalaim. Then Levi shouted:

'I curse you, God!'

In a rasping voice he shouted that he was convinced of God's injustice and did not intend to believe in him any longer.

'You are deaf!' growled Levi. 'If you were not deaf, you would have heard me and killed him straight away!'

Shutting his eyes, Levi waited for the fire that would fall from the sky and strike him instead. This did not happen, and Levi, without opening his eyes, went on shouting offensive and sarcastic things at the sky. He shouted about his total disappointment, about the existence of other gods and religions. Yes, another god would not have allowed it, he would never have allowed a man like Yeshua to be burnt by the sun on a post.

'I was mistaken!' Levi cried in a completely hoarse voice. 'You are a god of evil! Or are your eyes completely clouded by smoke from the temple censers, and have your ears ceased to hear anything but the trumpeting noises of the priests? You are not an almighty god! You are a black god! I curse you, god of robbers, their soul and their protector!'

Here something blew into the face of the former tax collector, and something rustled under his feet. It blew once more, and then, opening his eyes, Levi saw that, either under the influence of his curses, or owing to other reasons, everything in the world was changed. The sun had disappeared before reaching the sea, where it sank every evening. Having swallowed it, a storm cloud was rising menacingly and inexorably against the sky in the west. Its edges were already seething with white foam, its black smoky belly was tinged with yellow. The storm cloud was growling, threads of fire fell from it now and again. Down the Jaffa road, down the meagre Hinnom valley, over the tents of the pilgrims, driven by the suddenly risen wind, pillars of dust went flying.

Levi fell silent, trying to grasp whether the storm that was about to cover Yershalaim would bring any change in the fate of the unfortunate Yeshua. And straight away, looking at the threads of fire cutting up the cloud, he began to ask that lightning strike Yeshua's post. Repentantly looking into the clear sky that had not yet been devoured by the cloud, and where the vultures were veering on one wing to escape the storm, Levi thought he had been insanely hasty with his curses: now God was not going to listen to him.

Turning his gaze to the foot of the hill, Levi fixed on the place where the strung-out cavalry regiment stood, and saw that considerable changes had taken place there. From above, Levi was able to distinguish very well the soldiers bustling about, pulling spears out of the ground, throwing cloaks on, the horse-handlers trotting towards the road leading black horses by their bridles. The regiment was moving off, that was clear. Spitting and shielding himself with his hand from the dust blowing in his face, Levi tried to grasp what it might mean if the cavalry was about to leave. He shifted his gaze further up and made out a little figure in a crimson military chlamys climbing towards the place of execution. And here a chill came over the heart of the former tax collector in anticipation of the joyful end.

The man climbing the mountain in the fifth hour of the robbers' sufferings was the commander of the cohort, who had come galloping from Yershalaim accompanied by an aide. At a gesture from Ratslayer, the file of soldiers parted, and the centurion saluted the tribune. The latter, taking Ratslayer aside, whispered something to him. The centurion saluted him a second time and moved towards the group of executioners, who were sitting on stones at the foot of the posts. The tribune meanwhile directed his steps towards the one sitting on the three-legged stool, and the seated man politely rose to meet the tribune. And the tribune said something to him in a low voice, and the two went over to the posts. They were joined by the head of the temple guard.

Ratslayer, casting a squeamish sidelong glance at the dirty rags lying on the ground near the posts, rags that had recently been the criminals' clothing, and which the executioners had rejected, called two of them and ordered:

'Follow me!'

From the nearest post came a hoarse, senseless song. Gestas, hanging on it, had lost his mind from the flies and sun towards the end of the third hour, and was now quietly singing something about grapes, but his head, covered with a turban, occasionally swayed all the same, and then the flies rose sluggishly from his face and settled on it again.

Dysmas, on the second post, suffered more than the other two because he did not lose consciousness, and he swung his head constantly and rhythmically, right and left, so that his ears struck his shoulders.

Yeshua was more fortunate than the other two. In the very first hour, he began to have blackouts, and then he fell into oblivion, hanging his head in its unwound turban. The flies and horseflies therefore covered him completely, so that his face disappeared under the black swarming mass. In his groin, and on his belly, and in his armpits, fat horseflies sat sucking at his yellow naked body.

Obeying the gestures of the man in the hood, one of the executioners took a spear and another brought a bucket and a sponge to the post. The first executioner raised the spear and with it tapped first one, then the other of Yeshua's arms, stretched out and bound with ropes to the crossbar of the post. The body, with its protruding ribs, gave a start. The executioner passed the tip of the spear over the belly. Then Yeshua raised his head, and the flies moved off with a buzz, revealing the face of the hanged man, swollen with bites, the eyes puffy, an unrecognizable face.

Ungluing his eyelids, Ha-Nozri looked down. His eyes, usually clear, were slightly clouded.

'Ha-Nozri!' said the executioner.

Ha-Nozri moved his swollen lips and answered in a hoarse robber's voice:

'What do you want? Why have you come to me?'

'Drink!' said the executioner, and a water-soaked sponge on the tip of a spear rose to Yeshua's lips. Joy flashed in his eyes, he clung to the sponge and began greedily imbibing the moisture. From the neighbouring post came the voice of Dysmas:

'Injustice! I'm a robber just like him!'

Dysmas strained but was unable to move, his arms being bound to the crossbar in three places with loops of rope. He drew in his belly, clawed the ends of the crossbar with his nails, kept his head turned towards Yeshua's post, malice blazed in the eyes of Dysmas.

A dusty cloud covered the place, it became much darker. When the dust blew away, the centurion shouted:

'Silence on the second post!'

Dysmas fell silent. Yeshua tore himself away from the sponge, and trying to make his voice sound gentle and persuasive, but not succeeding, he begged the executioner hoarsely:

'Give him a drink.'

It was growing ever darker. The storm cloud had already poured across half the sky, aiming towards Yershalaim, boiling white clouds raced ahead of the storm cloud suffused with black moisture and fire. There was a flash and a thunderclap right over the hill. The executioner removed the sponge from the spear.

'Praise the magnanimous hegemon!' he whispered solemnly, and gently pricked Yeshua in the heart. He twitched and whispered:

'Hegemon . . .'

Blood ran down his belly, his lower jaw twitched convulsively and his head dropped.

At the second thunderclap, the executioner was already giving Dysmas a drink, and with the same words:

'Praise the hegemon!' – killed him as well.

Gestas, deprived of reason, cried out fearfully as soon as the executioner came near him, but when the sponge touched his lips, he growled something and seized it with his teeth. A few seconds later his body, too, slumped as much as the ropes would allow.

The man in the hood followed the executioner and the centurion, and after him came the head of the temple guard. Stopping at the first post, the man in the hood examined the blood-covered Yeshua attentively, touched his foot with his white hand, and said to his companions:

'Dead.'

The same was repeated at the other two posts.

After that the tribune motioned to the centurion and, turning, started off the hilltop together with the head of the temple guard and the man in the hood. Semi-darkness set in, and lightning furrowed the black sky. Fire suddenly sprayed out of it, and the centurion's shout: 'Raise the cordon!', was drowned in rumbling. The happy soldiers rushed headlong down the hill, putting on their helmets.

Darkness covered Yershalaim.

Torrents of rain poured down suddenly and caught the centuries halfway down the hill. The deluge fell so terribly that the soldiers were already pursued by raging streams as they ran downhill. Soldiers slipped and fell in the sodden clay, hurrying to get to the level road, along which – now barely visible through the sheet of water – the thoroughly drenched cavalry was heading for Yershalaim. A few minutes later only one man remained in the smoky brew of storm, water and fire on the hill.

Shaking the not uselessly stolen knife, falling from slippery ledges, clutching at whatever was there, sometimes crawling on his knees, he strained towards the posts. He now vanished in total darkness, now was suddenly illumined by a tremulous light.

Having made his way to the posts, already up to his ankles in water, he tore off his heavy water-soaked tallith, remaining just in his shirt, and clung to Yeshua's feet. He cut the ropes on his shins, stepped up on the lower crossbar, embraced Yeshua and freed his arms from the upper bonds. The naked, wet body of Yeshua collapsed on Levi and brought him to the ground. Levi wanted to heave it on to his shoulders straight away, but some thought stopped him. He left the body with its thrown-back head and outspread arms on the ground in the water, and ran, his feet slithering apart in the clayey mire, to the other posts. He cut the ropes on them as well, and the two bodies collapsed on the ground.

Several minutes passed, and all that remained on the top of the hill was these two bodies and the three empty posts. Water beat on the bodies and rolled them over.

By that time both Levi and the body of Yeshua were gone from the hilltop.

CHAPTER 17

An Unquiet Day

On Friday morning, that is, the day after the accursed séance, all the available staff of the Variety – the bookkeeper Vassily Stepanovich Lastochkin, two accountants, three typists, both box-office girls, the messengers, ushers, cleaning women – in short, all those available, were not at their places doing their jobs, but were all sitting on the window-sills looking out on Sadovaya and watching what was going on by the wall of the Variety. By this wall a queue of many thousands clung in two rows, its tail reaching to Kudrinskaya Square. At the head of the line stood some two dozen scalpers well known to theatrical Moscow.

The line behaved with much agitation, attracting the notice of the citizens streaming past, and was occupied with the discussion of inflammatory tales about yesterday's unprecedented séance of black magic. These same tales caused the greatest consternation in the book-keeper Vassily Stepanovich, who had not been present at the previous evening's performance. The ushers told of God knows what, among other things that after the conclusion of the famous séance, some female citizens went running around in the street looking quite indecent, and so on in the same vein. The modest and quiet Vassily Stepanovich merely blinked his eyes, listening to the tall tales of these wonders, and decidedly did not know what to undertake, and yet something had to be undertaken, and precisely by him, because he now turned out to be the senior member of the whole Variety team.

By ten o'clock the line of people desiring tickets had swelled so much that rumour of it reached the police, and with astonishing swiftness detachments were sent, both on foot and mounted, to bring this line into some sort of order. However, in itself even an orderly snake a half-mile long presented a great temptation, and caused utter amaze-ment in the citizens on Sadovaya.

That was outside, but inside the Variety things were also none too great. Early in the morning the telephones began to ring and went on ringing without interruption in Likhodeev's office, in Rimsky's office, at the bookkeeper's, in the box office, and in Varenukha's office.

Vassily Stepanovich at first made some answer, the box-office girl also answered, the ushers mumbled something into the telephones, but then they stopped altogether, because to questions of where Likhodeev, Varenukha and Rimsky were, there was decidedly no answer. At first they tried to get off by saying 'Likhodeev's at home', but the reply to this was that they had called him at home, and at home they said Likhodeev was at the Variety.

An agitated lady called, started asking for Rimsky, was advised to call his wife, to which the receiver, sobbing, answered that she was his wife and that Rimsky was nowhere to be found. Some sort of nonsense was beginning. The cleaning woman had already told everybody that when she came to the findirector's office to clean, she saw the door wide open, the lights on, the window to the garden broken, the armchair lying on the floor, and no one in the office.

Shortly after ten o'clock, Madame Rimsky burst into the Variety. She was sobbing and wringing her hands. Vassily Stepanovich was utterly at a loss and did not know how to counsel her. Then at half past ten came the police. Their first and perfectly reasonable question was:

'What's going on here, citizens? What's this all about?'

The team stepped back, bringing forward the pale and agitated Vassily Stepanovich. He had to call things by their names and confess that the administration of the Variety in the persons of the director, the findirector and the administrator had vanished and no one knew where, that the master of ceremonies had been taken to a psychiatric hospital after yesterday's séance, and that, to put it briefly, this séance yesterday had frankly been a scandalous séance.

The sobbing Madame Rimsky, having been calmed down as much as possible, was sent home, and the greatest interest was shown in the cleaning woman's story about the shape in which the findirector's office had been found. The staff were asked to go to their places and get busy, and in a short while the investigation appeared in the Variety building, accompanied by a sharp-eared, muscular, ash-coloured dog with extremely intelligent eyes. The whisper spread at once among the Variety staff that the dog was none other than the famous Ace of Diamonds. And so it was. His behaviour amazed them all. The moment Ace of Diamonds ran into the findirector's office, he growled, baring his monstrous yellow fangs, then crouched on his belly and, with some sort of look of anguish and at the same time of rage in his eyes, crawled towards the broken window. Overcoming his fear, he suddenly jumped up on the window-sill and, throwing back his sharp muzzle, howled savagely and angrily. He refused to leave the window, growled and twitched, and kept trying to jump out.

The dog was taken from the office and turned loose in the lobby, whence he walked out through the main entrance to the street and led those following him to the cab stand. There he lost the trail he had been pursuing. After that Ace of Diamonds was taken away.

The investigation settled in Varenukha's office, where they began summoning in turn all the Variety staff members who had witnessed yesterday's events during the séance. It must be said that the investigation had at every step to overcome unforeseen difficulties. The thread kept snapping off in their hands.

There had been posters, right? Right. But during the night they had been pasted over with new ones, and now, strike me dead, there wasn't a single one to be found! And the magician himself, where had he come from? Ah, who knows! But there was a contract drawn up with him?

'I suppose so,' the agitated Vassily Stepanovich replied.

'And if one was drawn up, it had to go through bookkeeping?'

'Most assuredly,' responded the agitated Vassily Stepanovich.

'Then where is it?'

'Not here,' the bookkeeper replied, turning ever more pale and spreading his arms.

And indeed no trace of the contract was found in the files of the bookkeeping office, nor at the findirector's, nor at Likhodeev's or Varenukha's.

And what was this magician's name? Vassily Stepanovich did not know, he had not been at the séance yesterday. The ushers did not know, the box-office girl wrinkled her brow, wrinkled it, thought and thought, and finally said:

'Wo ... Woland, seems like ...'

Or maybe not Woland? Maybe not Woland. Maybe Faland.

It turned out that in the foreigners' bureau they had heard precisely nothing either about any Woland, or for that matter any Faland, the magician.

The messenger Karpov said that this same magician was supposedly staying in Likhodeev's apartment. The apartment was, of course, visited at once – no magician was found there. Likhodeev himself was not there either. The housekeeper Grunya was not there, and where she had gone nobody knew. The chairman of the management, Nikanor Ivanovich, was not there, Bedsornev was not there!

Something utterly preposterous was coming out: the whole top administration had vanished, a strange, scandalous séance had taken place the day before, but who had produced it and at whose prompting, no one knew.

And meanwhile it was drawing towards noon, when the box office was to open. But, of course, there could be no talk of that! A huge piece of cardboard was straight away posted on the doors of the Variety reading: 'Today's Show Cancelled'. The line became agitated, beginning at its head, but after some agitation, it nevertheless began to break up, and about an hour later no trace of it remained on Sadovaya. The investigation departed to continue its work elsewhere, the staff was sent home, leaving only the watchmen, and the doors of the Variety were locked.

The bookkeeper Vassily Stepanovich had urgently to perform two tasks. First, to go to the Commission on Spectacles and Entertainment of the Lighter Type with a report on yesterday's events and, second, to visit the Finspectacle sector so as to turn over yesterday's receipts – 21,711 roubles.

The precise and efficient Vassily Stepanovich wrapped the money in newspaper, criss-crossed it with string, put it in his briefcase, and, knowing his instructions very well, set out, of course, not for a bus or a tram, but for the cab stand.

The moment the drivers of the three cabs saw a passenger hurrying towards the stand with a tightly stuffed briefcase, all three left empty right under his nose, looking back at him angrily for some reason.

Struck by this circumstance, the bookkeeper stood like a post for a long time, trying to grasp what it might mean.

About three minutes later, an empty cab drove up, but the driver's face twisted the moment he saw the passenger.

'Are you free?' Vassily Stepanovich asked with a cough of surprise.

'Show your money,' the driver replied angrily, without looking at the passenger.

With increasing amazement, the bookkeeper, pressing the precious briefcase under his arm, pulled a ten-rouble bill from his wallet and showed it to the driver.

'I won't go!' the man said curtly.

'I beg your pardon . . .' the bookkeeper tried to begin, but the driver interrupted him.

'Got any threes?'

The completely bewildered bookkeeper took two three-rouble bills from his wallet and showed them to the driver.

'Get in,' he shouted, and slapped down the flag of the meter so that he almost broke it. 'Let's go!'

'No change, is that it?' the bookkeeper asked timidly.

'A pocket full of change!' the driver bawled, and the eyes in the mirror went bloodshot. 'It's my third case today. And the same thing happened with the others, too. Some son of a bitch gives me a tenner, I give him change – four-fifty. He gets out, the scum! About five minutes later, I look: instead of a tenner, it's a label from a seltzer bottle!' Here the driver uttered several unprintable words. 'Another one, beyond Zubovskaya. A tenner. I give him three roubles change. He leaves. I go to my wallet, there's a bee there – zap in the finger! Ah, you! . . .' and again the driver pasted on some unprintable words. 'And no tenner. Yesterday, in the Variety here' (unprintable words), 'some vermin of a conjurer did a séance with ten-rouble bills' (unprintable words) . . .

The bookkeeper went numb, shrank into himself, and pretended it was the first time he had heard even the word 'Variety', while thinking to himself: 'Oh-oh! . . .'

Having got where he had to go, having paid satisfactorily, the bookkeeper entered the building and went down the corridor towards the manager's office, and realized on his way that he had come at the wrong time. Some sort of tumult reigned in the offices of the Spectacles Commission. A messenger girl ran past the bookkeeper, her kerchief all pushed back on her head and her eyes popping.

'Nothing, nothing, nothing, my dears!' she shouted, addressing no one knew whom. 'The jacket and trousers are there, but inside the jacket there's nothing!'

She disappeared through some door, and straight away from behind it came the noise of smashing dishes. The manager of the commission's first sector, whom the bookkeeper knew, ran out of the secretary's room, but he was in such a state that he did not recognize the book-keeper and disappeared without a trace.

Shaken by all this, the bookkeeper reached the secretary's room, which was the anteroom to the office of the chairman of the commission, and here he was definitively dumbfounded.

From behind the closed door of the office came a terrible voice, un-doubtedly belonging to Prokhor Petrovich, the chairman of the commission. 'Must be scolding somebody!' the consternated bookkeeper thought and, looking around, saw something else: in a leather armchair, her head thrown back, sobbing unrestrainedly, a wet handkerchief in her hand, legs stretched out into the middle of the room, lay Prokhor Petrovich's personal secretary – the beautiful Anna Richardovna.

Anna Richardovna's chin was all smeared with lipstick, and down her peachy cheeks black streams of sodden mascara flowed from her eyelashes.

Seeing someone come in, Anna Richardovna jumped up, rushed to the bookkeeper, clutched the lapels of his jacket, began shaking him and shouting:

'Thank God! At least one brave man has been found! Everybody ran away, everybody betrayed us! Let's go, let's go to him, I don't know what to do!' And, still sobbing, she dragged the bookkeeper into the office.

Once in the office, the bookkeeper first of all dropped his briefcase, and all the thoughts in his head turned upside-down. And, it must be said, not without reason.

At a huge writing desk with a massive inkstand an empty suit sat and with a dry pen, not dipped in ink, traced on a piece of paper. The suit was wearing a necktie, a fountain pen stuck from its pocket, but above the collar there was neither neck nor head, just as there were no hands sticking out of the sleeves. The suit was immersed in work and completely ignored the turmoil that reigned around it. Hearing someone come in, the suit leaned back and from above the collar came the voice, quite familiar to the bookkeeper, of Prokhor Petrovich:

'What is this? Isn't it written on the door that I'm not receiving?'

The beautiful secretary shrieked and, wringing her hands, cried out:

'You see? You see?! He's not there! He's not! Bring him back, bring him back!'

Here someone peeked in the door of the office, gasped, and flew out. The bookkeeper felt his legs trembling and sat on the edge of a chair, but did not forget to pick up his briefcase. Anna Richardovna hopped around the bookkeeper, worrying his jacket, and exclaiming:

'I always, always stopped him when he swore by the devil! So now the devil's got him!' Here the beauty ran to the writing desk and in a tender, musical voice, slightly nasal from weeping, called out:

'Prosha! Where are you!'

'Who here is "Prosha" to you?' the suit inquired haughtily, sinking still deeper into the armchair.

'He doesn't recognize me! Me he doesn't! Do you understand? . . .' the secretary burst into sobs.

'I ask you not to sob in the office!' the hot-tempered striped suit now said angrily, and with its sleeve it drew to itself a fresh stack of papers, with the obvious aim of appending its decision to them.

'No, I can't look at it, I can't!' cried Anna Richardovna, and she ran out to the secretary's room, and behind her, like a shot, flew the bookkeeper.

'Imagine, I'm sitting here,' Anna Richardovna recounted, shaking with agitation, again clutching at the bookkeeper's sleeve, 'and a cat walks in. Black, big as a behemoth. Of course, I shout "scat" to it. Out it goes, and in comes a fat fellow instead, also with a sort of cat-like mug, and says: "What are you doing, citizeness, shouting 'scat' at visitors?" And – whoosh – straight to Prokhor Petrovich. Of course, I run after him, shouting: "Are you out of your mind?" And this brazen-face goes straight to Prokhor Petrovich and sits down opposite him in the armchair. Well, that one . . . he's the kindest-hearted man, but edgy. He blew up, I don't deny it. An edgy man, works like an ox – he blew up. "Why do you barge in here unannounced?" he says. And that brazen-face, imagine, sprawls in the armchair and says, smiling: "I've come," he says, "to discuss a little business with you." Prokhor Petrovich blew up again: "I'm busy." And the other one, just think, answers: "You're not busy with anything . . ." Eh? Well, here, of course, Prokhor Petrovich's patience ran out, and he shouted: "What is all this? Get him out of here, devil take me!" And that one, imagine, smiles and says: "Devil take you? That, in fact, can be done!" And – bang! Before I had time to scream, I look: the one with the cat's mug is gone, and th . . . there . . . sits . . . the suit . . . Waaa! . . .' Stretching her mouth, which had lost all shape entirely, Anna Richardovna howled.

After choking with sobs, she caught her breath, but then began pouring out something completely incoherent:

'And it writes, writes, writes! You could lose your mind! Talks on the telephone! A suit! They all ran away like rabbits!'

The bookkeeper only stood and shook. But here fate came to his aid. Into the secretary's room, with calm, business-like strides, marched the police, to the number of two men. Seeing them, the beauty sobbed still harder, jabbing towards the door of the office with her hand.

'Let's not cry now, citizeness,' the first said calmly, and the bookkeeper, feeling himself quite superfluous there, ran out of the secretary's room and a minute later was already in the fresh air. There was some sort of draught in his head, a soughing as in a chimney, and through this soughing he heard scraps of the stories the ushers told about yesterday's cat, who had taken part in the séance. 'Oh-ho-ho! Might that not be our same little puss?'

Having got nowhere with the commission, the conscientious Vassily Stepanovich decided to visit its affiliate, located in Vagankovsky Lane, and to calm himself a little he walked the distance to the affiliate on foot.

The affiliate for city spectacles was housed in a peeling old mansion set back from the street, and was famous for the porphyry columns in its vestibule. But it was not the columns that struck visitors to the affiliate that day, but what was going on at the foot of them.

Several visitors stood in stupefaction and stared at a weeping girl sitting behind a small table on which lay special literature about various spectacles, which the girl sold. At that moment, the girl was not offering any of this literature to anyone, and only waved her hand at sympathetic inquiries, while at the same time, from above, from below, from the sides, and from all sections of the affiliate poured the ringing of at least twenty overwrought telephones.

After weeping for a while, the girl suddenly gave a start and cried out hysterically:

'Here it comes again!' and unexpectedly began singing in a tremulous soprano:

'Glorious sea, sacred Baikal . . .'[1]

A messenger appeared on the stairs, shook his fist at someone, and began singing along with the girl in a dull, weak-voiced baritone:

'Glorious boat, a barrel of cisco . . .'[2]

The messenger's voice was joined by distant voices, the choir began to swell, and finally the song resounded in all corners of the affiliate. In the neighbouring room no. 6, which housed the account comptroller's section, one powerful, slightly husky octave stood out particularly.

'Hey, Barguzin[3] . . . make the waves rise and fall! . . .' bawled the messenger on the stairs.

Tears flowed down the girl's face, she tried to clench her teeth, but her mouth opened of itself, as she sang an octave higher than the messenger:

'This young lad's ready to frisk-o!'

What struck the silent visitors to the affiliate was that the choristers, scattered in various places, sang quite harmoniously, as if the whole choir stood there with its eyes fixed on some invisible director.

Passers-by in Vagankovsky Lane stopped by the fence of the yard, wondering at the gaiety that reigned in the affiliate.

As soon as the first verse came to an end, the singing suddenly ceased, again as if to a director's baton. The messenger quietly swore and disappeared.

Here the front door opened, and in it appeared a citizen in a summer jacket, from under which protruded the skirts of a white coat, and with him a policeman.

'Take measures, doctor, I implore you!' the girl cried hysterically.

The secretary of the affiliate ran out to the stairs and, obviously burning with shame and embarrassment, began falteringly:

'You see, doctor, we have a case of some sort of mass hypnosis, and so it's necessary that . . .' He did not finish the sentence, began to choke on his words, and suddenly sang out in a tenor:

'Shilka and Nerchinsk . . .'[4]

'Fool!' the girl had time to shout, but, without explaining who she was abusing, produced instead a forced roulade and herself began singing about Shilka and Nerchinsk.

'Get hold of yourself! Stop singing!' the doctor addressed the secretary.

There was every indication that the secretary would himself have given anything to stop singing, but stop singing he could not, and together with the choir he brought to the hearing of passers-by in the lane the news that 'in the wilderness he was not touched by voracious beast, nor brought down by bullet of shooters.'

The moment the verse ended, the girl was the first to receive a dose of valerian from the doctor, who then ran after the secretary to give the others theirs.

'Excuse me, dear citizeness,' Vassily Stepanovich addressed the girl, 'did a black cat pay you a visit?'

'What cat?' the girl cried in anger. 'An ass, it's an ass we've got sitting in the affiliate!' And adding to that: 'Let him hear, I'll tell everything' – she indeed told what had happened.

It turned out that the manager of the city affiliate, 'who has made a perfect mess of lightened entertainment' (the girl's words), suffered from a mania for organizing all sorts of little clubs.

'Blew smoke in the authorities' eyes!' screamed the girl.

In the course of a year this manager had succeeded in organizing a club of Lermontov studies,[5] of chess and checkers, of ping-pong, and of horseback riding. For the summer, he was threatening to organize clubs of fresh-water canoeing and alpinism. And so today, during lunch-break, this manager comes in . . .

'. . . with some son of a bitch on his arm,' the girl went on, 'hailing from nobody knows where, in wretched checkered trousers, a cracked pince-nez, and . . . with a completely impossible mug! . . .'

And straight away, the girl said, he recommended him to all those eating in the affiliate's dining room as a prominent specialist in organizing choral-singing clubs.

The faces of the future alpinists darkened, but the manager immediately called on everyone to cheer up, while the specialist joked a little, laughed a little, and swore an oath that singing takes no time at all, but that, incidentally, there was a whole load of benefits to be derived from it.

Well, of course, as the girl said, the first to pop up were Fanov and Kosarchuk, well-known affiliate toadies, who announced that they would sign up. Here the rest of the staff realized that there was no way around the singing, and they, too, had to sign up for the club. They decided to sing during the lunch break, since the rest of the time was taken up by Lermontov and checkers. The manager, to set an example, declared that he was a tenor, and everything after that went as in a bad dream. The checkered specialist-choirmaster bawled out:

'Do, mi, sol, do!' – dragged the most bashful from behind the bookcases, where they had tried to save themselves from singing, told Kosarchuk he had perfect pitch, began whining, squealing, begging them to be kind to an old singing-master, tapped the tuning fork on his knuckle, beseeched them to strike up 'Glorious Sea'.

Strike up they did. And gloriously. The checkered one really knew his business. They finished the first verse. Here the director excused himself, said: 'Back in a minute . . .', and disappeared. They thought he would actually come back in a minute. But ten minutes went by and he was not there. The staff was overjoyed – he had run away!

Then suddenly, somehow of themselves, they began the second verse. They were all led by Kosarchuk, who may not have had perfect pitch, but did have a rather pleasant high tenor. They sang it through. No director! They moved to their places, but had not managed to sit down when, against their will, they began to sing. To stop was impossible. After three minutes of silence, they would strike up again. Silence – strike up! Then they realized that they were in trouble. The manager locked himself in his office from shame!

Here the girl's story was interrupted – the valerian had not done much good.

A quarter of an hour later, three trucks drove up to the fence in Vagankovsky, and the entire staff of the affiliate, the manager at its head, was loaded on to them.

As soon as the first truck, after lurching in the gateway, drove out into the lane, the staff members, who were standing on the platform holding each other's shoulders, opened their mouths, and the whole lane resounded with the popular song. The second truck picked it up, then the third. And so they drove on. Passers-by hurrying about their own business would cast only a fleeting glance at the trucks, not surprised in the least, thinking it was a group excursion to the country. And they were indeed going to the country, though not on an excursion, but to Professor Stravinsky's clinic.

Half an hour later, the bookkeeper, who had lost his head completely, reached the financial sector, hoping finally to get rid of the box-office money. Having learned from experience by now, he first peeked cautiously into the oblong hall where, behind frosted-glass windows with gold lettering, the staff was sitting. Here the bookkeeper discovered no signs of alarm or scandal. It was quiet, as it ought to be in a decent institution.

Vassily Stepanovich stuck his head through the window with 'Cash Deposits' written over it, greeted some unfamiliar clerk, and politely asked for a deposit slip.

'What do you need it for?' the clerk in the window asked.

The bookkeeper was amazed.

'I want to turn over some cash. I'm from the Variety.'

'One moment,' the clerk replied and instantly closed the opening in the window with a grille.

'Strange! . . .' thought the bookkeeper. His amazement was perfectly natural. It was the first time in his life that he had met with such a circumstance. Everybody knows how hard it is to get money; obstacles to it can always be found. But there had been no case in the book-keeper's thirty years of experience when anyone, either an official or a private person, had had a hard time accepting money.

But at last the little grille moved aside, and the bookkeeper again leaned to the window.

'Do you have a lot?' the clerk asked.

'Twenty-one thousand seven hundred and eleven roubles.'

'Oho!' the clerk answered ironically for some reason and handed the bookkeeper a green slip.

Knowing the form well, the bookkeeper instantly filled it out and began to untie the string on the bundle. When he unpacked his load, everything swam before his eyes, he murmured something painfully.

Foreign money flitted before his eyes: there were stacks of Canadian dollars, British pounds, Dutch guldens, Latvian lats, Estonian kroons . . .

'There he is, one of those tricksters from the Variety!' a menacing voice resounded over the dumbstruck bookkeeper. And straight away Vassily Stepanovich was arrested.

CHAPTER 18

Hapless Visitors

At the same time that the zealous bookkeeper was racing in a cab to his encounter with the self-writing suit, from first-class sleeping car no. 9 of the Kiev train, on its arrival in Moscow, there alighted, among others, a decent-looking passenger carrying a small fibreboard suitcase. This passenger was none other than the late Berlioz's uncle, Maximilian Andreevich Poplavsky, an industrial economist, who lived in Kiev on the former Institutsky Street. The reason for Maximilian Andreevich's coming to Moscow was a telegram received late in the evening two days before with the following content:

> Have just been run over by tram-car at Patriarch's Ponds
> funeral Friday three pm come. Berlioz.

Maximilian Andreevich was considered one of the most intelligent men in Kiev, and deservedly so. But even the most intelligent man might have been nonplussed by such a telegram. If someone sends a telegram saying he has been run over, it is clear that he has not died of it. But then, what was this about a funeral? Or was he in a bad way and foreseeing death? That was possible, but such precision was in the highest degree strange: how could he know he would be buried on Friday at three pm? An astonishing telegram!

However, intelligence is granted to intelligent people so as to sort out entangled affairs. Very simple. A mistake had been made, and the message had been distorted. The word 'have' had undoubtedly come there from some other telegram in place of the word 'Berlioz', which got moved and wound up at the end of the telegram. With such an emendation, the meaning of the telegram became clear, though, of course, tragic.

When the outburst of grief that struck Maximilian Andreevich's wife subsided, he at once started preparing to go to Moscow.

One secret about Maximilian Andreevich ought to be revealed. There is no arguing that he felt sorry for his wife's nephew, who had died in the bloom of life. But, of course, being a practical man, he realized that there was no special need for his presence at the funeral. And nevertheless Maximilian Andreevich was in great haste to go to Moscow. What was the point? The point was the apartment. An apartment in Moscow is a serious thing! For some unknown reason, Maximilian Andreevich did not like Kiev,[1] and the thought of moving to Moscow had been gnawing at him so much lately that he had even begun to sleep badly.

He did not rejoice in the spring flooding of the Dnieper, when, overflowing the islands by the lower bank, the water merged with the horizon. He did not rejoice in the staggeringly beautiful view which opened out from the foot of the monument to Prince Vladimir. He did not take delight in patches of sunlight playing in springtime on the brick paths of Vladimir's Hill. He wanted none of it, he wanted only one thing – to move to Moscow.

Advertising in the newspapers about exchanging an apartment on Institutsky Street in Kiev for smaller quarters in Moscow brought no results. No takers were found, or if they occasionally were, their offers were disingenuous.

The telegram staggered Maximilian Andreevich. This was a moment it would be sinful to let slip. Practical people know that such moments do not come twice.

In short, despite all obstacles, he had to succeed in inheriting his nephew's apartment on Sadovaya. Yes, it was difficult, very difficult, but these difficulties had to be overcome at whatever cost. The experienced Maximilian Andreevich knew that the first and necessary step towards that had to be the following: he must get himself registered, at least temporarily, as the tenant of his late nephew's three rooms.

On Friday afternoon, Maximilian Andreevich walked through the door of the room which housed the management of no. 302-bis on Sadovaya Street in Moscow.

In the narrow room, with an old poster hanging on the wall illustrating in several pictures the ways of resuscitating people who have drowned in the river, an unshaven, middle-aged man with anxious eyes sat in perfect solitude at a wooden table.

'May I see the chairman?' the industrial economist inquired politely, taking off his hat and putting his suitcase on a vacant chair.

This seemingly simple little question for some reason so upset the seated man that he even changed countenance. Looking sideways in anxiety, he muttered unintelligibly that the chairman was not there.

'Is he at home?' asked Poplavsky. 'I've come on the most urgent business.'

The seated man again replied quite incoherently, but all the same one could guess that the chairman was not at home.

'And when will he be here?'

The seated man made no reply to this and looked with a certain anguish out the window.

'Aha! . . .' the intelligent Poplavsky said to himself and inquired about the secretary.

The strange man at the table even turned purple with strain and said, again unintelligibly, that the secretary was not there either . . . he did not know when he would be back, and . . . that the secretary was sick . . .

'Aha! . . .' Poplavsky said to himself. 'But surely there's somebody in the management?'

'Me,' the man responded in a weak voice.

'You see,' Poplavsky began to speak imposingly, 'I am the sole heir of the late Berlioz, my nephew, who, as you know, died at the Patriarch's Ponds, and I am obliged, in accordance with the law, to take over the inheritance contained in our apartment no. 50 . . .'

'I'm not informed, comrade . . .' the man interrupted in anguish.

'But, excuse me,' Poplavsky said in a sonorous voice, 'you are a member of the management and are obliged . . .'

And here some citizen entered the room. At the sight of the entering man, the man seated at the table turned pale.

'Management member Pyatnazhko?' the entering man asked the seated man.

'Yes,' the latter said, barely audibly.

The entering one whispered something to the seated one, and he, thoroughly upset, rose from his chair, and a few seconds later Poplavsky found himself alone in the empty management room.

'Eh, what a complication! As if on purpose, all of them at once . . .' Poplavsky thought in vexation, crossing the asphalt courtyard and hurrying to apartment no. 50.

As soon as the industrial economist rang, the door was opened, and Maximilian Andreevich entered the semi-dark front hall. It was a somewhat surprising circumstance that he could not figure out who had let him in: there was no one in the front hall except an enormous black cat sitting on a chair.

Maximilian Andreevich coughed, stamped his feet, and then the door of the study opened and Koroviev came out to the front hall. Maximilian Andreevich bowed politely, but with dignity, and said:

'My name is Poplavsky. I am the uncle . . .'

But before he could finish, Koroviev snatched a dirty handkerchief from his pocket, buried his nose in it, and began to weep.

'. . . of the late Berlioz . . .'

'Of course, of course!' Koroviev interrupted, taking his handkerchief away from his face. 'Just one look and I knew it was you!' Here he was shaken with tears and began to exclaim: 'Such a calamity, eh? What's going on here, eh?'

'Run over by a tram-car?' Poplavsky asked in a whisper.

'Clean!' cried Koroviev, and tears flowed in streams from under his pince-nez. 'Run clean over! I was a witness. Believe me – bang! and the head's gone! Crunch – there goes the right leg! Crunch – there goes the left leg! That's what these trams have brought us to!' And, obviously unable to control himself, Koroviev pecked the wall beside the mirror with his nose and began to shake with sobs.

Berlioz's uncle was genuinely struck by the stranger's behaviour. 'And they say there are no warm-hearted people in our time!' he thought, feeling his own eyes beginning to itch. However, at the same time, an unpleasant little cloud came over his soul, and straight away the snake-like thought flashed in him that this warm-hearted man might perchance have registered himself in the deceased man's apartment, for such examples have been known in this life.

'Forgive me, were you a friend of my late Misha?' he asked, wiping his dry left eye with his sleeve, and with his right eye studying the racked-with-grief Koroviev. But the man was sobbing so much that one could understand nothing except the repeated word 'crunch!' Having sobbed his fill, Koroviev finally unglued himself from the wall and said:

'No, I can't take any more! I'll go and swallow three hundred drops of tincture of valerian . . .' And turning his completely tear-bathed face to Poplavsky, he added: 'That's trams for you!'

'Pardon me, but did you send me the telegram?' Maximilian

Andreevich asked, painfully puzzling over who this astonishing cry-baby might be.

'He did!' replied Koroviev, and he pointed his finger at the cat.

Poplavsky goggled his eyes, assuming he had not heard right.

'No, it's too much, I just can't,' Koroviev went on, snuffing his nose, 'when I remember: the wheel over the leg ... the wheel alone weighs three hundred pounds ... Crunch! ... I'll go to bed, forget myself in sleep.' And here he disappeared from the hall.

The cat then stirred, jumped off the chair, stood on his hind legs, front legs akimbo, opened his maw and said:

'Well, so I sent the telegram. What of it?'

Maximilian Andreevich's head at once began to spin, his arms and legs went numb, he dropped the suitcase and sat down on a chair facing the cat.

'I believe I asked in good Russian?' the cat said sternly. 'What of it?'

But Poplavsky made no reply.

'Passport!'[2] barked the cat, holding out a plump paw.

Understanding nothing and seeing nothing except the two sparks burning in the cat's eyes, Poplavsky snatched the passport from his pocket like a dagger. The cat picked up a pair of glasses in thick black frames from the pier-glass table, put them on his muzzle, thus acquiring a still more imposing air, and took the passport from Poplavsky's twitching hand.

'I wonder, am I going to faint or not? ...' thought Poplavsky. From far away came Koroviev's snivelling, the whole front hall filled with the smell of ether, valerian and some other nauseating vileness.

'What office issued this document?' the cat asked, peering at the page. No answer came.

'The 412th,' the cat said to himself, tracing with his paw on the passport, which he was holding upside down. 'Ah, yes, of course! I know that office, they issue passports to anybody. Whereas I, for instance, wouldn't issue one to the likes of you! Not on your life I wouldn't! I'd just take one look at your face and instantly refuse!' The cat got so angry that he flung the passport on the floor. 'Your presence at the funeral is cancelled,' the cat continued in an official voice. 'Kindly return to your place of residence.' And he barked through the door: 'Azazello!'

At his call a small man ran out to the front hall, limping, sheathed in black tights, with a knife tucked into his leather belt, red-haired, with a yellow fang and with albugo in his left eye.

Poplavsky felt he could not get enough air, rose from his seat and backed away, clutching his heart.

'See him off, Azazello!' the cat ordered and left the hall.

'Poplavsky,' the other twanged softly, 'I hope everything's understood now?'

Poplavsky nodded.

'Return immediately to Kiev,' Azazello went on. 'Sit there stiller than water, lower than grass, and don't dream of any apartments in Moscow. Clear?'

This small man, who drove Poplavsky to mortal terror with his fang, knife and blind eye, only came up to the economist's shoulder, but his actions were energetic, precise and efficient.

First of all, he picked up the passport and handed it to Maximilian Andreevich, and the latter took the booklet with a dead hand. Then the one named Azazello picked up the suitcase with one hand, with the other flung open the door, and, taking Berlioz's uncle under the arm, led him out to the landing of the stairway. Poplavsky leaned against the wall. Without any key, Azazello opened the suitcase, took out of it a huge roast chicken with a missing leg wrapped in greasy newspaper, and placed it on the landing. Then he took out two pairs of underwear, a razor-strop, some book and a case, and shoved it all down the stairwell with his foot, except for the chicken. The emptied suitcase went the same way. There came a crash from below and, judging by the sound of it, the lid broke off.

Then the red-haired bandit grabbed the chicken by the leg, and with this whole chicken hit Poplavsky on the neck, flat, hard, and so terribly that the body of the chicken tore off and the leg remained in Azazello's hand. 'Everything was confusion in the Oblonskys' home,'[3] as the famous writer Leo Tolstoy correctly put it. Precisely so he might have said on this occasion. Yes, everything was confusion in Poplavsky's eyes. A long spark flew before his eyes, then gave place to some funereal snake that momentarily extinguished the May day, and Poplavsky went hurtling down the stairs, clutching his passport in his hand.

Reaching the turn, he smashed the window on the landing with his foot and sat on a step. The legless chicken went bouncing past him and fell down the stairwell. Azazello, who stayed upstairs, instantly gnawed the chicken leg clean, stuck the bone into the side pocket of his tights, went back to the apartment, and shut the door behind him with a bang.

At that moment there began to be heard from below the cautious steps of someone coming up.

Having run down one more flight of stairs, Poplavsky sat on a wooden bench on the landing and caught his breath.

Some tiny elderly man with an extraordinarily melancholy face, in an old-fashioned tussore silk suit and a hard straw hat with a green band, on his way upstairs, stopped beside Poplavsky.

'May I ask you, citizen,' the man in tussore silk asked sadly, 'where apartment no. 50 is?'

'Further up,' Poplavsky replied curtly.

'I humbly thank you, citizen,' the little man said with the same sadness and went on up, while Poplavsky got to his feet and ran down.

The question arises whether it might have been the police that Maximilian Andreevich was hastening to, to complain about the bandits who had perpetrated savage violence upon him in broad daylight? No, by no means, that can be said with certainty. To go into a police station and tell them, look here, just now a cat in eyeglasses read my passport, and then a man in tights, with a knife ... no, citizens, Maximilian Andreevich was indeed an intelligent man.

He was already downstairs and saw just by the exit a door leading to some closet. The glass in the door was broken. Poplavsky hid his passport in his pocket and looked around, hoping to see his thrown-down belongings. But there was no trace of them. Poplavsky was even surprised himself at how little this upset him. He was occupied with another interesting and tempting thought: of testing the accursed apartment one more time on this little man. In fact, since he had inquired after its whereabouts, it meant he was going there for the first time. Therefore he was presently heading straight into the clutches of the company that had ensconced itself in apartment no. 50. Something told Poplavsky that the little man would be leaving this apartment very soon. Maximilian Andreevich was, of course, no longer going to any funeral of any nephew, and there was plenty of time before the train to Kiev. The economist looked around and ducked into the closet.

At that moment way upstairs a door banged. 'That's him going in . . .'

Poplavsky thought, his heart skipping a beat. The closet was cool, it smelled of mice and boots. Maximilian Andreevich settled on some stump of wood and decided to wait. The position was convenient, from the closet one looked directly on to the exit from the sixth stairway.

However, the man from Kiev had to wait longer than he supposed. The stairway was for some reason deserted all the while. One could hear well, and finally a door banged on the fifth floor. Poplavsky froze. Yes, those were his little steps. 'He's coming down . . .' A door one flight lower opened. The little steps ceased. A woman's voice. The voice of the sad man – yes, it's his voice . . . Saying something like 'leave me alone, for Christ's sake . . .' Poplavsky's ear stuck through the broken glass. This ear caught a woman's laughter. Quick and brisk steps coming down. And now a woman's back flashed by. This woman, carrying a green oilcloth bag, went out through the front hall to the courtyard. And the little man's steps came anew. 'Strange! He's going back up to the apartment! Does it mean he's part of the gang himself? Yes, he's going back. They've opened the door again upstairs. Well, then, let's wait a little longer . . .'

This time he did not have to wait long. The sound of the door. The little steps. The little steps cease. A desperate cry. A cat's miaowing. The little steps, quick, rapid, down, down, down!

Poplavsky had not waited in vain. Crossing himself and muttering something, the melancholy little man rushed past him, hatless, with a completely crazed face, his bald head all scratched and his trousers completely wet. He began tearing at the handle of the front door, unable in his fear to determine whether it opened out or in, managed at last, and flew out into the sun in the courtyard.

The testing of the apartment had been performed. Thinking no more either of the deceased nephew or of the apartment, shuddering at the thought of the risk he had been running, Maximilian Andreevich, whispering only the three words 'It's all clear, it's all clear!', ran out to the courtyard. A few minutes later the bus was carrying the industrial economist in the direction of the Kiev station.

As for the tiny little man, a most unpleasant story had gone on with him while the economist was sitting in the closet downstairs. The little man was barman at the Variety, and was called Andrei Fokich Sokov. While the investigation was going on in the Variety, Andrei Fokich kept himself apart from all that was happening, and only one thing could be noticed, that he became still sadder than he generally was, and, besides, that he inquired of the messenger Karpov where the visiting magician was staying.

And so, after parting with the economist on the landing, the barman went up to the fifth floor and rang at apartment no. 50.

The door was opened for him immediately, but the barman gave a start, backed away, and did not enter at once. This was understandable. The door had been opened by a girl who was wearing nothing but a coquettish little lacy apron and a white fichu on her head. On her feet, however, she had golden slippers. The girl was distinguished by an irreproachable figure, and the only thing that might have been considered a defect in her appearance was the purple scar on her neck.

'Well, come in then, since you rang,' said the girl, fixing her lewd green eyes on the barman.

Andrei Fokich gasped, blinked his eyes, and stepped into the front hall, taking off his hat. Just then the telephone in the front hall rang. The shameless maid put one foot on a chair, picked up the receiver, and into it said:

'Hello!'

The barman, not knowing where to look, stood shifting from one foot to the other, thinking: 'Some maid this foreigner's got! Pah, nasty thing!' And to save himself from the nasty thing, he began casting sidelong glances around him.

The whole big and semi-dark hall was cluttered with unusual objects and clothing. Thus, thrown over the back of a chair was a funereal cloak lined with fiery cloth, on the pier-glass table lay a long sword with a gleaming gold hilt. Three swords with silver hilts stood in the corner like mere umbrellas or canes. And on the stag-horns hung berets with eagle feathers.

'Yes,' the maid was saying into the telephone. 'How's that? Baron Meigel? I'm listening. Yes. Mister artiste is at home today. Yes, he'll be glad to see you. Yes, guests ... A tailcoat or a black suit. What? By twelve midnight.' Having finished the conversation, the maid hung up the receiver and turned to the barman: 'What would you like?'

'I must see the citizen artiste.'

'What? You mean him himself?'

'Himself,' the barman replied sorrowfully.

'I'll ask,' the maid said with visible hesitation and, opening the door to the late Berlioz's study, announced: 'Knight, there's a little man here who says he must see Messire.'

'Let him come in,' Koroviev's cracked voice came from the study.

'Go into the living room,' the girl said as simply as if she were dressed like anyone else, opened the door to the living room, and herself left the hall.

Going in where he was invited, the barman even forgot his business, so greatly was he struck by the decor of the room. Through the stained glass of the big windows (a fantasy of the jeweller's utterly vanished wife) poured an unusual, church-like light. Logs were blazing in the huge antique fireplace, despite the hot spring day. And yet it was not the least bit hot in the room, and even quite the contrary, on entering one was enveloped in some sort of dankness as in a cellar. On a tiger skin in front of the fireplace sat a huge black tom-cat, squinting good-naturedly at the fire. There was a table at the sight of which the God-fearing barman gave a start: the table was covered with church brocade. On the brocade tablecloth stood a host of bottles – round-bellied, mouldy and dusty. Among the bottles gleamed a dish, and it was obvious at once that it was of pure gold. At the fireplace a small red-haired fellow with a knife in his belt was roasting pieces of meat on a long steel sword, and the juice dripped into the fire, and the smoke went up the flue. There was a smell not only of roasting meat, but also of some very strong perfume and incense, and it flashed in the barman's mind, for he already knew of Berlioz's death and his place of residence from the newspapers, that this might, for all he knew, be a church panikhida[4] that was being served for Berlioz, which thought, however, he drove away at once as a priori absurd.

The astounded barman unexpectedly heard a heavy bass:

'Well, sir, what can I do for you?'

And here the barman discovered in the shadows the one he wanted.

The black magician was sprawled on some boundless sofa, low, with pillows scattered over it. As it seemed to the barman, the artiste was wearing only black underwear and black pointed shoes.

'I,' the barman began bitterly, 'am the manager of the buffet at the Variety Theatre . . .'

The artiste stretched out his hand, stones flashing on its fingers, as if stopping the barman's mouth, and spoke with great ardour:

'No, no, no! Not a word more! Never and by no means! Nothing from your buffet will ever pass my lips! I, my esteemed sir, walked past your stand yesterday, and even now I am unable to forget either the sturgeon or the feta cheese! My precious man! Feta cheese is never green in colour, someone has tricked you. It ought to be white. Yes, and the tea? It's simply swill! I saw with my own eyes some slovenly girl add tap water from a bucket to your huge samovar, while the tea went on being served. No, my dear, it's impossible!'

'I beg your pardon,' said Andrei Fokich, astounded by this sudden attack, 'but I've come about something else, and sturgeon has nothing to do with it . . .'

'How do you mean, nothing to do with it, when it's spoiled!'

'They supplied sturgeon of the second freshness,' the barman said.

'My dear heart, that is nonsense!'

'What is nonsense?'

'Second freshness – that's what is nonsense! There is only one freshness – the first – and it is also the last. And if sturgeon is of the second freshness, that means it is simply rotten.'

'I beg your pardon . . .' the barman again tried to begin, not knowing how to shake off the cavilling artiste.

'I cannot pardon you,' the other said firmly.

'I have come about something else,' the barman said, getting quite upset.

'About something else?' the foreign magician was surprised. 'And what else could have brought you to me? Unless memory deceives me, among people of a profession similar to yours, I have had dealings with only one sutler-woman, but that was long ago, when you were not yet in this world. However, I'm glad. Azazello! A tabouret for mister buffet-manager!'

The one who was roasting meat turned, horrifying the barman with his fangs, and deftly offered him one of the dark oaken tabourets. There were no other seats in the room.

The barman managed to say:

'I humbly thank you,' and lowered himself on to the stool. Its back leg broke at once with a crack, and the barman, gasping, struck his backside most painfully on the floor. As he fell, he kicked another stool in front of him with his foot, and from it spilled a full cup of red wine on his trousers.

The artiste exclaimed:

'Oh! Are you hurt?'

Azazello helped the barman up and gave him another seat. In a voice filled with grief, the barman declined his host's suggestion that he take off his trousers and dry them before the fire, and, feeling unbearably uncomfortable in his wet underwear and clothing, cautiously sat down on the other stool.

'I like sitting low down,' the artiste said, 'it's less dangerous falling from a low height. Ah, yes, so we left off at the sturgeon. Freshness, dear heart, freshness, freshness! That should be the motto of every barman. Here, wouldn't you like to try . . .'

In the crimson light of the fireplace a sword flashed in front of the barman, and Azazello laid a sizzling piece of meat on the golden dish, squeezed lemon juice over it, and handed the barman a golden two-pronged fork.

'My humble . . . I . . .'

'No, no, try it!'

The barman put a piece into his mouth out of politeness, and understood at once that he was chewing something very fresh indeed, and, above all, extraordinarily delicious. But as he was chewing the fragrant, juicy meat, the barman nearly choked and fell a second time. From the neighbouring room a big, dark bird flew in and gently brushed the barman's bald head with its wing. Alighting on the mantelpiece beside the clock, the bird turned out to be an owl. 'Oh, Lord God! . . .' thought Andrei Fokich, nervous like all barmen. 'A nice little apartment! . . .'

'A cup of wine? White, red? What country's wine do you prefer at this time of day?'

'My humble . . . I don't drink . . .'

'A shame! What about a game of dice, then? Or do you have some other favourite game? Dominoes? Cards?'

'I don't play games,' the already weary barman responded.

'Altogether bad,' the host concluded. 'As you will, but there's something not nice hidden in men who avoid wine, games, the society of charming women, table talk. Such people are either gravely ill or secretly hate everybody around them. True, there may be exceptions. Among persons sitting down with me at the banqueting table, there have been on occasion some extraordinary scoundrels! . . . And so, let me hear your business.'

'Yesterday you were so good as to do some conjuring tricks . . .'

'I?' the magician exclaimed in amazement. 'Good gracious, it's somehow even unbecoming to me!'

'I'm sorry,' said the barman, taken aback. 'I mean the séance of black magic . . .'

'Ah, yes, yes, yes! My dear, I'll reveal a secret to you. I'm not an artiste at all, I simply wanted to see the Muscovites *en masse*, and that could be done most conveniently in a theatre. And so my retinue,' he nodded in the direction of the cat, 'arranged for this séance, and I merely sat and looked at the Muscovites. Now, don't go changing countenance, but tell me, what is it in connection with this séance that has brought you to me?'

'If you please, you see, among other things there were banknotes flying down from the ceiling . . .' The barman lowered his voice and looked around abashedly. 'So they snatched them all up. And then a young man comes to my bar and gives me a ten-rouble bill, I give him eight-fifty in change . . . Then another one . . .'

'Also a young man?'

'No, an older one. Then a third, and a fourth . . . I keep giving them change. And today I went to check the cash box, and there, instead of money – cut-up paper. They hit the buffet for a hundred and nine roubles.'

'Ai-yai-yai!' the artiste exclaimed. 'But can they have thought those were real bills? I can't admit the idea that they did it knowingly.'

The barman took a somehow hunched and anguished look around him, but said nothing.

'Can they be crooks?' the magician asked worriedly of his visitor. 'Can there be crooks among the Muscovites?'

The barman smiled so bitterly in response that all doubts fell away: yes, there were crooks among the Muscovites.

'That is mean!' Woland was indignant. 'You're a poor man . . . You are a poor man?'

The barman drew his head down between his shoulders, making it evident that he was a poor man.

'How much have you got in savings?'

The question was asked in a sympathetic tone, but even so such a question could not but be acknowledged as indelicate. The barman faltered.

'Two hundred and forty-nine thousand roubles in five savings banks,' a cracked voice responded from the neighbouring room, 'and two hundred ten-rouble gold pieces at home under the floor.'

The barman became as if welded to his tabouret.

'Well, of course, that's not a great sum,' Woland said condescendingly to his visitor, 'though, as a matter of fact, you have no need of it anyway. When are you going to die?'

Here the barman became indignant.

'Nobody knows that and it's nobody's concern,' he replied.

'Sure nobody knows,' the same trashy voice came from the study. 'The binomial theorem, you might think! He's going to die in nine months, next February, of liver cancer, in the clinic of the First Moscow State University, in ward number four.'

The barman's face turned yellow.

'Nine months . . .' Woland calculated pensively. 'Two hundred and forty-nine thousand . . . rounding it off that comes to twenty-seven thousand a month . . . Not a lot, but enough for a modest life . . . Plus those gold pieces . . .'

'He won't get to realize the gold pieces,' the same voice mixed in, turning the barman's heart to ice. 'On Andrei Fokich's demise, the house will immediately be torn down, and the gold will be sent to the State Bank.'

'And I wouldn't advise you to go to the clinic,' the artiste went on. 'What's the sense of dying in a ward to the groans and wheezes of the hopelessly ill? Isn't it better to give a banquet on the twenty-seven thousand, then take poison and move on to the other world to the sounds of strings, surrounded by drunken beauties and dashing friends?'

The barman sat motionless and grew very old. Dark rings surrounded his eyes, his cheeks sagged, and his lower jaw hung down.

'However, we've started day-dreaming,' exclaimed the host. 'To business! Show me your cut-up paper.'

The barman, agitated, pulled a package from his pocket, unwrapped it, and was dumbfounded: the piece of paper contained ten-rouble bills.

'My dear, you really are unwell,' Woland said, shrugging his shoulders.

The barman, grinning wildly, got up from the tabouret.

'A-and . . .' he said, stammering, 'and if they . . . again . . . that is . . .'

'Hm . . .' the artiste pondered, 'well, then come to us again. You're always welcome. I'm glad of our acquaintance . . .'

Straight away Koroviev came bounding from the study, clutched the barman's hand, and began shaking it, begging Andrei Fokich to give his regards to everybody, everybody. Not thinking very well, the barman started for the front hall.

'Hella, see him out!' Koroviev shouted.

Again that naked redhead in the front hall! The barman squeezed through the door, squeaked 'Goodbye!', and went off like a drunk man. Having gone down a little way, he stopped, sat on a step, took out the packet and checked – the ten-rouble bills were in place.

Here a woman with a green bag came out of the apartment on that landing. Seeing a man sitting on a step and staring dully at some money, she smiled and said pensively:

'What a house we've got ... Here's this one drunk in the morning ... And the window on the stairway is broken again!'

Peering more attentively at the barman, she added:

'And you, citizen, are simply rolling in money! ... Give some to me, eh?'

'Let me alone, for Christ's sake!' the barman got frightened and quickly hid the money.

The woman laughed.

'To the hairy devil with you, skinflint! I was joking...' And she went downstairs.

The barman slowly got up, raised his hand to straighten his hat, and realized that it was not on his head. He was terribly reluctant to go back, but he was sorry about the hat. After some hesitation, he nevertheless went back and rang.

'What else do you want?' the accursed Hella asked him.

'I forgot my hat...' the barman whispered, pointing to his bald head. Hella turned around. The barman spat mentally and closed his eyes. When he opened them, Hella was holding out his hat to him and a sword with a dark hilt.

'Not mine...' the barman whispered, pushing the sword away and quickly putting on his hat.

'You came without a sword?' Hella was surprised.

The barman growled something and quickly went downstairs. His head for some reason felt uncomfortable and too warm in the hat. He took it off and, jumping from fear, cried out softly: in his hands was a velvet beret with a dishevelled cock's feather. The barman crossed himself. At the same moment, the beret miaowed, turned into a black kitten and, springing back on to Andrei Fokich's head, sank all its claws into his bald spot. Letting out a cry of despair, the barman dashed downstairs, and the kitten fell off and spurted back up the stairway.

Bursting outside, the barman trotted to the gates and left the devilish no. 302-bis for ever.

What happened to him afterwards is known perfectly well. Running out the gateway, the barman looked around wildly, as if searching for something. A minute later he was on the other side of the street in a pharmacy. He had no sooner uttered the words:

'Tell me, please . . .' when the woman behind the counter exclaimed:

'Citizen, your head is cut all over!'

Some five minutes later the barman was bandaged with gauze, knew that the best specialists in liver diseases were considered to be professors Bernadsky and Kuzmin, asked who was closer, lit up with joy on learning that Kuzmin lived literally across the courtyard in a small white house, and some two minutes later was in that house.

The premises were antiquated but very, very cosy. The barman remembered that the first one he happened to meet was an old nurse who wanted to take his hat, but as he turned out to have no hat, the nurse went off somewhere, munching with an empty mouth.

Instead of her, there turned up near the mirror and under what seemed some sort of arch, a middle-aged woman who said straight away that it was possible to make an appointment only for the nineteenth, not before. The barman at once grasped what would save him. Peering with fading eyes through the arch, where three persons were waiting in what was obviously some sort of anteroom, he whispered:

'Mortally ill . . .'

The woman looked in perplexity at the barman's bandaged head, hesitated, and said:

'Well, then . . .' and allowed the barman through the archway.

At that same moment the opposite door opened, there was the flash of a gold pince-nez. The woman in the white coat said:

'Citizens, this patient will go out of turn.'

And before the barman could look around him, he was in Professor Kuzmin's office. There was nothing terrible, solemn or medical in this oblong room.

'What's wrong with you?' Professor Kuzmin asked in a pleasant voice, and glanced with some alarm at the bandaged head.

'I've just learned from reliable hands,' the barman replied, casting wild glances at some group photograph under glass, 'that I'm going to die of liver cancer in February of this coming year. I beg you to stop it.'

Professor Kuzmin, as he sat there, threw himself against the high Gothic leather back of his chair.

'Excuse me, I don't understand you ... you've, what, been to the doctor? Why is your head bandaged?'

'Some doctor! ... You should've seen this doctor ...' the barman replied, and his teeth suddenly began to chatter. 'And don't pay any attention to the head, it has no connection ... Spit on the head, it has nothing to do with it ... Liver cancer, I beg you to stop it! ...'

'Pardon me, but who told you?!'

'Believe him!' the barman ardently entreated. 'He knows!'

'I don't understand a thing!' the professor said, shrugging his shoulders and pushing his chair back from the desk. 'How can he know when you're going to die? The more so as he's not a doctor!'

'In ward four of the clinic of the First MSU,' replied the barman.

Here the professor looked at his patient, at his head, at his damp trousers, and thought: 'Just what I needed, a madman ...' He asked:

'Do you drink vodka?'

'Never touch it,' the barman answered.

A moment later he was undressed, lying on the cold oilcloth of the couch, and the professor was kneading his stomach. Here, it must be said, the barman cheered up considerably. The professor categorically maintained that presently, at least for the given moment, the barman had no symptoms of cancer, but since it was so ... since he was afraid and had been frightened by some charlatan, he must perform all the tests ...

The professor was scribbling away on some sheets of paper, explaining where to go, what to bring. Besides that, he gave him a note for Professor Bouret, a neurologist, telling the barman that his nerves were in complete disorder.

'How much do I owe you, Professor?' the barman asked in a tender and trembling voice, pulling out a fat wallet.

'As much as you like,' the professor said curtly and drily.

The barman took out thirty roubles and placed them on the table, and then, with an unexpected softness, as if operating with a cat's paw, he placed on top of the bills a clinking stack wrapped in newspaper.

'And what is this?' Kuzmin asked, twirling his moustache.

'Don't scorn it, citizen Professor,' the barman whispered. 'I beg you – stop the cancer!'

'Take away your gold this minute,' said the professor, proud of himself. 'You'd better look after your nerves. Tomorrow have your urine analysed, don't drink a lot of tea, and don't put any salt in your food.'

'Not even in soup?' the barman asked.

'Not in anything,' ordered Kuzmin.

'Ahh! . . .' the barman exclaimed wistfully, gazing at the professor with tenderness, gathering up his gold pieces and backing towards the door.

That evening the professor had few patients, and as twilight approached the last one left. Taking off his white coat, the professor glanced at the spot where the barman had left his money and saw no banknotes there but only three labels from bottles of Abrau-Durso wine.

'Devil knows what's going on!' Kuzmin muttered, trailing the flap of his coat on the floor and feeling the labels. 'It turns out he's not only a schizophrenic but also a crook! But I can't understand what he needed me for! Could it be the prescription for the urine analysis? Oh-oh! . . . He's stolen my overcoat!' And the professor rushed for the front hall, one arm still in the sleeve of his white coat. 'Xenia Nikitishna!' he cried shrilly through the door to the front hall. 'Look and see if all the coats are there!'

The coats all turned out to be there. But instead, when the professor went back to his desk, having peeled off his white coat at last, he stopped as if rooted to the parquet beside his desk, his eyes riveted to it. In the place where the labels had been there sat an orphaned black kitten with a sorry little muzzle, miaowing over a saucer of milk.

'Wh-what's this, may I ask?! Now this is . . .' And Kuzmin felt the nape of his neck go cold.

At the professor's quiet and pitiful cry, Xenia Nikitishna came running and at once reassured him completely, saying that it was, of course, one of the patients who had abandoned the kitten, as happens not infrequently to professors.

'They probably have a poor life,' Xenia Nikitishna explained, 'well, and we, of course ...'

They started thinking and guessing who might have abandoned it. Suspicion fell on a little old lady with a stomach ulcer.

'It's she, of course,' Xenia Nikitishna said. 'She thinks: "I'll die anyway, and it's a pity for the kitten."'

'But excuse me!' cried Kuzmin. 'What about the milk? ... Did she bring that, too? And the saucer, eh?'

'She brought it in a little bottle, and poured it into the saucer here,' Xenia Nikitishna explained.

'In any case, take both the kitten and the saucer away,' said Kuzmin, and he accompanied Xenia Nikitishna to the door himself. When he came back, the situation had altered.

As he was hanging his coat on a nail, the professor heard guffawing in the courtyard. He glanced out and, naturally, was struck dumb. A lady was running across the yard to the opposite wing in nothing but a shift. The professor even knew her name – Marya Alexandrovna. The guffawing came from a young boy.

'What's this?' Kuzmin said contemptuously.

Just then, behind the wall, in the professor's daughter's room, a gramophone began to play the foxtrot 'Hallelujah,' and at the same moment a sparrow's chirping came from behind the professor's back. He turned around and saw a large sparrow hopping on his desk.

'Hm ... keep calm!' the professor thought. 'It flew in as I left the window. Everything's in order!' the professor told himself, feeling that everything was in complete disorder, and that, of course, owing chiefly to the sparrow. Taking a closer look at him, the professor became convinced at once that this was no ordinary sparrow. The obnoxious little sparrow dipped on its left leg, obviously clowning, dragging it, working it in syncopation – in short, it was dancing the foxtrot to the sounds of the gramophone, like a drunkard in a bar, saucy as could be, casting impudent glances at the professor.

Kuzmin's hand fell on the telephone, and he decided to call his old schoolmate Bouret, to ask what such little sparrows might mean at the age of sixty, especially when one's head suddenly starts spinning?

The sparrow meanwhile sat on the presentation inkstand, shat in it

(I'm not joking!), then flew up, hung in the air, and, swinging a steely beak, pecked at the glass covering the photograph portraying the entire university graduating class of '94, broke the glass to smithereens, and only then flew out the window.

The professor dialled again, and instead of calling Bouret, called a leech bureau,[5] said he was Professor Kuzmin, and asked them to send some leeches to his house at once. Hanging up the receiver, the professor turned to his desk again and straight away let out a scream. At this desk sat a woman in a nurse's headscarf, holding a handbag with the word 'Leeches' written on it. The professor screamed as he looked at her mouth: it was a man's mouth, crooked, stretching from ear to ear, with a single fang. The nurse's eyes were dead.

'This bit of cash I'll just pocket,' the nurse said in a male basso, 'no point in letting it lie about here.' She raked up the labels with a bird's claw and began melting into air.

Two hours passed. Professor Kuzmin sat in his bedroom on the bed, with leeches hanging from his temples, behind his ears, and on his neck. At Kuzmin's feet, on a quilted silk blanket, sat the grey-moustached Professor Bouret, looking at Kuzmin with condolence and comforting him, saying it was all nonsense. Outside the window it was already night.

What other prodigies occurred in Moscow that night we do not know and certainly will not try to find out – especially as it has come time for us to go on to the second part of this truthful narrative. Follow me, reader!

BOOK TWO

CHAPTER 19

Margarita

Follow me, reader! Who told you that there is no true, faithful, eternal love in this world! May the liar's vile tongue be cut out!

Follow me, my reader, and me alone, and I will show you such a love!

No! The master was mistaken when with bitterness he told Ivanushka in the hospital, at that hour when the night was falling past midnight, that she had forgotten him. That could not be. She had, of course, not forgotten him.

First of all let us reveal the secret which the master did not wish to reveal to Ivanushka. His beloved's name was Margarita[1] Nikolaevna. Everything the master told the poor poet about her was the exact truth. He described his beloved correctly. She was beautiful and intelligent. To that one more thing must be added: it can be said with certainty that many women would have given anything to exchange their lives for the life of Margarita Nikolaevna. The childless thirty-year-old Margarita was the wife of a very prominent specialist, who, moreover, had made a very important discovery of state significance. Her husband was young, handsome, kind, honest, and adored his wife. The two of them, Margarita and her husband, occupied the entire top floor of a magnificent house in a garden on one of the lanes near the Arbat. A charming place! Anyone can be convinced of it who wishes to visit this garden. Let them inquire of me, and I will give them the address, show them the way – the house stands untouched to this day.

Margarita Nikolaevna was not in need of money. Margarita Nikolaevna could buy whatever she liked. Among her husband's acquaintances there were some interesting people. Margarita Nikolaevna had never touched a primus stove. Margarita Nikolaevna knew nothing of the horrors of life in a communal apartment. In short . . . she was happy? Not for one minute! Never, since the age of nineteen, when she had married and wound up in this house, had she known any happiness. Gods, my gods! What, then, did this woman need?! What did this woman need, in whose eyes there always burned some enigmatic little fire? What did she need, this witch with a slight cast in one eye, who had adorned herself with mimosa that time in the spring? I do not know. I have no idea. Obviously she was telling the truth, she needed him, the master, and not at all some Gothic mansion, not a private garden, not money. She loved him, she was telling the truth.

Even I, the truthful narrator, though an outsider, feel my heart wrung at the thought of what Margarita endured when she came to the master's little house the next day (fortunately before she had time to talk with her husband, who had not come back at the appointed time) and discovered that the master was no longer there. She did everything to find out something about him, and, of course, found out nothing. Then she went back to her house and began living in her former place.

But as soon as the dirty snow disappeared from the sidewalks and streets, as soon as the slightly rotten, disquieting spring breeze wafted through the window, Margarita Nikolaevna began to grieve more than in winter. She often wept in secret, a long and bitter weeping. She did not know who it was she loved: a living man or a dead one? And the longer the desperate days went on, the more often, especially at twilight, did the thought come to her that she was bound to a dead man.

She had either to forget him or to die herself. It was impossible to drag on with such a life. Impossible! Forget him, whatever the cost – forget him! But he would not be forgotten, that was the trouble.

'Yes, yes, yes, the very same mistake!' Margarita said, sitting by the stove and gazing into the fire lit in memory of the fire that had burned while he was writing Pontius Pilate. 'Why did I leave him that night? Why? It was madness! I came back the next day, honestly, as I'd promised, but it was too late. Yes, like the unfortunate Matthew Levi, I came back too late!'

All these words were, of course, absurd, because what, in fact, would it have changed if she had stayed with the master that night? Would she have saved him? 'Ridiculous! . . .' we might exclaim, but we shall not do so before a woman driven to despair.

On that same day when all sorts of absurd turmoil took place, provoked by the appearance of the black magician in Moscow, on the Friday when Berlioz's uncle was chased back to Kiev, when the bookkeeper was arrested and a host of other quite stupid and incomprehensible things took place – Margarita woke up at around noon in her bedroom with bay windows in the tower of the house.

On awakening, Margarita did not weep, as she often did, because she awoke with a presentiment that today something was finally going to happen. Having felt this presentiment, she began to warm it and nurture it in her soul, for fear it might abandon her.

'I believe!' Margarita whispered solemnly. 'I believe! Something will happen! It cannot not happen, because for what, indeed, has lifelong torment been sent to me? I admit that I lied and deceived and lived a secret life, hidden from people, but all the same the punishment for it cannot be so cruel . . . Something is bound to happen, because it cannot be that anything will go on for ever. And besides, my dream was prophetic, I'll swear it was . . .'

So Margarita Nikolaevna whispered, looking at the crimson curtains as they filled with sun, dressing anxiously, combing her short curled hair in front of the triple mirror.

The dream that Margarita had dreamed that night was indeed unusual. The thing was that during her winter sufferings she had never seen the master in her dreams. He released her for the night, and she suffered only in the daylight hours. But now she had dreamed of him.

The dream was of a place unknown to Margarita – hopeless, dismal, under the sullen sky of early spring. In the dream there was this ragged, fleeting, grey sky, and under it a noiseless flock of rooks. Some gnarled little bridge, and under it a muddy spring runlet. Joyless, destitute, half-naked trees. A lone aspen, and further on, among the trees, beyond some vegetable patch, a little log structure – a separate kitchen, a bathhouse, devil knows what it was! Everything around somehow life-less and so dismal that one just longed to hang oneself from that aspen by the bridge. Not a puff of breeze, not a movement of the clouds, and not a living soul. What a hellish place for a living man!

And then, imagine, the door of this log structure is thrown open, and he appears. Rather far away, but clearly visible. He is in tatters, it is impossible to make out what he is wearing. Unshaven, hair dishev-elled. Sick, anxious eyes. He beckons with his hand, calling her. Gasping in the lifeless air, Margarita ran to him over the tussocks, and at that moment she woke up.

'This dream means only one of two things,' Margarita Nikolaevna reasoned with herself. 'If he's dead and beckoned to me, it means he has come for me, and I will die soon. And that's very good – because then my suffering will soon end. Or else he's alive, and then the dream can only mean one thing, that he's reminding me of himself! He wants to say that we will see each other again ... Yes, we will see each other very soon!'

Still in the same agitated state, Margarita got dressed and began impressing it upon herself that, essentially, everything was turning out very luckily, and one must know how to catch such lucky moments and take advantage of them. Her husband had gone on a business trip for a whole three days. During those three days she was at her own disposal, and no one could prevent her from thinking what she liked or dreaming what she liked. All five rooms on the top floor of the house, all of this apartment which in Moscow would be the envy of tens of thousands of people, was entirely at her disposal.

However, being granted freedom for a whole three days, Margarita chose from all this luxurious apartment what was far from the best place. After having tea, she went to a dark, windowless room where suitcases and all sorts of old stuff were kept in two large wardrobes. Squatting down, she opened the bottom drawer of the first of them and took from under a pile of silk scraps the only precious thing she had in life. Margarita held in her hands an old brown leather album which contained a photographic portrait of the master, a bank savings book with a deposit of ten thousand roubles in his name, the petals of a dried rose pressed between sheets of tissue paper, and part of a full-sized notebook covered with typescript and with a charred bottom edge.

Going back to her bedroom with these riches, Margarita Nikolaevna set the photograph up on the triple mirror and sat for about an hour holding the fire-damaged book on her knees, leafing through it and rereading that which, after the burning, had neither beginning nor end: '... The darkness that came from the Mediterranean Sea covered the city hated by the procurator. The hanging bridges connecting the temple with the dread Antonia Tower[2] disappeared, the abyss descended from the sky and flooded the winged gods over the hippodrome, the Hasmonaean Palace[3] with its loopholes, the bazaars, caravanserais, lanes, pools ... Yershalaim – the great city – vanished as if it had never existed in the world ...'

Margarita wanted to read further, but further there was nothing except an irregular, charred fringe.

Wiping her tears, Margarita Nikolaevna abandoned the notebook, rested her elbows on the dressing table and, reflected in the mirror, sat for a long time without taking her eyes from the photograph. Then the tears dried up. Margarita neatly folded her possessions, and a few minutes later they were again buried under silk rags, and the lock clicked shut in the dark room.

Margarita Nikolaevna was putting her coat on in the front hall in order to go for a walk. The beautiful Natasha, her housemaid, asked what to prepare for the main course, and, receiving the reply that it made no difference, got into conversation with her mistress for her own amusement, and began telling her God knows what, something about how yesterday in the theatre a conjurer began performing such tricks that everybody gasped, gave away two flacons of foreign perfume and a pair of stockings free to everybody, and then, when the séance ended, the audience came outside and – bang – everybody turned out to be naked! Margarita Nikolaevna dropped on to the chair in front of the hall mirror and burst out laughing.

'Natasha! You ought to be ashamed,' Margarita Nikolaevna said, 'you, a literate, intelligent girl . . . they tell devil knows what lies in the queues, and you go repeating them!'

Natasha flushed deeply and objected with great ardour that, no, they weren't lying, and that she herself had personally seen today, in a grocer's on the Arbat, one citizeness who came into the shop wearing shoes, but as she was paying at the cash register, the shoes disappeared from her feet, and she was left in just her stockings. Eyes popping out, and a hole in her heel! And the shoes were magic ones from that same séance.

'And she left like that?'

'And she left like that!' Natasha cried, blushing still more from not being believed. 'And yesterday, Margarita Nikolaevna, the police arrested around a hundred people in the evening. Women from this séance were running down Tverskaya in nothing but their bloomers.'

'Well, of course, it's Darya who told you that,' said Margarita Nikolaevna. 'I noticed long ago that she's a terrible liar.'

The funny conversation ended with a pleasant surprise for Natasha. Margarita Nikolaevna went to the bedroom and came back holding a pair of stockings and a flacon of eau-de-cologne. Telling Natasha that she, too, wanted to perform a trick, Margarita Nikolaevna gave her both the stockings and the bottle, and said her only request was that she not run around on Tverskaya in nothing but stockings and that she not listen to Darya. Having kissed each other, mistress and house-maid parted.

Leaning against the comfortable soft back of the trolley-bus seat, Margarita Nikolaevna rode down the Arbat, now thinking her own thoughts, now listening to the whispers of two citizens sitting in front of her.

They were exchanging whispers about some nonsense, looking around warily from time to time to make sure no one was listening. The hefty, beefy one with pert, piggish eyes, sitting by the window, was quietly telling his small neighbour that the coffin had to be covered with a black cloth . . .

'It can't be!' the small one whispered, amazed. 'This is something unheard-of! . . . And what has Zheldybin done?'

Amidst the steady humming of the trolley-bus, words came from the window:

'Criminal investigation . . . scandal . . . well, outright mysticism! . . .'

From these fragmentary scraps, Margarita Nikolaevna somehow put together something coherent. The citizens were whispering about some dead person (they did not name him) whose head had been stolen from the coffin that morning . . . This was the reason why Zheldybin was now so worried. And the two who were whispering on the trolley-bus also had some connection with the robbed dead man.

'Will we have time to stop for flowers?' the small one worried. 'The cremation is at two, you say?'

Margarita Nikolaevna finally got tired of listening to this mysterious palaver about a head stolen from a coffin, and she was glad it was time for her to get off.

A few minutes later Margarita Nikolaevna was sitting on one of the benches under the Kremlin wall, settling herself in such a way that she could see the Manège.[4]

Margarita squinted in the bright sunlight, remembered her last night's dream, remembered how, exactly a year ago to the day and the hour, she had sat next to him on this same bench. And in just the same way as then, her black handbag lay beside her on the bench. He was not beside her this day, but Margarita Nikolaevna mentally conversed with him all the same: 'If you've been exiled, why don't you send me word of yourself? People do send word. Have you stopped loving me? No, for some reason I don't believe that. It means you were exiled and died . . . Release me, then, I beg you, give me freedom to live, finally, to breathe the air! . . .' Margarita Nikolaevna answered for him herself: 'You are free . . . am I holding you?' Then she objected to him: 'No, what kind of answer is that? No, go from my memory, then I'll be free . . .'

People walked past Margarita Nikolaevna. Some man gave the well-dressed woman a sidelong glance, attracted by her beauty and her solitude. He coughed and sat down at the end of the same bench that Margarita Nikolaevna was sitting on. Plucking up his courage, he began:

'Definitely nice weather today . . .'

But Margarita gave him such a dark look that he got up and left.

'There, for example,' Margarita said mentally to him who possessed her. 'Why, in fact, did I chase that man away? I'm bored, and there's nothing bad about this Lovelace, unless it's the stupid word "definitely" . . . Why am I sitting alone under the wall like an owl? Why am I excluded from life?'

She became thoroughly sad and downcast. But here suddenly the same morning wave of expectation and excitement pushed at her chest. 'Yes, it will happen!' The wave pushed her a second time, and now she realized that it was a wave of sound. Through the noise of the city there came ever more distinctly the approaching beat of a drum and the sounds of slightly off-key trumpets.

The first to appear was a mounted policeman riding slowly past the garden fence, with three more following on foot. Then a slowly rolling truck with the musicians. After that, a new, open hearse moving slowly, a coffin on it all covered with wreaths, and at the corners of the platform four standing persons – three men and one woman.

Even from a distance, Margarita discerned that the faces of the people standing on the hearse, accompanying the deceased on his last journey, were somehow strangely bewildered. This was particularly noticeable with regard to the citizeness who stood at the left rear corner of the hearse. This citizeness's fat cheeks were as if pushed out still more from inside by some piquant secret, her puffy little eyes glinted with an ambiguous fire. It seemed that just a little longer and the citizeness, unable to help herself, would wink at the deceased and say: 'Have you ever seen the like? Outright mysticism! . . .' The same bewildered faces showed on those in the cortège, who, numbering three hundred or near it, slowly walked behind the hearse.

Margarita followed the procession with her eyes, listening to the dismal Turkish drum fading in the distance, producing one and the same 'boom, boom, boom', and thought: 'What a strange funeral . . . and what anguish from that "boom"! Ah, truly, I'd pawn my soul to the devil just to find out whether he's alive or not . . . It would be interesting to know who they're burying.'

'Berlioz, Mikhail Alexandrovich,' a slightly nasal male voice came from beside her, 'chairman of Massolit.'

The surprised Margarita Nikolaevna turned and saw a citizen on her bench, who had apparently sat down there noiselessly while Margarita was watching the procession and, it must be assumed, absent-mindedly asked her last question aloud.

The procession meanwhile was slowing down, probably delayed by traffic lights ahead.

'Yes,' the unknown citizen went on, 'they're in a surprising mood. They're accompanying the deceased and thinking only about what happened to his head.'

'What head?' asked Margarita, studying her unexpected neighbour. This neighbour turned out to be short of stature, a fiery redhead with a fang, in a starched shirt, a good-quality striped suit, patent leather shoes, and with a bowler hat on his head. His tie was brightly coloured. The surprising thing was that from the pocket where men usually carry a handkerchief or a fountain pen, this gentleman had a gnawed chicken bone sticking out.

'You see,' the redhead explained, 'this morning in the hall of Griboedov's, the deceased's head was filched from the coffin.'

'How can that be?' Margarita asked involuntarily, remembering at the same time the whispering on the trolley-bus.

'Devil knows how!' the redhead replied casually. 'I suppose, however, that it wouldn't be a bad idea to ask Behemoth about it. It was an awfully deft snatch! Such a scandal! . . . And, above all, it's incomprehensible – who needs this head and for what!'

Occupied though Margarita Nikolaevna was with her own thoughts, she was struck all the same by the unknown citizen's strange twaddle.

'Excuse me!' she suddenly exclaimed. 'What Berlioz? The one that today's newspapers ...'

'The same, the same ...'

'So it means that those are writers following the coffin!' Margarita asked, and suddenly bared her teeth.

'Well, naturally they are!'

'And do you know them by sight?'

'All of them to a man,' the redhead replied.

'Tell me,' Margarita began to say, and her voice became hollow, 'is the critic Latunsky among them?'

'How could he not be?' the redhead replied. 'He's there at the end of the fourth row.'

'The blond one?' Margarita asked, narrowing her eyes.

'Ash-coloured ... See, he's raising his eyes to heaven.'

'Looking like a parson?'

'That's him!'

Margarita asked nothing more, peering at Latunsky.

'And I can see,' the redhead said, smiling, 'that you hate this Latunsky!'

'There are some others I hate,' Margarita answered through her teeth, 'but it's not interesting to talk about it.'

The procession moved on just then, with mostly empty automobiles following the people on foot.

'Oh, well, of course there's nothing interesting in it, Margarita Niko-laevna!'

Margarita was surprised.

'Do you know me?'

In place of an answer, the redhead took off his bowler hat and held it out.

'A perfect bandit's mug!' thought Margarita, studying her street inter-locutor.

'Well, I don't know you,' Margarita said drily.

'Where could you know me from? But all the same I've been sent to you on a little business.'

Margarita turned pale and recoiled.

'You ought to have begun with that straight off,' she said, 'instead of pouring out devil knows what about some severed head! You want to arrest me?'

'Nothing of the kind!' the redhead exclaimed. 'What is it – you start a conversation, and right away it's got to be an arrest! I simply have business with you.'

'I don't understand, what business?'

The redhead looked around and said mysteriously:

'I've been sent to invite you for a visit this evening.'

'What are you raving about, what visit?'

'To a very distinguished foreigner,' the redhead said significantly, narrowing one eye.

Margarita became very angry.

'A new breed has appeared – a street pander!' she said, getting up to leave.

'Thanks a lot for such errands!' the redhead exclaimed grudgingly, and he muttered 'Fool!' to Margarita Nikolaevna's back.

'Scoundrel!' she replied, turning, and straight away heard the red-head's voice behind her:

'The darkness that came from the Mediterranean Sea covered the city hated by the procurator. The hanging bridges connecting the temple with the dread Antonia Tower disappeared ... Yershalaim – the great city – vanished as if it had never existed in the world ... So you, too, can just vanish away along with your burnt notebook and dried-up rose! Sit here on the bench alone and entreat him to set you free, to let you breathe the air, to go from your memory!'

Her face white, Margarita came back to the bench. The redhead was looking at her, narrowing his eyes.

'I don't understand any of this,' Margarita began quietly. 'It's possible to find out about the pages ... get in, snoop around ... You bribed Natasha, right? But how could you find out my thoughts?' She scowled painfully and added: 'Tell me, who are you? From which institution?'

'What a bore ...' the redhead muttered and then said aloud, 'I beg your pardon, didn't I tell you that I'm not from any institution? Sit down, please.'

Margarita obeyed unquestioningly, but even so, as she was sitting down, she asked once more:

'Who are you?'

'Well, all right, my name is Azazello, but anyhow that tells you nothing.'

'And you won't tell me how you found out about the pages and about my thoughts?'

'No, I won't,' Azazello replied drily.

'But do you know anything about him?' Margarita whispered imploringly.

'Well, suppose I do.'

'I implore you, tell me only one thing ... is he alive? ... Don't torment me!'

'Well, he's alive, he's alive,' Azazello responded reluctantly.

'Oh, God! ...'

'Please, no excitements and exclamations,' Azazello said, frowning.

'Forgive me, forgive me,' the now obedient Margarita murmured, 'of course, I got angry with you. But, you must agree, when a woman is invited in the street to pay a visit somewhere ... I have no prejudices, I assure you,' Margarita smiled joylessly, 'but I never see any foreigners, I have no wish to associate with them ... and, besides, my husband ... my drama is that I'm living with someone I don't love ... but I consider it an unworthy thing to spoil his life ... I've never seen anything but kindness from him ...'

Azazello heard out this incoherent speech with visible boredom and said sternly:

'I beg you to be silent for a moment.'

Margarita obediently fell silent.

'The foreigner to whom I'm inviting you is not dangerous at all. And not a single soul will know of this visit. That I can guarantee you.'

'And what does he need me for?' Margarita asked insinuatingly.

'You'll find that out later.'

'I understand ... I must give myself to him,' Margarita said pensively.

To which Azazello grunted somehow haughtily and replied thus:

'Any woman in the world, I can assure you, would dream of just that,' Azazello's mug twisted with a little laugh, 'but I must disappoint you, it won't happen.'

'What kind of foreigner is that?!' Margarita exclaimed in bewilderment, so loudly that people passing by turned to look at her. 'And what interest do I have in going to him?'

Azazello leaned towards her and whispered meaningfully:

'Well, a very great interest ... you'd better use the opportunity ...'

'What?' exclaimed Margarita, and her eyes grew round. 'If I understand you rightly, you're hinting that I may find out about him there?'

Azazello silently nodded.

'I'll go!' Margarita exclaimed with force and seized Azazello by the hand. 'I'll go wherever you like!'

Azazello, with a sigh of relief, leaned against the back of the bench, covering up the name 'Niura' carved on it in big letters, and saying ironically:

'Difficult folk, these women!' he put his hands in his pockets and stretched his legs way out. 'Why, for instance, was I sent on this business? Behemoth should have gone, he's a charmer ...'

Margarita said, with a crooked and bitter smile:

'Stop mystifying me and tormenting me with your riddles. I'm an unhappy person, and you're taking advantage of it ... I'm getting myself into some strange story, but I swear, it's only because you lured me with words about him! My head's spinning from all these puzzlements ...'

'No dramas, no dramas,' Azazello returned, making faces, 'you must also put yourself in my position. To give some administrator a pasting, or chuck an uncle out of the house, or gun somebody down, or any other trifle of the sort – that's right in my line. But talking with a woman in love, no thanks! ... It's half an hour now that I've been wangling you into it ... So you'll go?'

'I will,' Margarita Nikolaevna answered simply.

'Be so good as to accept this, then,' said Azazello, and, pulling a round little golden box from his pocket, he offered it to Margarita with the words: 'Hide it now, the passers-by are looking. It'll come in useful, Margarita Nikolaevna, you've aged a lot from grief in the last half-year.' Margarita flushed but said nothing, and Azazello went on: 'Tonight, at exactly half past nine, be so good as to take off all your clothes and rub your face and your whole body with this ointment. Then do whatever you like, only don't go far from the telephone. At ten I'll call you and tell you all you need to know. You won't have to worry about a thing, you'll be delivered where you need to go and won't be put to any trouble. Understood?'

Margarita was silent for a moment, then replied:

'Understood. This thing is pure gold, you can tell by the weight. So, then, I understand perfectly well that I'm being bribed and drawn into some shady story for which I'm going to pay dearly ...'

'What is all this?' Azazello almost hissed. 'You're at it again?'

'No, wait!'

'Give me back the cream!'

Margarita clutched the box more tightly in her hand and said:

'No, wait! . . . I know what I'm getting into. But I'm getting into it on account of him, because I have no more hope for anything in this world. But I want to tell you that if you're going to ruin me, you'll be ashamed! Yes, ashamed! I'm perishing on account of love!' – and striking herself on the breast, Margarita glanced at the sun.

'Give it back!' Azazello cried angrily. 'Give it back and devil take the whole thing. Let them send Behemoth!'

'Oh, no!' exclaimed Margarita, shocking the passers-by. 'I agree to everything, I agree to perform this comedy of rubbing in the ointment, agree to go to the devil and beyond! I won't give it back!'

'Hah!' Azazello suddenly shouted and, goggling his eyes at the garden fence, began pointing off somewhere with his finger.

Margarita turned to where Azazello was pointing, but found nothing special there. Then she turned back to Azazello, wishing to get an explanation of this absurd 'Hah!' but there was no one to give an explanation: Margarita Nikolaevna's mysterious interlocutor had disappeared.

Margarita quickly thrust her hand into her handbag, where she had put the box before this shouting, and made sure it was there. Then, without reflecting on anything, Margarita hurriedly ran out of the Alexandrovsky Garden.

CHAPTER 20

Azazello's Cream

The moon in the clear evening sky hung full, visible through the maple branches. Lindens and acacias drew an intricate pattern of spots on the ground in the garden. The triple bay window, open but covered by a curtain, was lit with a furious electric light. In Margarita Nikolaevna's bedroom all the lamps were burning, illuminating the total disorder in the room.

On the blanket on the bed lay shifts, stockings and underwear. Crumpled underwear was also simply lying about on the floor next to a box of cigarettes crushed in the excitement. Shoes stood on the night table next to an unfinished cup of coffee and an ashtray in which a butt was smoking. A black evening dress hung over the back of a chair. The room smelled of perfume. Besides that, the smell of a red-hot iron was coming from somewhere.

Margarita Nikolaevna sat in front of the pier-glass, with just a bath-robe thrown over her naked body, and in black suede shoes. A gold bracelet with a watch lay in front of Margarita Nikolaevna, beside the box she had received from Azazello, and Margarita did not take her eyes from its face.

At times it began to seem to her that the watch was broken and the hands were not moving. But they were moving, though very slowly, as if sticking, and at last the big hand fell on the twenty-ninth minute past nine. Margarita's heart gave a terrible thump, so that she could not even take hold of the box right away. Having mastered herself, Margarita opened it and saw in the box a rich, yellowish cream. It seemed to her that it smelled of swamp slime. With the tip of her finger, Margarita put a small dab of the cream on her palm, the smell of swamp grass and forest grew stronger, and then she began rubbing the cream into her forehead and cheeks with her palm.

The cream spread easily and, as it seemed to Margarita, evaporated at once. Having rubbed several times, Margarita glanced into the mirror and dropped the box right on her watch crystal, which became covered with cracks. Margarita closed her eyes, then glanced once again and burst into stormy laughter.

Her eyebrows, plucked to a thread with tweezers, thickened and lay in even black arches over her greening eyes. The thin vertical crease cutting the bridge of her nose, which had appeared back then, in October, when the master vanished, disappeared without a trace. So did the yellowish shadows at her temples and the two barely noticeable little webs of wrinkles at the outer corners of her eyes. The skin of her cheeks filled out with an even pink colour, her forehead became white and clear, and the hairdresser's waves in her hair came undone.

From the mirror a naturally curly, black-haired woman of about twenty was looking at the thirty-year-old Margarita, baring her teeth and shaking with laughter.

Having laughed her fill, Margarita jumped out of her bathrobe with a single leap, dipped freely into the light, rich cream, and with vigorous strokes began rubbing it into the skin of her body. It at once turned pink and tingly. That instant, as if a needle had been snatched from her brain, the ache she had felt in her temple all evening after the meeting in the Alexandrovsky Garden subsided, her leg and arm muscles grew stronger, and then Margarita's body became weightless.

She sprang up and hung in the air just above the rug, then was slowly pulled down and descended.

'What a cream! What a cream!' cried Margarita, throwing herself into an armchair.

The rubbings changed her not only externally. Now joy was boiling up in her, in all of her, in every particle of her body, which felt to her like bubbles prickling her body all over. Margarita felt herself free, free of everything. Besides, she understood with perfect clarity that what was happening was precisely what her presentiment had been telling her in the morning, and that she was leaving her house and her former life for ever. But, even so, a thought split off from this former life about the need of fulfilling just one last duty before the start of something new, extraordinary, which was pulling her upwards into the air. And, naked as she was, she ran from her bedroom, flying up in the air time and again, to her husband's study, and, turning on the light, rushed to the desk. On a page torn from a notebook, she pencilled a note quickly and in big letters, without any corrections:

Forgive me and forget me as soon as possible. I am leaving you for ever. Do not look for me, it is useless. I have become a witch from the grief and calamities that have struck me. It's time for me to go.

Farewell.

Margarita.

With a completely unburdened soul, Margarita came flying into the bedroom, and after her ran Natasha, loaded down with things. At once all these things – a wooden hanger with a dress, lace shawls, dark blue satin shoes on shoe-trees and a belt – all of it spilled on the floor, and Natasha clasped her freed hands.

'What, nice?' Margarita Nikolaevna cried loudly in a hoarse voice.

'How can it be?' Natasha whispered, backing away. 'How did you do it, Margarita Nikolaevna.'

'It's the cream! The cream, the cream!' answered Margarita, pointing to the glittering golden box and turning around in front of the mirror.

Natasha, forgetting the wrinkled dress lying on the floor, ran up to the pier-glass and fixed her greedy, lit-up eyes on the remainder of the cream. Her lips were whispering something. She again turned to Margarita and said with a sort of awe:

'And, oh, the skin! The skin! Margarita Nikolaevna, your skin is glowing!' But she came to her senses, ran to the dress, picked it up and began shaking it out.

'Leave it! Leave it!' Margarita shouted to her. 'Devil take it! Leave it all! Or, no, keep it as a souvenir. As a souvenir, I tell you. Take everything in the room!'

As if half-witted, the motionless Natasha looked at Margarita for some time, then hung on her neck, kissing her and crying out:

'Satin! Glowing! Satin! And the eyebrows, the eyebrows!'

'Take all these rags, take the perfume, drag it to your trunk, hide it,' cried Margarita, 'but don't take any valuables, they'll accuse you of stealing.'

Natasha grabbed and bundled up whatever came to her hand – dresses, shoes, stockings, underwear – and ran out of the bedroom.

Just then from somewhere at the other end of the lane a thundering, virtuoso waltz burst and flew out an open window, and the chugging of a car driving up to the gate was heard.

'Azazello will call now!' exclaimed Margarita, listening to the waltz spilling into the lane. 'He'll call! And the foreigner's not dangerous, yes, I understand now that he's not dangerous!'

There was the noise of a car driving away from the front gate. The garden gate banged, and steps were heard on the tiles of the path.

'It's Nikolai Ivanovich, I recognize his footsteps,' thought Margarita. 'I must do something funny and interesting in farewell.'

Margarita tore the curtain open and sat sideways on the window-sill, her arms around her knees. Moonlight licked her from the right side. Margarita raised her head towards the moon and made a pensive and poetic face. The steps tapped twice more, and then suddenly – silence. After admiring the moon a little longer, sighing for the sake of propriety, Margarita turned her head to the garden and indeed saw Nikolai Ivano-vich, who lived on the bottom floor of the same house. Moonlight poured down brightly on Nikolai Ivanovich. He was sitting on a bench, and there was every indication that he had sunk on to it suddenly. The pince-nez on his face was somehow askew, and he was clutching his briefcase in his hands.

'Ah, hello, Nikolai Ivanovich,' Margarita said in a melancholy voice. 'Good evening! Coming back from a meeting?'

Nikolai Ivanovich made no reply to that.

'And I,' Margarita went on, leaning further out into the garden, 'am sitting alone, as you see, bored, looking at the moon and listening to the waltz . . .'

Margarita passed her left hand over her temple, straightening a strand of hair, then said crossly:

'That is impolite, Nikolai Ivanovich! I'm still a woman after all! It's boorish not to reply when someone is talking to you.'

Nikolai Ivanovich, visible in the moonlight to the last button on his grey waistcoat, to the last hair of his blond, wedge-shaped beard, sud-denly smiled a wild smile, rose from the bench, and, apparently beside himself with embarrassment, instead of taking off his hat, waved his briefcase to the side and bent his knees as if about to break into a squatting dance.

'Ah, what a boring type you are, Nikolai Ivanovich!' Margarita went on. 'Generally, I'm so sick of you all that I can't even tell you, and I'm so happy to be parting with you! Well, go to the devil's dam!'

Just then, behind Margarita's back in the bedroom, the telephone exploded. Margarita tore from the window-sill and, forgetting Nikolai Ivanovich, snatched the receiver.

'Azazello speaking,' came from the receiver.

'Dear, dear Azazello!' cried Margarita.

'It's time. Take off,' Azazello spoke into the receiver, and it could be heard in his tone that he liked Margarita's sincere and joyful impulse. 'When you fly over the gate, shout "Invisible!" Then fly over the city a little, to get used to it, and after that head south, out of the city, and straight for the river. You're expected!'

Margarita hung up, and here something in the next room hobbled woodenly and started beating on the door. Margarita flung it open and a sweeping broom, bristles up, flew dancing into the bedroom. It drummed on the floor with its end, kicking and straining towards the window. Margarita squealed with delight and jumped astride the broom. Only now did the thought flash in the rider that amidst all this fracas she had forgotten to get dressed. She galloped over to the bed and grabbed the first thing she found, some light blue shift. Waving it like a banner, she flew out the window. And the waltz over the garden struck up louder.

From the window Margarita slipped down and saw Nikolai Ivanovich on the bench. He seemed to have frozen to it and listened completely dumbfounded to the shouting and crashing coming from the lighted bedroom of the upstairs tenants.

'Farewell, Nikolai Ivanovich!' cried Margarita, capering in front of Nikolai Ivanovich.

He gasped and crawled along the bench, pawing it with his hands and knocking down his briefcase.

'Farewell for ever! I'm flying away!' Margarita shouted above the waltz. Here she realized that she did not need any shift, and with a sinister guffaw threw it over Nikolai Ivanovich's head. The blinded Nikolai Ivanovich crashed from the bench on to the bricks of the path.

Margarita turned to take a last look at the house where she had suffered for so long, and saw in the blazing window Natasha's face distorted with amazement.

'Farewell, Natasha!' Margarita cried and reared up on the broom. 'Invisible! Invisible!' she cried still louder, and, flying over the front gates, between the maple branches, which lashed at her face, she flew out into the lane. And after her flew the completely insane waltz.

CHAPTER 21

Flight

Invisible and free! Invisible and free! ... After flying down her own lane, Margarita got into another that crossed the first at right angles. This patched up, darned, crooked and long lane, with the lopsided door of a kerosene shop where they sold paraffin by the cup and liquid against parasites in flacons, she cut across in an instant, and here she realized that, even while completely free and invisible, she still had to be at least somewhat reasonable in her pleasure. Having slowed down only by some miracle, she just missed smashing herself to death against an old lopsided street light at the corner. Dodging it, Margarita clutched the broom tighter and flew more slowly, studying the electric wires and the street signs hanging across the sidewalk.

The third lane led straight to the Arbat. Here Margarita became fully accustomed to controlling the broom, realized that it obeyed the slightest touch of her hands and legs, and that, flying over the city, she had to be very attentive and not act up too much. Besides, in the lane it had already become abundantly clear that passers-by did not see the lady flier. No one threw his head back, shouted 'Look! look!' or dashed aside, no one shrieked, swooned or guffawed with wild laughter.

Margarita flew noiselessly, very slowly, and not high up, approximately on second-floor level. But even with this slow flying, just at the entrance to the dazzlingly lit Arbat she misjudged slightly and struck her shoulder against some illuminated disc with an arrow on it. This angered Margarita. She reined in the obedient broom, flew a little aside, and then, suddenly hurling herself at the disc with the butt of the broom, smashed it to smithereens. Bits of glass rained down with a crash, passers-by shied away, a whistle came from somewhere, and Margarita, having accomplished this unnecessary act, burst out laughing.

'On the Arbat I must be more careful,' thought Margarita, 'everything's in such a snarl here, you can't figure it out.' She began dodging between the wires. Beneath Margarita floated the roofs of buses, trams and cars, and along the sidewalks, as it seemed to Margarita from above, floated rivers of caps. From these rivers little streams branched off and flowed into the flaming maws of night-time shops.

'Eh, what a mess!' Margarita thought angrily. 'You can't even turn around here.'

She crossed the Arbat, rose higher, to fourth-floor level, and, past the dazzlingly bright tubes on the theatre building at the corner, floated into a narrow lane with tall buildings. All the windows in them were open, and everywhere radio music came from the windows. Out of curiosity, Margarita peeked into one of them. She saw a kitchen. Two primuses were roaring on the range, and next to them stood two women with spoons in their hands, squabbling.

'You should turn the toilet light off after you, that's what I'm telling you, Pelageya Petrovna,' said the woman before whom there was a pot with some sort of eatables steaming in it, 'or else we'll apply to have you evicted.'

'You're a good one yourself,' the other woman answered.

'You're both good ones,' Margarita said loudly, clambering over the window-sill into the kitchen.

The two quarrelling women turned towards the voice and froze with their dirty spoons in their hands. Margarita carefully reached out between them, turned the knobs of both primuses, and extinguished them. The women gasped and opened their mouths. But Margarita was already bored with the kitchen and flew out into the lane.

Her attention was attracted by the magnificent hulk of an eight-storeyed, obviously just-constructed building at the end of it. Margarita dropped down and, alighting, saw that the façade of the building was covered in black marble, that the doors were wide, that behind their glass could be glimpsed a doorman's buttons and peaked cap with gold braid, and that over the door there was a gold inscription: 'Dramlit House'.

Margarita squinted at the inscription, trying to figure out what the word 'Dramlit' might mean. Taking her broom under her arm, Margarita walked into the lobby, shoving the surprised doorman with the door, and saw on the wall beside the elevator a huge black board and on it, written in white letters, apartment numbers and tenants' names. The heading 'House of Dramatists and Literary Workers' above the list provoked a suppressed predatory scream in Margarita. Rising in the air, she greedily began to read the last names: Khustov, Dvubratsky, Quant, Beskudnikov, Latunsky ...

'Latunsky!' shrieked Margarita. 'Latunsky! Why, he's the one ... he's the one who ruined the master!'

The doorman at the entrance, even hopping with astonishment, his eyes rolled out, gazed at the black board, trying to understand the marvel: why was the list of tenants suddenly shrieking?

But by that time Margarita was already going impetuously up the stairs, repeating in some sort of rapture:

'Latunsky eighty-four ... Latunsky eighty-four ...'

Here to the left – 82, to the right – 83, further up, to the left – 84! Here! And the name plate – 'O. Latunsky'.

Margarita jumped off the broom, and her hot soles felt the pleasant coolness of the stone landing. Margarita rang once, twice. But no one opened. Margarita began to push the button harder and could hear the jangling it set off in Latunsky's apartment. Yes, to his dying day the inhabitant of apartment no. 84 on the eighth floor should be grateful to the late Berlioz, chairman of Massolit, for having fallen under a tram-car, and that the memorial gathering had been appointed precisely for that evening. The critic Latunsky was born under a lucky star – it saved him from meeting Margarita, who that Friday became a witch.

No one opened the door. Then Margarita raced down at full swing, counting the floors, reached the bottom, burst out the door and, looking up, counted and checked the floors from outside, guessing which precisely were the windows of Latunsky's apartment. Undoubtedly they were the five dark windows at the corner of the building on the eighth floor. Convinced of it, Margarita rose into the air and in a few seconds was stepping through an open window into an unlit room, where only a narrow path from the moon shone silver. Margarita ran down it, felt for the switch. A moment later the whole apartment was lit up. The broom stood in a corner. After making sure that no one was home, Margarita opened the door to the stairs and checked whether the name plate was there. The name plate was in place. Margarita was where she wanted to be.

Yes, they say that to this day the critic Latunsky turns pale remembering that terrible evening, and to this day he utters the name of Berlioz with veneration. It is totally unknown what dark and vile criminal job would have marked this evening – returning from the kitchen, Margarita had a heavy hammer in her hands.

Naked and invisible, the lady flier tried to control and talk sense into herself; her hands trembled with impatience. Taking careful aim, Margarita struck at the keys of the grand piano, and a first plaintive wail passed all through the apartment. Becker's drawing-room instrument, not guilty of anything, cried out frenziedly. Its keys caved in, ivory veneer flew in all directions. The instrument howled, wailed, rasped and jangled. With the noise of a pistol shot, the polished upper soundboard split under a hammer blow. Breathing hard, Margarita tore and mangled the strings with the hammer. Finally getting tired, she left off and flopped into an armchair to catch her breath.

Water was roaring terribly in the bathroom, and in the kitchen as well. 'Seems it's already overflowing on the floor . . .' Margarita thought, and added aloud:

'No point sitting around, however.'

The stream was already running from the kitchen into the corridor. Splashing barefoot through the water, Margarita carried buckets of water from the kitchen to the critic's study and emptied them into his desk drawers. Then, after smashing the door of the bookcase in the same study with her hammer, she rushed to the bedroom. Shattering the mirror on the wardrobe, she took out the critic's dress suit and drowned it in the tub. A large bottle of ink, picked up in the study, she poured over the luxuriously plumped-up double bed.

The devastation she wrought afforded her a burning pleasure, and yet it seemed to her all the while that the results came out somehow meagre. Therefore she started doing whatever came along. She smashed pots of ficus in the room with the grand piano. Before finishing that, she went back to the bedroom, slashed the sheets with a kitchen knife, and broke the glass on the framed photographs. She felt no fatigue, only the sweat poured from her in streams.

Just then, in apartment no. 82, below Latunsky's apartment, the housekeeper of the dramatist Quant was having tea in the kitchen, perplexed by the clatter, running and jangling coming from above. Raising her head towards the ceiling, she suddenly saw it changing colour before her eyes from white to some deathly blue. The spot was widening right in front of her and drops suddenly swelled out on it. For about two minutes the housekeeper sat marvelling at this phenomenon, until finally a real rain began to fall from the ceiling, drumming on the floor. Here she jumped up, put a bowl under the stream, which did not help at all, because the rain expanded and began pouring down on the gas stove and the table with dishes. Then, crying out, Quant's housekeeper ran from the apartment to the stairs and at once the bell started ringing in Latunsky's apartment.

'Well, they're ringing . . . Time to be off,' said Margarita. She sat on the broom, listening to the female voice shouting through the keyhole:

'Open up, open up! Dusya, open the door! Is your water overflowing, or what? We're being flooded!'

Margarita rose up about a metre and hit the chandelier. Two bulbs popped and pendants flew in all directions. The shouting through the keyhole stopped, stomping was heard on the stairs. Margarita floated through the window, found herself outside it, swung lightly and hit the glass with the hammer. The pane sobbed, and splinters went cascading down the marble-faced wall. Margarita flew to the next window. Far below, people began running about on the sidewalk, one of the two cars parked by the entrance honked and drove off. Having finished with Latunsky's windows, Margarita floated to the neighbour's apartment. The blows became more frequent, the lane was filled with crashing and jingling. The doorman ran out of the main entrance, looked up, hesitated a moment, evidently not grasping at first what he ought to undertake, put the whistle to his lips, and started whistling furiously. To the sound of this whistle, Margarita, with particular passion, demolished the last window on the eighth floor, dropped down to the seventh, and started smashing the windows there.

Weary of his prolonged idleness behind the glass doors of the entrance, the doorman put his whole soul into his whistling, following Margarita precisely as if he were her accompanist. In the pauses as she flew from window to window, he would draw his breath, and at each of Margarita's strokes, he would puff out his cheeks and dissolve in whistling, drilling the night air right up to the sky.

His efforts, combined with the efforts of the infuriated Margarita, yielded great results. There was panic in the house. Those windows left intact were flung open, people's heads appeared in them and hid at once, while the open windows, on the contrary, were being closed. In the buildings across the street, against the lighted background of windows, there appeared the dark silhouettes of people trying to understand why the windows in the new Dramlit building were bursting for no reason at all.

In the lane people ran to Dramlit House, and inside, on all the stairways, there was the stamping of people rushing about with no reason or sense. Quant's housekeeper shouted to those running up the stairs that they were being flooded, and she was soon joined by Khustov's housekeeper from apartment no. 80, located just below Quant's apartment. At Khustov's it was pouring from the ceiling in both the kitchen and the toilet. Finally, in Quant's kitchen a huge slab of plaster fell from the ceiling, breaking all the dirty dishes, after which came a real downpour, the water gushing from the grid of wet, hanging lath as if from a bucket. Then on the steps of the main entrance shouting began.

Flying past the penultimate window of the fourth floor, Margarita peeked in and saw a man who in panic had pulled on a gas mask. Hitting his window with the hammer, Margarita scared him off, and he disappeared from the room.

And unexpectedly the wild havoc ceased. Slipping down to the third floor, Margarita peeked into the end window, covered by a thin, dark little curtain. In the room a little lamp was burning weakly under a shade. In a small bed with net sides sat a boy of about four, listening timorously. There were no grown-ups in the room, evidently they had all run out of the apartment.

'They're breaking the windows,' the boy said and called: 'Mama!'

No one answered, and then he said:

'Mama, I'm afraid.'

Margarita drew the little curtain aside and flew in.

'I'm afraid,' the boy repeated, and trembled.

'Don't be afraid, don't be afraid, little one,' said Margarita, trying to soften her criminal voice, grown husky from the wind. 'It's some boys breaking windows.'

'With a slingshot?' the boy asked, ceasing to tremble.

'With a slingshot, with a slingshot,' Margarita confirmed, 'and you go to sleep.'

'It's Sitnik,' said the boy, 'he's got a slingshot.'

'Well, of course it's he!'

The boy looked slyly somewhere to the side and asked:

'And where are you, ma'am?'

'I'm nowhere,' answered Margarita, 'I'm your dream.'

'I thought so,' said the boy.

'Lie down now,' Margarita ordered, 'put your hand under your cheek, and I'll go on being your dream.'

'Well, be my dream, then,' the boy agreed, and at once lay down and put his hand under his cheek.

'I'll tell you a story,' Margarita began, and placed her hot hand on his cropped head. 'Once there was a certain lady . . . And she had no children, and generally no happiness either. And so first she cried for a long time, and then she became wicked . . .' Margarita fell silent and took away her hand – the boy was asleep.

Margarita quietly placed the hammer on the window-sill and flew out the window. There was turmoil by the building. On the asphalt pavement strewn with broken glass, people were running and shouting something. Policemen were already flashing among them. Suddenly a bell rang, and a red fire-engine with a ladder drove into the lane from the Arbat.

But what followed no longer interested Margarita. Taking aim, so as not to brush against any wires, she clutched her broom more tightly and in a moment was high above the ill-fated house. The lane beneath her went askew and plunged away. In place of it a mass of roofs appeared under Margarita's feet, criss-crossed at various angles by shining paths. It all unexpectedly went off to one side, and the strings of lights smeared and merged.

Margarita made one more spurt and the whole mass of roofs fell through the earth, and in place of it a lake of quivering electric lights appeared below, and this lake suddenly rose up vertically and then appeared over Margarita's head, while the moon flashed under her feet. Realizing that she had flipped over, Margarita resumed a normal position and, glancing back, saw that there was no longer any lake, and that there behind her only a pink glow remained on the horizon. That, too, disappeared a second later, and Margarita saw that she was alone with the moon flying above and to the left of her. Margarita's hair had long been standing up in a shock, and the whistling moonlight bathed her body. Seeing two rows of widespread lights merge into two unbroken fiery lines, seeing how quickly they vanished behind her, Margarita realized that she was flying at an enormous speed and was amazed that she was not out of breath.

After a few seconds, a new glow of electric lights flared up far below in the earthly blackness and hurtled under the flying woman's feet, but immediately spun away like a whirligig and fell into the earth. A few seconds later – exactly the same phenomenon.

'Towns! Towns!' cried Margarita.

Two or three times after that she saw dully gleaming sabres lying in open black sheaths below her and realized that these were rivers.

Turning her head up and to the left, the flying woman admired the way the moon madly raced back over her towards Moscow, and at the same time strangely stayed in its place, so that there could be clearly seen on it something mysterious, dark – a dragon, or a little humpbacked horse, its sharp muzzle turned to the abandoned city.

Here the thought came to Margarita that, in fact, there was no need for her to drive her broom so furiously, that she was depriving herself of the opportunity of seeing anything properly, of revelling properly in her own flight. Something told her that she would be waited for in the place she was flying to, and that there was no need for her to become bored with this insane speed and height.

Margarita turned the broom's bristles forward, so that its tail rose up, and, slowing way down, headed right for the earth. This downward glide, as on an airy sled, gave her the greatest pleasure. The earth rose to meet her, and in its hitherto formless black density the charms and secrets of the earth on a moonlit night revealed themselves. The earth was coming to her, and Margarita was already enveloped in the scent of greening forests. Margarita was flying just above the mists of a dewy meadow, then over a pond. Under Margarita sang a chorus of frogs, and from somewhere far away, stirring her heart deeply for some reason, came the noise of a train. Soon Margarita saw it. It was crawling slowly along like a caterpillar, spraying sparks into the air. Going ahead of it, Margarita passed over yet another watery mirror, in which a second moon floated under her feet, dropped down lower still and went on, her feet nearly touching the tops of the huge pines.

A heavy noise of ripping air came from behind and began to overtake Margarita. To this noise of something flying like a cannon ball a woman's guffaw was gradually added, audible for many miles around. Margarita looked back and saw some complex dark object catching up with her. As it drew nearer to Margarita, it became more distinct – a mounted flying person could be seen. And finally it became quite distinct: slowing down, Natasha came abreast of Margarita.

Completely naked, her dishevelled hair flying in the air, she flew astride a fat hog, who was clutching a briefcase in his front hoofs, while his hind hoofs desperately threshed the air. Occasionally gleaming in the moonlight, then fading, the pince-nez that had fallen off his nose flew beside the hog on a string, and the hog's hat kept sliding down over his eyes. Taking a close look, Margarita recognized the hog as Nikolai Ivanovich, and then her laughter rang out over the forest, mingled with the laughter of Natasha.

'Natashka!' Margarita shouted piercingly. 'You rubbed yourself with the cream?'

'Darling!!' Natasha replied, awakening the sleeping pine forest with her shout. 'My French queen, I smeared it on him, too, on his bald head!'

'Princess!' the hog shouted tearfully, galloping along with his rider.

'Darling! Margarita Nikolaevna!' cried Natasha, riding beside Margarita, 'I confess, I took the cream! We, too, want to live and fly! Forgive me, my sovereign lady, I won't go back, not for anything! Ah, it's good, Margarita Nikolaevna! . . . He propositioned me,' Natasha began jabbing her finger into the neck of the abashedly huffing hog, 'propositioned me! What was it you called me, eh?' she shouted, leaning towards the hog's ear.

'Goddess!' howled the hog, 'I can't fly so fast! I may lose important papers, Natalya Prokofyevna, I protest!'

'Ah, devil take you and your papers!' Natasha shouted with a brazen guffaw.

'Please, Natalya Prokofyevna, someone may hear us!' the hog yelled imploringly.

Flying beside Margarita, Natasha laughingly told her what happened in the house after Margarita Nikolaevna flew off over the gates.

Natasha confessed that, without ever touching any of the things she had been given, she threw off her clothes, rushed to the cream, and immediately smeared herself with it. The same thing happened with her as with her mistress. Just as Natasha, laughing with joy, was revelling in her own magical beauty before the mirror, the door opened and Nikolai Ivanovich appeared before her. He was agitated; in his hands he was holding Margarita Nikolaevna's shift and his own hat and briefcase. Seeing Natasha, Nikolai Ivanovich was dumbfounded. Getting some control of himself, all red as a lobster, he announced that he felt it was his duty to pick up the little shift and bring it personally . . .

'The things he said, the blackguard!' Natasha shrieked and laughed. 'The things he said, the things he tempted me to do! The money he promised! He said Klavdia Petrovna would never learn of it. Well, speak, am I lying?' Natasha shouted to the hog, who only turned his muzzle away abashedly.

In the bedroom, carried away with her own mischief, Natasha dabbed some cream on Nikolai Ivanovich and was herself struck dumb with astonishment. The respectable ground-floor tenant's face shrank to a pig's snout, and his hands and feet acquired little hoofs. Looking at himself in the mirror, Nikolai Ivanovich let out a wild and desperate howl, but it was already too late. A few seconds later, saddled up, he was flying out of Moscow to devil knows where, sobbing with grief.

'I demand that my normal appearance be restored to me!' the hog suddenly grunted hoarsely, somewhere between frenzy and supplication. 'I'm not going to fly to any illegal gathering! Margarita Nikolaevna, it's your duty to call your housekeeper to order!'

'Ah, so now I'm a housekeeper? A housekeeper?' Natasha cried, pinching the hog's ear. 'And I used to be a goddess? What was it you called me?'

'Venus!' the hog replied tearfully, as he flew over a brook bubbling between stones, his little hoofs brushing the hazel bushes.

'Venus! Venus!' Natasha cried triumphantly, one hand on her hip, the other stretched out towards the moon. 'Margarita! Queen! Intercede for me so that I can stay a witch! They'll do anything for you, you have been granted power!'

And Margarita responded:

'All right, I promise.'

'Thank you!' exclaimed Natasha, and suddenly she cried out sharply and somehow longingly: 'Hey! Hey! Faster! Faster! Come on, speed it up!'

She dug her heels into the hog's sides, which had grown thinner during this insane ride, and he tore on, so that the air ripped open again, and a moment later Natasha could be seen only as a black speck in the distance, then vanished completely, and the noise of her flight melted away.

Margarita flew as slowly as before through the deserted and unfamiliar place, over hills strewn with occasional boulders among huge, widely spaced pines. Margarita now flew not over the tops of the pines but between their trunks, silvered on one side by the moon.

The light shadow of the flying woman glided over the ground ahead, the moon shining now on Margarita's back.

Margarita sensed the proximity of water, and guessed that her goal was near. The pines parted and Margarita rode slowly through the air up to a chalk cliff. Beyond this cliff, down in the shadows, lay a river. Mist hung clinging to the bushes on the cliff, but the opposite bank was flat and low. On it, under a solitary group of spreading trees, the light of a bonfire flickered and some small figures could be seen moving about. It seemed to Margarita that some nagging, merry little tune was coming from there. Further off, as far as the eye could see, there was no sign of habitation or people on the silvered plain.

Margarita leaped off the cliff and quickly descended to the water. The water enticed her after her airy race. Casting the broom aside, she ran and threw herself head first into the water. Her light body pierced the water's surface like an arrow, and the column of water thrown up almost reached the moon. The water turned out to be warm as in a bathhouse, and, emerging from the depths, Margarita swam her fill in the total solitude of night in this river.

There was no one near Margarita, but a little further away, behind the bushes, splashing and grunting could be heard – someone was also having a swim there.

Margarita ran out on to the bank. Her body was on fire after the swim. She felt no fatigue, and was joyfully capering about on the moist grass.

Suddenly she stopped dancing and pricked up her ears. The grunting came closer, and from behind the willow bushes some naked fat man emerged, with a black silk top hat pushed back on his head. His feet were covered with slimy mud, which made it seem that the swimmer was wearing black shoes. Judging by his huffing and hiccuping, he was properly drunk, as was confirmed, incidentally, by the fact that the river suddenly began to smell of cognac.

Seeing Margarita, the fat man peered at her and then shouted joyfully:

'What's this? Who is it I see? Claudine, it's you, the ungrieving widow! You're here, too?' and he came at her with his greetings.

Margarita stepped back and replied with dignity:

'Go to the devil! What sort of Claudine am I to you? Watch out who you're talking to,' and, after a moment's reflection, she added to her words a long, unprintable oath. All this had a sobering effect on the light-minded fat man.

'Ah!' he exclaimed softly and gave a start, 'magnanimously forgive me, bright Queen Margot! I mistook you for someone else. The cognac's to blame, curse it!' The fat man lowered himself to one knee, holding the top hat far out, made a bow, and started to prattle, mixing Russian phrases with French, some nonsense about the bloody wedding of his friend Guessard in Paris, and about the cognac, and about being mortified by his sad mistake.

'Why don't you put your trousers on, you son of a bitch,' Margarita said, softening.

The fat man grinned joyfully, seeing that Margarita was not angry, and rapturously declared that he found himself without trousers at the given moment only because in his absent-mindedness he had left them on the Yenisey River, where he had been swimming just before, but that he would presently fly there, since it was close at hand, and then, entrusting himself to her favour and patronage, he began to back away and went on backing away until he slipped and fell backwards into the water. But even as he fell, he kept on his face, framed in small side-whiskers, a smile of rapture and devotion.

Here Margarita gave a piercing whistle and, mounting the broom that flew up to her, crossed to the opposite bank of the river. The shadow of the chalk mountain did not reach that far, and the whole bank was flooded with moonlight.

As soon as Margarita touched the moist grass, the music under the pussy willows struck up louder, and a sheaf of sparks flew up more merrily from the bonfire. Under the pussy-willow branches, strewn with tender, fluffy catkins, visible in the moonlight, sat two rows of fat-faced frogs, puffing up as if they were made of rubber, playing a bravura march on wooden pipes. Glowing marsh-lights hung on willow twigs in front of the musicians, lighting up the music; the restless light of the bonfire danced on the frogs' faces.

The march was being played in honour of Margarita. She was given a most solemn reception. Transparent naiads stopped their round dance over the river and waved weeds at Margarita, and their far-audible greetings moaned across the deserted, greenish bank. Naked witches, jumping from behind the pussy willows, formed a line and began curtseying and making courtly bows. Someone goat-legged flew up and bent to her hand, spread silk on the grass, inquired whether the queen had had a good swim, and invited her to lie down and rest.

Margarita did just that. The goat-legged one offered her a glass of champagne, she drank it, and her heart became warm at once. Having inquired about Natasha's whereabouts, she received the reply that Natasha had already taken her swim and had flown ahead to Moscow on her hog, to warn them that Margarita would soon arrive and to help prepare her attire.

Margarita's short stay under the pussy willows was marked by one episode: there was a whistling in the air, and a black body, obviously missing its mark, dropped into the water. A few moments later there stood before Margarita that same fat side-whiskerist who had so unsuccessfully introduced himself on the other bank. He had apparently managed to get to the Yenisey and back, for he was in full evening dress, though wet from head to foot. The cognac had done him another bad turn: as he came down, he landed in the water after all. But he did not lose his smile even on this lamentable occasion, and the laughing Margarita admitted him to her hand.

Then they all started getting ready. The naiads finished their dance in the moonlight and melted into it. The goat-legged one deferentially inquired of Margarita how she had come to the river. On learning that she had come riding on a broom, he said:

'Oh, but why, it's so inconvenient!' He instantly slapped together some dubious-looking telephone from two twigs, and demanded of someone that a car be sent that very minute, which, that same minute, was actually done. An open, light sorrel car came down on the island, only in the driver's seat there sat no ordinary-looking driver, but a black, long-beaked rook in an oilcloth cap and gauntlets. The little island was becoming deserted. The witches flew off, melting into the moon-blaze. The bonfire was dying down, and the coals were covering over with hoary ash.

The goat-legged one helped Margarita in, and she sank on to the wide back seat of the sorrel car. The car roared, sprang up, and climbed almost to the moon; the island vanished, the river vanished, Margarita was racing to Moscow.

CHAPTER 22

By Candlelight

The steady humming of the car, flying high above the earth, lulled
Margarita, and the moonlight warmed her pleasantly. Closing her eyes,
she offered her face to the wind and thought with a certain sadness
about the unknown river bank she had left behind, which she sensed
she would never see again. After all the sorceries and wonders of that
evening, she could already guess precisely whom she was being taken
to visit, but that did not frighten her. The hope that there she would
manage to regain her happiness made her fearless. However, she was
not to dream of this happiness for long in the car. Either the rook
knew his job well, or the car was a good one, but Margarita soon
opened her eyes and saw beneath her not the forest darkness, but a
quivering sea of Moscow lights. The black bird-driver unscrewed the
right front wheel in flight, then landed the car in some completely
deserted cemetery in the Dorogomilovo area.

Having deposited the unquestioning Margarita by one of the graves
along with her broom, the rook started the car, aiming it straight into
the ravine beyond the cemetery. It tumbled noisily into it and there
perished. The rook saluted deferentially, mounted the wheel, and flew
off.

A black cloak appeared at once from behind one of the tombstones.
A fang flashed in the moonlight, and Margarita recognized Azazello.
He gestured to Margarita, inviting her to get on the broom, jumped
on to a long rapier himself, they both whirled up and in a few seconds,
unnoticed by anyone, landed near no. 302-bis on Sadovaya Street.

When the companions passed through the gateway, carrying the
broom and rapier under their arms, Margarita noticed a man languishing
there in a cap and high boots, probably waiting for someone. Light
though Azazello's and Margarita's footsteps were, the solitary man
heard them and twitched uneasily, not understanding who had produced
them.

By the sixth entrance they met a second man looking surprisingly
like the first. And again the same story repeated itself. Footsteps . . .

the man turned and frowned uneasily. And when the door opened and closed, he dashed after the invisible enterers, peeked into the front hall, but of course saw nothing.

A third man, the exact copy of the second, and therefore also of the first, stood watch on the third-floor landing. He smoked strong cigarettes, and Margarita had a fit of coughing as she walked past him. The smoker, as if pricked with a pin, jumped up from the bench he was sitting on, began turning around uneasily, went to the banister, looked down. Margarita and her companion were by that time already at the door of apartment no. 50. They did not ring the bell. Azazello noiselessly opened the door with his own key.

The first thing that struck Margarita was the darkness in which she found herself. It was as dark as underground, so that she involuntarily clutched at Azazello's cloak for fear of stumbling. But then, from far away and above, the light of some little lamp flickered and began to approach. Azazello took the broom from under Margarita's arm as they walked, and it disappeared without a sound in the darkness.

Here they started climbing some wide steps, and Margarita began to think there would be no end to them. She was struck that the front hall of an ordinary Moscow apartment could contain this extraordinary invisible, yet quite palpable, endless stairway. But the climb ended, and Margarita realized that she was on a landing. The light came right up to them, and Margarita saw in this light the face of a man, long and black, holding a little lamp in his hand. Those who in recent days had been so unfortunate as to cross paths with him, would certainly have recognized him even by the faint tongue of flame from the lamp. It was Koroviev, alias Fagott.

True, Koroviev's appearance was quite changed. The flickering light was reflected not in the cracked pince-nez, which it had long been time to throw in the trash, but in a monocle, which, true, was also cracked. The little moustache on his insolent face was twirled up and waxed, and Koroviev's blackness was quite simply explained – he was in formal attire. Only his chest was white.

The magician, choirmaster, sorcerer, interpreter – devil knows what he really was – Koroviev, in short, made his bows and, with a broad sweep of the lamp in the air, invited Margarita to follow him. Azazello disappeared.

'An amazingly strange evening,' thought Margarita, 'I expected anything but this. Has their electricity gone off, or what? But the most striking thing is the size of the place . . . How could it all be squeezed into a Moscow apartment? There's simply no way it could be! . . .'

However little light Koroviev's lamp gave out, Margarita realized that she was in an absolutely enormous hall, with a colonnade besides, dark and on first impression endless. Koroviev stopped by some sort of little settee, placed his lamp on some sort of post, gestured for Margarita to sit down, and settled himself beside her in a picturesque attitude, leaning his elbow on the post.

'Allow me to introduce myself to you,' creaked Koroviev, 'Koroviev. You are surprised there's no light? Economy, so you think, of course? Unh-unh! May the first executioner to come along, even one of those who later this evening will have the honour of kissing your knee, lop my head off on this very post if it's so! Messire simply doesn't like electric light, and we'll save it for the very last moment. And then, believe me, there'll be no lack of it. Perhaps it would even be better to have less.'

Margarita liked Koroviev, and his rattling chatter had a soothing effect on her.

'No,' replied Margarita, 'most of all I'm struck that there's room for all this.' She made a gesture with her hand, emphasizing the enormousness of the hall.

Koroviev grinned sweetly, which made the shadows stir in the folds of his nose.

'The most uncomplicated thing of all!' he replied. 'For someone well acquainted with the fifth dimension, it costs nothing to expand space to the desired proportions. I'll say more, respected lady – to devil knows what proportions! I, however,' Koroviev went on chattering, 'have known people who had no idea, not only of the fifth dimension, but generally of anything at all, and who nevertheless performed absolute wonders in expanding their space. Thus, for instance, one city-dweller, as I've been told, having obtained a three-room apartment on Zemlyanoy Val, transformed it instantly, without any fifth dimension or other things that addle the brain, into a four-room apartment by dividing one room in half with a partition.

'He forthwith exchanged that one for two separate apartments in different parts of Moscow: one of three rooms, the other of two. You must agree that that makes five. The three-room one he exchanged for two separate ones, each of two rooms, and became the owner, as you can see for yourself, of six rooms – true, scattered in total disorder all over Moscow. He was just getting ready to perform his last and most brilliant leap, by advertising in the newspapers that he wanted to exchange six rooms in different parts of Moscow for one five-room apartment on Zemlyanoy Val, when his activity ceased for reasons independent of him. He probably also has some sort of room now, only I venture to assure you it is not in Moscow. A real slicker, you see, ma'am, and you keep talking about the fifth dimension!'

Though she had never talked about the fifth dimension, and it was Koroviev himself who kept talking about it, Margarita laughed gaily, hearing the story of the adventures of the apartment slicker. Koroviev went on:

'But to business, to business, Margarita Nikolaevna. You're quite an intelligent woman, and of course have already guessed who our host is.'

Margarita's heart thumped, and she nodded.

'Well, and so, ma'am,' Koroviev said, 'and so, we're enemies of any sort of reticence and mysteriousness. Messire gives one ball annually. It is called the spring ball of the full moon, or the ball of the hundred kings. Such a crowd! . . .' here Koroviev held his cheek as if he had a toothache. 'However, I hope you'll be convinced of it yourself. Now, Messire is a bachelor, as you yourself, of course, understand. Yet a hostess is needed,' Koroviev spread his arms, 'without a hostess, you must agree . . .'

Margarita listened to Koroviev, trying not to miss a single word; she felt cold under her heart, the hope of happiness made her head spin.

'The tradition has been established,' Koroviev said further, 'that the hostess of the ball must without fail be named Margarita, first, and second, she must be a native of the place. And we, you will kindly note, are travelling and at the present moment are in Moscow. We found one hundred and twenty-one Margaritas in Moscow, and, would you believe it,' here Koroviev slapped himself on the thigh with despair, 'not one of them was suitable! And, at last, by a happy fate . . .'

Koroviev grinned expressively, inclining his body, and again Margarita's heart went cold.

'In short!' Koroviev cried out. 'Quite shortly: you won't refuse to take this responsibility upon yourself?'

'I won't refuse!' Margarita replied firmly.

'Done!' said Koroviev and, raising the little lamp, added: 'Please follow me.'

They walked between the columns and finally came to another hall, in which for some reason there was a strong smell of lemons, where some rustlings were heard and something brushed against Margarita's head. She gave a start.

'Don't be frightened,' Koroviev reassured her sweetly, taking Margarita under the arm, 'it's Behemoth's contrivances for the ball, that's all. And generally I will allow myself the boldness of advising you, Margarita Nikolaevna, never to be afraid of anything. It is unreasonable. The ball will be a magnificent one, I will not conceal it from you. We will see persons the scope of whose power in their own time was extremely great. But, really, once you think how microscopically small their possibilities were compared to those of him to whose retinue I have the honour of belonging, it seems ridiculous, and even, I would say, sad ... And, besides, you are of royal blood yourself.'

'Why of royal blood?' Margarita whispered fearfully, pressing herself to Koroviev.

'Ah, my Queen,' Koroviev rattled on playfully, 'questions of blood are the most complicated questions in the world! And if we were to question certain great-grandmothers, especially those who enjoyed a reputation as shrinking violets, the most astonishing secrets would be uncovered, my respected Margarita Nikolaevna! I would not be sinning in the least if, in speaking of that, I should make reference to a whimsically shuffled pack of cards. There are things in which neither barriers of rank nor even the borders between countries have any validity whatsoever. A hint: one of the French queens who lived in the sixteenth century would, one must suppose, be very amazed if someone told her that after all these years I would be leading her lovely great-great-great-granddaughter on my arm through the ballrooms of Moscow. But we've arrived!'

Here Koroviev blew out his lamp and it vanished from his hands, and Margarita saw lying on the floor in front of her a streak of light under some dark door. And on this door Koroviev softly knocked. Here Margarita became so agitated that her teeth chattered and a chill ran down her spine.

The door opened. The room turned out to be very small. Margarita saw a wide oak bed with dirty, rumpled and bunched-up sheets and pillows. Before the bed was an oak table with carved legs, on which stood a candelabrum with sockets in the form of a bird's claws. In these seven golden claws[1] burned thick wax candles. Besides that, there was on the table a large chessboard with pieces of extraordinarily artful workmanship. A little low bench stood on a small, shabby rug. There was yet another table with some golden bowl and another candelabrum with branches in the form of snakes. The room smelled of sulphur and pitch. Shadows from the lights criss-crossed on the floor.

Among those present Margarita immediately recognized Azazello, now dressed in a tailcoat and standing at the head of the bed. The dressed-up Azazello no longer resembled that bandit in whose form he had appeared to Margarita in the Alexandrovsky Garden, and his bow to Margarita was very gallant.

A naked witch, that same Hella who had so embarrassed the respectable barman of the Variety, and – alas – the same who had so fortunately been scared off by the cock on the night of the notorious séance, sat on a rug on the floor by the bed, stirring something in a pot which gave off a sulphurous steam.

Besides these, there was also a huge black tom-cat in the room, sitting on a high tabouret before the chess table, holding a chess knight in his right paw.

Hella rose and bowed to Margarita. The cat, jumping off the tabouret, did likewise. Scraping with his right hind paw, he dropped the knight and crawled under the bed after it.

Margarita, sinking with fear, nevertheless made all this out by the perfidious candlelight. Her eyes were drawn to the bed, on which sat he whom, still quite recently, at the Patriarch's Ponds, poor Ivan had tried to convince that the devil does not exist. It was this non-existent one who was sitting on the bed.

Two eyes were fixed on Margarita's face. The right one with a golden spark at its bottom, drilling anyone to the bottom of his soul, and the left one empty and black, like the narrow eye of a needle, like the entrance to the bottomless well of all darkness and shadow. Woland's face was twisted to one side, the right corner of the mouth drawn down, the high, bald forehead scored by deep wrinkles running parallel to the sharp eyebrows. The skin of Woland's face was as if burned for all eternity by the sun.

Woland, broadly sprawled on the bed, was wearing nothing but a long nightshirt, dirty and patched on the left shoulder. One bare leg was tucked under him, the other was stretched out on the little bench. It was the knee of this dark leg that Hella was rubbing with some smoking ointment.

Margarita also made out on Woland's bared, hairless chest a beetle artfully carved[2] from dark stone, on a gold chain and with some inscriptions on its back. Beside Woland, on a heavy stand, stood a strange globe, as if alive, lit on one side by the sun.

The silence lasted a few seconds. 'He's studying me,' thought Margarita, and with an effort of will she tried to control the trembling in her legs.

At last Woland began to speak, smiling, which made his sparkling eye as if to flare up.

'Greetings to you, Queen, and I beg you to excuse my homely attire.'

The voice of Woland was so low that on some syllables it drew out into a wheeze.

Woland took a long sword from the sheets, leaned down, poked it under the bed, and said:

'Out with you! The game is cancelled. The guest has arrived.'

'By no means,' Koroviev anxiously piped, prompter-like, at Margarita's ear.

'By no means . . .' began Margarita.

'Messire . . .' Koroviev breathed into her ear.

'By no means, Messire,' Margarita replied softly but distinctly, gaining control over herself, and she added with a smile: 'I beg you not to interrupt your game. I imagine the chess journals would pay good money for the chance to publish it.'

Azazello gave a low but approving grunt, and Woland, looking intently at Margarita, observed as if to himself:

'Yes, Koroviev is right. How whimsically the deck has been shuffled! Blood!'

He reached out and beckoned Margarita to him with his hand. She went up, not feeling the floor under her bare feet. Woland placed his hand, heavy as if made of stone and at the same time hot as fire, on Margarita's shoulder, pulled her towards him, and sat her on the bed by his side.

'Well,' he said, 'since you are so charmingly courteous – and I expected nothing else – let us not stand on ceremony.' He again leaned over the side of the bed and cried: 'How long will this circus under the bed continue? Come out, you confounded Hans!'[3]

'I can't find my knight,' the cat responded from under the bed in a muffled and false voice, 'it's ridden off somewhere, and I keep getting some frog instead.'

'You don't imagine you're at some fairground, do you?' asked Woland, pretending to be angry. 'There's no frog under the bed! Leave these cheap tricks for the Variety. If you don't appear at once, we'll consider that you've forfeited, you damned deserter!'

'Not for anything, Messire!' yelled the cat, and he got out from under the bed that same second, holding the knight in his paw.

'Allow me to present...' Woland began and interrupted himself: 'No, I simply cannot look at this buffoon. See what he's turned himself into under the bed!'

Standing on his hind legs, the dust-covered cat was meanwhile making his bows to Margarita. There was now a white bow-tie on the cat's neck, and a pair of ladies' mother-of-pearl opera glasses hung from a strap on his neck. What's more, the cat's whiskers were gilded.

'Well, what's all this now?' exclaimed Woland. 'Why have you gilded your whiskers? And what the devil do you need the bow-tie for, when you're not even wearing trousers?'

'A cat is not supposed to wear trousers, Messire,' the cat replied with great dignity. 'You're not going to tell me to wear boots, too, are you? Puss-in-Boots exists only in fairy tales, Messire. But have you ever seen anyone at a ball without a bow-tie? I do not intend to put myself in a ridiculous situation and risk being chucked out! Everyone adorns himself with what he can. You may consider what I've said as referring to the opera glasses as well, Messire!'

'But the whiskers?...'

'I don't understand,' the cat retorted drily. 'Why could Azazello and Koroviev put white powder on themselves as they were shaving today, and how is that better than gold? I powdered my whiskers, that's all! If I'd shaved myself, it would be a different matter! A shaved cat – now, that is indeed an outrage, I'm prepared to admit it a thousand times over. But generally,' here the cat's voice quavered touchily, 'I see I am being made the object of a certain captiousness, and I see that a serious problem stands before me – am I to attend the ball? What have you to say about that, Messire?'

And the cat got so puffed up with offence that it seemed he would burst in another second.

'Ah, the cheat, the cheat,' said Woland, shaking his head. 'Each time his game is in a hopeless situation, he starts addling your pate like the crudest mountebank on a street corner. Sit down at once and stop slinging this verbal muck.'

'I shall sit down,' replied the cat, sitting down, 'but I shall enter an objection with regard to your last. My speeches in no way resemble verbal muck, as you have been pleased to put it in the presence of a lady, but rather a sequence of tightly packed syllogisms, the merit of which would be appreciated by such connoisseurs as Sextus Empiricus, Martianus Capella,[4] and, for all I know, Aristotle himself.'

'Your king is in check,' said Woland.

'Very well, very well,' responded the cat, and he began studying the chessboard through his opera glasses.

'And so, donna,' Woland addressed Margarita, 'I present to you my retinue. This one who is playing the fool is the cat Behemoth. Azazello and Koroviev you have already met. I present to you my maid-servant, Hella: efficient, quick, and there is no service she cannot render.'

The beautiful Hella was smiling as she turned her green-tinged eyes to Margarita, without ceasing to dip into the ointment and apply it to Woland's knee.

'Well, that's the lot,' Woland concluded, wincing as Hella pressed especially hard on his knee. 'A small, mixed and guileless company, as you see.' He fell silent and began to spin the globe in front of him, which was so artfully made that the blue oceans moved on it and the cap at the pole lay like a real cap of ice and snow.

On the chessboard, meanwhile, confusion was setting in. A thoroughly upset king in a white mantle was shuffling on his square, desperately raising his arms. Three white pawn-mercenaries with halberds gazed in perplexity at the bishop brandishing his crozier and pointing forward to where, on two adjacent squares, white and black, Woland's black horsemen could be seen on two fiery chargers pawing the squares with their hoofs.

Margarita was extremely interested and struck by the fact that the chessmen were alive.

The cat, taking the opera glasses from his eyes, prodded his king lightly in the back. The king covered his face with his hands in despair.

'Things aren't so great, my dear Behemoth,' Koroviev said quietly in a venomous voice.

'The situation is serious but by no means hopeless,' Behemoth responded. 'What's more, I'm quite certain of final victory. Once I've analysed the situation properly.'

He set about this analysing in a rather strange manner – namely, by winking and making all sorts of faces at his king.

'Nothing helps,' observed Koroviev.

'Aie!' cried Behemoth, 'the parrots have flown away, just as I predicted!'

Indeed, from somewhere far away came the noise of many wings. Koroviev and Azazello rushed out of the room.

'Devil take you with your ball amusements!' Woland grunted without tearing his eyes from his globe.

As soon as Koroviev and Azazello disappeared, Behemoth's winking took on greater dimensions. The white king finally understood what was wanted of him. He suddenly pulled off his mantle, dropped it on the square, and ran off the board. The bishop covered himself with the abandoned royal garb and took the king's place.

Koroviev and Azazello came back.

'Lies, as usual,' grumbled Azazello, with a sidelong glance at Behemoth.

'I thought I heard it,' replied the cat.

'Well, is this going to continue for long?' asked Woland. 'Your king is in check.'

'I must have heard wrong, my master,' replied the cat. 'My king is not and cannot be in check.'

'I repeat, your king is in check!'

'Messire,' the cat responded in a falsely alarmed voice, 'you are overtired. My king is not in check.'

'The king is on square G-2,' said Woland, without looking at the board.

'Messire, I'm horrified!' howled the cat, showing horror on his mug. 'There is no king on that square!'

'What's that?' Woland asked in perplexity and began looking at the board, where the bishop standing on the king's square kept turning away and hiding behind his hand.

'Ah, you scoundrel,' Woland said pensively.

'Messire! Again I appeal to logic!' the cat began, pressing his paws to his chest. 'If a player announces that the king is in check, and meanwhile there's no trace of the king on the board, the check must be recognized as invalid!'

'Do you give up or not?' Woland cried in a terrible voice.

'Let me think it over,' the cat replied humbly, resting his elbows on the table, putting his paws over his ears, and beginning to think. He thought for a long time and finally said: 'I give up.'

'The obstinate beast should be killed,' whispered Azazello.

'Yes, I give up,' said the cat, 'but I do so only because I am unable to play in an atmosphere of persecution on the part of the envious!' He stood up and the chessmen climbed into their box.

'Hella, it's time,' said Woland, and Hella disappeared from the room. 'My leg hurts, and now this ball . . .' he continued.

'Allow me,' Margarita quietly asked.

Woland looked at her intently and moved his knee towards her.

The liquid, hot as lava, burned her hands, but Margarita, without wincing, and trying not to cause any pain, rubbed it into his knee.

'My attendants insist it's rheumatism,' Woland was saying, not taking his eyes off Margarita, 'but I strongly suspect that this pain in my knee was left me as a souvenir by a charming witch with whom I was closely acquainted in the year 1571, on Mount Brocken,[5] on the Devil's Podium.'

'Ah, can that be so!' said Margarita.

'Nonsense! In another three hundred years it will all go away! I've been recommended a host of medications, but I keep to my granny's old ways. Amazing herbs she left me, my grandam, that vile old thing! Incidentally, tell me, are you suffering from anything? Perhaps you have some sort of sorrow or soul-poisoning anguish?'

'No, Messire, none of that,' replied the clever Margarita, 'and now that I'm here with you, I feel myself quite well.'

'Blood is a great thing . . .' Woland said gaily, with no obvious point, and added: 'I see you're interested in my globe.'

'Oh, yes, I've never seen anything like it.'

'It's a nice little object. Frankly speaking, I don't enjoy listening to the news on the radio. It's always reported by some girls who pronounce the names of places inarticulately. Besides, every third one has some slight speech defect, as if they're chosen on purpose. My globe is much more convenient, especially since I need a precise knowledge of events. For instance, do you see this chunk of land, washed on one side by the ocean? Look, it's filling with fire. A war has started there. If you look closer, you'll see the details.'

Margarita leaned towards the globe and saw the little square of land spread out, get painted in many colours, and turn as it were into a relief map. And then she saw the little ribbon of a river, and some village near it. A little house the size of a pea grew and became the size of a matchbox. Suddenly and noiselessly the roof of this house flew up along with a cloud of black smoke, and the walls collapsed, so that nothing was left of the little two-storey box except a small heap with black smoke pouring from it. Bringing her eye still closer, Margarita made out a small female figure lying on the ground, and next to her, in a pool of blood, a little child with outstretched arms.

'That's it,' Woland said, smiling, 'he had no time to sin. Abaddon's[6] work is impeccable.'

'I wouldn't want to be on the side that this Abaddon is against,' said Margarita. 'Whose side is he on?'

'The longer I talk with you,' Woland responded amiably, 'the more I'm convinced that you are very intelligent. I'll set you at ease. He is of a rare impartiality and sympathizes equally with both sides of the fight. Owing to that, the results are always the same for both sides. Abaddon!' Woland called in a low voice, and here there emerged from the wall the figure of some gaunt man in dark glasses. These glasses produced such a strong impression on Margarita that she cried out softly and hid her face in Woland's leg. 'Ah, stop it!' cried Woland. 'Modern people are so nervous!' He swung and slapped Margarita on the back so that a ringing went through her whole body. 'Don't you see he's got his glasses on? Besides, there has never yet been, and never will be, an occasion when Abaddon appears before someone prematurely. And, finally, I'm here. You are my guest! I simply wanted to show him to you.'

Abaddon stood motionless.

'And is it possible for him to take off his glasses for a second?'

Margarita asked, pressing herself to Woland and shuddering, but now from curiosity.

'Ah, no, that's impossible,' Woland replied seriously and waved his hand at Abaddon, and he was no more. 'What do you wish to say, Azazello?'

'Messire,' replied Azazello, 'allow me to say – we've got two strangers here: a beauty who is whimpering and pleading to be allowed to stay with her lady, and with her, begging your pardon, there is also her hog.'

'Strange behaviour for a beauty!' observed Woland.

'It's Natasha, Natasha!' exclaimed Margarita.

'Well, let her stay with her lady. And the hog – to the cooks.'

'To slaughter him?' Margarita cried fearfully. 'For pity's sake, Messire, it's Nikolai Ivanovich, the ground-floor tenant. It's a misunderstanding, you see, she daubed him with the cream . . .'

'But wait,' said Woland, 'why the devil would anyone slaughter him? Let him stay with the cooks, that's all. You must agree, I cannot let him into the ballroom.'

'No, really . . .' Azazello added and announced: 'Midnight is approaching, Messire.'

'Ah, very good.' Woland turned to Margarita: 'And so, if you please . . . I thank you beforehand. Don't become flustered and don't be afraid of anything. Drink nothing but water, otherwise you'll get groggy and it will be hard for you. It's time!'

Margarita got up from the rug, and then Koroviev appeared in the doorway.

CHAPTER 23

The Great Ball at Satan's

Midnight was approaching; they had to hurry. Margarita dimly perceived her surroundings. Candles and a jewelled pool remained in her memory. As she stood in the bottom of this pool, Hella, with the assistance of Natasha, doused her with some hot, thick and red liquid. Margarita felt a salty taste on her lips and realized that she was being washed in blood. The bloody mantle was changed for another – thick, transparent, pinkish – and Margarita's head began to spin from rose oil. Then Margarita was laid on a crystal couch and rubbed with some big green leaves until she shone.

Here the cat burst in and started to help. He squatted down at Margarita's feet and began rubbing up her soles with the air of someone shining shoes in the street.

Margarita does not remember who stitched slippers for her from pale rose petals or how these slippers got fastened by themselves with golden clasps. Some force snatched Margarita up and put her before a mirror, and a royal diamond crown gleamed in her hair. Koroviev appeared from somewhere and hung a heavy, oval-framed picture of a black poodle by a heavy chain on Margarita's breast. This adornment was extremely burdensome to the queen. The chain at once began to chafe her neck, the picture pulled her down. But something compensated Margarita for the inconveniences that the chain with the black poodle caused her, and this was the deference with which Koroviev and Behemoth began to treat her.

'Never mind, never mind, never mind!' muttered Koroviev at the door of the room with the pool. 'No help for it, you must, must, must ... Allow me, Queen, to give you a last piece of advice. Among the guests there will be different sorts, oh, very different, but no one, Queen Margot, should be shown any preference! Even if you don't like someone ... I understand that you will not, of course, show it on your face – no, no, it's unthinkable! He'll notice it, he'll notice it instantly! You must love him, love him, Queen! The mistress of the ball will be rewarded a hundredfold for that. And also – don't ignore anyone! At least a little smile, if there's no time to drop a word, at least a tiny turn of the head! Anything you like, but not inattention, they'll sicken from that . . .'

Here Margarita, accompanied by Koroviev and Behemoth, stepped out of the room with the pool into total darkness.

'I, I,' whispered the cat, 'I give the signal!'

'Go ahead!' Koroviev replied from the darkness.

'The ball!!!!' shrieked the cat piercingly, and just then Margarita cried out and shut her eyes for a few seconds. The ball fell on her all at once in the form of light, and, with it, of sound and smell. Taken under the arm by Koroviev, Margarita saw herself in a tropical forest. Red-breasted, green-tailed parrots fluttered from liana to liana and cried out deafeningly: 'Delighted!' But the forest soon ended, and its bathhouse stuffiness changed at once to the coolness of a ballroom with columns of some yellowish, sparkling stone. This ballroom, just like the forest, was completely empty, except for some naked negroes with silver bands on their heads who were standing by the columns. Their faces turned a dirty brown from excitement when Margarita flew into the ballroom with her retinue, in which Azazello showed up from somewhere. Here Koroviev let go of Margarita's arm and whispered:

'Straight to the tulips.'

A low wall of white tulips had grown up in front of Margarita, and beyond it she saw numberless lamps under little shades and behind them the white chests and black shoulders of tailcoaters. Then Margarita understood where the sound of the ball was coming from. The roar of trumpets crashed down on her, and the soaring of violins that burst from under it doused her body as if with blood. The orchestra of about a hundred and fifty men was playing a polonaise.

The tailcoated man hovering over the orchestra paled on seeing Margarita, smiled, and suddenly, with a sweep of his arms, got the whole orchestra to its feet. Not interrupting the music for a moment, the orchestra, standing, doused Margarita with sound. The man over the orchestra turned from it and bowed deeply, spreading his arms wide, and Margarita, smiling, waved her hand to him.

'No, not enough, not enough,' whispered Koroviev, 'he won't sleep all night. Call out to him: "Greetings to you, waltz king!"'[1]

Margarita cried it out, and marvelled that her voice, full as a bell, was heard over the howling of the orchestra. The man started with happiness and put his left hand to his chest, while the right went on brandishing a white baton at the orchestra.

'Not enough, not enough,' whispered Koroviev, 'look to the left, to the first violins, and nod so that each one thinks you've recognized him individually. There are only world celebrities here. Nod to that one . . . at the first stand, that's Vieuxtemps!² . . . There, very good . . . Now, onward!'

'Who is the conductor?' Margarita asked, flying off.

'Johann Strauss!' cried the cat. 'And they can hang me from a liana in a tropical forest if such an orchestra ever played at any ball! I invited them! And, note, not one got sick or declined!'

In the next room there were no columns. Instead there stood walls of red, pink and milk-white roses on one side, and on the other a wall of Japanese double camellias. Between these walls fountains spurted up, hissing, and bubbly champagne seethed in three pools, the first of which was transparent violet, the second ruby, the third crystal. Next to them negroes in scarlet headbands dashed about, filling flat cups from the pools with silver dippers. The pink wall had a gap in it, where a man in a red swallowtail coat was flailing away on a platform. Before him thundered an unbearably loud jazz band. As soon as the conductor saw Margarita, he bent before her so that his hands touched the floor, then straightened up and cried piercingly:

'Hallelujah!'

He slapped himself on the knee – one! – then criss-cross on the other knee – two! – then snatched a cymbal from the hands of the end musician and banged it on a column.

As she flew off, Margarita saw only that the virtuoso jazzman, fighting against the polonaise blowing in Margarita's back, was beating his jazzmen on the heads with the cymbal while they cowered in comic fright.

Finally they flew out on to the landing where, as Margarita realized, she had been met in the dark by Koroviev with his little lamp. Now on this landing the light pouring from clusters of crystal grapes blinded the eye. Margarita was put in place, and under her left arm she found a low amethyst column.

'You may rest your arm on it if it becomes too difficult,' Koroviev whispered.

Some black man threw a pillow under Margarita's feet embroidered with a golden poodle, and she, obedient to someone's hands, bent her right leg at the knee and placed her foot on it.

Margarita tried to look around. Koroviev and Azazello stood beside her in formal poses. Next to Azazello stood another three young men, vaguely reminding Margarita of Abaddon. It blew cold in her back. Looking there, Margarita saw bubbly wine spurt from the marble wall behind her and pour into a pool of ice. At her left foot she felt something warm and furry. It was Behemoth.

Margarita was high up, and a grandiose stairway covered with carpet descended from her feet. Below, so far away that it was as if Margarita were looking the wrong way through binoculars, she saw a vast front hall with an absolutely enormous fireplace, into the cold and black maw of which a five-ton truck could easily have driven. The front hall and stairway, so flooded with light that it hurt the eyes, were empty. The sound of trumpets now came to Margarita from far away. Thus they stood motionless for about a minute.

'But where are the guests?' Margarita asked Koroviev.

'They'll come, Queen, they'll come, they'll come soon enough. There'll be no lack of them. And, really, I'd rather go and chop wood than receive them here on the landing.'

'Chop wood – hah!' picked up the garrulous cat. 'I'd rather work as a tram conductor, and there's no worse job in the world than that!'

'Everything must be made ready in advance, Queen,' explained Koroviev, his eye gleaming through the broken monocle. 'There's nothing more loathsome than when the first guest to arrive languishes, not knowing what to do, and his lawful beldame nags at him in a whisper for having come before everybody else. Such balls should be thrown in the trash, Queen.'

'Definitely in the trash,' confirmed the cat.

'No more than ten seconds till midnight,' said Koroviev. 'It'll start presently.'

Those ten seconds seemed extremely long to Margarita. Obviously they had already passed and precisely nothing had happened. But here something suddenly crashed downstairs in the huge fireplace, and from it leaped a gallows with some half-decayed remains dangling from it. The remains fell from the rope, struck the floor, and from it leaped a handsome dark-haired man in a tailcoat and patent leather shoes. A half-rotten little coffin ran out of the fireplace, its lid fell off, and another remains tumbled out of it. The handsome man gallantly leaped over to it and offered it his bent arm. The second remains put itself together into a fidgety woman in black shoes, with black feathers on her head, and then the man and the woman both hastened up the stairs.

'The first!' exclaimed Koroviev. 'Monsieur Jacques[3] and his spouse. I commend to you, Queen, one of the most interesting of men. A confirmed counterfeiter, a traitor to his government, but a rather good alchemist. Famous,' Koroviev whispered in Margarita's ear, 'for having poisoned a king's mistress. That doesn't happen to everyone! Look how handsome he is!'

The pale Margarita, her mouth open, watched as both gallows and coffin disappeared into some side passage in the front hall.

'Delighted!' the cat yelled right into the face of Monsieur Jacques as he came up the stairs.

At that moment a headless skeleton with a torn-off arm emerged from the fireplace, struck the ground, and turned into a man in a tailcoat.

Monsieur Jacques's spouse was already going on one knee before Margarita and, pale with excitement, was kissing Margarita's foot.

'Queen . . .' Monsieur Jacques's spouse murmured.

'The queen is delighted!' cried Koroviev.

'Queen . . .' the handsome Monsieur Jacques said quietly.

'We're delighted,' howled the cat.

The young men, Azazello's companions, smiling lifeless but affable smiles, were already shouldering Monsieur Jacques and his spouse to one side, towards the cups of champagne that the negroes were holding. The single man in the tailcoat was coming up the stairs at a run.

'Earl Robert,'[4] Koroviev whispered to Margarita, 'interesting as ever. Note how funny, Queen: the reverse case, this one was a queen's lover and poisoned his wife.'

'We're very glad, Earl,' cried Behemoth.

Out of the fireplace, bursting open and falling apart, three coffins tumbled one after another, then came someone in a black mantle, whom the next one to run out of the black maw stabbed in the back with a knife. A stifled cry was heard from below. An almost entirely decomposed corpse ran out of the fireplace. Margarita shut her eyes, and someone's hand held a flacon of smelling salts to her nose. Margarita thought the hand was Natasha's.

The stairway began to fill up. Now on each step there were tailcoaters, looking quite alike from afar, and naked women with them, who differed from each other only in the colour of their shoes and of the feathers on their heads.

Coming towards Margarita, hobbling, a strange wooden boot on her left foot, was a lady with nunnishly lowered eyes, thin and modest, and with a wide green band around her neck for some reason.

'Who is this ... green one?' Margarita asked mechanically.

'A most charming and respectable lady,' whispered Koroviev, 'I commend her to you: Madame Tofana.[5] Extremely popular among young, lovely Neapolitans, as well as the ladies of Palermo, especially those of them who had grown weary of their husbands. It does happen, Queen, that one grows weary of one's husband...'

'Yes,' Margarita replied in a hollow voice, smiling at the same time to two tailcoaters who bent before her one after the other, kissing her knee and hand.

'And so,' Koroviev managed to whisper to Margarita and at the same time to cry out to someone: 'Duke! A glass of champagne? I'm delighted! ... Yes, so then, Madame Tofana entered into the situation of these poor women and sold them some sort of water in little vials. The wife poured this water into her spouse's soup, he ate it, thanked her for being so nice, and felt perfectly well. True, a few hours later he would begin to get very thirsty, then go to bed, and a day later the lovely Neapolitan who had fed her husband soup would be free as the spring breeze.'

'But what's that on her foot?' asked Margarita, tirelessly offering her hand to the guests who came ahead of the hobbling Madame Tofana. 'And why that green band? A withered neck?'

'Delighted, Prince!' cried Koroviev, and at the same time whispered to Margarita: 'A beautiful neck, but an unpleasantness happened to her in prison. What she has on her foot, Queen, is a Spanish boot,[6] and the band is explained this way: when the prison guards learned that some five hundred ill-chosen husbands had departed Naples and Palermo for ever, in the heat of the moment they strangled Madame Tofana in prison.'

'How happy I am, O kindest Queen, that the high honour has fallen to me . . .' Tofana whispered nunnishly, trying to lower herself to one knee – the Spanish boot hindered her. Koroviev and Behemoth helped her up.

'I'm very glad,' Margarita answered her, at the same time offering her hand to others.

Now a steady stream was coming up the stairs from below. Margarita could no longer see what was going on in the front hall. She mechanically raised and lowered her hand and smiled uniformly to the guests. There was a hum in the air on the landing; from the ballrooms Margarita had left, music could be heard, like the sea.

'But this one is a boring woman,' Koroviev no longer whispered, but spoke aloud, knowing that in the hubbub of voices no one would hear him. 'She adores balls, and keeps dreaming of complaining about her handkerchief.'

Margarita's glance picked out among those coming up the woman at whom Koroviev was pointing. She was young, about twenty, of remarkably beautiful figure, but with somehow restless and importunate eyes.

'What handkerchief?' asked Margarita.

'She has a chambermaid assigned to her,' explained Koroviev, 'who for thirty years has been putting a handkerchief on her night table during the night. She wakes up and the handkerchief is there. She's tried burning it in the stove and drowning it in the river, but nothing helps.'

'What handkerchief?' whispered Margarita, raising and lowering her arm.

'A blue-bordered one. The thing is that when she worked in a café, the owner once invited her to the pantry, and nine months later she gave birth to a boy, took him to the forest, stuffed the handkerchief into his mouth, and then buried the boy in the ground. At the trial she said she had no way of feeding the child.'

'And where is the owner of the café?' asked Margarita.

'Queen,' the cat suddenly creaked from below, 'what, may I ask, does the owner have to do with it? It wasn't he who smothered the infant in the forest!'

Margarita, without ceasing to smile and proffer her right hand, dug the sharp nails of the left into Behemoth's ear and whispered to him:

'If you, scum, allow yourself to interfere in the conversation again . . .'

Behemoth squeaked in a not very ball-like fashion and rasped:

'Queen ... the ear will get swollen ... why spoil the ball with a swollen ear? ... I was speaking legally, from the legal point of view ... I say no more, I say no more. Consider me not a cat but a post, only let go of my ear!'

Margarita released his ear, and the importunate, gloomy eyes were before her.

'I am happy, Queen-hostess, to be invited to the great ball of the full moon!'

'And I am glad to see you,' Margarita answered her, 'very glad. Do you like champagne?'

'What are you doing, Queen?!' Koroviev cried desperately but soundlessly in Margarita's ear. 'There'll be a traffic jam!'

'Yes, I do,' the woman said imploringly, and suddenly began repeating mechanically: 'Frieda,[7] Frieda, Frieda! My name is Frieda, Queen!'

'Get drunk tonight, Frieda, and don't think about anything,' said Margarita.

Frieda reached out both arms to Margarita, but Koroviev and Behemoth very adroitly took her under the arms and she blended into the crowd.

Now people were coming in a solid wall from below, as if storming the landing where Margarita stood. Naked women's bodies came up between tailcoated men. Their swarthy, white, coffee-bean-coloured, and altogether black bodies floated towards Margarita. In their hair – red, black, chestnut, light as flax – precious stones glittered and danced, spraying sparkles into the flood of light. And as if someone had sprinkled the storming column of men with droplets of light, diamond studs sprayed light from their chests. Every second now Margarita felt lips touch her knee, every second she held out her hand to be kissed, her face was contracted into a fixed mask of greeting.

'I'm delighted,' Koroviev sang monotonously, 'we're delighted . . . the queen is delighted . . .'

'The queen is delighted . . .' Azazello echoed nasally behind her back.

'I'm delighted!' the cat kept exclaiming.

'The marquise . . .[8] muttered Koroviev, 'poisoned her father, two brothers and two sisters for the inheritance . . . The queen is delighted! . . . Madame Minkin . . .[9] Ah, what a beauty! A bit nervous. Why burn the maid's face with the curling-irons? Of course, in such conditions one gets stabbed ... The queen is delighted! ... Queen, one second of attention! The emperor Rudolf[10] – sorcerer and alchemist ... Another alchemist – got hanged ... Ah, here she is! Ah, what a wonderful brothel she ran in Strasbourg! ... We're delighted! ... A Moscow dressmaker,[11] we all love her for her inexhaustible fantasy ... She kept a shop and invented a terribly funny trick: drilled two round holes in the wall ...'

'And the ladies didn't know?' asked Margarita.

'Every one of them knew, Queen,' answered Koroviev. 'Delighted! ... This twenty-year-old boy was distinguished from childhood by strange qualities, a dreamer and an eccentric. A girl fell in love with him, and he went and sold her to a brothel ...'

A river came streaming from below, and there was no end to this river in sight. Its source – the enormous fireplace – continued to feed it. Thus one hour passed and a second commenced. Here Margarita began to notice that her chain had become heavier than before. Something strange also happened with her arm. Now, before raising it, Margarita had to wince. Koroviev's interesting observations ceased to amuse Margarita. Slant-eyed Mongolian faces, white faces and black became undifferentiated to her, they merged at times, and the air between them would for some reason begin to tremble and flow. A sharp pain, as if from a needle, suddenly pierced Margarita's right arm, and, clenching her teeth, she rested her elbow on the post. Some rustling, as if from wings against the walls, was now coming from the ballroom, and it was clear that unprecedented hordes of guests were dancing there, and it seemed to Margarita that even the massive marble, mosaic and crystal floors of this prodigious room were pulsing rhythmically.

Neither Gaius Caesar Caligula[12] nor Messalina[13] interested Margarita any longer, nor did any of the kings, dukes, cavaliers, suicides, poisoners, gallowsbirds, procuresses, prison guards and sharpers, executioners, informers, traitors, madmen, sleuths, seducers. All their names became jumbled in her head, the faces stuck together into one huge pancake, and only a single face lodged itself painfully in her memory – the face, framed in a truly fiery beard, of Maliuta Skuratov.[14] Margarita's legs kept giving way, she was afraid of bursting into tears at any moment. The worst suffering was caused by her right knee, which was being kissed. It became swollen, the skin turned blue, even though Natasha's hand appeared by this knee several times with a sponge, wiping it with something fragrant. At the end of the third hour, Margarita glanced down with completely desperate eyes and gave a joyful start – the stream of guests was thinning out.

'Balls always assemble according to the same laws, Queen,' whispered Koroviev. 'Presently the wave will begin to subside. I swear we're enduring the final minutes. Here's the group of revellers from Brocken, they always come last. Yes, here they are. Two drunken vampires . . . that's all? Ah, no, here's one more . . . no, two!'[15]

The last two guests were coming up the stairs!

'It's some new one,' Koroviev was saying, squinting through his lens. 'Ah, yes, yes. Azazello visited him once and, over the cognac, whispered some advice to him on how to get rid of a certain man whose exposures he was extremely afraid of. And so he told an acquaint-ance who was dependent on him to spray the walls of the office with poison . . .'

'What's his name?' asked Margarita.

'Ah, really, I myself don't know yet,' Koroviev replied, 'we'll have to ask Azazello.'

'And who is with him?'

'Why, that same efficient subordinate of his. Delighted!' cried Korov-iev to the last two.

The stairway was empty. They waited a little longer as a precaution. But no one else came from the fireplace.

A second later, without knowing how it happened, Margarita found herself in the same room with the pool, and there, bursting into tears at once from the pain in her arm and leg, she collapsed right on the floor. But Hella and Natasha, comforting her, again drew her under the bloody shower, again massaged her body, and Margarita revived.

'There's more, there's more, Queen Margot,' whispered Koroviev, appearing beside her. 'You must fly around the rooms, so that the honourable guests don't feel they've been abandoned.'

And once more Margarita flew out of the room with the pool. On the stage behind the tulips, where the waltz king's orchestra had been playing, there now raged an ape jazz band. A huge gorilla with shaggy side-whiskers, a trumpet in his hand, capering heavily, was doing the conducting. Orang-utans sat in a row blowing on shiny trumpets. Perched on their shoulders were merry chimpanzees with concertinas.

Two hamadryads with manes like lions played grand pianos, but these grand pianos were not heard amidst the thundering, squeaking and booming of saxophones, fiddles and drums in the paws of gibbons, mandrills and marmosets. On the mirror floor a countless number of couples, as if merged, amazing in the deftness and cleanness of their movements, all turning in the same direction, swept on like a wall threatening to clear away everything in its path. Live satin butterflies bobbed above the heads of the dancing hordes, flowers poured down from the ceiling. In the capitals of the columns, each time the electricity went off, myriads of fireflies lit up, and marsh-lights floated in the air.

Then Margarita found herself in a room with a pool of monstrous size bordered by a colonnade. A giant black Neptune spouted a wide pink stream from his maw. A stupefying smell of champagne rose from the pool. Here unconstrained merriment held sway. Ladies, laughing, gave their handbags to their cavaliers or the negroes who rushed about with towels in their hands, and with a cry dived swallow-like into the pool. Foamy columns shot up. The crystal bottom of the pool shone with light from below that broke through the density of the wine, and in it the silvery swimming bodies could be seen. The ladies got out of the pool completely drunk. Loud laughter resounded under the columns, booming like the jazz band.

All that was remembered from this turmoil was the completely drunken face of a woman with senseless and, even in their senselessness, imploring eyes, and only one name – Frieda – was recalled.

Margarita's head began to spin from the smell of the wine, and she was about to leave when the cat arranged a number in the pool that detained her. Behemoth performed some magic by Neptune's maw, and at once the billowing mass of champagne, hissing and gurgling, left the pool, and Neptune began spewing out a stream neither glittering nor foaming but of a dark-yellow colour. The ladies – shrieking and screaming 'Cognac!' – rushed from the pool-side and hid behind the columns. In a few seconds the pool was filled, and the cat, turning three times in the air, dropped into the heaving cognac. He crawled out, spluttering, his bow-tie limp, the gilding on his whiskers gone, along with the opera glasses. Only one woman dared to follow Behemoth's example – that same frolicsome dressmaker, with her cava-lier, an unknown young mulatto. The two threw themselves into the cognac, but here Koroviev took Margarita under the arm and they left the bathers.

It seemed to Margarita that she flew somewhere, where she saw mountains of oysters in huge stone basins. Then she flew over a glass floor with infernal furnaces burning under it and devilish white cooks darting among them. Then somewhere, already ceasing to comprehend anything, she saw dark cellars where some sort of lamps burned, where girls served meat sizzling on red-hot coals, where her health was drunk from big mugs. Then she saw polar bears playing concertinas and dancing the Kamarinsky[16] on a platform. A salamander-conjurer[17] who did not burn in the fireplace . . . And for the second time her strength began to ebb.

'One last appearance,' Koroviev whispered to her anxiously, 'and then we're free!'

Accompanied by Koroviev, she again found herself in the ballroom, but now there was no dancing in it, and the guests in a numberless throng pressed back between the columns, leaving the middle of the room open. Margarita did not remember who helped her to get up on the dais that appeared in the middle of this open space in the room. When she was up on it, to her own amazement, she heard a clock strike midnight somewhere, though by her reckoning it was long past. At the last stroke of the clock, which came from no one knew where, silence fell on the crowd of guests.

Then Margarita saw Woland again. He walked in surrounded by Abaddon, Azazello and several others who resembled Abaddon – dark-haired and young. Now Margarita saw that opposite her dais another had been prepared for Woland. But he did not make use of it. What struck Margarita was that Woland came out for this last great appearance at the ball looking just the same as he had looked in the bedroom. The same dirty, patched shirt[18] hung on his shoulders, his feet were in worn-out bedroom slippers. Woland had a sword, but he used this bare sword as a cane, leaning on it.

Limping, Woland stopped at his dais, and immediately Azazello was before him with a platter in his hands, and on this platter Margarita saw a man's severed head with the front teeth knocked out. Total silence continued to reign, broken only once by the far-off sound, inexplicable under the circumstances, of a doorbell, coming as if from the front hall.

'Mikhail Alexandrovich,' Woland addressed the head in a low voice, and then the slain man's eyelids rose, and on the dead face Margarita saw, with a shudder, living eyes filled with thought and suffering.

'Everything came to pass, did it not?' Woland went on, looking into the head's eyes. 'The head was cut off by a woman, the meeting did not take place, and I am living in your apartment. That is a fact. And fact is the most stubborn thing in the world. But we are now interested in what follows, and not in this already accomplished fact. You have always been an ardent preacher of the theory that, on the cutting off of his head, life ceases in a man, he turns to ashes and goes into non-being. I have the pleasure of informing you, in the presence of my guests, though they serve as proof of quite a different theory, that your theory is both solid and clever. However, one theory is as good as another. There is also one which holds that it will be given to each according to his faith.[19] Let it come true! You go into non-being, and from the cup into which you are to be transformed, I will joyfully drink to being!'

Woland raised his sword. Straight away the flesh of the head turned dark and shrivelled, then fell off in pieces, the eyes disappeared, and soon Margarita saw on the platter a yellowish skull with emerald eyes, pearl teeth and a golden foot. The lid opened on a hinge.

'Right this second, Messire,' said Koroviev, noticing Woland's questioning look, 'he'll appear before you. In this sepulchral silence I can hear the creaking of his patent leather shoes and the clink of the goblet he has just set down on the table, having drunk champagne for the last time in his life. Here he is.'

A solitary new guest was entering the room, heading towards Woland. Outwardly he did not differ in any way from the numerous other male guests, except for one thing: this guest was literally reeling with agitation, which could be seen even from afar. Flushed spots burned on his cheeks, and his eyes darted about in total alarm. The guest was dumbstruck, and that was perfectly natural: he was astounded by everything, and above all, of course, by Woland's attire.

However, the guest was met with the utmost kindness.

'Ah, my dearest Baron Meigel,' Woland, smiling affably, addressed the guest, whose eyes were popping out of his head. 'I'm happy to commend to you,' Woland turned to the other guests, 'the most esteemed Baron Meigel, an employee of the Spectacles Commission, in charge of acquainting foreigners with places of interest in the capital.'

Here Margarita froze, because she recognized this Meigel. She had come across him several times in Moscow theatres and restaurants. 'Excuse me . . .' thought Margarita, 'but that means – what – that he's also dead? . . .' But the matter straight away clarified itself.

'The dear baron,' Woland went on, smiling joyfully, 'was so charming that, having learned of my arrival in Moscow, he rang me up at once, offering his services along the line of his expertise, that is, acquainting people with places of interest. It goes without saying that I was happy to invite him here.'

Just then Margarita saw Azazello hand the platter with the skull to Koroviev.

'Ah, yes, incidentally, Baron,' Woland said, suddenly lowering his voice intimately, 'rumours have spread about your extreme curiosity. They say that, combined with your no less developed talkativeness, it was beginning to attract general attention. What's more, wicked tongues have already dropped the word – a stool-pigeon and a spy. And, what's still more, it is hinted that this will bring you to a sorry end in no more than a month. And so, in order to deliver you from this painful anticipation, we have decided to come to your aid, taking advantage of the fact that you invited yourself here precisely with the purpose of eavesdropping and spying out whatever you can.'

The baron turned paler than Abaddon, who was exceptionally pale by nature, and then something strange took place. Abaddon stood in front of the baron and took off his glasses for a second. At the same moment something flashed fire in Azazello's hand, something clapped softly, the baron began to fall backwards, crimson blood spurted from his chest and poured down his starched shirt and waistcoat. Koroviev put the cup to the spurt and handed the full cup to Woland. The baron's lifeless body was by that time already on the floor.

'I drink your health, ladies and gentlemen,' Woland said quietly and, raising the cup, touched it to his lips.

Then a metamorphosis occurred. The patched shirt and worn slippers disappeared. Woland was in some sort of black chlamys with a steel sword on his hip. He quickly approached Margarita, offered her the cup, and said imperiously:

'Drink!'

Margarita became dizzy, she swayed, but the cup was already at her lips, and voices, she could not make out whose, whispered in both her ears:

'Don't be afraid, Queen ... Don't be afraid, Queen, the blood has long since gone into the earth. And where it was spilled, grapevines are already growing.'

Margarita, without opening her eyes, took a gulp, and a sweet current ran through her veins, a ringing began in her ears. It seemed to her that cocks were crowing deafeningly, that somewhere a march was being played. The crowds of guests began to lose their shape: tailcoaters and women fell to dust. Decay enveloped the room before Margarita's eyes, a sepulchral smell flowed over it. The columns fell apart, the fires went out, everything shrank, there were no more fountains, no camellias, no tulips. And there was simply this: the modest living room of the jeweller's widow, and a strip of light falling from a slightly opened door. And Margarita went through this slightly opened door.

CHAPTER 24

The Extraction of the Master

In Woland's bedroom everything turned out to be as it had been before the ball. Woland was sitting on the bed in his nightshirt, only Hella was no longer rubbing his leg, but was setting out supper on the table on which they had been playing chess. Koroviev and Azazello, having removed their tailcoats, were sitting at the table, and next to them, of course, was the cat, who refused to part with his bow-tie, though it had turned into an utterly filthy rag. Margarita, swaying, came up to the table and leaned on it. Then Woland beckoned her to him like the other time and indicated that she should sit down beside him.

'Well, did they wear you out very much?' asked Woland.

'Oh, no, Messire,' Margarita answered, but barely audibly.

'Nobless obleege,' the cat observed and poured some transparent liquid into a goblet for Margarita.

'Is that vodka?' Margarita asked weakly.

The cat jumped up on his chair in resentment.

'Good heavens, Queen,' he croaked, 'would I allow myself to pour vodka for a lady? It's pure alcohol!'

Margarita smiled and made an attempt to push the glass away.

'Drink boldly,' said Woland, and Margarita took the glass in her hand at once.

'Hella, sit down,' Woland ordered and explained to Margarita: 'The night of the full moon is a festive night, and I have supper in the small company of my retinue and servants. And so, how do you feel? How did this tiring ball go?'

'Stupendous!' rattled Koroviev. 'Everybody's enchanted, infatuated, crushed! So much tact, so much skill, charm, and loveliness!'

Woland silently raised his glass and clinked with Margarita. Margarita drank obediently, thinking that this alcohol would be the end of her. But nothing bad happened. A living warmth flowed into her stomach, something struck her softly on the nape, her strength came back, as if she had got up after a long, refreshing sleep, with a wolfish appetite besides. And on recalling that she had eaten nothing since the previous morning, it flared up still more . . . She greedily began gulping down caviar.

Behemoth cut a slice of pineapple, salted it, peppered it, ate it, and then tossed off a second glass of alcohol so dashingly that everyone applauded.

After Margarita's second glass, the candles in the candelabra flared up more brightly, and the flame increased in the fireplace. Margarita did not feel drunk at all. Biting the meat with her white teeth, Margarita savoured the juice that ran from it, at the same time watching Behemoth spread mustard on an oyster.

'Why don't you put some grapes on top?' Hella said quietly, nudging the cat in the ribs.

'I beg you not to teach me,' replied Behemoth, 'I have sat at table, don't worry, that I have!'

'Ah, how nice it is to have supper like this, by the fireside, simply,' Koroviev clattered, 'in a small circle . . .'

'No, Fagott,' objected the cat, 'a ball has its own charm, and scope.'

'There's no charm in it, or scope either, and those idiotic bears and tigers in the bar almost gave me migraine with their roaring,' said Woland.

'I obey, Messire,' said the cat, 'if you find no scope, I will immediately begin to hold the same opinion.'

'Watch yourself!' Woland said to that.

'I was joking,' the cat said humbly, 'and as far as the tigers are concerned, I'll order them roasted.'

'One can't eat tiger,' said Hella.

'You think not? Then I beg you to listen,' responded the cat, and, narrowing his eyes with pleasure, he told how he had once wandered in the wilderness for nineteen days,[1] and the only thing he had to eat was the meat of a tiger he had killed. They all listened to this entertaining narrative with interest, and when Behemoth finished, exclaimed in chorus:

'Bunk!'

'And the most interesting thing about this bunk,' said Woland, 'is that it's bunk from first word to last.'

'Ah, bunk is it?' exclaimed the cat, and they all thought he would start protesting, but he only said quietly: 'History will judge.'

'And tell me,' Margot, revived after the vodka, addressed Azazello, 'did you shoot him, this former baron?'

'Naturally,' answered Azazello, 'how could I not shoot him? He absolutely had to be shot.'

'I got so excited!' exclaimed Margarita, 'it happened so unexpectedly!'

'There was nothing unexpected in it,' Azazello objected, but Koroviev started wailing and whining:

'How not get excited? I myself was quaking in my boots! Bang! Hup! Baron on his back!'

'I nearly had hysterics,' the cat added, licking the caviar spoon.

'Here's what I don't understand,' Margarita said, and golden sparks from the crystal glittered in her eyes. 'Can it be that the music and the noise of this ball generally weren't heard outside?'

'Of course they weren't, Queen,' explained Koroviev. 'It has to be done so that nothing is heard. It has to be done carefully.'

'Well, yes, yes ... But the thing is that that man on the stairs ... when Azazello and I passed by ... and the other one by the entrance ... I think he was watching your apartment ...'

'Right, right!' cried Koroviev, 'right, dear Margarita Nikolaevna! You confirm my suspicions! Yes, he was watching the apartment! I myself first took him for an absent-minded assistant professor or a lover languishing on the stairs. But no, no! Something kept gnawing at my heart! Ah, he was watching the apartment! And the other one by the entrance, too! And the same for the one in the gateway!'

'But, it's interesting, what if they come to arrest you?' Margarita asked.

'They're sure to come, charming Queen, they're sure to!' replied Koroviev, 'my heart tells me they'll come. Not now, of course, but in due time they'll certainly come. But I don't suppose it will be very interesting.'

'Ah, I got so excited when that baron fell!' said Margarita, evidently still reliving the murder, which was the first she had seen in her life. 'You must be a very good shot?'

'Passable,' replied Azazello.

'From how many paces?' Margarita asked Azazello a not entirely clear question.

'Depends on what,' Azazello replied reasonably. 'It's one thing to hit the critic Latunsky's window with a hammer, and quite another thing to hit him in the heart.'

'In the heart!' exclaimed Margarita, for some reason putting her hand to her own heart. 'In the heart!' she repeated in a hollow voice.

'Who is this critic Latunsky?' asked Woland, narrowing his eyes at Margarita.

Azazello, Koroviev and Behemoth dropped their eyes somehow abashedly, and Margarita answered, blushing:

'There is this certain critic. I destroyed his whole apartment tonight.'

'Just look at you! But what for? . . .'

'You see, Messire,' Margarita explained, 'he ruined a certain master.'

'But why go to such trouble yourself?' asked Woland.

'Allow me, Messire!' the cat cried out joyfully, jumping up.

'You sit down,' Azazello grunted, standing up. 'I'll go myself right now . . .'

'No!' exclaimed Margarita. 'No, I beg you, Messire, there's no need for that!'

'As you wish, as you wish,' Woland replied, and Azazello sat down in his place.

'So, where were we, precious Queen Margot?' said Koroviev. 'Ah, yes, the heart . . . He does hit the heart,' Koroviev pointed his long finger in Azazello's direction, 'as you choose – any auricle of the heart, or any ventricle.'

Margarita did not understand at first, and when she did, she exclaimed in surprise:

'But they're covered up!'

'My dear,' clattered Koroviev, 'that's the point, that they're covered up! That's the whole salt of it! Anyone can hit an uncovered object!'

Koroviev took a seven of spades from the desk drawer, offered it to Margarita, and asked her to mark one of the pips with her fingernail. Margarita marked the one in the upper right-hand corner. Hella hid the card under a pillow, crying:

'Ready!'

Azazello, who was sitting with his back to the pillow, drew a black automatic from the pocket of his tailcoat trousers, put the muzzle over his shoulder, and, without turning towards the bed, fired, provoking a merry fright in Margarita. The seven was taken from under the bullet-pierced pillow. The pip marked by Margarita had a hole in it.

'I wouldn't want to meet you when you're carrying a gun,' Margarita said, casting coquettish glances at Azazello. She had a passion for anyone who did something top-notch.

'Precious Queen,' squeaked Koroviev, 'I wouldn't advise anyone to meet him, even if he's not carrying a gun! I give you my word of honour as an ex-choirmaster and precentor that no one would congratulate the one doing the meeting.'

The cat sat scowling throughout the shooting trial, and suddenly announced:

'I undertake to beat the record with the seven.'

Azazello growled out something in reply to that. But the cat was stubborn, and demanded not one but two guns. Azazello took a second gun from the second back pocket of his trousers and, twisting his mouth disdainfully, handed it to the braggart together with the first. Two pips were marked on the seven. The cat made lengthy preparations, turning his back to the pillow. Margarita sat with her fingers in her ears and looked at the owl dozing on the mantelpiece. The cat fired both guns, after which Hella shrieked at once, the owl fell dead from the mantelpiece, and the smashed clock stopped. Hella, whose hand was all bloody, clutched at the cat's fur with a howl, and he clutched her hair in retaliation, and the two got tangled into a ball and rolled on the floor. One of the goblets fell from the table and broke.

'Pull this rabid hellion off me!' wailed the cat, fighting off Hella, who was sitting astride him. The combatants were separated, and Koroviev blew on Hella's bullet-pierced finger and it mended.

'I can't shoot when someone's talking at my elbow!' shouted Behemoth, trying to stick in place a huge clump of fur pulled from his back.

'I'll bet,' said Woland, smiling to Margarita, 'that he did this stunt on purpose. He's not a bad shot.'

Hella and the cat made peace and, as a sign of their reconciliation, exchanged kisses. The card was taken from under the pillow and checked. Not a single pip had been hit, except for the one shot through by Azazello.

'That can't be,' insisted the cat, holding the card up to the light of the candelabra.

The merry supper went on. The candles guttered in the candelabra, the dry, fragrant warmth of the fireplace spread waves over the room.

After eating, Margarita was enveloped in a feeling of bliss. She watched the blue-grey smoke-rings from Azazello's cigar float into the fireplace, while the cat caught them on the tip of a sword. She did not want to go anywhere, though according to her reckoning it was already late. By all tokens, it was getting on towards six in the morning. Taking advantage of a pause, Margarita turned to Woland and said timidly:

'I suppose it's time for me . . . it's late . . .'

'What's your hurry?' asked Woland, politely but a bit drily. The rest kept silent, pretending to be occupied with the smoke-rings.

'Yes, it's time,' Margarita repeated, quite embarrassed by it, and looked around as if searching for some cape or cloak. She was suddenly embarrassed by her nakedness. She got up from the table. Woland silently took his worn-out and greasy dressing-gown from the bed, and Koroviev threw it over Margarita's shoulders.

'I thank you, Messire,' Margarita said barely audibly, and looked questioningly at Woland. In reply, he smiled at her courteously and indifferently. Black anguish somehow surged up all at once in Margarita's heart. She felt herself deceived. No rewards would be offered her for all her services at the ball, apparently, just as no one was detaining her. And yet it was perfectly clear to her that she had nowhere to go. The fleeting thought of having to return to her house provoked an inward burst of despair in her. Should she ask, as Azazello had temptingly advised in the Alexandrovsky Garden? 'No, not for anything!' she said to herself.

'Goodbye, Messire,' she said aloud, and thought, 'I must just get out of here, and then I'll go to the river and drown myself.'

'Sit down now,' Woland suddenly said imperiously.

Margarita changed countenance and sat down.

'Perhaps you want to say something before you leave?'

'No, nothing, Messire,' Margarita answered proudly, 'except that if you still need me, I'm willing and ready to do anything you wish. I'm not tired in the least, and I had a very good time at the ball. So that if it were still going on, I would again offer my knee for thousands of gallowsbirds and murderers to kiss.' Margarita looked at Woland as if through a veil, her eyes filling with tears.

'True! You're perfectly right!' Woland cried resoundingly and terribly. 'That's the way!'

'That's the way!' Woland's retinue repeated like an echo.

'We've been testing you,' said Woland. 'Never ask for anything! Never for anything, and especially from those who are stronger than you. They'll make the offer themselves, and give everything themselves. Sit down, proud woman,' Woland tore the heavy dressing-gown from Margarita and again she found herself sitting next to him on the bed. 'And so, Margot,' Woland went on, softening his voice, 'what do you want for having been my hostess tonight? What do you wish for having spent the ball naked? What price do you put on your knee? What are your losses from my guests, whom you just called gallowsbirds? Speak! And speak now without constraint, for it is I who offer.'

Margarita's heart began to pound, she sighed heavily, started pondering something.

'Well, come, be braver!' Woland encouraged her. 'Rouse your fantasy, spur it on! Merely being present at the scene of the murder of that inveterate blackguard of a baron is worth a reward, particularly if the person is a woman. Well, then?'

Margarita's breath was taken away, and she was about to utter the cherished words prepared in her soul, when she suddenly turned pale, opened her mouth and stared: 'Frieda! . . . Frieda, Frieda!' someone's importunate, imploring voice cried in her ears, 'my name is Frieda!' And Margarita, stumbling over the words, began to speak:

'So, that means . . . I can ask . . . for one thing?'

'Demand, demand, my donna,' Woland replied, smiling knowingly, 'you may demand one thing.'

Ah, how adroitly and distinctly Woland, repeating Margarita's words, underscored that 'one thing'!

Margarita sighed again and said:

'I want them to stop giving Frieda that handkerchief with which she smothered her baby.'

The cat raised his eyes to heaven and sighed noisily, but said nothing, perhaps remembering how his ear had already suffered.

'In view of the fact,' said Woland, grinning, 'that the possibility of your having been bribed by that fool Frieda is, of course, entirely excluded – being incompatible with your royal dignity – I simply don't know what to do. One thing remains, perhaps: to procure some rags and stuff them in all the cracks of my bedroom.'

'What are you talking about, Messire?' Margarita was amazed, hearing these indeed incomprehensible words.

'I agree with you completely, Messire,' the cat mixed into the conversation, 'precisely with rags!' And the cat vexedly struck the table with his paw.

'I am talking about mercy,' Woland explained his words, not taking his fiery eye off Margarita. 'It sometimes creeps, quite unexpectedly and perfidiously, through the narrowest cracks. And so I am talking about rags . . .'

'And I'm talking about the same thing!' the cat exclaimed, and drew back from Margarita just in case, raising his paws to protect his sharp ears, covered with a pink cream.

'Get out,' said Woland.

'I haven't had coffee yet,' replied the cat, 'how can I leave? Can it be, Messire, that on a festive night the guests are divided into two sorts? One of the first, and the other, as that sad skinflint of a barman put it, of second freshness?'

'Quiet,' ordered Woland, and, turning to Margarita, he asked: 'You are, by all tokens, a person of exceptional kindness? A highly moral person?'

'No,' Margarita replied emphatically, 'I know that one can only speak frankly with you, and so I will tell you frankly: I am a light-minded person. I asked you for Frieda only because I was careless enough to give her firm hope. She's waiting, Messire, she believes in my power. And if she's left disappointed, I'll be in a terrible position. I'll have no peace in my life. There's no help for it, it just happened.'

'Ah,' said Woland, 'that's understandable.'

'Will you do it?' Margarita asked quietly.

'By no means,' answered Woland. 'The thing is, dear Queen, that a little confusion has taken place here. Each department must look after its own affairs. I don't deny our possibilities are rather great, they're much greater than some not very keen people may think . . .'

'Yes, a whole lot greater,' the cat, obviously proud of these possibilities, put in, unable to restrain himself.

'Quiet, devil take you!' Woland said to him, and went on addressing Margarita: 'But there is simply no sense in doing what ought to be done by another – as I just put it – department. And so, I will not do it, but you will do it yourself.'

'And will it be done at my word?'

Azazello gave Margarita an ironic look out of the corner of his blind eye, shook his red head imperceptibly, and snorted.

'Just do it, what a pain!' Woland muttered and, turning the globe, began peering into some detail on it, evidently also occupied with something else during his conversation with Margarita.

'So, Frieda . . .' prompted Koroviev.

'Frieda!' Margarita cried piercingly.

The door flew open and a dishevelled, naked woman, now showing no signs of drunkenness, ran into the room with frenzied eyes and stretched her arms out to Margarita, who said majestically:

'You are forgiven. The handkerchief will no longer be brought to you.'

Frieda's scream rang out, she fell face down on the floor and prostrated in a cross before Margarita. Woland waved his hand and Frieda vanished from sight.

'Thank you, and farewell,' Margarita said, getting up.

'Well, Behemoth,' began Woland, 'let's not take advantage of the action of an impractical person on a festive night.' He turned to Margarita: 'And so, that does not count, I did nothing. What do you want for yourself?'

Silence ensued, interrupted by Koroviev, who started whispering in Margarita's ear:

'Diamond donna, this time I advise you to be more reasonable! Or else fortune may slip away.'

'I want my beloved master to be returned to me right now, this second,' said Margarita, and her face was contorted by a spasm.

Here a wind burst into the room, so that the flames of the candles in the candelabra were flattened, the heavy curtain on the window moved aside, the window opened wide and revealed far away on high a full, not morning but midnight moon. A greenish kerchief of night light fell from the window-sill to the floor, and in it appeared Ivanushka's night visitor, who called himself a master. He was in his hospital clothes – robe, slippers and the black cap, with which he never parted. His unshaven face twitched in a grimace, he glanced sidelong with a crazy timorousness at the lights of the candles, and the torrent of moonlight seethed around him.

Margarita recognized him at once, gave a moan, clasped her hands, and ran to him. She kissed him on the forehead, on the lips, pressed herself to his stubbly cheek, and her long held-back tears now streamed down her face. She uttered only one word, repeating it senselessly:

'You ... you ... you ...'

The master held her away from him and said in a hollow voice:

'Don't weep, Margot, don't torment me, I'm gravely ill.' He grasped the window-sill with his hand, as if he were about to jump on to it and flee, and, peering at those sitting there, cried: 'I'm afraid, Margot! My hallucinations are beginning again ...'

Sobs stifled Margarita, she whispered, choking on the words:

'No, no, no ... don't be afraid of anything ... I'm with you ... I'm with you ...'

Koroviev deftly and inconspicuously pushed a chair towards the master, and he sank into it, while Margarita threw herself on her knees, pressed herself to the sick man's side, and so grew quiet. In her agitation she had not noticed that her nakedness was somehow suddenly over, that she was now wearing a black silk cloak. The sick man hung his head and began looking down with gloomy, sick eyes.

'Yes,' Woland began after a silence, 'they did a good job on him.' He ordered Koroviev: 'Knight, give this man something to drink.'

Margarita begged the master in a trembling voice:

'Drink, drink! You're afraid? No, no, believe me, they'll help you!'

The sick man took the glass and drank what was in it, but his hand twitched and the lowered glass smashed at his feet.

'It's good luck, good luck!' Koroviev whispered to Margarita. 'Look, he's already coming to himself.'

Indeed, the sick man's gaze was no longer so wild and troubled.

'But is it you, Margot?' asked the moonlit guest.

'Don't doubt, it's I,' replied Margarita.

'More!' ordered Woland.

After the master emptied the second glass, his eyes became alive and intelligent.

'Well, there, that's something else again,' said Woland, narrowing his eyes. 'Now let's talk. Who are you?'

'I'm nobody now,' the master replied, and a smile twisted his mouth.

'Where have you just come from?'

'From the house of sorrows. I am mentally ill,' replied the visitor.

These words Margarita could not bear, and she began to weep again. Then she wiped her eyes and cried out:

'Terrible words! Terrible words! He's a master, Messire, I'm letting you know that! Cure him, he's worth it!'

'Do you know with whom you are presently speaking?' Woland asked the visitor. 'On whom you have come calling?'

'I do,' replied the master, 'my neighbour in the madhouse was that boy, Ivan Homeless. He told me about you.'

'Ah, yes, yes,' Woland responded, 'I had the pleasure of meeting that young man at the Patriarch's Ponds. He almost drove me mad myself, proving to me that I don't exist. But you do believe that it is really I?'

'I must believe,' said the visitor, 'though, of course, it would be much more comforting to consider you the product of a hallucination. Forgive me,' the master added, catching himself.

'Well, so, if it's more comforting, consider me that,' Woland replied courteously.

'No, no!' Margarita said, frightened, shaking the master by the shoulder. 'Come to your senses! It's really he before you!'

The cat intruded here as well.

'And I really look like a hallucination. Note my profile in the moonlight.' The cat got into the shaft of moonlight and wanted to add something else, but on being asked to keep silent, replied: 'Very well, very well, I'm prepared to be silent. I'll be a silent hallucination,' and fell silent.

'But tell me, why does Margarita call you a master?' asked Woland.

The man smiled and said:

'That is an excusable weakness. She has too high an opinion of a novel I wrote.'

'What is this novel about?'

'It is a novel about Pontius Pilate.'

Here again the tongues of the candles swayed and leaped, the dishes on the table clattered, Woland burst into thunderous laughter, but neither frightened nor surprised anyone. Behemoth applauded for some reason.

'About what? About what? About whom?' said Woland, ceasing to laugh. 'And that – now? It's stupendous! Couldn't you have found some other subject? Let me see it.' Woland held out his hand, palm up.

'Unfortunately, I cannot do that,' replied the master, 'because I burned it in the stove.'

'Forgive me, but I don't believe you,' Woland replied, 'that cannot be: manuscripts don't burn.'[2] He turned to Behemoth and said, 'Come on, Behemoth, let's have the novel.'

The cat instantly jumped off the chair, and everyone saw that he had been sitting on a thick stack of manuscripts. With a bow, the cat gave the top copy to Woland. Margarita trembled and cried out, again shaken to the point of tears:

'It's here, the manuscript! It's here!'

She dashed to Woland and added in admiration:

'All-powerful! All-powerful!'

Woland took the manuscript that had been handed to him, turned it over, laid it aside, and silently, without smiling, stared at the master. But he, for some unknown reason, lapsed into anxiety and uneasiness, got up from the chair, wrung his hands, and, quivering as he addressed the distant moon, began to murmur:

'And at night, by moonlight, I have no peace ... Why am I being troubled? Oh, gods, gods ...'

Margarita clutched at the hospital robe, pressing herself to him, and began to murmur herself in anguish and tears:

'Oh, God, why doesn't the medicine help you?'

'It's nothing, nothing, nothing,' whispered Koroviev, twisting about the master, 'nothing, nothing ... One more little glass, I'll keep you company ...'

And the little glass winked and gleamed in the moonlight, and this little glass helped. The master was put back in his place, and the sick man's face assumed a calm expression.

'Well, it's all clear now,' said Woland, tapping the manuscript with a long finger.

'Perfectly clear,' confirmed the cat, forgetting his promise to be a silent hallucination. 'Now the main line of this opus is thoroughly clear to me. What do you say, Azazello?' he turned to the silent Azazello.

'I say,' the other twanged, 'that it would be a good thing to drown you.'

'Have mercy, Azazello,' the cat replied to him, 'and don't suggest the idea to my sovereign. Believe me, every night I'd come to you in the same moonlight garb as the poor master, and nod and beckon to you to follow me. How would that be, Azazello?'

'Well, Margarita,' Woland again entered the conversation, 'tell me everything you need.'

Margarita's eyes lit up, and she said imploringly to Woland:

'Allow me to whisper something to him.'

Woland nodded his head, and Margarita, leaning to the master's ear, whispered something to him. They heard him answer her.

'No, it's too late. I want nothing more in my life, except to see you. But again I advise you to leave me, or you'll perish with me.'

'No, I won't leave you,' Margarita answered and turned to Woland: 'I ask that we be returned to the basement in the lane off the Arbat, and that the lamp be burning, and that everything be as it was.'

Here the master laughed and, embracing Margarita's long-since-uncurled head, said:

'Ah, don't listen to the poor woman, Messire! Someone else has long been living in the basement, and generally it never happens that anything goes back to what it used to be.' He put his cheek to his friend's head, embraced Margarita, and began muttering: 'My poor one ... my poor one ...'

'Never happens, you say?' said Woland. 'That's true. But we shall try.' And he called out: 'Azazello!'

At once there dropped from the ceiling on to the floor a bewildered and nearly delirious citizen in nothing but his underwear, though with a suitcase in his hand for some reason and wearing a cap. This man trembled with fear and kept cowering.

'Mogarych?' Azazello asked of the one fallen from the sky.

'Aloisy Mogarych,'[3] the man answered, shivering.

'Was it you who, after reading Latunsky's article about this man's novel, wrote a denunciation saying that he kept illegal literature?' asked Azazello.

The newly arrived citizen turned blue and dissolved in tears of repentance.

'You wanted to move into his rooms?' Azazello twanged as soulfully as he could.

The hissing of an infuriated cat was heard in the room, and Margarita, with a howl of 'Know a witch when you see one!', sank her nails into Aloisy Mogarych's face.

A commotion ensued.

'What are you doing?' the master cried painfully. 'Margot, don't disgrace yourself!'

'I protest! It's not a disgrace!' shouted the cat.

Koroviev pulled Margarita away.

'I put in a bathroom . . .' the bloodied Mogarych cried, his teeth chattering, and, terrified, he began pouring out some balderdash, 'the whitewashing alone . . . the vitriol . . .'

'Well, it's nice that you put in a bathroom,' Azazello said approvingly, 'he needs to take baths.' And he yelled: 'Out!'

Then Mogarych was turned upside down and left Woland's bedroom through the open window.

The master goggled his eyes, whispering:

'Now that's maybe even neater than what Ivan described!' Thoroughly struck, he looked around and finally said to the cat: 'But, forgive me, was it you . . . was it you, sir . . .' he faltered, not knowing how to address a cat, 'are you that same cat, sir, who got on the tram?'

'I am,' the flattered cat confirmed and added: 'It's pleasing to hear you address a cat so politely. For some reason, cats are usually addressed familiarly, though no cat has ever drunk *bruderschaft*[4] with anyone.'

'It seems to me that you're not so much a cat . . .' the master replied hesitantly. 'Anyway, they'll find me missing at the hospital,' he added timidly to Woland.

'Well, how are they going to find you missing?' Koroviev soothed him, and some papers and ledgers turned up in his hands. 'By your medical records?'

'Yes . . .'

Koroviev flung the medical records into the fireplace.

'No papers, no person,' Koroviev said with satisfaction. 'And this is your landlord's house register?'

'Y-yes . . .'

'Who is registered in it? Aloisy Mogarych?' Koroviev blew on the page of the house register. 'Hup, two! He's not there, and, I beg you to notice, never has been. And if this landlord gets surprised, tell him he dreamed Aloisy up! Mogarych? What Mogarych? There was never any Mogarych!' Here the loose-leafed book evaporated from Koroviev's hands. 'And there it is, already back in the landlord's desk.'

'What you say is true,' the master observed, struck by the neatness of Koroviev's work, 'that if there are no papers, there's no person. I have no papers, so there's precisely no me.'

'I beg your pardon,' Koroviev exclaimed, 'but that precisely is a hallucination, your papers are right here.' And Koroviev handed the master his papers. Then he rolled up his eyes and whispered sweetly to Margarita: 'And here is your property, Margarita Nikolaevna,' and Koroviev handed Margarita the notebook with charred edges, the dried rose, the photograph, and, with particular care, the savings book. 'Ten thousand, as you kindly deposited, Margarita Nikolaevna. We don't need what belongs to others.'

'Sooner let my paws wither than touch what belongs to others,' the cat exclaimed, all puffed up, dancing on the suitcase to stamp down all the copies of the ill-fated novel.

'And your little papers as well,' Koroviev continued, handing Margarita her papers and then turning to report deferentially to Woland: 'That's all, Messire!'

'No, not all,' replied Woland, tearing himself away from the globe. 'What, dear donna, will you order me to do with your retinue? I personally don't need them.'

Here the naked Natasha ran through the open door, clasped her hands, and cried out to Margarita:

'Be happy, Margarita Nikolaevna!' She nodded to the master and again turned to Margarita: 'I knew all about where you used to go.'

'Domestics know everything,' observed the cat, raising a paw significantly. 'It's a mistake to think they're blind.'

'What do you want, Natasha?' asked Margarita. 'Go back to the house.'

'Darling Margarita Nikolaevna,' Natasha began imploringly and knelt down, 'ask them' – she cast a sidelong glance at Woland – 'to let me stay a witch. I don't want any more of that house! I won't marry an engineer or a technician! Yesterday at the ball Monsieur Jacques proposed to me.' Natasha opened her fist and showed some gold coins.

Margarita turned a questioning look to Woland. He nodded. Then Natasha threw herself on Margarita's neck, gave her a smacking kiss, and with a victorious cry flew out the window.

In Natasha's place Nikolai Ivanovich now stood. He had regained his former human shape, but was extremely glum and perhaps even annoyed.

'This is someone I shall dismiss with special pleasure,' said Woland, looking at Nikolai Ivanovich with disgust, 'with exceptional pleasure, so superfluous he is here.'

'I earnestly beg that you issue me a certificate,' Nikolai Ivanovich began with great insistence, but looking around wildly, 'as to where I spent last night.'

'For what purpose?' the cat asked sternly.

'For the purpose of presenting it to the police and to my wife,' Nikolai Ivanovich said firmly.

'We normally don't issue certificates,' the cat replied, frowning, 'but, very well, for you we'll make an exception.'

And before Nikolai Ivanovich had time to gather his wits, the naked Hella was sitting at a typewriter and the cat was dictating to her.

'It is hereby certified that the bearer, Nikolai Ivanovich, spent the said night at Satan's ball, having been summoned there in the capacity of a means of transportation . . . make a parenthesis, Hella, in the parenthesis put "hog". Signed – Behemoth.'

'And the date?' squeaked Nikolai Ivanovich.

'We don't put dates, with a date the document becomes invalid,' responded the cat, setting his scrawl to it. Then he got himself a stamp from somewhere, breathed on it according to all the rules, stamped the word 'payed' on the paper, and handed it to Nikolai Ivanovich. After which Nikolai Ivanovich disappeared without a trace, and in his place appeared a new, unexpected guest.

'And who is this one?' Woland asked squeamishly, shielding himself from the candlelight with his hand.

Varenukha hung his head, sighed, and said softly:

'Let me go back, I can't be a vampire. I almost did Rimsky in that time with Hella. And I'm not bloodthirsty. Let me go!'

'What is all this raving!' Woland said with a wince. 'Which Rimsky? What is this nonsense?'

'Kindly do not worry, Messire,' responded Azazello, and he turned to Varenukha: 'Mustn't be rude on the telephone. Mustn't tell lies on the telephone. Understand? Will you do it again?'

Everything went giddy with joy in Varenukha's head, his face beamed, and, not knowing what he was saying, he began to murmur:

'Verily . . . that is, I mean to say . . . Your ma . . . right after dinner . . .' Varenukha pressed his hands to his chest, looking beseechingly at Azazello.

'All right. Home with you!' the latter said, and Varenukha dissolved.

'Now all of you leave me alone with them,' ordered Woland, pointing to the master and Margarita.

Woland's order was obeyed instantly. After some silence, Woland said to the master:

'So it's back to the Arbat basement? And who is going to write? And the dreams, the inspiration?'

'I have no more dreams, or inspiration either,' replied the master. 'No one around me interests me, except her.' He again put his hand on Margarita's head. 'I'm broken, I'm bored, and I want to be in the basement.'

'And your novel? Pilate?'

'It's hateful to me, this novel,' replied the master, 'I went through too much because of it.'

'I implore you,' Margarita begged plaintively, 'don't talk like that. Why do you torment me? You know I put my whole life into this work.' Turning to Woland, Margarita also added: 'Don't listen to him, Messire, he's too worn out.'

'But you must write about something,' said Woland. 'If you've exhausted the procurator, well, then why not start portraying, say, this Aloisy . . .'

The master smiled.

'Lapshennikova wouldn't publish that, and, besides, it's not interesting.'

'And what are you going to live on? You'll have a beggarly existence.'

'Willingly, willingly,' replied the master, drawing Margarita to him. He put his arm around her shoulders and added: 'She'll see reason, she'll leave me . . .'

'I doubt that,' Woland said through his teeth and went on: 'And so, the man who wrote the story of Pontius Pilate goes to the basement with the intention of settling by the lamp and leading a beggarly existence?'

Margarita separated herself from the master and began speaking very ardently:

'I did all I could. I whispered the most tempting thing to him. And he refused.'

'I know what you whispered to him,' Woland retorted, 'but it is not the most tempting thing. And to you I say,' he turned, smiling, to the master, 'that your novel will still bring you surprises.'

'That's very sad,' replied the master.

'No, no, it's not sad,' said Woland, 'nothing terrible. Well, Margarita Nikolaevna, it has all been done. Do you have any claims against me?'

'How can you, oh, how can you, Messire! . . .'

'Then take this from me as a memento,' said Woland, and he drew from under the pillow a small golden horseshoe studded with diamonds.

'No, no, no, why on earth!'

'You want to argue with me?' Woland said, smiling.

Since Margarita had no pockets in her cloak, she put the horseshoe in a napkin and tied it into a knot. Here something amazed her. She looked at the window through which the moon was shining and said:

'And here's something I don't understand . . . How is it midnight, midnight, when it should have been morning long ago?'

'It's nice to prolong the festive night a little,' replied Woland. 'Well, I wish you happiness!'

Margarita prayerfully reached out both hands to Woland, but did not dare approach him and softly exclaimed:

'Farewell! Farewell!'

'Goodbye,' said Woland.

And, Margarita in the black cloak, the master in the hospital robe, they walked out to the corridor of the jeweller's wife's apartment, where a candle was burning and Woland's retinue was waiting for them. When they left the corridor, Hella was carrying the suitcase containing the novel and Margarita Nikolaevna's few possessions, and the cat was helping Hella.

At the door of the apartment, Koroviev made his bows and disappeared, while the rest went to accompany them downstairs. The stairway was empty. As they passed the third-floor landing, something thudded softly, but no one paid any attention to it. Just at the exit from the sixth stairway, Azazello blew upwards, and as soon as they came out to the courtyard, where the moonlight did not reach, they saw a man in a cap and boots asleep, and obviously dead asleep, on the doorstep, as well as a big black car by the entrance with its lights turned off. Through the windshield could be dimly seen the silhouette of a rook.

They were just about to get in when Margarita cried softly in despair:

'Oh, God, I've lost the horseshoe!'

'Get into the car,' said Azazello, 'and wait for me. I'll be right back, I only have to see what's happened.' And he went back in.

What had happened was the following: shortly before Margarita and the master left with their escort, a little dried-up woman carrying a can and a bag came out of apartment no. 48, which was located just under the jeweller's wife's apartment. This was that same Annushka who on Wednesday, to Berlioz's misfortune, had spilled sunflower oil by the turnstile.

No one knew, and probably no one will ever know, what this woman did in Moscow or how she maintained her existence. The only thing known about her is that she could be seen every day either with the can, or with bag and can together, in the kerosene shop, or in the market, or under the gateway, or on the stairs, but most often in the kitchen of apartment no. 48, of which this Annushka was one of the tenants. Besides that and above all it was known that wherever she was or wherever she appeared, a scandal would at once break out, and, besides, that she bore the nickname of 'the Plague'.

Annushka the Plague always got up very early for some reason, and today something got her up in the wee hours, just past midnight. The key turned in the door, Annushka's nose stuck out of it, then the whole of her stuck out, she slammed the door behind her, and was about to set off somewhere when a door banged on the landing above, someone hurtled down the stairs and, bumping into Annushka, flung her aside so that she struck the back of her head against the wall.

'Where's the devil taking you in nothing but your underpants?' Annushka shrieked, clutching her head.

The man in nothing but his underwear, carrying a suitcase and wearing a cap, his eyes shut, answered Annushka in a wild, sleepy voice:

'The boiler ... the vitriol ... the cost of the whitewashing alone ...' And, bursting into tears, he barked: 'Out!'

Here he dashed, not further down, but back up to where the window had been broken by the economist's foot, and out this window he flew, legs up, into the courtyard. Annushka even forgot about her head, gasped, and rushed to the window herself. She lay down on her stomach on the landing and stuck her head into the yard, expecting to see the man with the suitcase smashed to death on the asphalt, lit up by the courtyard lantern. But on the asphalt courtyard there was precisely nothing.

It only remained to suppose that a sleepy and strange person had flown out of the house like a bird, leaving not a trace behind him. Annushka crossed herself and thought: 'Yes, indeed, a nice little apartment, that number fifty! It's not for nothing people say . . . Oh, a nice little apartment!'

Before she had time to think it through, the door upstairs slammed again, and a second someone came running down. Annushka pressed herself to the wall and saw a rather respectable citizen with a little beard, but, as it seemed to Annushka, with a slightly piggish face, dart past her and, like the first one, leave the house through the window, again without ever thinking of smashing himself on the asphalt. Annushka had already forgotten the purpose of her outing and stayed on the stairway, crossing herself, gasping, and talking to herself.

A third one, without a little beard, with a round, clean-shaven face, in a Tolstoy blouse, came running down a short while later and fluttered out the window in just the same way.

To Annushka's credit it must be said that she was inquisitive and decided to wait and see whether any new miracles would occur. The door above was opened again, and now a whole company started down, not at a run, but normally, as everybody walks. Annushka darted away from the window, went to her own door, opened it in a trice, hid behind it, and her eye, frenzied with curiosity, glittered in the chink she left for herself.

Someone, possibly sick or possibly not, but strange, pale, with a stubbly beard, in a black cap and some sort of robe, walked down with unsteady steps. He was led carefully under the arm by a lady in a black cassock, as it seemed to Annushka in the darkness. The lady was possibly barefoot, possibly wearing some sort of transparent, obviously imported, shoes that were torn to shreds. Pah! Shoes my eye! . . . The lady is naked! Yes, the cassock has been thrown right over her naked body! . . . 'A nice little apartment! . . .' Everything in Annushka's soul sang in anticipation of what she was going to tell the neighbours the next day.

The strangely dressed lady was followed by a completely naked one carrying a suitcase, and next to the suitcase a huge black cat was knocking about. Annushka almost squeaked something out loud, rubbing her eyes.

Bringing up the rear of the procession was a short, limping foreigner, blind in one eye, without a jacket, in a white formal waistcoat and tie. This whole company marched downstairs past Annushka. Here something thudded on the landing.

As the steps died away, Annushka slipped like a snake from behind the door, put the can down by the wall, dropped to the floor on her stomach, and began feeling around. Her hands came upon a napkin with something heavy in it. Annushka's eyes started out of her head when she unwrapped the package. Annushka kept bringing the precious thing right up to her eyes, and these eyes burned with a perfectly wolfish fire. A whirlwind formed in Annushka's head:

'I see nothing, I know nothing! ... To my nephew? Or cut it in pieces? ... I could pick the stones out, and then one by one: one to Petrovka, another to Smolensky ... And – I see nothing, I know nothing!'

Annushka hid the found object in her bosom, grabbed the can, and was about to slip back into her apartment, postponing her trip to town, when that same one with the white chest, without a jacket, emerged before her from devil knows where and quietly whispered:

'Give me the horseshoe and napkin!'

'What napkin horseshoe?' Annushka asked, shamming very artfully. 'I don't know about any napkins. Are you drunk, citizen, or what?'

With fingers as hard as the handrails of a bus, and as cold, the white-chested one, without another word, squeezed Annushka's throat so that he completely stopped all access of air to her chest. The can dropped from Annushka's hand on to the floor. After keeping Annushka without air for some time, the jacketless foreigner removed his fingers from her throat. Gulping air, Annushka smiled.

'Ah, the little horseshoe?' she said. 'This very second! So it's your little horseshoe? And I see it lying there in a napkin, I pick it up so that no one takes it, and then just try finding it!'

Having received the little horseshoe and napkin, the foreigner started bowing and scraping before Annushka, shook her hand firmly, and thanked her warmly, with the strongest of foreign accents, in the following terms:

'I am deeply grateful to you, ma'am. This little horseshoe is dear to me as a memento. And, for having preserved it, allow me to give you two hundred roubles.' And he took the money from his waistcoat pocket at once and handed it to Annushka.

She, smiling desperately, could only keep exclaiming:

'Ah, I humbly thank you! Merci! Merci!'

The generous foreigner cleared a whole flight of stairs in one leap, but, before decamping definitively, shouted from below, now without any accent:

'You old witch, if you ever pick up somebody else's stuff again, take it to the police, don't hide it in your bosom!'

Feeling a ringing and commotion in her head from all these events on the stairs, Annushka went on shouting for some time by inertia:

'Merci! Merci! Merci! . . .' But the foreigner was long gone.

And so was the car in the courtyard. Having returned Woland's gift to Margarita, Azazello said goodbye to her and asked if she was comfortably seated, Hella exchanged smacking kisses with Margarita, the cat kissed her hand, everyone waved to the master, who collapsed lifelessly and motionlessly in the corner of the seat, waved to the rook, and at once melted into air, considering it unnecessary to take the trouble of climbing the stairs. The rook turned the lights on and rolled out through the gates, past the man lying dead asleep under the archway. And the lights of the big black car disappeared among the other lights on sleepless and noisy Sadovaya.

An hour later, in the basement of the small house in the lane off the Arbat, in the front room, where everything was the same as it had been before that terrible autumn night last year, at the table covered with a velvet tablecloth, under the shaded lamp, near which stood a little vase of lilies of the valley, Margarita sat and wept quietly from the shock she had experienced and from happiness. The notebook disfigured by fire lay before her, and next to it rose a pile of intact notebooks. The little house was silent. On a sofa in the small adjoining room, covered with the hospital robe, the master lay in a deep sleep. His even breathing was noiseless.

Having wept her fill, Margarita went to the intact notebooks and found the place she had been rereading before she met Azazello under the Kremlin wall. Margarita did not want to sleep. She caressed the manuscript tenderly, as one caresses a favourite cat, and kept turning it in her hands, examining it from all sides, now pausing at the title page, now opening to the end. A terrible thought suddenly swept over her, that this was all sorcery, that the notebooks would presently disappear from sight, and she would be in her bedroom in the old house, and that on waking up she would have to go and drown herself. But this was her last terrible thought, an echo of the long suffering she had lived through. Nothing disappeared, the all-powerful Woland really was all powerful, and as long as she liked, even till dawn itself, Margarita could rustle the pages of the notebooks, gaze at them, kiss them, and read over the words:

'The darkness that came from the Mediterranean Sea covered the city hated by the procurator . . .' Yes, the darkness . . .

CHAPTER 25

How the Procurator Tried to Save Judas of Kiriath

The darkness that came from the Mediterranean Sea covered the city hated by the procurator. The hanging bridges connecting the temple with the dread Antonia Tower disappeared, the abyss descended from the sky and flooded the winged gods over the hippodrome, the Hasmonaean Palace with its loopholes, the bazaars, caravanserais, lanes, pools ... Yershalaim – the great city – vanished as if it had never existed in the world. Everything was devoured by the darkness, which frightened every living thing in Yershalaim and round about. The strange cloud was swept from seaward towards the end of the day, the fourteenth day of the spring month of Nisan.

It was already heaving its belly over Bald Skull, where the executioners hastily stabbed the condemned men, it heaved itself over the temple of Yershalaim, crept in smoky streams down the temple hill, and flooded the Lower City. It poured through windows and drove people from the crooked streets into the houses. It was in no hurry to yield up its moisture and gave off only light. Each time the black smoky brew was ripped by fire, the great bulk of the temple with its glittering scaly roof flew up out of the pitch darkness. But the fire would instantly go out, and the temple would sink into the dark abyss. Time and again it grew out of it and fell back, and each time its collapse was accompanied by the thunder of catastrophe.

Other tremulous glimmers called out of the abyss the palace of Herod the Great, standing opposite the temple on the western hill, and its dread, eyeless golden statues flew up into the black sky, stretching their arms out to it. But again the heavenly fire would hide, and heavy claps of thunder would drive the golden idols into the darkness.

The downpour burst unexpectedly, and then the storm turned into a hurricane. In the very place where the procurator and the high priest had had their talk around noon, by the marble bench in the garden, with the sound of a cannon shot, a cypress snapped like a reed. Along with the watery spray and hail, broken-off roses, magnolia leaves, small twigs and sand were swept on to the balcony under the columns. The hurricane racked the garden.

At that time there was only one man under the columns, and that man was the procurator.

Now he was not sitting in the chair but lying on a couch by a small, low table set with food and jugs of wine. Another couch, empty, stood on the other side of the table. By the procurator's feet spread an unwiped red puddle, as if of blood, with pieces of a broken jug. The servant who was setting the table for the procurator before the storm became disconcerted for some reason under his gaze, grew alarmed at having displeased him in some way, and the procurator, getting angry with him, smashed the jug on the mosaic floor, saying:

'Why don't you look me in the face when you serve me? Have you stolen something?'

The African's black face turned grey, mortal fear showed in his eyes, he trembled and almost broke a second jug, but the procurator's wrath flew away as quickly as it had flown in. The African rushed to remove the pieces and wipe up the puddle, but the procurator waved his hand and the slave ran away. The puddle remained.

Now, during the hurricane, the African was hiding near a niche in which stood the statue of a white, naked woman with a drooping head, afraid of appearing before the procurator's eyes at the wrong time, and at the same time fearing to miss the moment when the procurator might call for him.

Lying on the couch in the storm's twilight, the procurator poured wine into the cup himself, drank it in long draughts, occasionally touched the bread, crumbled it, swallowed small pieces, sucked out an oyster from time to time, chewed a lemon, and drank again.

Had it not been for the roaring of the water, had it not been for the thunderclaps that seemed to threaten to lay flat the roof of the palace, had it not been for the rattle of hail hammering on the steps of the balcony, one might have heard that the procurator was muttering something, talking to himself. And if the unsteady glimmering of the heavenly fire had turned into a constant light, an observer would have been able to see that the procurator's face, with eyes inflamed by recent insomnia and wine, showed impatience, that the procurator was not only looking at the two white roses drowned in the red puddle, but constantly turned his face towards the garden, meeting the watery spray and sand, that he was waiting for someone, impatiently waiting.

Time passed, and the veil of water before the procurator's eyes began to thin. Furious as it was, the hurricane was weakening. Branches no longer cracked and fell. The thunderclaps and flashes came less frequently. It was no longer a violet coverlet trimmed with white, but an ordinary, grey rear-guard cloud that floated over Yershalaim. The storm was being swept towards the Dead Sea.

Now it was possible to hear separately the noise of the rain and the noise of water rushing along the gutters and also straight down the steps of that stairway upon which the procurator had walked in the afternoon to announce the sentence in the square. And finally the hitherto drowned-out fountain made itself heard. It was growing lighter. Blue windows appeared in the grey veil fleeing eastward.

Here, from far off, breaking through the patter of the now quite weakened rainfall, there came to the procurator's ears a weak sound of trumpets and the tapping of several hundred hoofs. Hearing this, the procurator stirred, and his face livened up. The ala was coming back from Bald Mountain. Judging by the sound, it was passing through the same square where the sentence had been announced.

At last the procurator heard the long-awaited footsteps and a slapping on the stairs leading to the upper terrace of the garden, just in front of the balcony. The procurator stretched his neck and his eyes glinted with an expression of joy.

Between the two marble lions there appeared first a hooded head, then a completely drenched man with his cloak clinging to his body. It was the same man who had exchanged whispers with the procurator in a darkened room of the palace before the sentencing, and who during the execution had sat on a three-legged stool playing with a twig.

Heedless of puddles, the man in the hood crossed the garden terrace, stepped on to the mosaic floor of the balcony, and, raising his arm, said in a high, pleasant voice:

'Health and joy to the procurator!' The visitor spoke in Latin.

'Gods!' exclaimed Pilate. 'There's not a dry stitch on you! What a hurricane! Eh? I beg you to go inside immediately. Do me a favour and change your clothes.'

The visitor threw back his hood, revealing a completely wet head with hair plastered to the forehead, and, showing a polite smile on his clean-shaven face, began refusing to change, insisting that a little rain would not hurt him.

'I won't hear of it,' Pilate replied and clapped his hands. With that he called out the servants who were hiding from him, and told them to take care of the visitor and then serve the hot course immediately.

The procurator's visitor required very little time to dry his hair, change his clothes and shoes, and generally put himself in order, and he soon appeared on the balcony in dry sandals, a dry crimson military cloak, and with slicked-down hair.

Just then the sun returned to Yershalaim, and, before going to drown in the Mediterranean Sea, sent farewell rays to the city hated by the procurator and gilded the steps of the balcony. The fountain revived completely and sang away with all its might, doves came out on the sand, cooing, hopping over broken branches, pecking at something in the wet sand. The red puddle was wiped up, the broken pieces were removed, meat steamed on the table.

'I wait to hear the procurator's orders,' said the visitor, approaching the table.

'But you won't hear anything until you sit down and drink some wine,' Pilate replied courteously and pointed to the other couch.

The visitor reclined, a servant poured some thick red wine into his cup. Another servant, leaning cautiously over Pilate's shoulder, filled the procurator's cup. After that, he motioned for the two servants to withdraw.

While the visitor drank and ate, Pilate, sipping his wine, kept glancing with narrowed eyes at his guest. The man who had come to Pilate was middle-aged, with a very pleasant, rounded and neat face and a fleshy mouth. His hair was of some indeterminate colour. Now, as it dried, it became lighter. It would be difficult to establish the man's nationality. The chief determinant of his face was perhaps its good-natured expression, which, however, was not in accord with his eyes, or, rather, not his eyes but the visitor's way of looking at his interlocutor. Ordinarily he kept his small eyes under his lowered, somewhat strange, as if slightly swollen eyelids. Then the slits of these eyes shone with an unspiteful slyness. It must be supposed that the procurator's guest had a propensity for humour. But occasionally, driving this glittering humour from the slits entirely, the procurator's present guest would open his eyelids wide and look at his interlocutor suddenly and point-blank, as if with the purpose of rapidly scrutinizing some inconspicuous spot on his interlocutor's nose. This lasted only an instant, after which the eyelids would lower again, the slits would narrow, and once again they would begin to shine with good-naturedness and sly intelligence.

The visitor did not decline a second cup of wine, swallowed a few oysters with obvious pleasure, tried some steamed vegetables, ate a piece of meat. Having eaten his fill, he praised the wine:

'An excellent vintage, Procurator, but it is not Falerno?'[1]

'Caecuba,[2] thirty years old,' the procurator replied courteously.

The guest put his hand to his heart, declined to eat more, declared that he was full. Then Pilate filled his own cup, and the guest did the same. Both diners poured some wine from their cups on to the meat platter, and the procurator, raising his cup, said loudly:

'For us, for thee, Caesar, father of the Romans, best and dearest of men! . . .'

After this they finished the wine, and the Africans removed the food from the table, leaving the fruit and the jugs. Again the procurator motioned for the servants to withdraw and remained alone with his guest under the colonnade.

'And so,' Pilate began in a low voice, 'what can you tell me about the mood of this city?'

He inadvertently turned his eyes to where the colonnades and flat roofs below, beyond the terraces of the garden, were drying out, gilded by the last rays.

'I believe, Procurator,' the guest replied, 'that the mood of Yershalaim is now satisfactory.'

'So it can be guaranteed that there is no threat of further disorders?'

'Only one thing can be guaranteed in this world,' the guest replied, glancing tenderly at the procurator, 'the power of great Caesar.'

'May the gods grant him long life!' Pilate picked up at once, 'and universal peace!' He paused and then continued: 'So you believe the troops can now be withdrawn?'

'I believe that the cohort of the Lightning legion can go,' the guest replied and added: 'It would be good if it paraded through the city in farewell.'

'A very good thought,' the procurator approved, 'I will dismiss it the day after tomorrow, and go myself, and – I swear to you by the feast of the twelve gods,[3] by the lares[4] I swear – I'd give a lot to be able to do so today!'

'The procurator doesn't like Yershalaim?' the guest asked good-naturedly.

'Good heavens,' the procurator exclaimed, smiling, 'there's no more hopeless place on earth. I'm not even speaking of natural conditions – I get sick every time I have to come here – but that's only half the trouble! ... But these feasts! ... Magicians, sorcerers, wizards, these flocks of pilgrims! ... Fanatics, fanatics! ... Just take this messiah[5] they suddenly started expecting this year! Every moment you think you're about to witness the most unpleasant bloodshed ... The shifting of troops all the time, reading denunciations and calumnies, half of which, moreover, are written against yourself! You must agree, it's boring. Oh, if it weren't for the imperial service!'

'Yes, the feasts are hard here,' agreed the guest.

'I wish with all my heart that they should be over soon,' Pilate added energetically. 'I will finally have the possibility of going back to Caesarea. Believe me, this delirious construction of Herod's' – the procurator waved his arm along the colonnade, to make clear that he was speaking of the palace – 'positively drives me out of my mind! I cannot spend my nights in it. The world has never known a stranger architecture! ... Well, but let's get back to business. First of all, this cursed Bar-Rabban – you're not worried about him?'

And here the guest sent his peculiar glance at the procurator's cheek. But the latter, frowning squeamishly, gazed into the distance with bored eyes, contemplating the part of the city that lay at his feet and was fading into the twilight. The guest's eyes also faded, and his eyelids lowered.

'It may be supposed that Bar has now become as harmless as a lamb,' the guest began to say, and wrinkles appeared on his round face. 'It would be awkward for him to rebel now.'

'Too famous?' Pilate asked with a smirk.

'The procurator has subtly understood the problem, as always.'

'But in any case,' the procurator observed with concern, and the thin, long finger with the black stone of its ring was raised, 'there must be ...'

'Oh, the procurator can be certain that as long as I am in Judea,

Bar will not take a step without having someone on his heels.'

'Now I am at peace – as I always am, incidentally, when you are here.'

'The procurator is too kind!'

'And now I ask you to tell me about the execution,' said the procurator.

'What precisely interests the procurator?'

'Were there any attempts on the part of the crowd to display rebelliousness? That is the main thing, of course.'

'None,' replied the guest.

'Very good. Did you personally establish that death took place?'

'The procurator may be certain of it.'

'And tell me ... were they given the drink before being hung on the posts?'[6]

'Yes. But he,' here the guest closed his eyes, 'refused to drink it.'

'Who, precisely?' asked Pilate.

'Forgive me, Hegemon!' the guest exclaimed. 'Did I not name him? Ha-Nozri!'

'Madman!' said Pilate, grimacing for some reason. A little nerve began to twitch under his left eye. 'To die of sunburn! Why refuse what is offered by law! In what terms did he refuse it?'

'He said,' the guest answered, again closing his eyes, 'that he was grateful and laid no blame for the taking of his life.'

'On whom?' Pilate asked in a hollow voice.

'That he did not say, Hegemon ...'

'Did he try to preach anything in the soldiers' presence?'

'No, Hegemon, he was not loquacious this time. The only thing he said was that among human vices he considered cowardice one of the first.'[7]

'This was said with regard to what?' the guest heard a suddenly cracked voice.

'That was impossible to understand. He generally behaved himself strangely – as always, however.'

'What was this strangeness?'

'He kept trying to peer into the eyes of one or another of those around him, and kept smiling some sort of lost smile.'

'Nothing else?' asked the hoarse voice.

'Nothing else.'

The procurator knocked against the cup as he poured himself some wine. After draining it to the very bottom, he spoke:

'The matter consists in the following: though we have been unable – so far at least – to discover any admirers or followers of his, it is none the less impossible to guarantee that there are none.'

The guest listened attentively, inclining his head.

'And so, to avoid surprises of any sort,' the procurator continued, 'I ask you to remove the bodies of all three executed men from the face of the earth, immediately and without any noise, and to bury them in secrecy and silence, so that not another word or whisper is heard of them.'

'Understood, Hegemon,' replied the guest, and he got up, saying: 'In view of the complexity and responsibility of the matter, allow me to go immediately.'

'No, sit down again,' said Pilate, stopping his guest with a gesture, 'there are two more questions. First, your enormous merits in this most difficult job at the post of head of the secret service for the procurator of Judea give me the pleasant opportunity of reporting them to Rome.'

Here the guest's face turned pink, he rose and bowed to the procurator, saying:

'I merely fulfil my duty in the imperial service.'

'But I wanted to ask you,' the hegemon continued, 'in case you're offered a transfer elsewhere with a raise – to decline it and remain here. I wouldn't want to part with you for anything. Let them reward you in some other way.'

'I am happy to serve under your command, Hegemon.'

'That pleases me very much. And so, the second question. It concerns this ... what's his name ... Judas of Kiriath.'

Here the guest sent the procurator his glance, and at once, as was his custom, extinguished it.

'They say,' the procurator continued, lowering his voice, 'that he supposedly got some money for receiving this madman so cordially?'

'Will get,' the head of the secret service quietly corrected Pilate.

'And is it a large sum?'

'That no one can say, Hegemon.'

'Not even you?' said the hegemon, expressing praise by his amazement.

'Alas, not even I,' the guest calmly replied. 'But he will get the money this evening, that I do know. He is to be summoned tonight to the palace of Kaifa.'

'Ah, that greedy old man of Kiriath!' the procurator observed, smiling. 'He is an old man, isn't he?'

'The procurator is never mistaken, but he is mistaken this time,' the guest replied courteously, 'the man from Kiriath is a young man.'

'You don't say! Can you describe his character for me? A fanatic?'

'Oh, no, Procurator.'

'So. And anything else?'

'Very handsome.'

'What else? He has some passion, perhaps?'

'It is difficult to have such precise knowledge about everyone in this huge city, Procurator . . .'

'Ah, no, no, Aphranius! Don't play down your merits.'

'He has one passion, Procurator.' The guest made a tiny pause. 'A passion for money.'

'And what is his occupation?'

Aphranius raised his eyes, thought, and replied:

'He works in the money-changing shop of one of his relatives.'

'Ah, so, so, so, so.' Here the procurator fell silent, looked around to be sure there was no one on the balcony, and then said quietly: 'The thing is this – I have just received information that he is going to be killed tonight.'

This time the guest not only cast his glance at the procurator, but even held it briefly, and after that replied:

'You spoke too flatteringly of me, Procurator. In my opinion, I do not deserve your report. This information I do not have.'

'You deserve the highest reward,' the procurator replied. 'But there is such information.'

'May I be so bold as to ask who supplied it?'

'Permit me not to say for the time being, the more so as it is accidental, obscure and uncertain. But it is my duty to foresee everything. That is my job, and most of all I must trust my presentiment, for it has never yet deceived me. The information is that one of Ha-Nozri's secret friends, indignant at this money-changer's monstrous betrayal, is plotting with his accomplices to kill him tonight, and to foist the money paid for the betrayal on the high priest, with a note: "I return the cursed money."'

The head of the secret service cast no more of his unexpected glances at the hegemon, but went on listening to him, narrowing his eyes, as Pilate went on:

'Imagine, is it going to be pleasant for the high priest to receive such a gift on the night of the feast?'

'Not only not pleasant,' the guest replied, smiling, 'but I believe, Procurator, that it will cause a very great scandal.'

'I am of the same opinion myself. And therefore I ask you to occupy yourself with this matter – that is, to take all measures to protect Judas of Kiriath.'

'The hegemon's order will be carried out,' said Aphranius, 'but I must reassure the hegemon: the evil-doers' plot is very hard to bring off. Only think,' the guest looked over his shoulder as he spoke and went on, 'to track the man down, to kill him, and besides that to find out how much he got, and manage to return the money to Kaifa, and all that in one night? Tonight?'

'And none the less he will be killed tonight,' Pilate stubbornly repeated. 'I have a presentiment, I tell you! Never once has it deceived me.' Here a spasm passed over the procurator's face, and he rubbed his hands briskly.

'Understood,' the guest obediently replied, stood up, straightened out, and suddenly asked sternly: 'So they will kill him, Hegemon?'

'Yes,' answered Pilate, 'and all hope lies in your efficiency alone, which amazes everyone.'

The guest adjusted the heavy belt under his cloak and said:

'I salute you and wish you health and joy!'

'Ah, yes,' Pilate exclaimed softly, 'I completely forgot! I owe you something! . . .'

The guest was amazed.

'Really, Procurator, you owe me nothing.'

'But of course! As I was riding into Yershalaim, remember, the crowd of beggars . . . I wanted to throw them some money, but I didn't have any, and so I took it from you.'

'Oh, Procurator, it was a trifle!'

'One ought to remember trifles, too.' Here Pilate turned, picked up the cloak that lay on the chair behind him, took a leather bag from under it, and handed it to the guest. The man bowed, accepting it, and put the bag under his cloak.

'I expect a report on the burial,' said Pilate, 'and also on the matter to do with Judas of Kiriath, this same night, do you hear, Aphranius, this night. The convoy will have orders to awaken me the moment you appear. I'll be expecting you.'

'I salute you,' the head of the secret service said and, turning, left the balcony. One could hear the wet sand crunch under his feet, then the stamp of his boots on the marble between the lions, then his legs were cut off, then his body, and finally the hood also disappeared. Only here did the procurator notice that the sun was gone and twilight had come.

CHAPTER 26

The Burial

And perhaps it was the twilight that caused such a sharp change in the procurator's appearance. He aged, grew hunched as if before one's eyes, and, besides that, became alarmed. Once he looked around and gave a start for some reason, casting an eye on the empty chair with the cloak thrown over its back. The night of the feast was approaching, the evening shadows played their game, and the tired procurator probably imagined that someone was sitting in the empty chair. Yielding to his faint-heartedness and ruffling the cloak, the procurator let it drop and began rushing about the balcony, now rubbing his hands, now rushing to the table and seizing the cup, now stopping and staring senselessly at the mosaics of the floor, as if trying to read something written there . . .

It was the second time in the same day that anguish came over him. Rubbing his temple, where only a dull, slightly aching reminder of the morning's infernal pain lingered, the procurator strained to understand what the reason for his soul's torments was. And he quickly understood it, but attempted to deceive himself. It was clear to him that that afternoon he had lost something irretrievably, and that he now wanted to make up for the loss by some petty, worthless and, above all, belated actions. The deceiving of himself consisted in the procurator's trying to convince himself that these actions, now, this evening, were no less important than the morning's sentence. But in this the procurator succeeded very poorly.

At one of his turns, he stopped abruptly and whistled. In response to this whistle, a low barking resounded in the twilight, and a gigantic sharp-eared dog with a grey pelt and a gold-studded collar sprang from the garden on to the balcony.

'Banga, Banga,' the procurator cried weakly.

The dog rose on his hind legs, placed his front paws on his master's shoulders, nearly knocking him to the floor, and licked his cheek. The procurator sat down in the armchair. Banga, his tongue hanging out, panting heavily, lay down at his master's feet, and the joy in the dog's eyes meant that the storm was over, the only thing in the world that the fearless dog was afraid of, and also that he was again there, next to the man whom he loved, respected, and considered the most powerful man in the world, the ruler of all men, thanks to whom the dog considered himself a privileged, lofty and special being. Lying down at his master's feet without even looking at him, but looking into the dusky garden, the dog nevertheless realized at once that trouble had befallen his master. He therefore changed his position, got up, came from the side and placed his front paws and head on the procurator's knees, smearing the bottom of his cloak with wet sand. Banga's actions were probably meant to signify that he comforted his master and was ready to meet misfortune with him. He also attempted to express this with his eyes, casting sidelong glances at his master, and with his alert, pricked-up ears. Thus the two of them, the dog and man who loved each other, met the night of the feast on the balcony.

Just then the procurator's guest was in the midst of a great bustle. After leaving the upper terrace of the garden before the balcony, he went down the stairs to the next terrace of the garden, turned right and came to the barracks which stood on the palace grounds. In these barracks the two centuries that had come with the procurator for the feast in Yershalaim were quartered, as was the procurator's secret guard, which was under the command of this very guest. The guest did not spend much time in the barracks, no more than ten minutes, but at the end of these ten minutes, three carts drove out of the barracks yard loaded with entrenching tools and a barrel of water. The carts were escorted by fifteen mounted men in grey cloaks. Under their escort the carts left the palace grounds by the rear gate, turned west, drove through gates in the city wall, and followed a path first to the Bethlehem road, then down this road to the north, came to the intersection by the Hebron gate, and then moved down the Jaffa road, along which the procession had gone during the day with the men condemned to death. By that time it was already dark, and the moon appeared on the horizon.

Soon after the departure of the carts with their escorting detachment, the procurator's guest also left the palace grounds on horseback, having changed into a dark, worn chiton. The guest went not out of the city but into it. Some time later he could be seen approaching the Antonia Fortress, located to the north and in the vicinity of the great temple.

The guest did not spend much time in the fortress either, and then his tracks turned up in the Lower City, in its crooked and tangled streets. Here the guest now came riding a mule.

Knowing the city well, the guest easily found the street he wanted. It was called Greek Street, because there were several Greek shops on it, among them one that sold carpets. Precisely by this shop, the guest stopped his mule, dismounted, and tied it to the ring by the gate. The shop was closed by then. The guest walked through the little gate beside the entrance to the shop and found himself in a small square courtyard surrounded on three sides by sheds. Turning a corner inside the yard, the guest came to the stone terrace of a house all twined with ivy and looked around. Both the little house and the sheds were dark, no lamps were lit yet. The guest called softly:

'Niza!'

At this call a door creaked, and in the evening twilight a young woman without a veil appeared on the terrace. She leaned over the railing, peering anxiously, wishing to know who had come. Recognizing the visitor, she smiled amiably to him, nodded her head, waved her hand.

'Are you alone?' Aphranius asked softly in Greek.

'Yes,' the woman on the terrace whispered, 'my husband left for Caesarea in the morning.' Here the woman looked back at the door and added in a whisper: 'But the serving-woman is at home.' Here she made a gesture meaning 'Come in'.

Aphranius looked around and went up the stone steps. After which both he and the woman disappeared into the house. With this woman Aphranius spent very little time, certainly no more than five minutes. After which he left the house and the terrace, pulled the hood down lower on his eyes, and went out to the street. Just then the lamps were being lit in the houses, the pre-festive tumult was still considerable, and Aphranius on his mule lost himself in the stream of riders and passers-by. His subsequent route is not known to anyone.

The woman Aphranius called 'Niza', left alone, began changing her clothes, and was hurrying greatly. But difficult though it was for her to find the things she needed in the dark room, she did not light a lamp or call the serving-woman. Only after she was ready and her head was covered by a dark veil did the sound of her voice break the silence in the little house:

'If anyone asks for me, say I went to visit Enanta.'

The old serving-woman's grumbling was heard in the darkness:

'Enanta? Ah, this Enanta! Didn't your husband forbid you to visit her? She's a procuress, your Enanta! Wait till I tell your husband ...'

'Well, well, be quiet,' Niza replied and, like a shadow, slipped out of the house. Niza's sandals pattered over the stone flags of the yard. The serving-woman, grumbling, shut the door to the terrace. Niza left her house.

Just at that time, from another lane in the Lower City, a twisting lane that ran down from ledge to ledge to one of the city pools, from the gates of an unsightly house with a blank wall looking on to the lane and windows on the courtyard, came a young man with a neatly trimmed beard, wearing a white kefia falling to his shoulders, a new pale blue festive tallith with tassels at the bottom, and creaking new sandals. The handsome, aquiline-nosed young fellow, all dressed up for the great feast, walked briskly, getting ahead of passers-by hurrying home for the solemn meal, and watched as one window after another lit up. The young man took the street leading past the bazaar to the palace of the high priest Kaifa, located at the foot of the temple hill.

Some time later he could be seen entering the gates of Kaifa's courtyard. And a bit later still, leaving the same courtyard.

After visiting the palace, where the lamps and torches already blazed, and where the festive bustle had already begun, the young man started walking still more briskly, still more joyfully, hastening back to the Lower City. At the corner where the street flowed into the market-place, amidst the seething and tumult, he was overtaken by a slight woman, walking with a dancer's gait, in a black veil that came down over her eyes. As she overtook the handsome young man, this woman raised her veil for a moment, cast a glance in the young man's direction, yet not only did not slow her pace, but quickened it, as if trying to escape from the one she had overtaken.

The young man not only noticed this woman, no, he also recognized her, and, having recognized her, gave a start, halted, looking perplexedly into her back, and at once set out after her. Almost knocking over some passer-by carrying a jug, the young man caught up with the woman, and, breathing heavily with agitation, called out to her:

'Niza!'

The woman turned, narrowed her eyes, her face showing cold vexation, and replied drily in Greek:

'Ah, it's you, Judas? I didn't recognize you at once. That's good, though. With us, if someone's not recognized, it's a sign he'll get rich . . .'

So agitated that his heart started leaping like a bird under a black cloth, Judas asked in a faltering whisper, for fear passers-by might overhear:

'Where are you going, Niza?'

'And what do you want to know that for?' replied Niza, slowing her pace and looking haughtily at Judas.

Then some sort of childish intonations began to sound in Judas's voice, he whispered in bewilderment:

'But why? . . . We had it all arranged . . . I wanted to come to you, you said you'd be home all evening . . .'

'Ah, no, no,' answered Niza, and she pouted her lower lip capriciously, which made it seem to Judas that her face, the most beautiful face he had ever seen in his life, became still more beautiful. 'I was bored. You're having a feast, and what am I supposed to do? Sit and listen to you sighing on the terrace? And be afraid, on top of it, that the serving-woman will tell him about it? No, no, I decided to go out of town and listen to the nightingales.'

'How, out of town?' the bewildered Judas asked. 'Alone?'

'Of course, alone,' answered Niza.

'Let me accompany you,' Judas asked breathlessly. His mind clouded, he forgot everything in the world and looked with imploring eyes into the blue eyes of Niza, which now seemed black.

Niza said nothing and quickened her pace.

'Why are you silent, Niza?' Judas said pitifully, adjusting his pace to hers.

'Won't I be bored with you?' Niza suddenly asked and stopped. Here Judas's thoughts became totally confused.

'Well, all right,' Niza finally softened, 'come along.'

'But where, where?'

'Wait . . . let's go into this yard and arrange it, otherwise I'm afraid some acquaintance will see me and then they'll tell my husband I was out with my lover.'

And here Niza and Judas were no longer in the bazaar, they were whispering under the gateway of some yard.

'Go to the olive estate,' Niza whispered, pulling the veil over her eyes and turning away from a man who was coming through the gateway with a bucket, 'to Gethsemane, beyond the Kedron, understand?'

'Yes, yes, yes . . .'

'I'll go ahead,' Niza continued, 'but don't follow on my heels. Keep separate from me. I'll go ahead . . . When you cross the stream . . . you know where the grotto is?'

'I know, I know . . .'

'Go up past the olive press and turn to the grotto. I'll be there. Only don't you dare come after me at once, be patient, wait here,' and with these words Niza walked out the gateway as though she had never spoken with Judas.

Judas stood for some time alone, trying to collect his scattering thoughts. Among them was the thought of how he was going to explain his absence from the festal family meal. Judas stood thinking up some lie, but in his agitation was unable to think through or prepare anything properly, and slowly walked out the gateway.

Now he changed his route, he was no longer heading towards the Lower City, but turned back to Kaifa's palace. The feast had already entered the city. In the windows around Judas, not only were lights shining, but hymns of praise were heard. On the pavement, belated passers-by urged their donkeys on, whipping them up, shouting at them. Judas's legs carried him by themselves, and he did not notice how the terrible, mossy Antonia Towers flew past him, he did not hear the roar of trumpets in the fortress, did not pay attention to the mounted Roman patrol and its torch that flooded his path with an alarming light.

Turning after he passed the tower, Judas saw that in the terrible height above the temple two gigantic five-branched candlesticks blazed. But even these Judas made out vaguely. It seemed to him that ten lamps of an unprecedented size lit up over Yershalaim, competing with the light of the single lamp that was rising ever higher over Yershalaim – the moon.

Now Judas could not be bothered with anything, he headed for the Gethsemane gate, he wanted to leave the city quickly. At times it seemed to him that before him, among the backs and faces of passers-by, the dancing little figure flashed, leading him after her. But this was an illusion. Judas realized that Niza was significantly ahead of him. Judas rushed past the money-changing shops and finally got to the Gethsemane gate. There, burning with impatience, he was still forced to wait. Camels were coming into the city, and after them rode a Syrian military patrol, which Judas cursed mentally . . .

But all things come to an end. The impatient Judas was already beyond the city wall. To the left of him Judas saw a small cemetery, next to it several striped pilgrims' tents. Crossing the dusty road flooded with moonlight, Judas headed for the stream of the Kedron with the intention of wading across it. The water babbled quietly under Judas's feet. Jumping from stone to stone, he finally came out on the Gethsemane bank opposite and saw with great joy that here the road below the gardens was empty. The half-ruined gates of the olive estate could already be seen not far away.

After the stuffy city, Judas was struck by the stupefying smell of the spring night. From the garden a wave of myrtle and acacia from the Gethsemane glades poured over the fence.

No one was guarding the gateway, there was no one in it, and a few minutes later Judas was already running under the mysterious shade of the enormous, spreading olive trees. The road went uphill. Judas ascended, breathing heavily, at times emerging from the darkness on to patterned carpets of moonlight, which reminded him of the carpets he had seen in the shop of Niza's jealous husband.

A short time later there flashed at Judas's left hand, in a clearing, an olive press with a heavy stone wheel and a pile of barrels. There was no one in the garden, work had ended at sunset, and now over Judas choirs of nightingales pealed and trilled.

Judas's goal was near. He knew that on his right in the darkness he would presently begin to hear the soft whisper of water falling in the grotto. And so it happened, he heard it. It was getting cooler. Then he slowed his pace and called softly:

'Niza!'

But instead of Niza, a stocky male figure, detaching itself from a thick olive trunk, leaped out on the road, and something gleamed in its hand and at once went out. With a weak cry, Judas rushed back, but a second man barred his way.

The first man, in front of him, asked Judas:

'How much did you just get? Speak, if you want to save your life!'

Hope flared up in Judas's heart, and he cried out desperately:

'Thirty tetradrachmas![1] Thirty tetradrachmas! I have it all with me! Here's the money! Take it, but grant me my life!'

The man in front instantly snatched the purse from Judas's hands. And at the same instant a knife flew up behind Judas's back and struck the lover under the shoulder-blade. Judas was flung forward and thrust out his hands with clawed fingers into the air. The front man caught Judas on his knife and buried it up to the hilt in Judas's heart.

'Ni . . . za . . .' Judas said, not in his own high and clear young voice, but in a low and reproachful one, and uttered not another sound. His body struck the earth so hard that it hummed.

Then a third figure appeared on the road. This third one wore a cloak with a hood.

'Don't linger,' he ordered. The killers quickly wrapped the purse together with a note handed to them by the third man in a piece of hide and criss-crossed it with twine. The second put the bundle into his bosom, and then the two killers plunged off the roadsides and the darkness between the olive trees ate them. The third squatted down by the murdered man and looked at his face. In the darkness it appeared white as chalk to the gazing man and somehow spiritually beautiful.

A few seconds later there was not a living man on the road. The lifeless body lay with outstretched arms. The left foot was in a spot of moonlight, so that each strap of the sandal could be seen distinctly. The whole garden of Gethsemane was just then pealing with the song of nightingales.

Where the two who had stabbed Judas went, no one knows, but the route of the third man in the hood is known. Leaving the road, he headed into the thick of the olive trees, making his way south. He climbed over the garden fence far from the main gate, in the southern corner, where the upper stones of the masonry had fallen out. Soon he was on the bank of the Kedron. Then he entered the water and for some time made his way in it, until he saw ahead the silhouettes of two horses and a man beside them. The horses were also standing in the stream. The water flowed, washing their hoofs. The horse-handler mounted one of the horses, the man in the hood jumped on to the other, and the two slowly walked in the stream, and one could hear the pebbles crunching under the horses' hoofs. Then the riders left the water, came out on the Yershalaim bank, and rode slowly under the city wall. Here the horse-handler separated himself, galloped ahead, and disappeared from view, while the man in the hood stopped his horse, dismounted on the deserted road, removed his cloak, turned it inside out, took from under the cloak a flat helmet without plumes and put it on. Now it was a man in a military chlamys with a short sword at his hip who jumped on to the horse. He touched the reins and the fiery cavalry horse set off at a trot, jolting its rider. It was not a long way – the rider was approaching the southern gate of Yershalaim.

Under the arch of the gateway the restless flame of torches danced and leaped. The soldiers on guard from the second century of the Lightning legion sat on stone benches playing dice. Seeing a military man ride in, the soldiers jumped up, the man waved his hand to them and rode on into the city.

The city was flooded with festive lights. The flames of lamps played in all the windows, and from everywhere, merging into one dissonant chorus, came hymns of praise. Occasionally glancing into windows that looked on to the street, the rider could see people at tables set with roast kid and cups of wine amidst dishes of bitter herbs. Whistling some quiet song, the rider made his way at an unhurried trot through the deserted streets of the Lower City, heading for the Antonia Tower, glancing occasionally at the five-branched candlesticks, such as the world had never seen, blazing above the temple, or at the moon that hung still higher than the five-branched candlesticks.

The palace of Herod the Great took no part in the solemnities of the Passover night. In the auxiliary quarters of the palace, facing to the south, where the officers of the Roman cohort and the legate of the legion were stationed, lights burned and there was a feeling of some movement and life. But the front part, the formal part, which housed the sole and involuntary occupant of the palace – the procurator – all of it, with its columns and golden statues, was as if blind under the brightest moon. Here, inside the palace, darkness and silence reigned.

And the procurator, as he had told Aphranius, would not go inside. He ordered his bed made up on the balcony, there where he had dined and where he had conducted the interrogation in the morning. The procurator lay on the made-up couch, but sleep would not come to him. The bare moon hung high in the clear sky, and the procurator did not take his eyes off it for several hours.

Approximately at midnight, sleep finally took pity on the hegemon. With a spasmodic yawn, the procurator unfastened and threw off his cloak, removed the belt girded over his shirt, with a broad steel knife in a sheath, placed it on the chair by his couch, took off his sandals, and stretched out. Banga got on the bed at once and lay down next to him, head to head, and the procurator, placing his hand on the dog's neck, finally closed his eyes. Only then did the dog also fall asleep.

The couch was in semi-darkness, shielded from the moon by a column, but a ribbon of moonlight stretched from the porch steps to the bed. And once the procurator lost connection with what surrounded him in reality, he immediately set out on the shining road and went up it straight towards the moon. He even burst out laughing in his sleep from happiness, so wonderful and inimitable did everything come to be on the transparent, pale blue road. He walked in the company of Banga, and beside him walked the wandering philosopher. They were arguing about something very complex and important, and neither of them could refute the other. They did not agree with each other in anything, and that made their argument especially interesting and endless. It went without saying that today's execution proved to be a sheer misunderstanding: here this philosopher, who had thought up such an incredibly absurd thing as that all men are good, was walking beside him, therefore he was alive. And, of course, it would be terrible even to think that one could execute such a man. There had been no execution! No execution! That was the loveliness of this journey up the stairway of the moon.

There was as much free time as they needed, and the storm would come only towards evening, and cowardice was undoubtedly one of the most terrible vices. Thus spoke Yeshua Ha-Nozri. No, philosopher, I disagree with you: it is the most terrible vice!

He, for example, the present procurator of Judea and former tribune of a legion, had been no coward that time, in the Valley of the Virgins, when the fierce Germani had almost torn Ratslayer the Giant to pieces. But, good heavens, philosopher! How can you, with your intelligence, allow yourself to think that, for the sake of a man who has committed a crime against Caesar, the procurator of Judea would ruin his career?

'Yes, yes . . .' Pilate moaned and sobbed in his sleep. Of course he would. In the morning he still would not, but now, at night, after weighing everything, he would agree to ruin it. He would do everything to save the decidedly innocent, mad dreamer and healer from execution!

'Now we shall always be together,'[2] said the ragged wandering philosopher in his dream, who for some unknown reason had crossed paths with the equestrian of the golden spear. 'Where there's one of us, straight away there will be the other! Whenever I am remembered, you will at once be remembered, too! I, the foundling, the son of unknown parents, and you, the son of an astrologer-king and a miller's daughter, the beautiful Pila.'[3]

'Yes, and don't you forget to remember me, the astrologer's son,' Pilate asked in his dream. And securing in his dream a nod from the En-Sarid[4] beggar who was walking beside him, the cruel procurator of Judea wept and laughed from joy in his dream.

This was all very good, but the more terrible was the hegemon's awakening. Banga growled at the moon, and the pale-blue road, slippery as though smoothed with oil, fell away before the procurator. He opened his eyes, and the first thing he remembered was that the execution had been. The first thing the procurator did was to clutch Banga's collar with a habitual gesture, then with sick eyes he began searching for the moon and saw that it had moved slightly to the side and turned silvery. Its light was being interfered with by an unpleasant, restless light playing on the balcony right before his eyes. A torch blazed and smoked in the hand of the centurion Ratslayer. The holder of it glanced sidelong with fear and spite at the dangerous beast preparing itself to leap.

'Stay, Banga,' the procurator said in a sick voice and coughed. Shielding himself from the flame with his hand, he went on: 'Even at night, even by moonlight, I have no peace! . . . Oh, gods! . . . Yours is also a bad job, Mark. You cripple soldiers . . .'

Mark gazed at the procurator in great amazement, and the man recollected himself. To smooth over the unwarranted words, spoken while not quite awake, the procurator said:

'Don't be offended, centurion. My position, I repeat, is still worse. What do you want?'

'The head of the secret guard is waiting to see you,' Mark reported calmly.

'Call him, call him,' the procurator ordered, clearing his throat with a cough, and he began feeling for his sandals with his bare feet. The flame played on the columns, the centurion's caligae tramped across the mosaics. The centurion went out to the garden.

'Even by moonlight I have no peace,' the procurator said to himself, grinding his teeth.

Instead of the centurion, a man in a hood appeared on the balcony.

'Stay, Banga,' the procurator said quietly and pressed the back of the dog's head.

Before beginning to speak, Aphranius, as was his custom, looked around and stepped into the shadow, and having made sure that, besides Banga, there were no extra persons on the balcony, he said quietly:

'I ask to be tried, Procurator. You turned out to be right. I was unable to protect Judas of Kiriath, he has been stabbed to death. I ask to be tried and retired.'

It seemed to Aphranius that four eyes were looking at him – a dog's and a wolf's.

Aphranius took from under his chlamys a purse stiff with blood, sealed with two seals.

'This is the bag of money the killers left at the high priest's house. The blood on this bag is the blood of Judas of Kiriath.'

'How much is there, I wonder?' asked Pilate, bending over the bag.

'Thirty tetradrachmas.'

The procurator grinned and said:

'Not much.'

Aphranius was silent.

'Where is the murdered man?'

'That I do not know,' the visitor, who never parted with his hood, said with calm dignity. 'We will begin a search in the morning.'

The procurator started, abandoning a sandal strap that refused to be fastened.

'But you do know for certain that he was killed?'

To this the procurator received a dry response:

'I have been working in Judea for fifteen years, Procurator. I began my service under Valerius Gratus.[5] I do not have to see the corpse in order to say that a man has been killed, and so I report to you that the one who was called Judas of Kiriath was stabbed to death several hours ago.'

'Forgive me, Aphranius,' answered Pilate, 'I'm not properly awake yet, that's why I said it. I sleep badly,' the procurator grinned, 'I keep seeing a moonbeam in my sleep. Quite funny, imagine, it's as if I'm walking along this moonbeam . . . And so, I would like to know your thoughts on this matter. Where are you going to look for him? Sit down, head of the secret service.'

Aphranius bowed, moved the chair closer to the bed, and sat down, clanking his sword.

'I am going to look for him not far from the oil press in the garden of Gethsemane.'

'So, so. And why there, precisely?'

'As I figure it, Hegemon, Judas was not killed in Yershalaim itself, nor anywhere very far from it, he was killed near Yershalaim.'

'I regard you as one of the outstanding experts in your business. I don't know how things are in Rome, but in the colonies you have no equal . . . But, explain to me, why are you going to look for him precisely there?'

'I will by no means admit the notion,' Aphranius spoke in a low voice, 'of Judas letting himself be caught by any suspicious people within city limits. It's impossible to put a knife into a man secretly in the street. That means he was lured to a basement somewhere. But the service has already searched for him in the Lower City and undoubtedly would have found him. He is not in the city, I can guarantee that. If he was killed far from the city, this packet of money could not have been dropped off so quickly. He was killed near the city. They managed to lure him out of the city.'

'I cannot conceive how that could have been done!'

'Yes, Procurator, that is the most difficult question in the whole affair, and I don't even know if I will succeed in resolving it.'

'It is indeed mysterious! A believer, on the eve of the feast, goes out of the city for some unknown reason, leaving the Passover meal, and perishes there. Who could have lured him, and how? Could it have been done by a woman?' the procurator asked on a sudden inspiration.

Aphranius replied calmly and weightily:

'By no means, Procurator. That possibility is utterly excluded. One must reason logically. Who was interested in Judas's death. Some wandering dreamers, some circle in which, first of all, there weren't any women. To marry, Procurator, one needs money. To bring a person into the world, one needs the same. But to put a knife into a man with the help of a woman, one needs very big money, and no vagabond has got it. There was no woman in this affair, Procurator. Moreover, I will say that such an interpretation of the murder can only throw us off the track, hinder the investigation, and confuse me.'

'Ah, yes! I forgot to ask,' the procurator rubbed his forehead, 'how did they manage to foist the money on Kaifa?'

'You see, Procurator ... that is not especially complicated. The avengers came from behind Kaifa's palace, where the lane is higher than the yard. They threw the packet over the fence.'

'With a note?'

'Yes, exactly as you suspected, Procurator.'

'I see that you are perfectly right, Aphranius,' said Pilate, 'and I merely allowed myself to express a supposition.'

'Alas, it is erroneous, Procurator.'

'But what is it, then, what is it?' exclaimed the procurator, peering into Aphranius's face with greedy curiosity.

'I suppose it's money again.'

'An excellent thought! But who could have offered him money at night, outside the city, and for what?'

'Oh, no, Procurator, it's not that. I have only one supposition, and if it is wrong, I may not find any other explanations.' Aphranius leaned closer to the procurator and finished in a whisper: 'Judas wanted to hide his money in a secluded place known only to himself.'

'A very subtle explanation. That, apparently, is how things were. Now I understand you: he was lured out not by others, but by his own purpose. Yes, yes, that's so.'

'So. Judas was mistrustful, he was hiding the money from others.'

'Yes, in Gethsemane, you said ... And why you intend to look for him precisely there – that, I confess, I do not understand.'

'Oh, Procurator, that is the simplest thing of all. No one would hide money on the roads, in open and empty places. Judas was neither on the road to Hebron, nor on the road to Bethany. He had to be in a protected, secluded place with trees. It's as simple as that. And except for Gethsemane, there are no such places near Yershalaim. He couldn't have gone far.'

'You have utterly convinced me. And so, what are we to do now?'

'I will immediately start a search for the murderers who tracked Judas out of the city, and I myself, meanwhile, as I have already reported to you, will stand trial.'

'What for?'

'My guards lost him in the bazaar last evening, after he left Kaifa's palace. How it happened, I cannot comprehend. It has never happened before in my life. He was put under surveillance just after our conversation. But in the neighbourhood of the bazaar he doubled back somewhere, and made such a strange loop that he escaped without a trace.'

'So. I declare to you that I do not consider it necessary to try you. You did all you could, and no one in the world' – here the procurator smiled – 'could do more than you! Penalize the sleuths who lost Judas. But here, too, I warn you, I would not want it to be anything of a severe sort. In the last analysis, we did everything to take care of the blackguard!'

'Yes, although . . .' Here Aphranius tore the seal off the packet and showed its contents to Pilate.

'Good heavens, what are you doing, Aphranius, those must be temple seals!'

'The procurator needn't trouble himself with that question,' Aphranius replied, closing the packet.

'Can it be that you have all the seals?' Pilate asked, laughing.

'It couldn't be otherwise, Procurator,' Aphranius replied very sternly, not laughing at all.

'I can imagine the effect at Kaifa's!'

'Yes, Procurator, it caused great agitation. They summoned me immediately.'

Even in the semi-darkness one could see how Pilate's eyes flashed.

'That's interesting, interesting . . .'

'I venture to disagree, Procurator, it was not interesting. A most boring and tiresome business. To my question whether anyone had been paid money in Kaifa's palace, I was told categorically that there had been nothing of the sort.'

'Ah, yes? Well, so, if no one was paid, no one was paid. It will be that much harder to find the killers.'

'Absolutely right, Procurator.'

'It suddenly occurs to me, Aphranius: might he not have killed himself?'[6]

'Oh, no, Procurator,' Aphranius replied, even leaning back in his chair from astonishment, 'excuse me, but that is entirely unlikely!'

'Ah, everything is likely in this city. I'm ready to bet that in a very short time rumours of it will spread all over the city.'

Here Aphranius again darted his look at the procurator, thought for a moment, and replied:

'That may be, Procurator.'

The procurator was obviously still unable to part with this question of the killing of the man from Kiriath, though everything was already clear, and he said even with a sort of reverie:

'But I'd like to have seen how they killed him.'

'He was killed with great art, Procurator,' Aphranius replied, glancing somewhat ironically at the procurator.

'How do you know that?'

'Kindly pay attention to the bag, Procurator,' Aphranius replied. 'I guarantee you that Judas's blood gushed out in a stream. I've seen murdered people in my time, Procurator.'

'So, of course, he won't rise?'

'No, Procurator, he will rise,' replied Aphranius, smiling philosophically, 'when the trumpet of the messiah they're expecting here sounds over him. But before then he won't rise.'

'Enough, Aphranius, the question is clear. Let's go on to the burial.'

'The executed men have been buried, Procurator.'

'Oh, Aphranius, it would be a crime to try you. You're deserving of the highest reward. How was it?'

Aphranius began to tell about it: while he himself was occupied with Judas's affair, a detachment of the secret guard, under the direction of his assistant, arrived at the hill as evening came. One of the bodies was not found on the hilltop. Pilate gave a start and said hoarsely:

'Ah, how did I not foresee it! . . .'

'No need to worry, Procurator,' said Aphranius, and he went on with his narrative: 'The bodies of Dysmas and Gestas, their eyes pecked out by carrion birds, were taken up, and they immediately rushed in search of the third body. It was discovered in a very short time. A certain man . . .'

'Matthew Levi,' said Pilate, not questioningly, but rather affirmatively.

'Yes, Procurator . . . Matthew Levi was hiding in a cave on the northern slope of Bald Skull, waiting for darkness. The naked body of

Yeshua Ha-Nozri was with him. When the guards entered the cave with a torch, Levi fell into despair and wrath. He shouted about having committed no crime, and about every man's right by law to bury an executed criminal if he so desires. Matthew Levi said he did not want to part with the body. He was agitated, cried out something incoherent, now begging, now threatening and cursing . . .'

'Did they have to arrest him?' Pilate asked glumly.

'No, Procurator, no,' Aphranius replied very soothingly, 'they managed to quiet the impudent madman, explaining to him that the body would be buried. Levi, having grasped what was being said to him, calmed down, but announced that he would not leave and wished to take part in the burial. He said he would not leave even if they started to kill him, and even offered for that purpose a bread knife he had with him.'

'Was he chased away?' Pilate asked in a stifled voice.

'No, Procurator, no. My assistant allowed him to take part in the burial.'

'Which of your assistants was in charge of it?' asked Pilate.

'Tolmai,' Aphranius answered and added in alarm: 'Perhaps he made a mistake?'

'Go on,' answered Pilate, 'there was no mistake. Generally, I am beginning to feel a bit at a loss, Aphranius, I am apparently dealing with a man who never makes mistakes. That man is you.'

'Matthew Levi was taken in the cart with the bodies of the executed men, and in about two hours they reached a solitary ravine north of Yershalaim. There the detachment, working in shifts, dug a deep hole within an hour and buried all three executed men in it.'

'Naked?'

'No, Procurator, the detachment brought chitons with them for that purpose. They put rings on the buried men's fingers. Yeshua's with one notch, Dysmas's with two, and Gestas's with three. The hole has been covered over and heaped with stones. The landmark is known to Tolmai.'

'Ah, if only I had foreseen it!' Pilate spoke, wincing. 'I needed to see this Matthew Levi . . .'

'He is here, Procurator.'

Pilate, his eyes wide open, stared at Aphranius for some time, and then said:

'I thank you for everything that has been done in this affair. I ask you to send Tolmai to me tomorrow, and to tell him beforehand that I am pleased with him. And you, Aphranius,' here the procurator took a seal ring from the pouch of the belt lying on the table and gave it to the head of the secret service, 'I beg you to accept this as a memento.'

Aphranius bowed and said:

'A great honour, Procurator.'

'I request that the detachment that performed the burial be given rewards. The sleuths who let Judas slip – a reprimand. Have Matthew Levi sent to me right now. I must have the details on Yeshua's case.'

'Understood, Procurator,' Aphranius replied and began retreating and bowing, while the procurator clapped his hands and shouted:

'To me, here! A lamp to the colonnade!'

Aphranius was going out to the garden when lights began to flash in the hands of servants behind Pilate's back. Three lamps appeared on the table before the procurator, and the moonlit night at once retreated to the garden, as if Aphranius had led it away with him. In place of Aphranius, an unknown man, small and skinny, stepped on to the balcony beside the gigantic centurion. The latter, catching the procurator's eye, withdrew to the garden at once and there disappeared.

The procurator studied the newcomer with greedy and slightly frightened eyes. So one looks at a man of whom one has heard a great deal, of whom one has been thinking, and who finally appears.

The newcomer, a man of about forty, was black-haired, ragged, covered with caked mud, and looked wolf-like from under his knitted brows. In short, he was very unsightly, and rather resembled a city beggar, of whom there were many hanging about on the porches of the temple or in the bazaars of the noisy and dirty Lower City.

The silence continued for a long time, and was broken by the strange behaviour of the man brought to Pilate. His countenance changed, he swayed, and if he had not grasped the edge of the table with his dirty hand, he would have fallen.

'What's wrong with you?' Pilate asked him.

'Nothing,' answered Matthew Levi, and he made a movement as if he were swallowing something. His skinny, bare, grey neck swelled out and then slackened again.

'What's wrong, answer me,' Pilate repeated.

'I'm tired,' Levi answered and looked sullenly at the floor.

'Sit down,' said Pilate, pointing to the armchair.

Levi looked at the procurator mistrustfully, moved towards the arm-chair, gave a timorous sidelong glance at the gilded armrests, and sat down not in the chair but beside it on the floor.

'Explain to me, why did you not sit in the chair?' asked Pilate.

'I'm dirty, I'd soil it,' said Levi, looking at the ground.

'You'll presently be given something to eat.'

'I don't want to eat,' answered Levi.

'Why lie?' Pilate asked quietly. 'You haven't eaten for the whole day, and maybe even longer. Very well, don't eat. I've summoned you so that you could show me the knife you had with you.'

'The soldiers took it from me when they brought me here,' Levi replied and added sullenly: 'You must give it back to me, I have to return it to its owner, I stole it.'

'What for?'

'To cut the ropes,' answered Levi.

'Mark!' cried the procurator, and the centurion stepped in under the columns. 'Give me his knife.'

The centurion took a dirty bread knife from one of the two cases on his belt, handed it to the procurator, and withdrew.

'Who did you take the knife from?'

'From the bakery by the Hebron gate, just as you enter the city, on the left.'

Pilate looked at the broad blade, for some reason tried the sharpness of the edge with his finger, and said:

'Concerning the knife you needn't worry, the knife will be returned to the shop. But now I want a second thing – show me the charta you carry with you, on which Yeshua's words are written down.'

Levi looked at Pilate with hatred and smiled such an inimical smile that his face became completely ugly.

'You want to take away the last thing?' he asked.

'I didn't say "give me",' answered Pilate, 'I said "show me".'

Levi fumbled in his bosom and produced a parchment scroll. Pilate took it, unrolled it, spread it out between the lights, and, squinting, began to study the barely legible ink marks. It was difficult to understand these crabbed lines, and Pilate kept wincing and leaning right to the parchment, running his finger over the lines. He did manage to make out that the writing represented an incoherent chain of certain utterances, certain dates, household records, and poetic fragments. Some of it Pilate could read: '... there is no death ... yesterday we ate sweet spring baccuroth ...'[7]

Grimacing with the effort, Pilate squinted as he read: '... we shall see the pure river of the water of life[8] ... mankind shall look at the sun through transparent crystal ...' Here Pilate gave a start. In the last lines of the parchment he made out the words: '... greater vice ... cowardice ...'

Pilate rolled up the parchment and with an abrupt movement handed it to Levi.

'Take it,' he said and, after a pause, added: 'You're a bookish man, I see, and there's no need for you to go around alone, in beggar's clothing, without shelter. I have a big library in Caesarea, I am very rich and want to take you to work for me. You will sort out and look after the papyri, you will be fed and clothed.'

Levi stood up and replied:

'No, I don't want to.'

'Why?' the procurator asked, his face darkening. 'Am I disagreeable to you? ... Are you afraid of me?'

The same bad smile distorted Levi's face, and he said:

'No, because you'll be afraid of me. It won't be very easy for you to look me in the face now that you've killed him.'

'Quiet,' replied Pilate. 'Take some money.'

Levi shook his head negatively, and the procurator went on:

'I know you consider yourself a disciple of Yeshua, but I can tell you that you learned nothing of what he taught you. For if you had, you would certainly take something from me. Bear in mind that before he died he said he did not blame anyone.' Pilate raised a finger significantly, Pilate's face was twitching. 'And he himself would surely have taken something. You are cruel, and he was not cruel. Where will you go?'

Levi suddenly came up to the table, leaned both hands on it, and, gazing at the procurator with burning eyes, whispered to him:

'Know, Hegemon, that I am going to kill a man in Yershalaim. I wanted to tell you that, so you'd know there will be more blood.'

'I, too, know there will be more of it,' replied Pilate, 'you haven't surprised me with your words. You want, of course, to kill me?'

'You I won't manage to kill,' replied Levi, baring his teeth and smiling, 'I'm not such a foolish man as to count on that. But I'll kill Judas of Kiriath, I'll devote the rest of my life to it.'

Here pleasure showed in the procurator's eyes, and beckoning Matthew Levi to come closer, he said:

'You won't manage to do it, don't trouble yourself. Judas has already been killed this night.'

Levi sprang away from the table, looking wildly around, and cried out:

'Who did it?'

'Don't be jealous,' Pilate answered, his teeth bared, and rubbed his hands, 'I'm afraid he had other admirers besides you.'

'Who did it?' Levi repeated in a whisper.

Pilate answered him:

'I did it.'

Levi opened his mouth and stared at the procurator, who said quietly:

'It is, of course, not much to have done, but all the same I did it.' And he added: 'Well, and now will you take something?'

Levi considered, relented, and finally said:

'Have them give me a piece of clean parchment.'

An hour went by. Levi was not in the palace. Now the silence of the dawn was broken only by the quiet noise of the sentries' footsteps in the garden. The moon was quickly losing its colour, one could see at the other edge of the sky the whitish dot of the morning star. The lamps had gone out long, long ago. The procurator lay on the couch. Putting his hand under his cheek, he slept and breathed soundlessly. Beside him slept Banga.

Thus was the dawn of the fifteenth day of Nisan met by the fifth procurator of Judea, Pontius Pilate.

CHAPTER 27

The End of Apartment No. 50

When Margarita came to the last words of the chapter – '. . . Thus was the dawn of the fifteenth day of Nisan met by the fifth procurator of Judea, Pontius Pilate' – it was morning.

Sparrows could be heard in the branches of the willows and lindens in the little garden, conducting a merry, excited morning conversation.

Margarita got up from the armchair, stretched, and only then felt how broken her body was and how much she wanted to sleep. It is interesting to note that Margarita's soul was in perfect order. Her thoughts were not scattered, she was quite unshaken by having spent the night supernaturally. She was not troubled by memories of having been at Satan's ball, or that by some miracle the master had been returned to her, that the novel had risen from the ashes, that everything was back in place in the basement in the lane, from which the snitcher Aloisy Mogarych had been expelled. In short, acquaintance with Woland had caused her no psychic damage. Everything was as if it ought to have been so.

She went to the next room, convinced herself that the master was soundly and peacefully asleep, turned off the unnecessary table lamp, and stretched out by the opposite wall on a little couch covered with an old, torn sheet. A minute later she was asleep, and that morning she had no dreams. The basement rooms were silent, the builder's whole little house was silent, and it was quiet in the solitary lane.

But just then, that is, at dawn on Saturday, an entire floor of a certain Moscow institution was not asleep, and its windows, looking out on a big asphalt-paved square which special machines, driving around slowly and droning, were cleaning with brushes, shone with their full brightness, cutting through the light of the rising sun.

The whole floor was occupied with the investigation of the Woland case, and the lights had burned all night in dozens of offices.

Essentially speaking, the matter had already become clear on the previous day, Friday, when the Variety had had to be closed, owing to the disappearance of its administration and all sorts of outrages which had taken place during the notorious séance of black magic the day before. But the thing was that more and more new material kept arriving all the time and incessantly on the sleepless floor.

Now the investigators of this strange case, which smacked of obvious devilry, with an admixture of some hypnotic tricks and distinct criminality, had to shape into one lump all the many-sided and tangled events that had taken place in various parts of Moscow.

The first to visit the sleepless, electrically lit-up floor was Arkady Apollonovich Sempleyarov, chairman of the Acoustics Commission.

After dinner on Friday, in his apartment located in a house by the Kamenny Bridge, the telephone rang and a male voice asked for Arkady Apollonovich. Arkady Apollonovich's wife, who picked up the phone, replied sullenly that Arkady Apollonovich was unwell, had retired for the night, and could not come to the phone. However, Arkady Apollonovich came to the phone all the same. To the question of where Arkady Apollonovich was being called from, the voice in the telephone had said very briefly where it was from.

'This second ... at once ... this minute ...' babbled the ordinarily very haughty wife of the chairman of the Acoustics Commission, and she flew to the bedroom like an arrow to rouse Arkady Apollonovich from his bed, where he lay experiencing the torments of hell at the recollection of yesterday's séance and the night's scandal, followed by the expulsion of his Saratov niece from the apartment.

Not in a second, true, yet not in a minute either, but in a quarter of a minute, Arkady Apollonovich, with one slipper on his left foot, in nothing but his underwear, was already at the phone, babbling into it:

'Yes, it's me ... I'm listening, I'm listening ...'

His wife, forgetting for these moments all the loathsome crimes against fidelity in which the unfortunate Arkady Apollonovich had been exposed, kept sticking herself out the door to the corridor with a frightened face, poking a slipper at the air and whispering:

'Put the slipper on, the slipper ... you'll catch cold ...' At which Arkady Apollonovich, waving his wife away with his bare foot and making savage eyes at her, muttered into the telephone:

'Yes, yes, yes, surely ... I understand ... I'll leave at once ...'

Arkady Apollonovich spent the whole evening on that same floor where the investigation was being conducted.

It was a difficult conversation, a most unpleasant conversation, for he had to tell with complete sincerity not only about this obnoxious séance and the fight in the box, but along with that – as was indeed necessary – also about Militsa Andreevna Pokobatko from Yelokhovskaya Street, and about the Saratov niece, and about much else, the telling of which caused Arkady Apollonovich inexpressible torments.

Needless to say, the testimony of Arkady Apollonovich, an intelligent and cultivated man, who had been a witness to the outrageous séance, a sensible and qualified witness, who gave an excellent description of the mysterious masked magician himself and of his two scoundrelly assistants, a witness who remembered perfectly well that the magician's name was indeed Woland, advanced the investigation considerably. And the juxtaposition of Arkady Apollonovich's testimony with the testimony of others – among whom were some ladies who had suffered after the séance (the one in violet underwear who had shocked Rimsky and, alas, many others), and the messenger Karpov, who had been sent to apartment no. 50 on Sadovaya Street – at once essentially established the place where the culprit in all these adventures was to be sought.

Apartment no. 50 was visited, and not just once, and not only was it looked over with extreme thoroughness, but the walls were also tapped and the fireplace flues checked, in search of hiding places. However, none of these measures yielded any results, and no one was discovered in the apartment during any of these visits, though it was perfectly clear that there was someone in the apartment, despite the fact that all persons who in one way or another were supposed to be in charge of foreign artistes coming to Moscow decidedly and categorically insisted that there was not and could not be any black magician Woland in Moscow.

He had decidedly not registered anywhere on arrival, had not shown anyone his passport or other papers, contracts, or agreements, and no one had heard anything about him! Kitaitsev, head of the programme department of the Spectacles Commission, swore to God that the vanished Styopa Likhodeev had never sent him any performance programme of any Woland for approval and had never telephoned him about the arrival of such a Woland. So that he, Kitaitsev, utterly failed to see and understand how Styopa could have allowed such a séance in the Variety. And when told that Arkady Apollonovich had seen this magician at the séance with his own eyes, Kitaitsev only spread his arms and raised his eyes to heaven. And from Kitaitsev's eyes alone one could see and say confidently that he was as pure as crystal.

That same Prokhor Petrovich, chairman of the main Spectacles Commission . . .

Incidentally, he returned to his suit immediately after the police came into his office, to the ecstatic joy of Anna Richardovna and the great perplexity of the needlessly troubled police.

Also, incidentally, having returned to his place, into his grey striped suit, Prokhor Petrovich fully approved of all the resolutions the suit had written during his short-term absence.

. . . So, then, this same Prokhor Petrovich knew decidedly nothing about any Woland.

Whether you will or no, something preposterous was coming out: thousands of spectators, the whole staff of the Variety, and finally Sempleyarov, Arkady Apollonovich, a most educated man, had seen this magician, as well as his thrice-cursed assistants, and yet it was absolutely impossible to find him anywhere. What was it, may I ask, had he fallen through the ground right after his disgusting séance, or, as some affirm, had he not come to Moscow at all? But if the first is allowed, then undoubtedly, in falling through, he had taken along the entire top administration of the Variety, and if the second, then would it not mean that the administration of the luckless theatre itself, after first committing some vileness (only recall the broken window in the study and the behaviour of Ace of Diamonds!), had disappeared from Moscow without a trace?

We must do justice to the one who headed the investigation. The vanished Rimsky was found with amazing speed. One had only to put together the behaviour of Ace of Diamonds at the cab stand by the movie theatre with certain given times, such as when the séance ended, and precisely when Rimsky could have disappeared, and then immediately send a telegram to Leningrad. An hour later (towards evening on Friday) came the reply that Rimsky had been discovered in number four-twelve on the fourth floor of the Hotel Astoria, next to the room in which the repertory manager of one of the Moscow theatres, then on tour in Leningrad, was staying – that same room which, as is known, had gilded grey-blue furniture and a wonderful bathroom.[1]

Discovered hiding in the wardrobe of number four-twelve of the Astoria, Rimsky was questioned right there in Leningrad. After which a telegram came to Moscow reporting that findirector Rimsky was in an unanswerable state, that he could not or did not wish to give sensible replies to questions and begged only to be hidden in a bulletproof room and provided with an armed guard.

A telegram from Moscow ordered that Rimsky be delivered to Moscow under guard, as a result of which Rimsky departed Friday evening, under said guard, on the evening train.

Towards evening on that same Friday, Likhodeev's trail was also found. Telegrams of inquiry about Likhodeev were sent to all cities, and from Yalta came the reply that Likhodeev had been in Yalta but had left on a plane for Moscow.

The only one whose trail they failed to pick up was Varenukha. The famous theatre administrator known to decidedly all of Moscow had vanished into thin air.

In the meantime, there was some bother with things happening in other parts of Moscow, outside the Variety Theatre. It was necessary to explain the extraordinary case of the staff all singing 'Glorious Sea' (incidentally, Professor Stravinsky managed to put them right within two hours, by means of some subcutaneous injections), of persons presenting other persons or institutions with devil knows what in the guise of money, and also of persons who had suffered from such presentations.

As goes without saying, the most unpleasant, the most scandalous and insoluble of all these cases was the case of the theft of the head of the deceased writer Berlioz right from the coffin in the hall of Griboedov's, carried out in broad daylight.

Twelve men conducted the investigation, gathering as on a knitting-needle the accursed stitches of this complicated case scattered all over Moscow.

One of the investigators arrived at Professor Stravinsky's clinic and first of all asked to be shown a list of the persons who had checked in to the clinic over the past three days. Thus they discovered Nikanor Ivanovich Bosoy and the unfortunate master of ceremonies whose head had been torn off. However, little attention was paid to them. By now it was easy to establish that these two had fallen victim to the same gang, headed by that mysterious magician. But to Ivan Nikolaevich Homeless the investigator paid great attention.

The door of Ivanushka's room no. 117 opened towards evening

on Friday, and into the room came a young, round-faced, calm and mild-mannered man, who looked quite unlike an investigator and yet was one of the best in Moscow. He saw lying on the bed a pale and pinched young man, in whose eyes one could read a lack of interest in what went on around him, whose eyes looked now somewhere into the distance, over his surroundings, now into the young man himself. The investigator gently introduced himself and said he had stopped at Ivan Nikolaevich's to talk over the events at the Patriarch's Ponds two days ago.

Oh, how triumphant Ivan would have been if the investigator had come to him earlier – say, on Wednesday night, when Ivan had striven so violently and passionately to make his story about the Patriarch's Ponds heard! Now his dream of helping to catch the consultant had come true, there was no longer any need to run after anyone, they had come to him on their own, precisely to hear his story about what had happened on Wednesday evening.

But, alas, Ivanushka had changed completely in the time that had passed since the moment of Berlioz's death: he was ready to answer all of the investigator's questions willingly and politely, but indifference could be sensed both in Ivan's eyes and in his intonation. The poet was no longer concerned with Berlioz's fate.

Before the investigator's arrival, Ivanushka lay dozing, and certain visions passed before him. Thus, he saw a city, strange, incomprehensible, non-existent, with marble masses, eroded colonnades, roofs gleaming in the sun, with the black, gloomy and merciless Antonia Tower, with the palace on the western hill sunk almost up to its rooftops in the tropical greenery of the garden, with bronze statues blazing in the sunset above this greenery, and he saw armour-clad Roman centuries moving along under the walls of the ancient city.

As he dozed, there appeared before Ivan a man, motionless in an armchair, clean-shaven, with a harried yellow face, a man in a white mantle with red lining, gazing hatefully into the luxurious and alien garden. Ivan also saw a treeless yellow hill with empty cross-barred posts.

And what had happened at the Patriarch's Ponds no longer interested the poet Ivan Homeless.

'Tell me, Ivan Nikolaevich, how far were you from the turnstile yourself when Berlioz slipped under the tram-car?'

A barely noticeable, indifferent smile touched Ivan's lips for some reason, and he replied:

'I was far away.'

'And the checkered one was right by the turnstile?'

'No, he was sitting on a little bench nearby.'

'You clearly recall that he did not go up to the turnstile at the moment when Berlioz fell?'

'I recall. He didn't go up to it. He sat sprawled on the bench.'

These questions were the investigator's last. After them he got up, gave Ivanushka his hand, wished him a speedy recovery, and expressed the hope that he would soon be reading his poetry again.

'No,' Ivan quietly replied, 'I won't write any more poetry.'

The investigator smiled politely, allowed himself to express his certainty that, while the poet was presently in a state of some depression, it would soon pass.

'No,' Ivan responded, looking not at the investigator but into the distance, at the fading sky, 'it will never pass. The poems I used to write were bad poems, and now I understand it.'

The investigator left Ivanushka, having obtained some quite important material. Following the thread of events from the end to the beginning, they finally succeeded in reaching the source from which all the events had come. The investigator had no doubt that these events began with the murder at the Patriarch's Ponds. Of course, neither Ivanushka nor this checkered one had pushed the unfortunate chairman of Massolit under the tram-car; physically, so to speak, no one had contributed to his falling under the wheels. But the investigator was convinced that Berlioz had thrown himself under the tram-car (or tumbled under it) while hypnotized.

Yes, there was already a lot of material, and it was known who had to be caught and where. But the thing was that it proved in no way possible to catch anyone. We must repeat, there undoubtedly was someone in the thrice-cursed apartment no. 50. Occasionally the apartment answered telephone calls, now in a rattling, now in a nasal voice, occasionally one of its windows was opened, what's more, the sounds of a gramophone came from it. And yet each time it was visited, decidedly no one was found there. And it had already been visited more than once and at different times of day. And not only that, but they had gone through it with a net, checking every corner. The apartment had long been under suspicion. Guards were placed not just at the way to the courtyard through the gates, but at the back entrance as well. Not only that, but guards were placed on the roof by the chimneys. Yes, apartment no. 50 was acting up, and it was impossible to do anything about it.

So the thing dragged on until midnight on Friday, when Baron Meigel, dressed in evening clothes and patent-leather shoes, solemnly proceeded into apartment no. 50 in the quality of a guest. One could hear the baron being let in to the apartment. Exactly ten minutes later, without any ringing of bells, the apartment was visited, yet not only were the hosts not found in it, but, which was something quite bizarre, no signs of Baron Meigel were found in it either.

And so, as was said, the thing dragged on in this fashion until dawn on Saturday. Here new and very interesting data were added. A six-place passenger plane, coming from the Crimea, landed at the Moscow airport. Among the other passengers, one strange passenger got out of it. This was a young citizen, wildly overgrown with stubble, unwashed for three days, with inflamed and frightened eyes, carrying no luggage and dressed somewhat whimsically. The citizen was wearing a tall sheepskin hat, a Georgian felt cape over a nightshirt, and new, just-purchased, blue leather bedroom slippers. As soon as he separated from the ladder by which they descended from the plane, he was approached. This citizen had been expected, and in a little while the unforgettable director of the Variety, Stepan Bogdanovich Likhodeev, was standing before the investigators. He threw in some new data. It now became clear that Woland had penetrated the Variety in the guise of an artiste, having hypnotized Styopa Likhodeev, and had then contrived to fling this same Styopa out of Moscow and God knows how many miles away. The material was thus augmented, yet that did not make things easier, but perhaps even a bit harder, because it was becoming obvious that to lay hold of a person who could perform such stunts as the one of which Stepan Bogdanovich had been the victim would not be so easy. Incidentally, Likhodeev, at his own request, was confined in a secure cell, and next before the investigators stood Varenukha, just arrested in his own apartment, to which he had returned after a blank disappearance of almost two days.

Despite the promise he had given Azazello not to lie any more, the administrator began precisely with a lie. Though, by the way, he cannot be judged very harshly for it. Azazello had forbidden him to lie and be rude on the telephone, but in the present case the administrator spoke without the assistance of this apparatus. His eyes wandering, Ivan Savelyevich declared that on Thursday afternoon he had got drunk in his office at the Variety, all by himself, after which he went somewhere, but where he did not remember, drank starka[2] somewhere, but where he did not remember, lay about somewhere under a fence, but where he again did not remember. Only after the administrator was told that with his behaviour, stupid and senseless, he was hindering the investigation of an important case and would of course have to answer for it, did Varenukha burst into sobs and whisper in a trembling voice, looking around him, that he had lied solely out of fear, apprehensive of the revenge of Woland's gang, into whose hands he had already fallen, and that he begged, implored and yearned to be locked up in a bulletproof cell.

'Pah, the devil! Really, them and their bulletproof cells!' grumbled one of the investigators.

'They've been badly frightened by those scoundrels,' said the investigator who had visited Ivanushka.

They calmed Varenukha down the best they could, said they would protect him without any cell, and here it was learned that he had not drunk any starka under a fence, and that he had been beaten by two, one red-haired and with a fang, the other fat . . .

'Ah, resembling a cat?'

'Yes, yes, yes,' whispered the administrator, sinking with fear and looking around him every second, coming out with further details of how he had existed for some two days in apartment no. 50 in the quality of a tip-off vampire, who had all but caused the death of the findirector Rimsky . . .

Just then Rimsky, brought on the Leningrad train, was being led in. However, this mentally disturbed, grey-haired old man, trembling with fear, in whom it was very difficult to recognize the former findirector, would not tell the truth for anything, and proved to be very stubborn in this respect. Rimsky insisted that he had not seen any Hella in his office window at night, nor any Varenukha, but had simply felt bad and in a state of unconsciousness had left for Leningrad. Needless to say, the ailing findirector concluded his testimony with a request that he be confined to a bulletproof cell.

Annushka was arrested just as she made an attempt to hand a ten-dollar bill to the cashier of a department store on the Arbat. Annushka's story about people flying out the window of the house on Sadovaya and about the little horseshoe which Annushka, in her own words, had picked up in order to present it to the police, was listened to attentively.

'The horseshoe was really made of gold and diamonds?' Annushka was asked.

'As if I don't know diamonds,' replied Annushka.

'But he gave you ten-rouble bills, you say?'

'As if I don't know ten-rouble bills,' replied Annushka.

'Well, and when did they turn into dollars?'

'I don't know anything about any dollars, I never saw any dollars!' Annushka replied shrilly. 'I'm in my rights! I got recompensed, I was buying cloth with it,' and she went off into some balderdash about not being answerable for the house management that allowed unclean powers on to the fifth floor, making life unbearable.

Here the investigator waved at Annushka with his pen, because everyone was properly sick of her, and wrote a pass for her to get out on a green slip of paper, after which, to everyone's pleasure, Annushka disappeared from the building.

Then there followed one after another a whole series of people, Nikolai Ivanovich among them, just arrested owing solely to the foolishness of his jealous wife, who towards morning had informed the police that her husband had vanished. Nikolai Ivanovich did not surprise the investigators very much when he laid on the table the clownish certificate of his having spent the time at Satan's ball. In his stories of how he had carried Margarita Nikolaevna's naked housekeeper on his back through the air, somewhere to hell and beyond, for a swim in a river, and of the preceding appearance of the bare Margarita Nikolaevna in the window, Nikolai Ivanovich departed somewhat from the truth. Thus, for instance, he did not consider it necessary to mention that he had arrived in the bedroom with the discarded shift in his hands, or that he had called Natasha 'Venus'. From his words it looked as if Natasha had flown out the window, got astride him, and dragged him away from Moscow . . .

'Obedient to constraint, I was compelled to submit,' Nikolai Ivanovich said, and finished his tale with a request that not a word of it be told to his wife. Which was promised him.

The testimony of Nikolai Ivanovich provided an opportunity for establishing that Margarita Nikolaevna as well as her housekeeper Natasha had vanished without a trace. Measures were taken to find them.

Thus every second of Saturday morning was marked by the unrelenting investigation. In the city during that time, completely impossible rumours emerged and floated about, in which a tiny portion of truth was embellished with the most luxuriant lies. It was said that there had been a séance at the Variety after which all two thousand spectators ran out to the street in their birthday suits, that a press for making counterfeit money of a magic sort had been nabbed on Sadovaya Street, that some gang had kidnapped five managers from the entertainment sector, but the police had immediately found them all, and many other things that one does not even wish to repeat.

Meanwhile it was getting on towards dinner time, and then, in the place where the investigation was being conducted, the telephone rang. From Sadovaya came a report that the accursed apartment was again showing signs of life. It was said that its windows had been opened from inside, that sounds of a piano and singing were coming from it, and that a black cat had been seen in a window, sitting on the sill and basking in the sun.

At around four o'clock on that hot day, a big company of men in civilian clothes got out of three cars a short distance from no. 302-bis on Sadovaya Street. Here the big group divided into two small ones, the first going under the gateway of the house and across the courtyard directly to the sixth entrance, while the second opened the normally boarded-up little door leading to the back entrance, and both started up separate stairways to apartment no. 50.

Just then Koroviev and Azazello – Koroviev in his usual outfit and not the festive tailcoat – were sitting in the dining room of the apartment finishing breakfast. Woland, as was his wont, was in the bedroom, and where the cat was nobody knew. But judging by the clatter of dishes coming from the kitchen, it could be supposed that Behemoth was precisely there, playing the fool, as was his wont.

'And what are those footsteps on the stairs?' asked Koroviev, toying with the little spoon in his cup of black coffee.

'That's them coming to arrest us,' Azazello replied and drank off a glass of cognac.

'Ahh ... well, well ...' Koroviev replied to that.

The ones going up the front stairway were already on the third-floor landing. There a couple of plumbers were pottering over the harmonica of the steam heating. The newcomers exchanged significant glances with the plumbers.

'They're all at home,' whispered one of the plumbers, tapping a pipe with his hammer.

Then the one walking at the head openly took a black Mauser from under his coat, and another beside him took out the skeleton keys. Generally, those going to apartment no. 50 were properly equipped. Two of them had fine, easily unfolded silk nets in their pockets. Another of them had a lasso, another had gauze masks and ampoules of chloroform.

In a second the front door to apartment no. 50 was open and all the visitors were in the front hall, while the slamming of the door in the kitchen at the same moment indicated the timely arrival of the second group from the back stairs.

This time there was, if not complete, at least some sort of success. The men instantly dispersed through all the rooms and found no one anywhere, but instead on the table of the dining room they discovered the remains of an apparently just-abandoned breakfast, and in the living room, on the mantelpiece, beside a crystal pitcher, sat an enormous black cat. He was holding a primus in his paws.

Those who entered the living room contemplated this cat for quite a long time in total silence.

'Hm, yes . . . that's quite something . . .' one of the men whispered.

'Ain't misbehaving, ain't bothering anybody, just reparating my primus,' said the cat with an unfriendly scowl, 'and I also consider it my duty to warn you that the cat is an ancient and inviolable animal.'

'Exceptionally neat job,' whispered one of the men, and another said loudly and distinctly:

'Well, come right in, you inviolable, ventriloquous cat!'

The net unfolded and soared upwards, but the man who cast it, to everyone's utter astonishment, missed and only caught the pitcher, which straight away smashed ringingly.

'You lose!' bawled the cat. 'Hurrah!' and here, setting the primus aside, he snatched a Browning from behind his back. In a trice he aimed it at the man standing closest, but before the cat had time to shoot, fire blazed in the man's hand, and at the blast of the Mauser the cat plopped head first from the mantelpiece on to the floor, dropping the Browning and letting go of the primus.

'It's all over,' the cat said in a weak voice, sprawled languidly in a pool of blood, 'step back from me for a second, let me say farewell to the earth. Oh, my friend Azazello,' moaned the cat, bleeding profusely, 'where are you?' The cat rolled his fading eyes in the direction of the dining-room door. 'You did not come to my aid in the moment of unequal battle, you abandoned poor Behemoth, exchanging him for a glass of – admittedly very good – cognac! Well, so, let my death be on your conscience, and I bequeath you my Browning . . .'

'The net, the net, the net . . .' was anxiously whispered around the cat. But the net, devil knows why, got caught in someone's pocket and refused to come out.

'The only thing that can save a mortally wounded cat,' said the cat, 'is a swig of benzene.' And taking advantage of the confusion, he bent to the round opening in the primus and had a good drink of benzene. The blood at once stopped flowing from under his left front leg. The cat jumped up, alive and cheerful, seized the primus under his paw, shot back on to the mantelpiece with it, and from there, shredding the wallpaper, climbed the wall and some two seconds later was high above the visitors and sitting on a metal curtain rod.

Hands instantly clutched the curtain and tore it off together with the rod, causing sunlight to flood the shaded room. But neither the fraudulently recovered cat nor the primus fell down. The cat, without parting with his primus, managed to shoot through the air and land on the chandelier hanging in the middle of the room.

'A stepladder!' came from below.

'I challenge you to a duel!' bawled the cat, sailing over their heads on the swinging chandelier, and the Browning was again in his paw, and the primus was lodged among the branches of the chandelier. The cat took aim and, flying like a pendulum over the heads of the visitors, opened fire on them. The din shook the apartment. Crystal shivers poured down from the chandelier, the mantelpiece mirror was cracked into stars, plaster dust flew, spent cartridges bounced over the floor, window-panes shattered, benzene spouted from the bullet-pierced primus. Now there was no question of taking the cat alive, and the visitors fiercely and accurately returned his fire from the Mausers, aiming at his head, stomach, chest and back. The shooting caused panic on the asphalt courtyard.

But this shooting did not last long and began to die down of itself. The thing was that it caused no harm either to the cat or to the visitors. Not only was no one killed, but no one was even wounded. Everyone, including the cat, remained totally unharmed. One of the visitors, to verify it definitively, sent some five bullets at the confounded animal's head, while the cat smartly responded with a full clip, but it was the same – no effect was produced on anybody. The cat swayed on the chandelier, which swung less and less, blowing into the muzzle of his Browning and spitting on his paw for some reason.

The faces of those standing silently below acquired an expression of utter bewilderment. This was the only case, or one of the only cases, when shooting proved to be entirely inefficacious. One might allow, of course, that the cat's Browning was some sort of toy, but one could by no means say the same of the visitors' Mausers. The cat's very first wound – there obviously could not be the slightest doubt of it – was nothing but a trick and a swinish sham, as was the drinking of the benzene.

One more attempt was made to get hold of the cat. The lasso was thrown, it caught on one of the candles, the chandelier fell down. The crash seemed to shake the whole structure of the house, but it was no use. Those present were showered with splinters, and the cat flew through the air over them and settled high under the ceiling on the upper part of the mantelpiece mirror's gilded frame. He had no intention of escaping anywhere, but, on the contrary, while sitting in relative safety, even started another speech:

'I utterly fail to comprehend,' he held forth from on high, 'the reasons for such harsh treatment of me . . .'

And here at its very beginning this speech was interrupted by a heavy, low voice coming from no one knew where:

'What's going on in the apartment? They prevent me from working . . .'

Another voice, unpleasant and nasal, responded:

'Well, it's Behemoth, of course, devil take him!'

A third, rattling voice said:

'Messire! It's Saturday. The sun is setting. Time to go.'

'Excuse me, I can't talk any more,' the cat said from the mirror, 'time to go.' He hurled his Browning and knocked out both panes in the window. Then he splashed down some benzene, and this benzene caught fire by itself, throwing a wave of flame up to the very ceiling.

Things caught fire somehow unusually quickly and violently, as does not happen even with benzene. The wallpaper at once began to smoke, the torn-down curtain started burning on the floor, and the frames of the broken windows began to smoulder. The cat crouched, miaowed, shot from the mirror to the window-sill, and disappeared through it together with his primus. Shots rang out outside. A man sitting on the iron fire-escape at the level of the jeweller's wife's windows fired at the cat as he flew from one window-sill to another, making for the corner drainpipe of the house which, as has been said, was built in the form of a 'U'. By way of this pipe, the cat climbed up to the roof. There, unfortunately also without any result, he was shot at by the sentries guarding the chimneys, and the cat cleared off into the setting sun that was flooding the city.

Just then in the apartment the parquet blazed up under the visitors' feet, and in that fire, on the same spot where the cat had sprawled with his sham wound, there appeared, growing more and more dense, the corpse of the former Baron Meigel with upthrust chin and glassy eyes. To get him out was no longer possible.

Leaping over the burning squares of parquet, slapping themselves on their smoking chests and shoulders, those who were in the living room retreated to the study and front hall. Those who were in the dining room and bedroom ran out through the corridor. Those in the kitchen also came running and rushed into the front hall. The living room was already filled with fire and smoke. Someone managed, in flight, to dial the number of the fire department and shout briefly into the receiver:

'Sadovaya, three-oh-two-bis! . . .'

To stay longer was impossible. Flames gushed out into the front hall. Breathing became difficult.

As soon as the first little spurts of smoke pushed through the broken windows of the enchanted apartment, desperate human cries arose in the courtyard:

'Fire! Fire! We're burning!'

In various apartments of the house, people began shouting into telephones:

'Sadovaya! Sadovaya, three-oh-two-bis!'

Just then, as the heart-quailing bells were heard on Sadovaya, ringing from long red engines racing quickly from all parts of the city, the people rushing about the yard saw how, along with the smoke, there flew out of the fifth-storey window three dark, apparently male silhouettes and one silhouette of a naked woman.

CHAPTER 28

The Last Adventures of Koroviev and Behemoth

Whether these silhouettes were there, or were only imagined by the fear-struck tenants of the ill-fated house on Sadovaya, is, of course, impossible to say precisely. If they were there, where they set out for is also known to no one. Nor can we say where they separated, but we do know that approximately a quarter of an hour after the fire started on Sadovaya, there appeared by the mirrored doors of a currency store[1] on the Smolensky market-place a long citizen in a checkered suit, and with him a big black cat.

Deftly slithering between the passers-by, the citizen opened the outer door of the shop. But here a small, bony and extremely ill-disposed doorman barred his way and said irritably:

'No cats allowed!'

'I beg your pardon,' rattled the long one, putting his gnarled hand to his ear as if he were hard of hearing, 'no cats, you say? And where do you see any cats?'

The doorman goggled his eyes, and well he might: there was no cat at the citizen's feet now, but instead, from behind his shoulder, a fat fellow in a tattered cap, whose mug indeed somewhat resembled a cat's, stuck out, straining to get into the store. There was a primus in the fat fellow's hands.

The misanthropic doorman for some reason disliked this pair of customers.

'We only accept currency,' he croaked, gazing vexedly from under his shaggy, as if moth-eaten, grizzled eyebrows.

'My dear man,' rattled the long one, flashing his eye through the broken pince-nez, 'how do you know I don't have any? Are you judging by my clothes? Never do so, my most precious custodian! You may make a mistake, and a big one at that. At least read the story of the famous caliph Harun al-Rashid[2] over again. But in the present case, casting that story aside temporarily, I want to tell you that I am going to make a complaint about you to the manager and tell him such tales about you that you may have to surrender your post between the shining mirrored doors.'

'Maybe I've got a whole primus full of currency,' the cat-like fat fellow, who was simply shoving his way into the store, vehemently butted into the conversation.

Behind them the public was already pushing and getting angry. Looking at the prodigious pair with hatred and suspicion, the doorman stepped aside, and our acquaintances, Koroviev and Behemoth, found themselves in the store. Here they first of all looked around, and then, in a ringing voice heard decidedly in every corner, Koroviev announced:

'A wonderful store! A very, very fine store!'

The public turned away from the counters and for some reason looked at the speaker in amazement, though he had all grounds for praising the store.

Hundreds of bolts of cotton in the richest assortment of colours could be seen in the pigeon-holes of the shelves. Next to them were piled calicoes, and chiffons, and flannels for suits. In receding perspective endless stacks of shoeboxes could be seen, and several citizenesses sat on little low chairs, one foot shod in an old, worn-out shoe, the other in a shiny new pump, which they stamped on the carpet with a preoccupied air. Somewhere in the depths, around a corner, gramophones sang and played music.

But, bypassing all these enchantments, Koroviev and Behemoth made straight for the junction of the grocery and confectionery departments. Here there was plenty of room, no citizenesses in scarves and little berets were pushing against the counters, as in the fabric department.

A short, perfectly square man with blue shaven jowls, horn-rimmed glasses, a brand-new hat, not crumpled and with no sweat stains on the band, in a lilac coat and orange kid gloves, stood by the counter grunting something peremptorily. A sales clerk in a clean white smock and a blue hat was waiting on the lilac client. With the sharpest of knives, much like the knife stolen by Matthew Levi, he was removing from a weeping, plump pink salmon its snake-like, silvery skin.

'This department is splendid, too,' Koroviev solemnly acknowledged, 'and the foreigner is a likeable fellow,' he benevolently pointed his finger at the lilac back.

'No, Fagott, no,' Behemoth replied pensively, 'you're mistaken, my friend: the lilac gentleman's face lacks something, in my opinion.'

The lilac back twitched, but probably by chance, for the foreigner was surely unable to understand what Koroviev and his companion were saying in Russian.

'Is good?' the lilac purchaser asked sternly.

'Top-notch!' replied the sales clerk, cockily slipping the edge of the knife under the skin.

'Good I like, bad I don't,' the foreigner said sternly.

'Right you are!' the sales clerk rapturously replied.

Here our acquaintances walked away from the foreigner and his salmon to the end of the confectionery counter.

'It's hot today,' Koroviev addressed a young, red-cheeked salesgirl and received no reply to his words. 'How much are the mandarins?' Koroviev then inquired of her.

'Fifteen kopecks a pound,' replied the salesgirl.

'Everything's so pricey,' Koroviev observed with a sigh, 'hm . . . hm . . .' He thought a little longer and then invited his companion: 'Eat up, Behemoth.'

The fat fellow put his primus under his arm, laid hold of the top mandarin on the pyramid, straight away gobbled it up skin and all, and began on a second.

The salesgirl was overcome with mortal terror.

'You're out of your mind!' she shouted, losing her colour. 'Give me the receipt! The receipt!' and she dropped the confectionery tongs.

'My darling, my dearest, my beauty,' Koroviev rasped, leaning over the counter and winking at the salesgirl, 'we're out of currency today . . . what can we do? But I swear to you, by next time, and no later than Monday, we'll pay it all in pure cash! We're from near by, on Sadovaya, where they're having the fire . . .'

Behemoth, after swallowing a third mandarin, put his paw into a clever construction of chocolate bars, pulled out the bottom one, which of course made the whole thing collapse, and swallowed it together with its gold wrapper.

The sales clerks behind the fish counter stood as if petrified, their knives in their hands, the lilac foreigner swung around to the robbers, and here it turned out that Behemoth was mistaken: there was nothing lacking in the lilac one's face, but, on the contrary, rather some super-fluity of hanging jowls and furtive eyes.

Turning completely yellow, the salesgirl anxiously cried for the whole store to hear:

'Palosich![3] Palosich!'

The public from the fabric department came thronging at this cry, while Behemoth, stepping away from the confectionery temptations, thrust his paw into a barrel labelled 'Choice Kerch Herring',[4] pulled out a couple of herring, and swallowed them, spitting out the tails.

'Palosich!' the desperate cry came again from behind the confectionery counter, and from behind the fish counter a sales clerk with a goatee barked:

'What's this you're up to, vermin?'

Pavel Yosifovich was already hastening to the scene of the action. He was an imposing man in a clean white smock, like a surgeon, with a pencil sticking out of the pocket. Pavel Yosifovich was obviously an experienced man. Seeing the tail of the third herring in Behemoth's mouth, he instantly assessed the situation, understood decidedly everything, and, without getting into any arguments with the insolent louts, waved his arm into the distance, commanding:

'Whistle!'

The doorman flew from the mirrored door out to the corner of the Smolensky market-place and dissolved in a sinister whistling. The public began to surround the blackguards, and then Koroviev stepped into the affair.

'Citizens!' he called out in a high, vibrating voice, 'what's going on here? Eh? Allow me to ask you that! The poor man' – Koroviev let some tremor into his voice and pointed to Behemoth, who immediately concocted a woeful physiognomy – 'the poor man spends all day reparating primuses. He got hungry ... and where's he going to get currency?'

To this Pavel Yosifovich, usually restrained and calm, shouted sternly:

'You just stop that!' and waved into the distance, impatiently now. Then the trills by the door resounded more merrily.

But Koroviev, unabashed by Pavel Yosifovich's pronouncement, went on:

'Where? – I ask you all this question! He's languishing with hunger and thirst, he's hot. So the hapless fellow took and sampled a mandarin. And the total worth of that mandarin is three kopecks. And here they go whistling like spring nightingales in the woods, bothering the police, tearing them away from their business. But he's allowed, eh?' and here Koroviev pointed to the lilac fat man, which caused the strongest alarm to appear on his face. 'Who is he? Eh? Where did he come from? And why? Couldn't we do without him? Did we invite him, or what? Of course,' the ex-choirmaster bawled at the top of his lungs, twisting his mouth sarcastically, 'just look at him, in his smart lilac suit, all swollen with salmon, all stuffed with currency – and us, what about the likes of us?! . . . I'm bitter! Bitter, bitter!'[5] Koroviev wailed, like the best man at an old-fashioned wedding.

This whole stupid, tactless, and probably politically harmful speech made Pavel Yosifovich shake with wrath, but, strange as it may seem, one could see by the eyes of the crowding public that it provoked sympathy in a great many people. And when Behemoth, putting a torn, dirty sleeve to his eyes, exclaimed tragically:

'Thank you, my faithful friend, you stood up for the sufferer!' – a miracle occurred. A most decent, quiet little old man, poorly but cleanly dressed, a little old man buying three macaroons in the confectionery department, was suddenly transformed. His eyes flashed with bellicose fire, he turned purple, hurled the little bag of macaroons on the floor, and shouted 'True!' in a child's high voice. Then he snatched up a tray, throwing from it the remains of the chocolate Eiffel Tower demolished by Behemoth, brandished it, tore the foreigner's hat off with his left hand, and with his right swung and struck the foreigner flat on his bald head with the tray. There was a roll as of the noise one hears when sheets of metal are thrown down from a truck. The fat man, turning white, fell backwards and sat in the barrel of Kerch herring, spouting a fountain of brine from it. Straight away a second miracle occurred. The lilac one, having fallen into the barrel, shouted in pure Russian, with no trace of any accent:

'Murder! Police! The bandits are murdering me!' evidently having mastered, owing to the shock, this language hitherto unknown to him.

Then the doorman's whistling ceased, and amid the crowds of agitated shoppers two military helmets could be glimpsed approaching. But the perfidious Behemoth doused the confectionery counter with benzene from his primus, as one douses a bench in a bathhouse with a tub of water, and it blazed up of itself. The flame spurted upwards and ran along the counter, devouring the beautiful paper ribbons on the fruit baskets. The salesgirls dashed shrieking from behind the counters, and as soon as they came from behind them, the linen curtains on the windows blazed up and the benzene on the floor ignited.

The public, at once raising a desperate cry, shrank back from the confectionery department, running down the no longer needed Pavel Yosifovich, and from behind the fish counter the sales clerks with their whetted knives trotted in single file towards the door of the rear exit.

The lilac citizen, having extracted himself from the barrel, thoroughly drenched with herring juice, heaved himself over the salmon on the counter and followed after them. The glass of the mirrored front doors clattered and spilled down, pushed out by fleeing people, while the two blackguards, Koroviev and the glutton Behemoth, got lost somewhere, but where – it was impossible to grasp. Only afterwards did eyewitnesses who had been present at the starting of the fire in the currency store in Smolensky market-place tell how the two hooligans supposedly flew up to the ceiling and there popped like children's balloons. It is doubtful, of course, that things happened that way, but what we don't know, we don't know.

But we do know that exactly one minute after the happening in Smolensky market-place, Behemoth and Koroviev both turned up on the sidewalk of the boulevard just by the house of Griboedov's aunt. Koroviev stood by the fence and spoke:

'Hah! This is the writers' house! You know, Behemoth, I've heard many good and flattering things about this house. Pay attention to this house, my friend. It's pleasant to think how under this roof no end of talents are being sheltered and nurtured.'

'Like pineapples in a greenhouse,' said Behemoth and, the better to admire the cream-coloured building with columns, he climbed the concrete footing of the cast-iron fence.

'Perfectly correct,' Koroviev agreed with his inseparable companion, 'and a sweet awe creeps into one's heart at the thought that in this house there is now ripening the future author of a *Don Quixote* or a *Faust*, or, devil take me, a *Dead Souls*![6] Eh?'

'Frightful to think of,' agreed Behemoth.

'Yes,' Koroviev went on, 'one can expect astonishing things from the hotbeds of this house, which has united under its roof several thousand zealots resolved to devote their lives to the service of Melpomene, Polyhymnia and Thalia.[7] You can imagine the noise that will arise when one of them, for starters, offers the reading public *The Inspector General*[8] or, if worse comes to worst, *Evgeny Onegin*.'[9]

'Quite easily,' Behemoth again agreed.

'Yes,' Koroviev went on, anxiously raising his finger, 'but! ... But, I say, and I repeat this *but*! ... Only if these tender hothouse plants are not attacked by some micro-organism that gnaws at their roots so that they rot! And it does happen with pineapples! Oh, my, does it!'

'Incidentally,' inquired Behemoth, putting his round head through an opening in the fence, 'what are they doing on the veranda?'

'Having dinner,' explained Koroviev, 'and to that I will add, my dear, that the restaurant here is inexpensive and not bad at all. And, by the way, like any tourist before continuing his trip, I feel a desire to have a bite and drink a big, ice-cold mug of beer.'

'Me, too,' replied Behemoth, and the two blackguards marched down the asphalt path under the lindens straight to the veranda of the unsuspecting restaurant.

A pale and bored citizeness in white socks and a white beret with a nib sat on a Viennese chair at the corner entrance to the veranda, where amid the greenery of the trellis an opening for the entrance had been made. In front of her on a simple kitchen table lay a fat book of the ledger variety, in which the citizeness, for unknown reasons, wrote down all those who entered the restaurant. It was precisely this citizeness who stopped Koroviev and Behemoth.

'Your identification cards?' She was gazing in amazement at Koroviev's pince-nez, and also at Behemoth's primus and Behemoth's torn elbow.

'A thousand pardons, but what identification cards?' asked Koroviev in surprise.

'You're writers?' the citizeness asked in her turn.

'Unquestionably,' Koroviev answered with dignity.

'Your identification cards?' the citizeness repeated.

'My sweetie ...' Koroviev began tenderly.

'I'm no sweetie,' interrupted the citizeness.

'More's the pity,' Koroviev said disappointedly and went on: 'Well, so, if you don't want to be a sweetie, which would be quite pleasant, you don't have to be. So, then, to convince yourself that Dostoevsky was a writer, do you have to ask for his identification card? Just take any five pages from any one of his novels and you'll be convinced, without any identification card, that you're dealing with a writer. And I don't think he even had any identification card! What do you think?' Koroviev turned to Behemoth.

'I'll bet he didn't,' replied Behemoth, setting the primus down on the table beside the ledger and wiping the sweat from his sooty forehead with his hand.

'You're not Dostoevsky,' said the citizeness, who was getting muddled by Koroviev.

'Well, who knows, who knows,' he replied.

'Dostoevsky's dead,' said the citizeness, but somehow not very confidently.

'I protest!' Behemoth exclaimed hotly. 'Dostoevsky is immortal!'

'Your identification cards, citizens,' said the citizeness.

'Good gracious, this is getting to be ridiculous!' Koroviev would not give in. 'A writer is defined not by any identity card, but by what he writes. How do you know what plots are swarming in my head? Or in this head?' and he pointed at Behemoth's head, from which the latter at once removed the cap, as if to let the citizeness examine it better.

'Step aside, citizens,' she said, nervously now.

Koroviev and Behemoth stepped aside and let pass some writer in a grey suit with a tie-less, summer white shirt, the collar of which lay wide open on the lapels of his jacket, and with a newspaper under his arm. The writer nodded affably to the citizeness, in passing put some flourish in the proffered ledger, and proceeded to the veranda.

'Alas, not to us, not to us,' Koroviev began sadly, 'but to him will go that ice-cold mug of beer, which you and I, poor wanderers, so dreamed of together. Our position is woeful and difficult, and I don't know what to do.'

Behemoth only spread his arms bitterly and put his cap on his round head, covered with thick hair very much resembling a cat's fur.

And at that moment a low but peremptory voice sounded over the head of the citizeness:

'Let them pass, Sofya Pavlovna.'[10]

The citizeness with the ledger was amazed. Amidst the greenery of the trellis appeared the white tailcoated chest and wedge-shaped beard of the freebooter. He was looking affably at the two dubious ragamuffins and, moreover, even making inviting gestures to them. Archibald Archibaldovich's authority was something seriously felt in the restaurant under his management, and Sofya Pavlovna obediently asked Koroviev:

'What is your name?'

'Panaev,'[11] he answered courteously. The citizeness wrote this name down and raised a questioning glance to Behemoth.

'Skabichevsky,'[12] the latter squeaked, for some reason pointing to his primus. Sofya Pavlovna wrote this down, too, and pushed the book towards the visitors for them to sign. Koroviev wrote 'Skabichevsky' next to the name 'Panaev', and Behemoth wrote 'Panaev' next to 'Skabichevsky'.

Archibald Archibaldovich, to the utter amazement of Sofya Pavlovna, smiled seductively, and led the guests to the best table, at the opposite end of the veranda, where the deepest shade lay, a table next to which the sun played merrily through one of the gaps in the trellis greenery, while Sofya Pavlovna, blinking with amazement, studied for a long time the strange entry made in the book by the unexpected visitors.

Archibald Archibaldovich surprised the waiters no less than he had Sofya Pavlovna. He personally drew a chair back from the table, inviting Koroviev to sit down, winked to one, whispered something to the other, and the two waiters began bustling around the new guests, one of whom set his primus down on the floor next to his scuffed shoe.

The old yellow-stained tablecloth immediately disappeared from the table, another shot up into the air, crackling with starch, white as a Bedouin's burnous, and Archibald Archibaldovich was already whispering softly but very significantly, bending right to Koroviev's ear:

'What may I treat you to? I have a special little *balyk*[13] here ... bagged at the architects' congress ...'

'Oh ... just give us a bite of something ... eh? ...' Koroviev mumbled good-naturedly, sprawling on the chair.

'I understand ...' Archibald Archibaldovich replied meaningfully, closing his eyes.

Seeing the way the chief of the restaurant treated the rather dubious visitors, the waiters laid aside their suspicions and got seriously down to business. One was already offering a match to Behemoth, who had taken a butt from his pocket and put it in his mouth, the other raced up clinking with green glass and at their places arranged goblets, tumblers, and those thin-walled glasses from which it is so nice to drink seltzer under the awning ... no, skipping ahead, let us say: it used to be so nice to drink seltzer under the awning of the unforgettable Griboedov veranda.

'I might recommend a little fillet of hazel-grouse,' Archibald

Archibaldovich murmured musically. The guest in the cracked pince-nez fully approved the commander of the brig's suggestions and gazed at him benevolently through the useless bit of glass.

The fiction writer Petrakov-Sukhovey, dining at the next table with his wife, who was finishing a pork chop, noticed with the keenness of observation proper to all writers the wooing of Archibald Archibaldovich, and was quite, quite surprised. And his wife, a very respectable lady, even simply became jealous of Koroviev over the pirate, and even rapped with her teaspoon, as if to say: why are we kept waiting? . . . It's time the ice cream was served. What's the matter? . . .

However, after sending Mrs Petrakov a seductive smile, Archibald Archibaldovich dispatched a waiter to her, but did not leave his dear guests himself. Ah, how intelligent Archibald Archibaldovich was! And his powers of observation were perhaps no less keen than those of the writers themselves! Archibald Archibaldovich knew about the séance at the Variety, and about many other events of those days; he had heard, but, unlike the others, had not closed his ears to, the word 'checkered' and the word 'cat'. Archibald Archibaldovich guessed at once who his visitors were. And, having guessed, naturally did not start quarrelling with them. And that Sofya Pavlovna was a good one! To come up with such a thing – barring the way to the veranda for those two! Though what could you expect of her! . . .

Haughtily poking her little spoon into the slushy ice cream, Mrs Petrakov, with displeased eyes, watched the table in front of the two motley buffoons become overgrown with dainties as if by magic. Shiny clean lettuce leaves were already sticking from a bowl of fresh caviar . . . an instant later a sweating silver bucket appeared, brought especially on a separate little table . . .

Only when convinced that everything had been done impeccably, only when there came flying in the waiter's hands a covered pan with something gurgling in it, did Archibald Archibaldovich allow himself to leave the two mysterious visitors, and that after having first whispered to them:

'Excuse me! One moment! I'll see to the fillets personally!'

He flew away from the table and disappeared into an inner passage of the restaurant. If any observer had been able to follow the further actions of Archibald Archibaldovich, they would undoubtedly have seemed somewhat mysterious to him.

The chief did not go to the kitchen to supervise the fillets at all, but went to the restaurant pantry. He opened it with his own key, locked himself inside, took two hefty *balyks* from the icebox, carefully, so as not to soil his cuffs, wrapped them in newspaper, tied them neatly with string, and set them aside. Then he made sure that his hat and silk-lined summer coat were in place in the next room, and only after that proceeded to the kitchen, where the chef was carefully boning the fillets the pirate had promised his visitors.

It must be said that there was nothing strange or incomprehensible in any of Archibald Archibaldovich's actions, and that they could seem strange only to a superficial observer. Archibald Archibaldovich's behaviour was the perfectly logical result of all that had gone before. A knowledge of the latest events, and above all Archibald Archibaldovich's phenomenal intuition, told the chief of the Griboedov restaurant that his two visitors' dinner, while abundant and sumptuous, would be of extremely short duration. And his intuition, which had never yet deceived the former freebooter, did not let him down this time either.

Just as Koroviev and Behemoth were clinking their second glasses of wonderful, cold, double-distilled Moskovskaya vodka, the sweaty and excited chronicler Boba Kandalupsky, famous in Moscow for his astounding omniscience, appeared on the veranda and at once sat down with the Petrakovs. Placing his bulging briefcase on the table, Boba immediately put his lips to Petrakov's ear and whispered some very tempting things into it. Madame Petrakov, burning with curiosity, also put her ear to Boba's plump, greasy lips. And he, with an occasional furtive look around, went on whispering and whispering, and one could make out separate words, such as:

'I swear to you! On Sadovaya, on Sadovaya! . . .' Boba lowered his voice still more, 'bullets have no effect! . . . bullets . . . bullets . . . benzene . . . fire . . . bullets . . .'

'It's the liars that spread these vile rumours,' Madame Petrakov boomed in a contralto voice, somewhat louder in her indignation than Boba would have liked, 'they're the ones who ought to be explained! Well, never mind, that's how it will be, they'll be called to order! Such pernicious lies!'

'Why lies, Antonida Porfirievna!' exclaimed Boba, upset by the disbelief of the writer's wife, and again began spinning: 'I tell you, bullets have no effect! . . . And then the fire . . . they went up in the air . . .

in the air!' Boba went on hissing, not suspecting that those he was talking about were sitting next to him, delighting in his yarn.

However, this delight soon ceased: from an inner passage of the restaurant three men, their waists drawn in tightly by belts, wearing leggings and holding revolvers in their hands, strode precipitously on to the veranda. The one in front cried ringingly and terribly:

'Don't move!' And at once all three opened fire on the veranda, aiming at the heads of Koroviev and Behemoth. The two objects of the shooting instantly melted into air, and a pillar of fire spurted from the primus directly on to the tent roof. It was as if a gaping maw with black edges appeared in the tent and began spreading in all directions. The fire leaping through it rose up to the roof of Griboedov House. Folders full of papers lying on the window-sill of the editorial office on the second floor suddenly blazed up, followed by the curtains, and now the fire, howling as if someone were blowing on it, went on in pillars to the interior of the aunt's house.

A few seconds later, down the asphalt paths leading to the cast-iron fence on the boulevard, whence Ivanushka, the first herald of the disaster, understood by no one, had come on Wednesday evening, various writers, Sofya Pavlovna, Boba, Petrakov's wife and Petrakov, now went running, leaving their dinners unfinished.

Having stepped out through a side entrance beforehand, not fleeing or hurrying anywhere, like a captain who must be the last to leave his burning brig, Archibald Archibaldovich stood calmly in his summer coat with silk lining, the two *balyk* logs under his arm.

CHAPTER 29

The Fate of the Master and Margarita is Decided

At sunset, high over the city, on the stone terrace of one of the most beautiful houses in Moscow, a house built about a hundred and fifty years ago, there were two: Woland and Azazello. They could not be seen from the street below, because they were hidden from unwanted eyes by a balustrade with plaster vases and plaster flowers. But they could see the city almost to its very edges.

Woland was sitting on a folding stool, dressed in his black soutane. His long and broad sword was stuck vertically into a crack between two flags of the terrace so as to make a sundial. The shadow of the sword lengthened slowly and steadily, creeping towards the black shoes on Satan's feet. Resting his sharp chin on his fist, hunched on the stool with one leg drawn under him, Woland stared fixedly[1] at the endless collection of palaces, gigantic buildings and little hovels destined to be pulled down.

Azazello, having parted with his modern attire – that is, jacket, bowler hat and patent-leather shoes – and dressed, like Woland, in black, stood motionless not far from his sovereign, like him with his eyes fixed on the city.

Woland began to speak:

'Such an interesting city, is it not?'

Azazello stirred and replied respectfully:

'I like Rome better, Messire.'

'Yes, it's a matter of taste,' replied Woland.

After a while, his voice resounded again:

'And what is that smoke there on the boulevard?'

'That is Griboedov's burning,' replied Azazello.

'It must be supposed that that inseparable pair, Koroviev and Behemoth, stopped by there?'

'Of that there can be no doubt, Messire.'

Again silence fell, and the two on the terrace gazed at the fragmented, dazzling sunlight in the upper-floor windows of the huge buildings facing west. Woland's eye burned like one of those windows, though Woland had his back to the sunset.

But here something made Woland turn his attention to the round tower behind him on the roof. From its wall stepped a tattered, clay-covered, sullen man in a chiton, in home-made sandals, black-bearded.

'Hah!' exclaimed Woland, looking mockingly at the newcomer. 'Least of all would I expect you here! What have you come with, uninvited guest?'

'I have come to see you, spirit of evil and sovereign of shadows,' the newcomer replied, glowering inimically at Woland.

'If you've come to see me, why didn't you wish me a good evening, former tax collector?' Woland said sternly.

'Because I don't wish you a good anything,' the newcomer replied insolently.

'But you'll have to reconcile yourself to that,' Woland objected, and a grin twisted his mouth. 'You no sooner appear on the roof than you produce an absurdity, and I'll tell you what it is – it's your intonation. You uttered your words as if you don't acknowledge shadows, or evil either. Kindly consider the question: what would your good do if evil did not exist, and what would the earth look like if shadows disappeared from it? Shadows are cast by objects and people. Here is the shadow of my sword. Trees and living beings also have shadows. Do you want to skin the whole earth, tearing all the trees and living things off it, because of your fantasy of enjoying bare light? You're a fool.'

'I won't argue with you, old sophist,' replied Matthew Levi.

'You also cannot argue with me, for the reason I've already mentioned: you're a fool,' Woland replied and asked: 'Well, make it short, don't weary me, why have you appeared?'

'He sent me.'

'What did he tell you to say, slave?'

'I'm not a slave,' Matthew Levi replied, growing ever angrier, 'I'm his disciple.'

'You and I speak different languages, as usual,' responded Woland, 'but the things we say don't change for all that. And so? . . .'

'He has read the master's work,' said Matthew Levi, 'and asks you to take the master with you and reward him with peace. Is that hard for you to do, spirit of evil?'

'Nothing is hard for me to do,' answered Woland, 'you know that very well.' He paused and added: 'But why don't you take him with you into the light?'

'He does not deserve the light, he deserves peace,' Levi said in a sorrowful voice.

'Tell him it will be done,' Woland replied and added, his eye flashing: 'And leave me immediately.'

'He asks that she who loved him and suffered because of him also be taken with him,' Levi addressed Woland pleadingly for the first time.

'We would never have thought of it without you. Go.'

Matthew Levi disappeared after that, and Woland called Azazello and ordered him:

'Fly to them and arrange it all.'

Azazello left the terrace, and Woland remained alone.

But his solitude did not last. Over the flags of the terrace came the sound of footsteps and animated voices, and before Woland stood Koroviev and Behemoth. But now the fat fellow had no primus with him, but was loaded with other things. Thus, under his arm he had a small landscape in a gold frame, from one hand hung a half-burnt cook's smock, and in the other he held a whole salmon with skin and tail. Koroviev and Behemoth reeked of fire, Behemoth's mug was all sooty and his cap was badly burnt.

'Greetings, Messire!' cried the irrepressible pair, and Behemoth waved the salmon.

'A fine sight,' said Woland.

'Imagine, Messire!' Behemoth cried excitedly and joyfully, 'I was taken for a looter!'

'Judging by the things you've brought,' Woland replied, glancing at the landscape, 'you are a looter!'

'Believe me, Messire . . .' Behemoth began in a soulful voice.

'No, I don't,' Woland replied curtly.

'Messire, I swear, I made heroic efforts to save everything I could, and this is all I was able to rescue.'

'You'd better tell me, why did Griboedov's catch fire?' asked Woland.

Both Koroviev and Behemoth spread their arms, raised their eyes to heaven, and Behemoth cried out:

'I can't conceive why! We were sitting there peacefully, perfectly quiet, having a bite to eat . . .'

'And suddenly – bang, bang!' Koroviev picked up, 'gunshots! Crazed with fear, Behemoth and I ran out to the boulevard, our pursuers followed, we rushed to Timiriazev! . . .'[2]

'But the sense of duty,' Behemoth put in, 'overcame our shameful fear and we went back.'

'Ah, you went back?' said Woland. 'Well, then of course the building was reduced to ashes.'

'To ashes!' Koroviev ruefully confirmed, 'that is, Messire, literally to ashes, as you were pleased to put it so aptly. Nothing but embers!'

'I hastened,' Behemoth narrated, 'to the meeting room, the one with the columns, Messire, hoping to bring out something valuable. Ah, Messire, my wife, if only I had one, was twenty times in danger of being left a widow! But happily, Messire, I'm not married, and, let me tell you, I'm really happy that I'm not. Ah, Messire, how can one trade a bachelor's freedom for the burdensome yoke . . .'

'Again some gibberish gets going,' observed Woland.

'I hear and continue,' the cat replied. 'Yes, sir, this landscape here! It was impossible to bring anything more out of the meeting room, the flames were beating in my face. I ran to the pantry and rescued the salmon. I ran to the kitchen and rescued the smock. I think, Messire, that I did everything I could, and I don't understand how to explain the sceptical expression on your face.'

'And what did Koroviev do while you were looting?' asked Woland.

'I was helping the firemen, Messire,' replied Koroviev, pointing to his torn trousers.

'Ah, if so, then of course a new building will have to be built.'

'It will be built, Messire,' Koroviev responded, 'I venture to assure you of that.'

'Well, so it remains for us to wish that it be better than the old one,' observed Woland.

'It will be, Messire,' said Koroviev.

'You can believe me,' the cat added, 'I'm a regular prophet.'

'In any case, we're here, Messire,' Koroviev reported, 'and await your orders.'

Woland got up from his stool, went over to the balustrade, and alone, silently, his back turned to his retinue, gazed into the distance for a long time. Then he stepped away from the edge, lowered himself on to his stool, and said:

'There will be no orders, you have fulfilled all you could, and for the moment I no longer need your services. You may rest. Right now a storm is coming, the last storm, it will complete all that needs completing, and we'll be on our way.'

'Very well, Messire,' the two buffoons replied and disappeared somewhere behind the round central tower, which stood in the middle of the terrace.

The storm of which Woland had spoken was already gathering on the horizon. A black cloud rose in the west and cut off half the sun. Then it covered it entirely. The air became cool on the terrace. A little later it turned dark.

This darkness which came from the west covered the vast city. Bridges and palaces disappeared. Everything vanished as if it had never existed in the world. One fiery thread ran across the whole sky. Then a thunderclap shook the city. It was repeated, and the storm began. Woland could no longer be seen in its gloom.

CHAPTER 30

It's Time! It's Time!

'You know,' said Margarita, 'just as you fell asleep last night, I was reading about the darkness that came from the Mediterranean Sea . . . and those idols, ah, the golden idols! For some reason they never leave me in peace. I think it's going to rain now, too. Do you feel how cool it's getting?'

'That's all well and good,' replied the master, smoking and breaking up the smoke with his hand, 'and as for the idols, God be with them . . . but what will happen further on is decidedly unclear!'

This conversation occurred at sunset, just at the moment when Matthew Levi came to Woland on the terrace. The basement window was open, and if anyone had looked through it, he would have been astonished at how strange the talkers looked. Margarita had a black cloak thrown directly over her naked body, and the master was in his hospital underwear. The reason for this was that Margarita had decidedly nothing to put on, because all her clothes had stayed in her house, and though this house was very near by, there was, of course, no question of going there to take her clothes. And the master, whose clothes were all found in the wardrobe as if he had never gone anywhere, simply did not want to get dressed, developing before Margarita the thought that some perfect nonsense was about to begin at any moment. True, he was clean-shaven for the first time since that autumn night (in the clinic his beard had been cut with clippers).

The room also had a strange look, and it was very hard to make anything out in its chaos. Manuscripts were lying on the rug, and on the sofa as well. A book sat humpbacked on an armchair. And dinner was set out on the round table, with several bottles standing among the dishes of food. Where all this food and drink came from was known neither to Margarita nor to the master. On waking up they found everything already on the table.

Having slept until sunset Saturday, the master and his friend felt themselves thoroughly fortified, and only one thing told of the previous day's adventure – both had a slight ache in the left temple. But with regard to their minds, there were great changes in both of them, as anyone would have been convinced who was able to eavesdrop on the conversation in the basement. But there was decidedly no one to eavesdrop. That little courtyard was good precisely for being always empty. With each day the greening lindens and the ivy outside the window exuded an ever stronger smell of spring, and the rising breeze carried it into the basement.

'Pah, the devil!' exclaimed the master unexpectedly. 'But, just think, it's . . .' he put out his cigarette butt in the ashtray and pressed his head with his hands. 'No, listen, you're an intelligent person and have never been crazy . . . are you seriously convinced that we were at Satan's yesterday?'

'Quite seriously,' Margarita replied.

'Of course, of course,' the master said ironically, 'so now instead of one madman there are two – husband and wife!' He raised his hands to heaven and cried: 'No, the devil knows what this is! The devil, the devil . . .'

Instead of answering, Margarita collapsed on the sofa, burst out laughing, waved her bare legs, and only then cried out:

'Aie, I can't . . . I can't! You should see what you look like! . . .'

Having finished laughing, while the master bashfully pulled up his hospital drawers, Margarita became serious.

'You unwittingly spoke the truth just now,' she began, 'the devil knows what it is, and the devil, believe me, will arrange everything!' Her eyes suddenly flashed, she jumped up and began dancing on the spot, crying out: 'How happy I am, how happy I am, how happy I am that I struck a bargain with him! Oh, Satan, Satan! . . . You'll have to live with a witch, my dear!' Then she rushed to the master, put her arms around his neck, and began kissing his lips, his nose, his cheeks. Strands of unkempt black hair leaped at the master, and his cheeks and forehead burned under the kisses.

'And you've really come to resemble a witch.'

'And I don't deny it,' answered Margarita, 'I'm a witch and I'm very glad of it.'

'Well, all right,' said the master, 'so you're a witch, very nice, splendid! And I've been stolen from the hospital . . . also very nice! I've been brought here, let's grant that, too. Let's even suppose that we won't be missed . . . But tell me, by all that's holy, how and on what are we going to live? My concern is for you when I say that, believe me!'

At that moment round-toed shoes and the lower part of a pair of pinstriped trousers appeared in the window. Then the trousers bent at the knee and somebody's hefty backside blocked the daylight.

'Aloisy, are you home?' asked a voice somewhere up above the trousers, outside the window.

'There, it's beginning,' said the master.

'Aloisy?' asked Margarita, going closer to the window. 'He was arrested yesterday. Who's asking for him? What's your name?'

That instant the knees and backside vanished, there came the bang of the gate, after which everything returned to normal. Margarita collapsed on the sofa and laughed so that tears poured from her eyes. But when she calmed down, her countenance changed greatly, she began speaking seriously, and as she spoke she slipped down from the couch, crept over to the master's knees, and, looking into his eyes, began to caress his head.

'How you've suffered, how you've suffered, my poor one! I'm the only one who knows it. Look, you've got white threads in your hair, and an eternal crease by your lips! My only one, my dearest, don't think about anything! You've had to think too much, and now I'll think for you. And I promise you, I promise, that everything will be dazzlingly well!'

'I'm not afraid of anything, Margot,' the master suddenly answered her and raised his head, and he seemed to her the same as he had been when he was inventing that which he had never seen, but of which he knew for certain that it had been, 'not afraid, because I've already experienced it all. They tried too hard to frighten me, and cannot frighten me with anything any more. But I pity you, Margot, that's the trick, that's why I keep saying it over and over. Come to your senses! Why do you have to ruin your life with a sick man and a beggar? Go back! I pity you, that's why I say it.'

'Oh, you, you . . .' Margarita whispered, shaking her dishevelled head, 'oh, you faithless, unfortunate man! . . . Because of you I spent the whole night yesterday shivering and naked. I lost my nature and replaced it with a new one, I spent several months sitting in a dark closet thinking about one thing, about the storm over Yershalaim, I cried my eyes out, and now, when happiness has befallen us, you drive me away! Well, then I'll go, I'll go, but you should know that you are a cruel man! They've devastated your soul!'

Bitter tenderness rose up in the master's heart, and, without knowing why, he began to weep, burying his face in Margarita's hair. Weeping herself, she whispered to him, and her fingers trembled on the master's temples.

'Yes, threads, threads . . . before my eyes your head is getting covered with snow . . . ah, my much-suffering head! Look what eyes you've got! There's a desert in them . . . and the shoulders, the shoulders with their burden . . . crippled, crippled . . .' Margarita's speech was becoming incoherent, Margarita was shaking with tears.

Then the master wiped his eyes, raised Margarita from her knees, got up himself and said firmly:

'Enough. You've shamed me. Never again will I yield to faint-heartedness, or come back to this question, be reassured. I know that we're both the victims of our mental illness, which you perhaps got from me . . . Well, so we'll bear it together.'

Margarita put her lips close to the master's ear and whispered:

'I swear to you by your life, I swear by the astrologer's son whom you guessed, that all will be well!'

'Fine, fine,' responded the master, and he added, laughing: 'Of course, when people have been robbed of everything, like you and me, they seek salvation from other-worldly powers! Well, so, I agree to seek there.'

'Well, there, there, now you're your old self, you're laughing,' replied Margarita, 'and devil take you with your learned words. Other-worldly or not other-worldly, isn't it all the same? I want to eat!' And she dragged the master to the table by the hand.

'I'm not sure this food isn't about to fall through the floor or fly out the window,' he said, now completely calm.

'It won't fly out.'

And just then a nasal voice came through the window:

'Peace be unto you.'[1]

The master gave a start, but Margarita, already accustomed to the extraordinary, exclaimed:

'Why, it's Azazello! Ah, how nice, how good!' and, whispering to the master: 'You see, you see, we're not abandoned!' – she rushed to open the door.

'Cover yourself at least,' the master called after her.

'Spit on it,' answered Margarita, already in the corridor.

And there was Azazello bowing, greeting the master, and flashing his blind eye, while Margarita exclaimed:

'Ah, how glad I am! I've never been so glad in my life! But forgive me, Azazello, for being naked!'

Azazello begged her not to worry, assuring her that he had seen not only naked women, but even women with their skin flayed clean off, and willingly sat down at the table, having first placed some package wrapped in dark brocade in the corner by the stove.

Margarita poured Azazello some cognac, and he willingly drank it. The master, not taking his eyes off him, quietly pinched his own left hand under the table. But the pinches did not help. Azazello did not melt into air, and, to tell the truth, there was no need for that. There was nothing terrible in the short, reddish-haired man, unless it was his eye with albugo, but that occurs even without sorcery, or unless his clothes were not quite ordinary – some sort of cassock or cloak – but again, strictly considered, that also happens. He drank his cognac adroitly, too, as all good people do, by the glassful and without nibbling. From this same cognac the master's head became giddy, and he began to think:

'No, Margarita's right ... Of course, this is the devil's messenger sitting before me. No more than two nights ago, I myself tried to prove to Ivan that it was precisely Satan whom he had met at the Patriarch's Ponds, and now for some reason I got scared of the thought and started babbling something about hypnotists and hallucinations ... Devil there's any hypnotists in it! ...'

He began looking at Azazello more closely and became convinced that there was some constraint in his eyes, some thought that he would not reveal before its time. 'This is not just a visit, he's come on some errand,' thought the master.

His powers of observation did not deceive him. After drinking a third glass of cognac, which produced no effect in Azazello, the visitor spoke thus:

'A cosy little basement, devil take me! Only one question arises – what is there to do in this little basement?'

'That's just what I was saying,' the master answered, laughing.

'Why do you trouble me, Azazello?' asked Margarita. 'We'll live somehow or other!'

'Please, please!' cried Azazello, 'I never even thought of troubling you. I say the same thing – somehow or other! Ah, yes! I almost forgot . . . Messire sends his regards and has also asked me to tell you that he invites you to go on a little excursion with him – if you wish, of course. What do you say to that?'

Margarita nudged the master under the table with her leg.

'With great pleasure,' replied the master, studying Azazello, who continued:

'We hope that Margarita Nikolaevna will also not decline the invitation?'

'I certainly will not,' said Margarita, and again her leg brushed against the master's.

'A wonderful thing!' exclaimed Azazello. 'I like that! One, two, and it's done! Not like that time in the Alexandrovsky Garden!'

'Ah, don't remind me, Azazello, I was stupid then. And anyhow you mustn't blame me too severely for it – you don't meet unclean powers every day!'

'That you don't!' agreed Azazello. 'Wouldn't it be pleasant if it was every day!'

'I like quickness myself,' Margarita said excitedly, 'I like quickness and nakedness . . . Like from a Mauser – bang! Ah, how he shoots!' Margarita cried, turning to the master. 'A seven under the pillow – any pip you like! . . .' Margarita was getting drunk, and it made her eyes blaze.

'And again I forgot!' cried Azazello, slapping himself on the forehead. 'I'm quite frazzled! Messire sends you a present,' here he adverted precisely to the master, 'a bottle of wine. I beg you to note that it's the same wine the procurator of Judea drank. Falernian wine.'

It was perfectly natural that such a rarity should arouse great attention in both Margarita and the master. Azazello drew from the piece of dark coffin brocade a completely mouldy jug. The wine was sniffed, poured into glasses, held up to the light in the window, which was disappearing before the storm.

'To Woland's health!' exclaimed Margarita, raising her glass.

All three put their glasses to their lips and took big gulps. At once the pre-storm light began to fade in the master's eyes, his breath failed him, and he felt the end coming. He could still see the deathly pale Margarita, helplessly reaching her arms out to him, drop her head to the table and then slide down on the floor.

'Poisoner . . .' the master managed to cry out. He wanted to snatch the knife from the table and strike Azazello with it, but his hand slid strengthlessly from the tablecloth, everything around the master in the basement took on a black colour and then vanished altogether. He fell backwards and in falling cut the skin of his temple on the corner of his desk.

When the poisoned ones lay still, Azazello began to act. First of all, he rushed out of the window and a few instants later was in the house where Margarita Nikolaevna lived. The ever precise and accurate Azazello wanted to make sure that everything was carried out properly. And everything turned out to be in perfect order. Azazello saw a gloomy woman, who was waiting for her husband's return, come out of her bedroom, suddenly turn pale, clutch her heart, and cry helplessly:

'Natasha ... somebody ... come ...' and fall to the floor in the living room before reaching the study.

'Everything's in order,' said Azazello. A moment later he was beside the fallen lovers. Margarita lay with her face against the little rug. With his iron hands, Azazello turned her over like a doll, face to him, and peered at her. The face of the poisoned woman was changing before his eyes. Even in the gathering dusk of the storm, one could see the temporary witch's cast in her eyes and the cruelty and violence of her features disappear. The face of the dead woman brightened and finally softened, and the look of her bared teeth was no longer predatory but simply that of a suffering woman. Then Azazello unclenched her white teeth and poured into her mouth several drops of the same wine with which he had poisoned her. Margarita sighed, began to rise without Azazello's help, sat up and asked weakly:

'Why, Azazello, why? What have you done to me?'

She saw the outstretched master, shuddered, and whispered:

'I didn't expect this ... murderer!'

'Oh, no, no,' answered Azazello, 'he'll rise presently. Ah, why are you so nervous?'

Margarita believed him at once, so convincing was the red-headed demon's voice. She jumped up, strong and alive, and helped to give the outstretched man a drink of wine. Opening his eyes, he gave a dark look and with hatred repeated his last word:

'Poisoner ...'

'Ah, insults are the usual reward for a good job!' replied Azazello. 'Are you blind? Well, quickly recover your sight!'

Here the master rose, looked around with alive and bright eyes, and asked:

'What does this new thing mean?'

'It means,' replied Azazello, 'that it's time for us to go. The storm is already thundering, do you hear? It's getting dark. The steeds are pawing the ground, your little garden is shuddering. Say farewell, quickly say farewell to your little basement.'

'Ah, I understand . . .' the master said, glancing around, 'you've killed us, we're dead. Oh, how intelligent that is! And how timely! Now I understand everything.'

'Oh, for pity's sake,' replied Azazello, 'is it you I hear talking? Your friend calls you a master, you can think, so how can you be dead? Is it necessary, in order to consider yourself alive, to sit in a basement and dress yourself in a shirt and hospital drawers? It's ridiculous! . . .'

'I understand everything you're saying,' the master cried out, 'don't go on! You're a thousand times right!'

'Great Woland!' Margarita began to echo him. 'Great Woland! He thought it out much better than I did! But the novel, the novel,' she shouted to the master, 'take the novel with you wherever you fly!'

'No need,' replied the master, 'I remember it by heart.'

'But you won't . . . you won't forget a single word of it?' Margarita asked, pressing herself to her lover and wiping the blood from his cut temple.

'Don't worry. I'll never forget anything now,' he replied.

'Fire, then!' cried Azazello. 'Fire, with which all began and with which we end it all.'

'Fire!' Margarita cried terribly. The little basement window banged, the curtain was beaten aside by the wind. The sky thundered merrily and briefly. Azazello thrust his clawed hand into the stove, pulled out a smoking brand, and set fire to the tablecloth. Then he set fire to the stack of old newspapers on the sofa, and next to the manuscripts and the window curtain.

The master, already drunk with the impending ride, flung some book from the shelf on to the table, ruffled its pages in the flame of the tablecloth, and the book blazed up merrily.

'Burn, burn, former life!'

'Burn, suffering!' cried Margarita.

The room was already swaying in crimson pillars, and along with the smoke the three ran out of the door, went up the stone steps, and came to the yard. The first thing they saw there was the landlord's cook sitting on the ground. Beside her lay spilled potatoes and several bunches of onions. The cook's state was comprehensible. Three black steeds snorted by the shed, twitching, sending up fountains of earth. Margarita mounted first, then Azazello, and last the master. The cook moaned and wanted to raise her hand to make the sign of the cross, but Azazello shouted menacingly from the saddle:

'I'll cut your hand off!' He whistled, and the steeds, breaking through the linden branches, soared up and pierced the low black cloud. Smoke poured at once from the basement window. From below came the weak, pitiful cry of the cook:

'We're on fire . . .'

The steeds were already racing over the rooftops of Moscow.

'I want to bid farewell to the city,' the master cried to Azazello, who rode at their head. Thunder ate up the end of the master's phrase. Azazello nodded and sent his horse into a gallop. The dark cloud flew precipitously to meet the fliers, but as yet gave not a sprinkle of rain.

They flew over the boulevards, they saw little figures of people scatter, running for shelter from the rain. The first drops were falling. They flew over smoke – all that remained of Griboedov House. They flew over the city which was already being flooded by darkness. Over them lightning flashed. Soon the roofs gave place to greenery. Only then did the rain pour down, transforming the fliers into three huge bubbles in the water.

Margarita was already familiar with the sensation of flight, but the master was not, and he marvelled at how quickly they reached their goal, the one to whom he wished to bid farewell, because he had no one else to bid farewell to. He immediately recognized through the veil of rain the building of Stravinsky's clinic, the river, and the pine woods on the other bank, which he had studied so well. They came down in the clearing of a copse not far from the clinic.

'I'll wait for you here,' cried Azazello, his hands to his mouth, now lit up by lightning, now disappearing behind the grey veil. 'Say your farewells, but be quick!'

The master and Margarita jumped from their saddles and flew, flickering like watery shadows, through the clinic garden. A moment later the master, with an accustomed hand, was pushing aside the balcony grille of room no. 117. Margarita followed after him. They stepped into Ivanushka's room, unseen and unnoticed in the rumbling and howling of the storm. The master stopped by the bed.

Ivanushka lay motionless, as before, when for the first time he had watched a storm in the house of his repose. But he was not weeping as he had been then. Once he had taken a good look at the dark silhouette that burst into his room from the balcony, he raised himself, held out his hands, and said joyfully:

'Ah, it's you! And I kept waiting and waiting for you! And here you are, my neighbour!'

To this the master replied:

'I'm here, but unfortunately I cannot be your neighbour any longer. I'm flying away for ever, and I've come to you only to say farewell.'

'I knew that, I guessed it,' Ivan replied quietly and asked: 'You met him?'

'Yes,' said the master. 'I've come to say farewell to you, because you are the only person I've talked with lately.'

Ivanushka brightened up and said:

'It's good that you stopped off here. I'll keep my word, I won't write any more poems. I'm interested in something else now,' Ivanushka smiled and with mad eyes looked somewhere past the master. 'I want to write something else. You know, while I lay here, a lot became clear to me.'

The master was excited by these words and, sitting on the edge of Ivanushka's bed, said:

'Ah, but that's good, that's good. You'll write a sequel about him.'

Ivanushka's eyes lit up.

'But won't you do that yourself?' Here he hung his head and added pensively: 'Ah, yes ... what am I asking?' Ivanushka looked sidelong at the floor, his eyes fearful.

'Yes,' said the master, and his voice seemed unfamiliar and hollow to Ivanushka, 'I won't write about him any more now. I'll be occupied with other things.'

A distant whistle cut through the noise of the storm.

'Do you hear?' asked the master.

'The noise of the storm . . .'

'No, I'm being called, it's time for me to go,' explained the master, and he got up from the bed.

'Wait! One word more,' begged Ivan. 'Did you find her? Did she remain faithful to you?'

'Here she is,' the master replied and pointed to the wall. The dark Margarita separated from the white wall and came up to the bed. She looked at the young man lying there and sorrow could be read in her eyes.

'Poor boy, poor boy...' Margarita whispered soundlessly and bent down to the bed.

'She's so beautiful,' Ivan said, without envy, but sadly, and with a certain quiet tenderness. 'Look how well everything has turned out for you. But not so for me.' Here he thought a little and added thoughtfully: 'Or else maybe it is so...'

'It is so, it is so,' whispered Margarita, and she bent closer to him. 'I'm going to kiss you now, and everything will be as it should be with you ... believe me in that, I've seen everything, I know everything...' The young man put his arms around her neck and she kissed him.

'Farewell, disciple,' the master said barely audibly and began melting into air. He disappeared, and Margarita disappeared with him. The balcony grille was closed.

Ivanushka fell into anxiety. He sat up in bed, looked around uneasily, even moaned, began talking to himself, got up. The storm raged more and more, and evidently stirred up his soul. He was also upset by the troubling footsteps and muted voices that his ear, accustomed to the constant silence, heard outside the door. He called out, now nervous and trembling:

'Praskovya Fyodorovna!'

Praskovya Fyodorovna was already coming into the room, looking at Ivanushka questioningly and uneasily.

'What? What is it?' she asked. 'The storm upsets you? Never mind, never mind ... we'll help you now ... I'll call the doctor now...'

'No, Praskovya Fyodorovna, you needn't call the doctor,' said Ivanushka, looking anxiously not at Praskovya Fyodorovna but into the wall. 'There's nothing especially the matter with me. I can sort things out now, don't worry. But you'd better tell me,' Ivan begged soulfully, 'what just happened in room one-eighteen?'

'Eighteen?' Praskovya Fyodorovna repeated, and her eyes became furtive. 'Why, nothing happened there.' But her voice was false, Ivanushka noticed it at once and said:

'Eh, Praskovya Fyodorovna! You're such a truthful person ... You think I'll get violent? No, Praskovya Fyodorovna, that won't happen. You'd better speak directly, for I can feel everything through the wall.'

'Your neighbour has just passed away,' whispered Praskovya Fyodorovna, unable to overcome her truthfulness and kindness, and, all clothed in a flash of lightning, she looked fearfully at Ivanushka. But nothing terrible happened to Ivanushka. He only raised his finger significantly and said:

'I knew it! I assure you, Praskovya Fyodorovna, that yet another person has just passed away in the city. I even know who,' here Ivanushka smiled mysteriously. 'It's a woman!'

CHAPTER 31

On Sparrow Hills[1]

The storm was swept away without a trace, and a multicoloured rainbow, its arch thrown across all of Moscow, stood in the sky, drinking water from the Moscow River. High up, on a hill between two copses, three dark silhouettes could be seen. Woland, Koroviev and Behemoth sat in the saddle on three black horses, looking at the city spread out beyond the river, with the fragmented sun glittering in thousands of windows facing west, and at the gingerbread towers of the Devichy Convent.[2]

There was a noise in the air, and Azazello, who had the master and Margarita flying in the black tail of his cloak, alighted with them beside the waiting group.

'We had to trouble you a little, Margarita Nikolaevna and master,' Woland began after some silence, 'but you won't grudge me that. I don't think you will regret it. So, then,' he addressed the master alone, 'bid farewell to the city. It's time for us to go,' Woland pointed with his black-gauntleted hand to where numberless suns melted the glass beyond the river, to where, above these suns, stood the mist, smoke and steam of the city scorched all day.

The master threw himself out of the saddle, left the mounted ones, and ran to the edge of the hillside. The black cloak dragged on the ground behind him. The master began to look at the city. In the first moments a wringing sadness crept over his heart, but it very quickly gave way to a sweetish anxiety, a wondering gypsy excitement.

'For ever! ... That needs to be grasped,' the master whispered and licked his dry, cracked lips. He began to heed and take precise note of everything that went on in his soul. His excitement turned, as it seemed to him, into a feeling of deep and grievous offence. But it was unstable, vanished, and gave way for some reason to a haughty indifference, and that to a foretaste of enduring peace.

The group of riders waited silently for the master. The group of riders watched the black, long figure on the edge of the hillside gesticulate, now raising his head, as if trying to reach across the whole city with his eyes, to peer beyond its limits, now hanging his head down, as if studying the trampled, meagre grass under his feet.

The silence was broken by the bored Behemoth.

'Allow me, maître,' he began, 'to give a farewell whistle before the ride.'

'You may frighten the lady,' Woland answered, 'and, besides, don't forget that all your outrages today are now at an end.'

'Ah, no, no, Messire,' responded Margarita, who sat side-saddle, arms akimbo, the sharp corner of her train hanging to the ground, 'allow him, let him whistle. I'm overcome with sadness before the long journey. Isn't it true, Messire, it's quite natural even when a person knows that happiness is waiting at the end of the road? Let him make us laugh, or I'm afraid it will end in tears, and everything will be spoiled before the journey!'

Woland nodded to Behemoth, who became all animated, jumped down from the saddle, put his fingers in his mouth, puffed out his cheeks, and whistled. Margarita's ears rang. Her horse reared, in the copse dry twigs rained down from the trees, a whole flock of crows and sparrows flew up, a pillar of dust went sweeping down to the river, and, as an excursion boat was passing the pier, one could see several of the passengers' caps blow off into the water.

The whistle made the master start, yet he did not turn, but began gesticulating still more anxiously, raising his hand to the sky as if threatening the city. Behemoth gazed around proudly.

'That was whistled, I don't argue,' Koroviev observed condescendingly, 'whistled indeed, but, to be impartial, whistled rather middlingly.'

'I'm not a choirmaster,' Behemoth replied with dignity, puffing up, and he winked unexpectedly at Margarita.

'Give us a try, for old times' sake,' Koroviev said, rubbed his hand, and breathed on his fingers.

'Watch out, watch out,' came the stern voice of Woland on his horse, 'no inflicting of injuries.'

'Messire, believe me,' Koroviev responded, placing his hand on his heart, 'in fun, merely in fun . . .' Here he suddenly stretched himself upwards, as if he were made of rubber, formed the fingers of his right hand into some clever arrangement, twisted himself up like a screw, and then, suddenly unwinding, whistled.

This whistle Margarita did not hear, but she saw it in the moment when she, together with her fiery steed, was thrown some twenty yards away. An oak tree beside her was torn up by the roots, and the ground was covered with cracks all the way to the river. A huge slab of the bank, together with the pier and the restaurant, sagged into the river. The water boiled, shot up, and the entire excursion boat with its perfectly unharmed passengers was washed on to the low bank opposite. A jackdaw, killed by Fagott's whistle, was flung at the feet of Margarita's snorting steed.

The master was startled by this whistle. He clutched his head and ran back to the group of waiting companions.

'Well, then,' Woland addressed him from the height of his steed, 'is your farewell completed?'

'Yes, it's completed,' the master replied and, having calmed down, looked directly and boldly into Woland's face.

And then over the hills like a trumpet blast rolled Woland's terrible voice:

'It's time!!' – and with it the sharp whistle and guffaw of Behemoth.

The steeds tore off, and the riders rose into the air and galloped. Margarita felt her furious steed champing and straining at the bit. Woland's cloak billowed over the heads of the cavalcade; the cloak began to cover the evening sky. When the black shroud was momentarily blown aside, Margarita looked back as she rode and saw that there not only were no multicoloured towers behind them, but the city itself had long been gone. It was as if it had fallen through the earth – only mist and smoke were left . . .

CHAPTER 32

Forgiveness and Eternal Refuge

Gods, my gods! How sad the evening earth! How mysterious the mists over the swamps! He who has wandered in these mists, he who has suffered much before death, he who has flown over this earth bearing on himself too heavy a burden, knows it. The weary man knows it. And without regret he leaves the mists of the earth, its swamps and rivers, with a light heart he gives himself into the hands of death, knowing that she alone can bring him peace.

The magical black horses also became tired and carried their riders slowly, and ineluctable night began to overtake them. Sensing it at his back, even the irrepressible Behemoth quieted down and, his claws sunk into the saddle, flew silent and serious, puffing up his tail.

Night began to cover forests and fields with its black shawl, night lit melancholy little lights somewhere far below – now no longer interesting and necessary either for Margarita or for the master – alien lights. Night was outdistancing the cavalcade, it sowed itself over them from above, casting white specks of stars here and there in the saddened sky.

Night thickened, flew alongside, caught at the riders' cloaks and, tearing them from their shoulders, exposed the deceptions. And when Margarita, blown upon by the cool wind, opened her eyes, she saw how the appearance of them all was changing as they flew to their goal. And when, from beyond the edge of the forest, the crimson and full moon began rising to meet them, all deceptions vanished, fell into the swamp, the unstable magic garments drowned in the mists.

Hardly recognizable as Koroviev-Fagott, the self-appointed interpreter to the mysterious consultant who needed no interpreting, was he who now flew just beside Woland, to the right of the master's friend. In place of him who had left Sparrow Hills in a ragged circus costume under the name of Koroviev-Fagott, there now rode, softly clinking the golden chains of the bridle, a dark-violet knight with a most gloomy and never-smiling face. He rested his chin on his chest, he did not look at the moon, he was not interested in the earth, he was thinking something of his own, flying beside Woland.

'Why has he changed so?' Margarita quietly asked Woland to the whistling of the wind.

'This knight once made an unfortunate joke,' replied Woland, turning his face with its quietly burning eye to Margarita. 'The pun he thought up, in a discussion about light and darkness, was not altogether good. And after that the knight had to go on joking a bit more and longer than he supposed. But this is one of the nights when accounts are settled. The knight has paid up and closed his account.'

Night also tore off Behemoth's fluffy tail, pulled off his fur and scattered it in tufts over the swamps. He who had been a cat, entertaining the prince of darkness, now turned out to be a slim youth, a demon-page, the best jester the world has ever seen. Now he, too, grew quiet and flew noiselessly, setting his young face towards the light that streamed from the moon.

At the far side, the steel of his armour glittering, flew Azazello. The moon also changed his face. The absurd, ugly fang disappeared without a trace, and the albugo on his eye proved false. Azazello's eyes were both the same, empty and black, and his face was white and cold. Now Azazello flew in his true form, as the demon of the waterless desert, the killer-demon.

Margarita could not see herself, but she saw very well how the master had changed. His hair was now white in the moonlight and gathered behind in a braid, and it flew on the wind. When the wind blew the cloak away from the master's legs, Margarita saw the stars of spurs on his jackboots, now going out, now lighting up. Like the demon-youth, the master flew with his eyes fixed on the moon, yet smiling to it, as to a close and beloved friend, and, from a habit acquired in room no. 118, murmuring something to himself.

And, finally, Woland also flew in his true image. Margarita could not have said what his horse's bridle was made of, but thought it might be chains of moonlight, and the horse itself was a mass of darkness, and the horse's mane a storm cloud, and the rider's spurs the white flecks of stars.

Thus they flew in silence for a long time, until the place itself began to change below them. The melancholy forests drowned in earthly darkness and drew with them the dim blades of the rivers. Boulders appeared and began to gleam below, with black gaps between them where the moonlight did not penetrate.

Woland reined in his horse on a stony, joyless, flat summit, and the riders then proceeded at a walk, listening to the crunch of flint and stone under the horses' shoes. Moonlight flooded the platform greenly and brightly, and soon Margarita made out an armchair in this deserted place and in it the white figure of a seated man. Possibly the seated man was deaf, or else too sunk in his own thoughts. He did not hear the stony earth shudder under the horses' weight, and the riders approached him without disturbing him.

The moon helped Margarita well, it shone better than the best electric lantern, and Margarita saw that the seated man, whose eyes seemed blind, rubbed his hands fitfully, and peered with those same unseeing eyes at the disc of the moon. Now Margarita saw that beside the heavy stone chair, on which sparks glittered in the moonlight, lay a dark, huge, sharp-eared dog, and, like its master, it gazed anxiously at the moon. Pieces of a broken jug were scattered by the seated man's feet and an undrying black-red puddle spread there.

The riders stopped their horses.

'Your novel has been read,' Woland began, turning to the master, 'and the only thing said about it was that, unfortunately, it is not finished. So, then, I wanted to show you your hero. For about two thousand years he has been sitting on this platform and sleeping, but when the full moon comes, as you see, he is tormented by insomnia. It torments not only him, but also his faithful guardian, the dog. If it is true that cowardice is the most grievous vice, then the dog at least is not guilty of it. Storms were the only thing the brave dog feared. Well, he who loves must share the lot of the one he loves.'

'What is he saying?' asked Margarita, and her perfectly calm face clouded over with compassion.

'He says one and the same thing,' Woland replied. 'He says that even the moon gives him no peace, and that his is a bad job. That is what he always says when he is not asleep, and when he sleeps, he dreams one and the same thing: there is a path of moonlight, and he wants to walk down it and talk with the prisoner Ha-Nozri, because, as he insists, he never finished what he was saying that time, long ago, on the fourteenth day of the spring month of Nisan. But, alas, for some reason he never manages to get on to this path, and no one comes to him. Then there's no help for it, he must talk to himself. However, one does need some diversity, and to his talk about the moon he often adds that of all things in the world, he most hates his immortality and his unheard-of fame. He maintains that he would willingly exchange his lot for that of the ragged tramp Matthew Levi.'

'Twelve thousand moons for one moon long ago, isn't that too much?' asked Margarita.

'Repeating the story with Frieda?' said Woland. 'But don't trouble yourself here, Margarita. Everything will turn out right, the world is built on that.'

'Let him go!' Margarita suddenly cried piercingly, as she had cried once as a witch, and at this cry a stone fell somewhere in the mountains and tumbled down the ledges into the abyss, filling the mountains with rumbling. But Margarita could not have said whether it was the rumbling of its fall or the rumbling of satanic laughter. In any case, Woland was laughing as he glanced at Margarita and said:

'Don't shout in the mountains, he's accustomed to avalanches anyway, and it won't rouse him. You don't need to ask for him, Margarita, because the one he so yearns to talk with has already asked for him.' Here Woland turned to the master and said: 'Well, now you can finish your novel with one phrase!'

The master seemed to have been expecting this, as he stood motionless and looked at the seated procurator. He cupped his hands to his mouth and cried out so that the echo leaped over the unpeopled and unforested mountains:

'You're free! You're free! He's waiting for you!'

The mountains turned the master's voice to thunder, and by this same thunder they were destroyed. The accursed rocky walls collapsed. Only the platform with the stone armchair remained. Over the black abyss into which the walls had gone, a boundless city lit up, dominated by gleaming idols above a garden grown luxuriously over many thousands of moons. The path of moonlight so long awaited by the procurator stretched right to this garden, and the first to rush down it was the sharp-eared dog. The man in the white cloak with blood-red lining rose from the armchair and shouted something in a hoarse, cracked voice. It was impossible to tell whether he was weeping or laughing, or what he shouted. It could only be seen that, following his faithful guardian, he, too, rushed headlong down the path of moonlight.

'I'm to follow him there?' the master asked anxiously, holding the bridle.

'No,' replied Woland, 'why run after what is already finished?'

'There, then?' the master asked, turning and pointing back, where the recently abandoned city with the gingerbread towers of its convent, with the sun broken to smithereens in its windows, now wove itself behind them.

'Not there, either,' replied Woland, and his voice thickened and flowed over the rocks. 'Romantic master! He, whom the hero you invented and have just set free so yearns to see, has read your novel.' Here Woland turned to Margarita: 'Margarita Nikolaevna! It is impossible not to believe that you have tried to think up the best future for the master, but, really, what I am offering you, and what Yeshua has asked for you, is better still! Leave them to each other,' Woland said, leaning towards the master's saddle from his own, pointing to where the procurator had gone, 'let's not interfere with them. And maybe they'll still arrive at something.' Here Woland waved his arm in the direction of Yershalaim, and it went out.

'And there, too,' Woland pointed behind them, 'what are you going to do in the little basement?' Here the sun broken up in the glass went out. 'Why?' Woland went on persuasively and gently, 'oh, thrice-romantic master, can it be that you don't want to go strolling with your friend in the daytime under cherry trees just coming into bloom, and in the evening listen to Schubert's music? Can it be that you won't like writing with a goose quill by candlelight? Can it be that you don't want to sit over a retort like Faust, in hopes that you'll succeed in forming a new homunculus? There! There! The house and the old servant are already waiting for you, the candles are already burning, and soon they will go out, because you will immediately meet the dawn. Down this path, master, this one! Farewell! It's time for me to go!'

'Farewell!' Margarita and the master answered Woland in one cry. Then the black Woland, heedless of any road, threw himself into a gap, and his retinue noisily hurtled down after him. There were no rocks, no platform, no path of moonlight, no Yershalaim around. The black steeds also vanished. The master and Margarita saw the promised dawn. It began straight away, immediately after the midnight moon.

The master walked with his friend in the brilliance of the first rays of morning over a mossy little stone bridge. They crossed it. The faithful lovers left the stream behind and walked down the sandy path.

'Listen to the stillness,' Margarita said to the master, and the sand rustled under her bare feet, 'listen and enjoy what you were not given in life – peace. Look, there ahead is your eternal home, which you have been given as a reward. I can already see the Venetian window and the twisting vine, it climbs right up to the roof. Here is your home, your eternal home. I know that in the evenings you will be visited by those you love, those who interest you and who will never trouble you. They will play for you, they will sing for you, you will see what light is in the room when the candles are burning. You will fall asleep, having put on your greasy and eternal nightcap, you will fall asleep with a smile on your lips. Sleep will strengthen you, you will reason wisely. And you will no longer be able to drive me away. I will watch over your sleep.'

Thus spoke Margarita, walking with the master to their eternal home, and it seemed to the master that Margarita's words flowed in the same way as the stream they had left behind flowed and whispered, and the master's memory, the master's anxious, needled memory began to fade. Someone was setting the master free, as he himself had just set free the hero he had created. This hero had gone into the abyss, gone irrevocably, the son of the astrologer-king, forgiven on the eve of Sunday, the cruel fifth procurator of Judea, the equestrian Pontius Pilate.

Epilogue

But all the same – what happened later in Moscow, after that Saturday evening when Woland left the capital, having disappeared from Sparrow Hills at sunset with his retinue?

Of the fact that, for a long time, a dense hum of the most incredible rumours went all over the capital and very quickly spread to remote and forsaken provincial places as well, nothing need be said. It is even nauseating to repeat such rumours.

The writer of these truthful lines himself, personally, on a trip to Feodosiya, heard a story on the train about two thousand persons in Moscow coming out of a theatre stark-naked in the literal sense of the word and in that fashion returning home in taxi-cabs.

The whisper 'unclean powers' was heard in queues waiting at dairy stores, in tram-cars, shops, apartments, kitchens, on trains both suburban and long-distance, in stations big and small, at summer resorts and on beaches.

The most developed and cultured people, to be sure, took no part in this tale-telling about the unclean powers that had visited Moscow, even laughed at them and tried to bring the tellers to reason. But all the same a fact, as they say, is a fact, and to brush it aside without explanations is simply impossible: someone had visited the capital. The nice little cinders left over from Griboedov's, and many other things as well, confirmed that only too eloquently.

Cultured people adopted the view of the investigation: it had been the work of a gang of hypnotists and ventriloquists with a superb command of their art.

Measures for catching them, in Moscow as well as outside it, were of course immediately and energetically taken, but, most regrettably, produced no results. The one calling himself Woland disappeared with all his company and neither returned to Moscow nor appeared anywhere else, and did not manifest himself in any way. Quite naturally, the suggestion emerged that he had fled abroad, but there, too, he gave no signs of himself.

The investigation of his case continued for a long time. Because, i[n] truth, it was a monstrous case! Not to mention four burned-dow[n] buildings and hundreds of people driven mad, there had been murder[s] Of two this could be said with certainty: of Berlioz, and of that ill-fate[d] employee of the bureau for acquainting foreigners with places of intere[st] in Moscow, the former Baron Meigel. They had been murdered. Th[e] charred bones of the latter were discovered in apartment no. 50 o[f] Sadovaya Street after the fire was put out. Yes, there were victims, an[d] these victims called for investigation.

But there were other victims as well, even after Woland left th[e] capital, and these victims, sadly enough, were black cats.

Approximately a hundred of these peaceful and useful anima[ls] devoted to mankind, were shot or otherwise exterminated in vario[us] parts of the country. About a dozen cats, some badly disfigured, we[re] delivered to police stations in various cities. For instance, in Armav[ir] one of these perfectly guiltless beasts was brought to the police b[y] some citizen with its front paws tied.

This cat had been ambushed by the citizen at the very moment wh[en] the animal, with a thievish look (how can it be helped if cats have th[is] look? It is not because they are depraved, but because they are afra[id] lest some beings stronger than themselves – dogs or people – cau[se] them some harm or offence. Both are very easy to do, but I assu[re] you there is no credit in doing so, no, none at all!), so, then, with [a] thievish look the cat was for some reason about to dash into t[he] burdock.

Falling upon the cat and tearing his necktie off to bind it, the citiz[en] muttered venomously and threateningly:

'Aha! So now you've been so good as to come to our Armav[ir,] mister hypnotist? Well, we're not afraid of you here. Don't pretend [to] be dumb! We know what kind of goose you are!'

The citizen brought the cat to the police, dragging the poor be[ast] by its front paws, bound with a green necktie, giving it little kicks [to] make the cat walk not otherwise than on its hind legs.

'You quit that,' cried the citizen, accompanied by whistling bo[ys,] 'quit playing the fool! It won't do! Kindly walk like everybo[dy] else!'

The black cat only rolled its martyred eyes. Being deprived by nat[ure] of the gift of speech, it could not vindicate itself in any way. The po[or]

beast owed its salvation first of all to the police, and then to its owner
– a venerable old widow. As soon as the cat was delivered to the police
station, it was realized that the citizen smelled rather strongly of alcohol,
as a result of which his evidence was at once subject to doubt. And
the little old lady, having meanwhile learned from neighbours that her
cat had been hauled in, rushed to the station and arrived in the nick
of time. She gave the most flattering references for the cat, explained
that she had known it for five years, since it was a kitten, that she
vouched for it as for her own self, and proved that it had never been
known to do anything bad and had never been to Moscow. As it had
been born in Armavir, so there it had grown up and learned the catching
of mice.

The cat was untied and returned to its owner, having tasted grief,
it's true, and having learned by experience the meaning of error and
slander.

Besides cats, some minor unpleasantnesses befell certain persons.
Detained for a short time were: in Leningrad, the citizens Wolman and
Wolper; in Saratov, Kiev and Kharkov, three Volodins; in Kazan, one
Volokh; and in Penza – this for totally unknown reasons – doctor of
chemical sciences Vetchinkevich. True, he was enormously tall, very
swarthy and dark-haired.

In various places, besides that, nine Korovins, four Korovkins and
two Karavaevs were caught.

A certain citizen was taken off the Sebastopol train and bound at
the Belgorod station. This citizen had decided to entertain his fellow
passengers with card tricks.

In Yaroslavl, a citizen came to a restaurant at lunch-time carrying a
primus which he had just picked up from being repaired. The moment
they saw him, the two doormen abandoned their posts in the coatroom
and fled, and after them fled all the restaurant's customers and person-
nel. With that, in some inexplicable fashion, the girl at the cash register
had all the money disappear on her.

There was much else, but one cannot remember everything.

Again and again justice must be done to the investigation. Every
attempt was made not only to catch the criminals, but to explain all
their mischief. And it all was explained, and these explanations cannot
but be acknowledged as sensible and irrefutable.

Representatives of the investigation and experienced psychiatrists established that members of the criminal gang, or one of them perhaps (suspicion fell mainly on Koroviev), were hypnotists of unprecedented power, who could show themselves not in the place where they actually were, but in imaginary, shifted positions. Along with that, they could freely suggest to those they encountered that certain things or people were where they actually were not, and, contrariwise, could remove from the field of vision things or people that were in fact to be found within that field of vision.

In the light of such explanations, decidedly everything was clear, even what the citizens found most troublesome, the apparently quite inexplicable invulnerability of the cat, shot at in apartment no. 50 during the attempt to put him under arrest.

There had been no cat on the chandelier, naturally, nor had anyone even thought of returning their fire, the shooters had been aiming at an empty spot, while Koroviev, having suggested that the cat was acting up on the chandelier, was free to stand behind the shooters' backs, mugging and enjoying his enormous, albeit criminally employed, capacity for suggestion. It was he, of course, who had set fire to the apartment by spilling the benzene.

Styopa Likhodeev had, of course, never gone to any Yalta (such a stunt was beyond even Koroviev's powers), nor had he sent any telegrams from there. After fainting in the jeweller's wife's apartment, frightened by a trick of Koroviev's, who had shown him a cat holding a pickled mushroom on a fork, he lay there until Koroviev, jeering at him, capped him with a shaggy felt hat and sent him to the Moscow airport, having first suggested to the representatives of the investigation who went to meet Styopa that Styopa would be getting off the plane from Sebastopol.

True, the criminal investigation department in Yalta maintained that they had received the barefoot Styopa, and had sent telegrams concerning Styopa to Moscow, but no copies of these telegrams were found in the files, from which the sad but absolutely invincible conclusion was drawn that the hypnotizing gang was able to hypnotize at an enormous distance, and not only individual persons but even whole groups of them.

Under these circumstances, the criminals were able to drive people of the most sturdy psychic make-up out of their minds. To say nothing of such trifles as the pack of cards in the pocket of someone in the stalls, the women's disappearing dresses, or the miaowing beret, or other things of that sort! Such stunts can be pulled by any professional hypnotist of average ability on any stage, including the uncomplicated trick of tearing the head off the master of ceremonies. The talking cat was also sheer nonsense. To present people with such a cat, it is enough to have a command of the basic principles of ventriloquism, and scarcely anyone will doubt that Koroviev's art went significantly beyond those principles.

Yes, the point here lay not at all in packs of cards, or the false letters in Nikanor Ivanovich's briefcase! These were all trifles! It was he, Koroviev, who had sent Berlioz to certain death under the tram-car. It was he who had driven the poor poet Ivan Homeless crazy, he who had made him have visions, see ancient Yershalaim in tormenting dreams, and sun-scorched, waterless Bald Mountain with three men hanging on posts. It was he and his gang who had made Margarita Nikolaevna and her housekeeper Natasha disappear from Moscow. Incidentally, the investigation considered this matter with special attention. It had to find out if the two women had been abducted by the gang of murderers and arsonists or had fled voluntarily with the criminal company. On the basis of the absurd and incoherent evidence of Nikolai Ivanovich, and considering the strange and insane note Margarita Nikolaevna had left for her husband, the note in which she wrote that she had gone off to become a witch, as well as the circumstance that Natasha had disappeared leaving all her clothes behind, the investigation concluded that both mistress and housekeeper, like many others, had been hypnotized, and had thus been abducted by the band. There also emerged the probably quite correct thought that the criminals had been attracted by the beauty of the two women.

Yet what remained completely unclear to the investigation was the gang's motive in abducting the mental patient who called himself the master from the psychiatric clinic. This they never succeeded in establishing, nor did they succeed in obtaining the abducted man's last name. Thus he vanished for ever under the dead alias of number one-eighteen from the first building.

And so, almost everything was explained, and the investigation came to an end, as everything generally comes to an end.

Several years passed, and the citizens began to forget Woland, Koroviev and the rest. Many changes took place in the lives of those who suffered from Woland and his company, and however trifling and insignificant those changes are, they still ought to be noted.

Georges Bengalsky, for instance, after spending three months in the clinic, recovered and left it, but had to give up his work at the Variety, and that at the hottest time, when the public was flocking after tickets: the memory of black magic and its exposure proved very tenacious. Bengalsky left the Variety, for he understood that to appear every night before two thousand people, to be inevitably recognized and endlessly subjected to jeering questions of how he liked it better, with or without his head, was much too painful.

And, besides that, the master of ceremonies had lost a considerable dose of his gaiety, which is so necessary in his profession. He remained with the unpleasant, burdensome habit of falling, every spring during the full moon, into a state of anxiety, suddenly clutching his neck, looking around fearfully and weeping. These fits would pass, but all the same, since he had them, he could not continue in his former occupation, and so the master of ceremonies retired and started living on his savings, which, by his modest reckoning, were enough to last him fifteen years.

He left and never again met Varenukha, who has gained universal popularity and affection by his responsiveness and politeness, incredible even among theatre administrators. The free-pass seekers, for instance, never refer to him otherwise than as father-benefactor. One can call the Variety at any time and always hear in the receiver a soft but sad voice: 'May I help you?' And to the request that Varenukha be called to the phone, the same voice hastens to answer: 'At your service.' And, oh, how Ivan Savelyevich has suffered from his own politeness!

Styopa Likhodeev was to talk no more over the phone at the Variety. Immediately after his release from the clinic, where he spent eight days, Styopa was transferred to Rostov, taking up the position of manager of a large food store. Rumour has it that he has stopped drinking cheap wine altogether and drinks only vodka with blackcurrant buds, which has greatly improved his health. They say he has become taciturn and keeps away from women.

The removal of Stepan Bogdanovich from the Variety did not bring Rimsky the joy of which he had been so greedily dreaming over the past several years. After the clinic and Kislovodsk, old, old as could be, his head wagging, the findirector submitted a request to be dismissed from the Variety. The interesting thing was that this request was brought to the Variety by Rimsky's wife. Grigory Danilovich himself found it beyond his strength to visit, even during the daytime, the building where he had seen the cracked window-pane flooded with moonlight and the long arm making its way to the lower latch.

Having left the Variety, the findirector took a job with a children's marionette theatre in Zamoskvorechye. In this theatre he no longer had to run into the much esteemed Arkady Apollonovich Sempleyarov on matters of acoustics. The latter had been promptly transferred to Briansk and appointed manager of a mushroom cannery. The Muscovites now eat salted and pickled mushrooms and cannot praise them enough, and they rejoice exceedingly over this transfer. Since it is a bygone thing, we may now say that Arkady Apollonovich's relations with acoustics never worked out very well, and as they had been, so they remained, no matter how he tried to improve them.

Among persons who have broken with the theatre, apart from Arkady Apollonovich, mention should be made of Nikanor Ivanovich Bosoy, though he had been connected with the theatre in no other way than by his love for free tickets. Nikanor Ivanovich not only goes to no sort of theatre, either paying or free, but even changes countenance at any theatrical conversation. Besides the theatre, he has come to hate, not to a lesser but to a still greater degree, the poet Pushkin and the talented actor Savva Potapovich Kurolesov. The latter to such a degree that last year, seeing a black-framed announcement in the newspaper that Savva Potapovich had suffered a stroke in the full bloom of his career, Nikanor Ivanovich turned so purple that he almost followed after Savva Potapovich, and bellowed: 'Serves him right!' Moreover, that same evening Nikanor Ivanovich, in whom the death of the popular actor had evoked a great many painful memories, alone, in the sole company of the full moon shining on Sadovaya, got terribly drunk. And with each drink, the cursed line of hateful figures got longer, and in this line were Dunchil, Sergei Gerardovich, and the beautiful Ida Herculanovna, and that red-haired owner of fighting geese, and the candid Kanavkin, Nikolai.

Well, and what on earth happened to them? Good heavens! Precisely nothing happened to them, or could happen, since they never actually existed, as that affable artiste, the master of ceremonies, never existed, nor the theatre itself, nor that old pinchfist of an aunt Porokhovnikova, who kept currency rotting in the cellar, and there certainly were no golden trumpets or impudent cooks. All this Nikanor Ivanovich merely dreamed under the influence of the nasty Koroviev. The only living person to fly into this dream was precisely Savva Potapovich, the actor, and he got mixed up in it only because he was ingrained in Nikanor Ivanovich's memory owing to his frequent performances on the radio. He existed, but the rest did not.

So, maybe Aloisy Mogarych did not exist either? Oh, no! He not only existed, but he exists even now and precisely in the post given up by Rimsky, that is, the post of findirector of the Variety.

Coming to his senses about twenty-four hours after his visit to Woland, on a train somewhere near Vyatka, Aloisy realized that, having for some reason left Moscow in a darkened state of mind, he had forgotten to put on his trousers, but instead had stolen, with an unknown purpose, the completely useless household register of the builder. Paying a colossal sum of money to the conductor, Aloisy acquired from him an old and greasy pair of pants, and in Vyatka he turned back. But, alas, he did not find the builder's little house. The decrepit trash had been licked clean away by a fire. But Aloisy was an extremely enterprising man. Two weeks later he was living in a splendid room on Briusovsky Lane, and a few months later he was sitting in Rimsky's office. And as Rimsky had once suffered because of Styopa, so now Varenukha was tormented because of Aloisy. Ivan Savelyevich's only dream is that this Aloisy should be removed somewhere out of sight, because, as Varenukha sometimes whispers in intimate company, he supposedly has never in his life met 'such scum as this Aloisy', and he supposedly expects anything you like from this Aloisy.

However, the administrator is perhaps prejudiced. Aloisy has not been known for any shady business, or for any business at all, unless of course we count his appointing someone else to replace the barman Sokov. For Andrei Fokich died of liver cancer in the clinic of the First MSU some ten months after Woland's appearance in Moscow.

Yes, several years have passed, and the events truthfully described in this book have healed over and faded from memory. But not for everyone, not for everyone.

Each year, with the festal spring full moon,[1] a man of about thirty or thirty-odd appears towards evening under the lindens at the Patriarch's Ponds. A reddish-haired, green-eyed, modestly dressed man. He is a researcher at the Institute of History and Philosophy, Professor Ivan Nikolaevich Ponyrev.

Coming under the lindens, he always sits down on the same bench on which he sat that evening when Berlioz, long forgotten by all, saw the moon breaking to pieces for the last time in his life. Whole now, white at the start of the evening, then gold with a dark horse-dragon, it floats over the former poet Ivan Nikolaevich and at the same time stays in place at its height.

Ivan Nikolaevich is aware of everything, he knows and understands everything. He knows that as a young man he fell victim to criminal hypnotists and was afterwards treated and cured. But he also knows that there are things he cannot manage. He cannot manage this spring full moon. As soon as it begins to approach, as soon as the luminary that once hung higher than the two five-branched candlesticks begins to swell and fill with gold, Ivan Nikolaevich becomes anxious, nervous, he loses appetite and sleep, waiting till the moon ripens. And when the full moon comes, nothing can keep Ivan Nikolaevich at home. Towards evening he goes out and walks to the Patriarch's Ponds.

Sitting on the bench, Ivan Nikolaevich openly talks to himself, smokes, squints now at the moon, now at the memorable turnstile.

Ivan Nikolaevich spends an hour or two like this. Then he leaves his place and, always following the same itinerary, goes with empty and unseeing eyes through Spiridonovka to the lanes of the Arbat.

He passes the kerosene shop, turns by a lopsided old gaslight, and steals up to a fence, behind which he sees a luxuriant, though as yet unclothed, garden, and in it a Gothic mansion, moon-washed on the side with the triple bay window and dark on the other.

The professor does not know what draws him to the fence or who lives in the mansion, but he does know that there is no fighting with himself on the night of the full moon. Besides, he knows that he will inevitably see one and the same thing in the garden behind the fence.

He will see an elderly and respectable man with a little beard, wearing a pince-nez, and with slightly piggish features, sitting on a bench. Ivan Nikolaevich always finds this resident of the mansion in one and the same dreamy pose, his eyes turned towards the moon. It is known to Ivan Nikolaevich that, after admiring the moon, the seated man will unfailingly turn his gaze to the bay windows and fix it on them, as if

393

expecting that they would presently be flung open and something extraordinary would appear on the window-sill. The whole sequel Ivan Nikolaevich knows by heart. Here he must bury himself deeper behind the fence, for presently the seated man will begin to turn his head restlessly, to snatch at something in the air with a wandering gaze, to smile rapturously, and then he will suddenly clasp his hands in a sort of sweet anguish, and then he will murmur simply and rather loudly:

'Venus! Venus! ... Ah, fool that I am! ...'

'Gods, gods!' Ivan Nikolaevich will begin to whisper, hiding behind the fence and never taking his kindling eyes off the mysterious stranger. 'Here is one more of the moon's victims ... Yes, one more victim, like me ...'

And the seated man will go on talking:

'Ah, fool that I am! Why, why didn't I fly off with her? What were you afraid of, old ass? Got yourself a certificate! Ah, suffer now, you old cretin! ...'

It will go on like this until a window in the dark part of the mansion bangs, something whitish appears in it, and an unpleasant female voice rings out:

'Nikolai Ivanovich, where are you? What is this fantasy? Want to catch malaria? Come and have tea!'

Here, of course, the seated man will recover his senses and reply in a lying voice:

'I wanted a breath of air, a breath of air, dearest! The air is so nice! ...'

And here he will get up from the bench, shake his fist on the sly at the closing ground-floor window, and trudge back to the house.

'Lying, he's lying! Oh, gods, how he's lying!' Ivan Nikolaevich mutters as he leaves the fence. 'It's not the air that draws him to the garden, he sees something at the time of this spring full moon, in the garden, up there! Ah, I'd pay dearly to penetrate his mystery, to know who this Venus is that he's lost and now fruitlessly feels for in the air, trying to catch her! ...'

And the professor returns home completely ill. His wife pretends not to notice his condition and urges him to go to bed. But she herself does not go to bed and sits by the lamp with a book, looking with grieving eyes at the sleeper. She knows that Ivan Nikolaevich will wake up at dawn with a painful cry, will begin to weep and thrash. Therefore there lies before her, prepared ahead of time, on the tablecloth, under the lamp, a syringe in alcohol and an ampoule of liquid the colour of dark tea.

The poor woman, tied to a gravely ill man, is now free and can sleep without apprehensions. After the injection, Ivan Nikolaevich will sleep till morning with a blissful face, having sublime and blissful dreams unknown to her.

It is always one and the same thing that awakens the scholar and draws pitiful cries from him on the night of the full moon. He sees some unnatural, noseless executioner who, leaping up and hooting somehow with his voice, sticks his spear into the heart of Gestas, who is tied to a post and has gone insane. But it is not the executioner who is frightening so much as the unnatural lighting in this dream, caused by some dark cloud boiling and heaving itself upon the earth, as happens only during world catastrophes.

After the injection, everything changes before the sleeping man. A broad path of moonlight stretches from his bed to the window, and a man in a white cloak with blood-red lining gets on to this path and begins to walk towards the moon. Beside him walks a young man in a torn chiton and with a disfigured face. The walkers talk heatedly about something, they argue, they want to reach some understanding.

'Gods, gods!' says that man in the cloak, turning his haughty face to his companion. 'Such a banal execution! But, please,' here the face turns from haughty to imploring, 'tell me it never happened! I implore you, tell me, it never happened?'

'Well, of course it never happened,' his companion replies in a hoarse voice, 'you imagined it.'

'And you can swear it to me?' the man in the cloak asks ingratiatingly.

'I swear it!' replies his companion, and his eyes smile for some reason.

'I need nothing more!' the man in the cloak exclaims in a husky voice and goes ever higher towards the moon, drawing his companion along. Behind them a gigantic, sharp-eared dog walks calmly and majestically.

Then the moonbeam boils up, a river of moonlight begins to gush from it and pours out in all directions. The moon rules and plays, the moon dances and frolics. Then a woman of boundless beauty forms herself in the stream, and by the hand she leads out to Ivan a man overgrown with beard who glances around fearfully. Ivan Nikolaevich recognizes him at once. It is number one-eighteen, his nocturnal guest. In his dream Ivan Nikolaevich reaches his arms out to him and asks greedily:

'So it ended with that?'

'It ended with that, my disciple,' answers number one-eighteen, and then the woman comes up to Ivan and says:

'Of course, with that. Everything has ended, and everything ends ... And I will kiss you on the forehead, and everything with you will be as it should be ...'

She bends over Ivan and kisses him on the forehead, and Ivan reaches out to her and peers into her eyes, but she retreats, retreats, and together with her companion goes towards the moon ...

Then the moon begins to rage, it pours streams of light down right on Ivan, it sprays light in all directions, a flood of moonlight engulfs the room, the light heaves, rises higher, drowns the bed. It is then that Ivan Nikolaevich sleeps with a blissful face.

The next morning he wakes up silent but perfectly calm and well. His needled memory grows quiet, and until the next full moon no one will trouble the professor – neither the noseless killer of Gestas, nor the cruel fifth procurator of Judea, the equestrian Pontius Pilate.

[1928–1940]

Notes

Epigraph

1. The epigraph comes from the scene entitled 'Faust's Study' in the first part of the drama *Faust* by Johann Wolfgang von Goethe (1749–1842). The question is asked by Faust; the answer comes from the demon Mephistopheles.

Book One

Chapter 1: Never Talk with Strangers

1. *the Patriarch's Ponds*: Bulgakov uses the old name for what in 1918 was rechristened 'Pioneer Ponds'. Originally these were three ponds, only one of which remains, on the place where Philaret, eighteenth-century patriarch of the Russian Orthodox Church, had his residence.

2. *Berlioz*: Bulgakov names several of his characters after composers. In addition to Berlioz, there will be the financial director Rimsky and the psychiatrist Stravinsky. The efforts of critics to find some meaning behind this fact seem rather strained.

3. *Massolit*: An invented but plausible contraction parodying the many contractions introduced in post-revolutionary Russia. There will be others further on – Dramlit House (House for Dramatists and Literary Workers), findirector (financial director), and so on.

4. *Homeless*: In early versions of the novel, Bulgakov called his poet Bezrodny ('Pastless' or 'Familyless'). Many 'proletarian' writers adopted such pen-names, the most famous being Alexei Peshkov, who called himself Maxim Gorky (*gorky* meaning 'bitter'). Others called themselves Golodny ('Hungry'), Besposhchadny ('Merciless'), Pribludny ('Stray'). Worthy of special note here is the poet Efim Pridvorov, who called himself Demian Bedny ('Poor'), author of violent anti-religious poems. It may have been the reading of Bedny that originally sparked Bulgakov's impulse to write *The Master and Margarita*. In his *Journal* of 1925 (the so-called 'Confiscated Journal' which turned up in the files of the KGB and was published in 1990), Bulgakov noted: 'Jesus Christ is presented as a scoundrel and swindler ... There is no name for this crime.'

5. *Kislovodsk*: Literally 'acid waters', a popular resort in the northern Caucasus, famous for its mineral springs.

6. *Philo of Alexandria*: (20 BC–AD 54), Greek philosopher of Jewish origin, a

biblical exegete and theologian, influenced both the Neo-Platonists and early Christian thinkers.

7. *Flavius Josephus*: (AD 37–100), Jewish general and historian, born in Jerusalem, the author of *The Jewish War* and *Antiquities of the Jews*. Incidentally, Berlioz is mistaken: Christ is mentioned in the latter work.

8. *Tacitus's [famous] Annals*: A work, covering the years AD 14–66, by Roman historian Cornelius Tacitus (AD 55–120). He also wrote a *History* of the years AD 69–70, among other works. Modern scholarship rejects the opinion that the passage Berlioz refers to here is a later interpolation.

9. *Osiris*: Ancient Egyptian protector of the dead, brother and husband of Isis, and father of the hawk-headed Horus, a 'corn god', annually killed and resurrected.

10. *Tammuz*: A Syro-Phoenician demi-god, like Osiris a spirit of annual vegetation.

11. *Marduk*: Babylonian sun-god, leader of a revolt against the old deities and institutor of a new order.

12. *Vitzliputzli*: Also known as Huitzilopochtli, the Aztec god of war, to whom human sacrifices were offered.

13. *a poodle's head*: In Goethe's *Faust*, Mephistopheles first gets to Faust by taking the form of a black poodle.

14. *a foreigner*: Foreigners aroused both curiosity and suspicion in Soviet Russia, representing both the glamour of 'abroad' and the possibility of espionage.

15. *Adonis*: Greek version of the Syro-Phoenician demi-god Tammuz.

16. *Attis*: Phrygian god, companion to Cybele. He was castrated and bled to death.

17. *Mithras*: God of light in ancient Persian Mazdaism.

18. *Magi*: The three wise men from the east (a *magus* was a member of the Persian priestly caste) who visited the newborn Jesus (Matt. 2:1–12).

19. *restless old Immanuel*: Immanuel Kant (1724–1804), German idealist philosopher, thought that the moral law innate in man implied freedom, immortality and the existence of God.

20. *Schiller*: Friedrich Schiller (1759–1805), German poet and playwright, a liberal idealist.

21. *Strauss*: David Strauss (1808–74), German theologian, author of a *Life of Jesus*, considered the Gospel story as belonging to the category of myth.

22. *Solovki*: A casual name for the 'Solovetsky Special Purpose Camps' located on the site of a former monastery on the Solovetsky Islands in the White Sea. They were of especially terrible renown during the thirties. The last prisoners were loaded on a barge and drowned in the White Sea in 1939.

23. *Enemies? Interventionists?*: There was constant talk in the early Soviet period of 'enemies of the revolution' and 'foreign interventionists' seeking to subvert the new workers' state.